Includes Bor
Faithful Traitor
by Jill Stengl

Love's Betrayal

DIANN
MILLS

BARBOUR BOOKS
An Imprint of Barbour Publishing, Inc.

Prologue

1776

Henry O'Neill studied the blue waves slapping against the sides of the British war vessel as it sailed into Boston Harbor. The wind gathered momentum and rocked the vessel from side to side. Glancing above the sails and tall masts to a gray, turbulent sky, he watched the clouds roll toward the bay. At least they would land soon on the American soil and be free of nature's pending fury. Henry believed in God, not omens, but a clear blue sky and a sparkling ray of sunlight flitting off the waters would have suited him much better.

Glancing at his bright red jacket with its deep blue facing and white metal buttons, he could not help but feel proud of what his uniform represented. As a foot soldier in Colonel Hamilton's Twenty-first Regiment, he shared in the objective to help squelch the rebellion. These colonists were an unruly lot, but they were no match for King George's army.

No matter what lay ahead in the line of duty, serving the king provided the distinction of being a part of the world's strongest fighting force. The distinction also kept clothes on his back and food in his belly, although the latter hadn't settled well during the lengthy voyage. Henry cringed. His stomach had wretched more times than he cared to recall, and he could not wait to set foot on solid ground.

A twinge of excitement and fear raced up his spine. Henry never thought of himself as a hero. His livelihood before enlisting depended on weaving cloth, an honorable trade taught to him by his father. Unfortunately, his father couldn't feed all twelve of his brood in Ireland, and Henry had vowed not to go without food, clothing, and proper shelter again. This new land offered so many opportunities for a skilled craftsman, and he eagerly anticipated setting up his loom for business once he had fulfilled his responsibilities to His Majesty.

He stiffened. Yes, he'd fight for King George. Henry had declared his allegiance, his very life if necessary, to defend the crown and uphold the king's edicts.

A few short months should manage the rebellion quite nicely. Then on to his new life.

Chapter 1

January 1776

Delight Butler stuffed a folded piece of paper into her apron pocket and peered to the right and to the left of Boston's bricked street for any sign of redcoats. A gust of wind whipped around and caught her unaware, and she pulled her coat tighter to fight the biting chill. A few soldiers emerged from down the street and marched toward her and her sixteen-year-old sister, Charity. Although she believed they would not harm them, a measure of anxiety nipped at her heels nonetheless.

Where is he?

Sometimes she read the papers before delivering them to the designated patriot or member of the Continental army, but not today. William Taylor needed this as soon as possible.

"How much farther to the Taylor home?" Charity said with a sigh. "Mama will be expecting us."

Delight frowned at her sister and adjusted the wooden bucket dangling from her arms. "Papa promised this to Mr. Taylor. We only have to cross over to Hanover Street."

Charity tossed her dark head, her mobcap trimmed in lace bobbing like a chicken pecking for grain. "I don't like walking with the redcoats marching by."

Delight stopped in the street, her attention focused on the approaching soldiers. Just the mere sight of them infuriated her, and the thought of flinging a jeer their way teased her mind.

"Sister?" Charity said with a stamp of her foot.

Delight found her senses. "We shan't be much longer, and I must say the walk home will be more pleasant without the sight of the British soldiers."

"I agree. I am simply thinking of the work awaiting us at home, and this cold has my fingers and toes numb."

Delight ignored her. She didn't have the time or the whim to indulge Charity. The soldiers moved closer. Their hands gripped their muskets, poised and ready for a fight. Their boots pounded a rhythm against the packed snow, leaving the impression they stomped every patriot in Boston. A twinge of fear assaulted her, although not for her safety but for those defending freedom. She held her breath as they passed, not wanting to offer any respect for their pompous mannerisms, least of all for King George and his outrageous demands.

Will these despised soldiers ever leave Boston? "Let us hurry on," Delight said. She recoiled when the five soldiers turned onto Hanover Street. Suspicion crept over her. She picked up her pace in an effort to make Charity think she was obliging her.

"Has Mr. Taylor paid Papa for the buckets?" her sister said.

"He traded with Papa for an iron pot. We only need to make the delivery." How could she give him the document with Charity nailed to her side? She should have anticipated this problem when Mama suggested Charity accompany her and carry the second bucket for Mr. Taylor.

While they hastened their pace, Delight's gaze fixed on the soldiers who marched past Mr. Taylor's blacksmith shop. *Thank Thee, Lord.* She'd delivered more than one message to Mr. Taylor and knew his boldness. While soldiers waited for him to shoe their horses, they talked among themselves, and he forgot nary a word. Delight knew only one of his contacts, the man who'd given her the document today—a close friend of her father's who was a tanner by trade and lived on the outskirts of the city.

Once at the blacksmith, Delight peered into the darkness. "Mr. Taylor," she called out. "This is Delight and Charity Butler. We have come to deliver your two buckets."

The lean-looking man stepped out of the shadows and smiled broadly. "Good afternoon." He took the pieces and admired the craftsmanship. "What a fine job your father does, and I sorely needed these today."

"Papa will be pleased." Delight touched the crisp document in her pocket. Now, how would she be able to distract her sister?

"Do you have a favorite piece of scripture?" Mr. Taylor said.

6

Her code. If Charity had not been with her, she wouldn't have had to deal with procedures. Mr. Taylor needed to be assured of her purpose, and in the past she had been alone. "Yes sir, I most certainly do. It is from Psalm 37:4. 'Delight thyself also in the Lord; and he shall give thee the desires of thine heart.' "

"Ah, commendable. Your namesake verse, perhaps?"

We are using all our formalities today. I wonder why. "Yes sir. All of my sisters have one in accordance with their name."

"I've finished with the iron pot your mother requested. Would you like to take it with you?" Mr. Taylor gestured toward a bench in the corner, crowded with tools, nails, ox- and horseshoes, and her mother's pot.

"Of course." Delight stepped over to retrieve the pot—a bit heavy, but she had Charity to help her carry it back. Spying a pile of nails, she elected to slip the message under them. Her fingers grasped the paper.

"William Taylor!" a man's voice boomed.

Charity gasped, and Delight whirled around to see British soldiers pointing their bayonets at the blacksmith. *Oh no. He has been found out.*

"That be my name," he replied without reservation.

Delight took her sister's arm and pulled her away from the soldiers' path. She could feel Charity trembling and feared the young woman might faint.

"The colonel would like to speak with you," the same soldier said. "He does not like to be kept waiting."

"About what matter?" Mr. Taylor crossed his arms over his chest.

"It matters naught to you. It is the king's business. Come along without another moment's delay."

Mr. Taylor laid his leather apron aside and glanced at Delight. In the dim light she could not read his eyes, but the document still rested in her pocket. "Go ahead and take the pot—and give my utmost to Mistress Butler."

Delight nodded and lifted the pot from the bench. "Godspeed, sir. Our prayers will be with you."

"He will need them," another soldier said with a chuckle.

Elijah Butler pounded his fist onto the table, his round face and bald head flushed crimson. "How dare those lobsterbacks seize our friends and frighten my daughters! I wish I had the likes of King George for five minutes. I'd tell him to keep his soldiers out of our country!"

He plopped down onto his chair while Delight and her sisters set wooden bowls on the table for the evening meal. The tantalizing aroma of an oyster stew and hot bread with freshly churned butter filled the air. Once he had calmed and the family had taken their places on the benches, he thanked God for His bountiful blessings and asked Him to take care of William Taylor.

Delight lifted her gaze and glanced around the table at her mother and six sisters: Charity, Remember, Faith, Patience, Mercy, and Hope. *I am the oldest and expected to be a Christian example to my younger sisters. How would Mama and Papa feel about my assisting the patriot cause?*

The precious document in her pocket plagued her mind. She would have to leave in the dark of night in order to deliver it, and she hadn't the opportunity to read the contents or know where it should be delivered.

"I have made up my mind," Papa lifted his chin.

Stirred from her musings, Delight gave him her full attention. Papa never made rash decisions.

"We shall leave Boston. It is no longer safe for my family." He nodded at Mama with a slight smile. "We shall go to Chesterfield, where my brother tells me there is need for a cooper." He leaned in closer, peered from side to side. "And if the British soldiers continue to disturb our lives, then I shall join the patriot army," he whispered.

Mama drew in a sharp breath. "Praise God," she said, then moistened her lips. "Not that you might consider such foolishness as enlisting at your age, but that you have seen fit to rescue us from the yoke of the British soldiers."

Delight's heart pounded harder than Mr. Taylor's hammer against his anvil. *Chesterfield. How can I help the cause there? Who will be the courier here?* She looked at her father, searching his face for answers. "How will we be able to leave?"

Papa nodded his understanding. "We cannot leave together, and it must be done in secrecy to avoid the soldiers."

Charity gasped at Papa's words. Because she was given to fainting, everyone looked expectantly at her pale face. "I'm fine, Papa."

He glanced at Mama. "You, Mercy, and Hope will leave tomorrow. I will give you detailed instructions later."

Delight picked at her stew. She was foolish to have her thoughts linger on her own importance. Of course the patriots would find someone else to deliver messages. Boston was full of those committed to the cause, those who longed to see liberty in the colonies. Indeed she thought too highly of herself. Perhaps she had fulfilled the destiny God intended, but she'd found meaning in her life by combining her faith in God with the efforts of the colonies to unite for freedom. Disappointment raged through her.

"Delight, have the happenings today stolen your appetite?" her mother said. "Perhaps the soldiers frightened you more than you revealed to us."

"No, Mama. I am merely thinking." She wanted to voice her concern over the move but dare not sound disrespectful. "Papa, are you sure leaving our home is necessary? Can't we stay and be wary of the British?"

He shook his head. "I think not. When I look around the table, I see seven beautiful, brown-eyed daughters and their lovely mother. Our home is to be peaceful, not surrounded by strife and oppression. We will pack our belongings and sojourn to Chesterfield."

"When will all of us be together for the journey, Papa?" Mercy, the eight year old, said. Tears filled her eyes.

"Four days hence," Papa said and downed his buttermilk.

"We know you have friends here." Mama's gentle tone seemed to appease Mercy. Even after seven children, her face bore few lines, and tenderness prevailed in her spirit. "But you will find new ones in Chesterfield."

Papa cleared his throat, an indication of the importance of his words. "Let us all be in constant prayer for a safe journey and a prosperous life in a new home."

"May we bring Bear?" Little Hope reached down to stroke the dog's sleek coat.

"Of course," Papa said. "We shall try to take all we can. I have made arrangements with your uncle Matthew to secure us a good house and means for me to continue in building buckets and barrels once we arrive."

Delight's sisters chatted on. Some were excited and relieved, and others were not. Luckily Papa was not of the mind that children should always be seen and not heard.

"One question at a time," he said. "What you have to say is important to me."

But the discussion of the move only firmed Delight's resolve that at the first possible opportunity, she needed to read the document in her pocket and learn its destination. Only then could she consider what God intended by uprooting her world.

Long after the small house quieted and the only sounds were the even breathing of her family, Delight rose, dressed, and tiptoed to the fire, where the embers had not yet died. She carefully opened the document and squinted to read only enough to determine that it should be delivered to the owner of one of the taverns near the wharf. The British had closed Boston's port. Even so, it was not safe for a young woman to be out alone after dark. Papa would be terribly angry if he discovered she was venturing toward such a rowdy place. But she must.

Oh heavenly Father. Protect me this night from the perils lurking where I must walk. Guide my feet, and shelter me in the shadow of Thy grace.

Somehow Delight found the courage to step out into the dark with a lantern turned down low and hooded. She must not be seen—either by the town crier or by soldiers. She shivered in the frigid temperatures and stole toward the tavern, slipping on the ice and praying she didn't fall. Although she silenced her feet against the street, every sound alerted her to possible danger and reminded her of the vital information concealed in her right shoe.

She glanced at the starless night hosted by only a quarter

moon. How wonderful if God had blessed her with light. Her deliberations told her He had done so. She simply had to believe He honored her cause.

The time was long after midnight, and the tavern would be closed. Still, the area alarmed her. Every sound alerted her: the bark of a dog, the distant laughter, and the rowdy talk of soldiers. An eerie sensation trickled through her, as if someone trailed her steps. She had perceived this before and ignored it, but tonight the sensation felt so true. Nonsense, fear would not rule over her responsibilities.

When the establishment came in sight and the pronounced smell of fish met her nostrils, she didn't know whether to let out a sigh of relief or pray harder. To reach the back door of the tavern, she would have to risk attracting the attention of anyone who might be hiding in wait for a victim or wallowing in drunkenness. Worse yet, she might be detected by a redcoat. Chills raced up her arms, and she longed to turn and hurry home. Only her sense of mission enabled her to keep one foot in front of the other.

Delight realized she had held her breath until she felt faint. For the first time in her life, she wished she'd held the thoughts and desires of other young women her age—a home and family. Not that she didn't want those admirable blessings, but she felt duty-bound not to seek such a future until the war for independence had been won. Perhaps God had made a mistake, and she should have been born a man.

Clenching her fists, she rapped on the tavern's door. The deafening sound caused her to hastily glance into the darkness. Along with the smells of the wharf, she inhaled the odor of sour ale. When no one appeared at the door, she knocked again a little louder.

"Who goes there?" a gruff voice called.

Delight took a deep breath. "One bearing scripture fitting for the times to Cavin Sullivan."

The latch lifted with a squeak, and she stood before a man who in the shadows resembled a huge beast. "For all that is just and right," he whispered. In the next moment he grabbed her arm and flung her inside. "Lass, do you not know how dangerous it is to

11

be out and about?" His stern voice, laced with a thick Irish accent, frightened her. In the darkness, this man could do anything.

"Are you not expecting something?" she said. *Oh dear, I sound like an unscrupulous woman.*

He said nothing for several moments, but oh how conscious she was of this giant of a man. "Did you tell me you brought scripture?"

"Yes sir." Her voice sounded shaky, not at all courageous. "'Delight thyself also in the Lord—'"

"Aye, you've said enough," he whispered. "What bring ye?"

"Mr. Taylor was seized by the soldiers today."

"Indeed."

"I could not deliver my message, and I saw it goes to you."

She heard him expel a heavy breath.

"You are brave to risk the night for our cause," he said. "I expected a man."

She stiffened. "I am able to go undetected in most places." Delight reached down to unlace her shoe and to retrieve the document for Mr. Sullivan.

"Thank you, lass," he whispered and took the folded paper. "Now, let me escort you home. It is not safe for you to be unescorted."

"I would be most obliged."

Suddenly his hand clamped over her mouth.

Chapter 2

Terror reigned through Delight's body along with a measure of foolishness. She knew stealing out into the night to the wharf area without an escort invited peril.

Someone pounded on the door. "Open up. We are in need of spirits."

Mr. Sullivan moved not a muscle.

"Open up, or we will beat down the door. Our captain requests a bottle."

Redcoats! I've been followed. Caught!

Mr. Sullivan released her mouth and led her backwards. Surely all of Boston could hear her heart pound. "Just a minute. Can't a man sleep?" Mr. Sullivan called. He pushed her behind what she thought was a barrel.

"You can go back to bed once you have given us what we need."

The door creaked open. "And what would you like?" Mr. Sullivan said.

"Rum!"

"And do you have payment?" Mr. Sullivan demanded.

A laugh rose from what must have been two, possibly three soldiers. "Talk to our captain in the morning. We were told to get a bottle of rum, that's all."

"Not without payment."

Silence invaded the room. *Please, give them what they want.*

"Either give it to us or we will take two bottles."

Loathsome redcoats.

"I'll get your rum," Mr. Sullivan shouted. Shortly thereafter the door closed. "Are you all right, lass?" He bent to help her to her feet—this man whose face she had not yet viewed.

"I am well," she whispered.

"Come, this has been a hard night, and no doubt you seek the comforts of your home." A candlelight's flicker opened the darkness, and she saw his face.

13

Once they silently disappeared into the streets, Delight gave thanks for her escort, and she prayed Papa had not detected her absence. Enough excitement had transpired for one day.

"I daresay this is the last time I can help," she said. Without waiting for him to question, she continued, "Papa is moving us to Chesterfield in three days. I fear I am of no service there."

"You have done more than your duty for the cause," he said. "We are greatly indebted."

"I would like to continue, sir. Please let those know who might need assistance in Chesterfield."

"I understand, and I will extend your concern."

When she saw the outline of her two-story home, she stopped. "I am quite safe now. Thank you for the escort."

"Good evening, and may your father's decision to leave Boston be a prosperous one."

Delight straightened her shoulders and moved toward the back of her home, for now she faced the ardent task of slipping inside without detection. In three days, all of this would be memories. But tonight, vivid sights and sounds raced across her heart. She longed to do so much more, but God obviously saw fit for her to cease in her work.

She held her breath and lifted the latch. Setting foot on the plank floor of her home somehow relieved the burden of the night's dangers. Only the stillness of sleeping inhabitants greeted her. *I thank Thee, Lord.*

Stealing up the stairs, Delight realized she would never forget the night's happenings. Weariness threatened to overtake her. Alas, it would take a long time before her heart slowed its incessant pounding.

❧

For more than sixteen months, Delight tried to appreciate the small town of Chesterfield, but it lacked the excitement of Boston. She'd hoped Papa would want to move back to their home city once the British deserted Boston in March of '76, but he elected to remain in the quieter town. News of the war trickled in, although the patriots of Chesterfield eagerly strove to fight for their beliefs.

Tories disgusted her, for she felt their loyalty to Britain was out of fear. She refused to listen to their viewpoint and wished all of them would board the next ship back to England.

She listened and took note of a few patriots who held the qualities of leaders, all the while praying she could again be of assistance to the cause.

In the past, Papa had attempted to take the middle ground, as though they were Quakers who dared not take up arms. But even before they left Boston, she saw him lean heavily toward the patriot cause. The incident at Mr. Taylor's blacksmith shop was the turning point.

In Chesterfield, Papa often left the house in the evening and didn't return until quite late. Mama fretted constantly, and once Delight heard them arguing about the war efforts when he returned. She quickly assessed her father had joined the revolutionary cause and wanted to enlist in the Continental army. However, Mama stood her ground and insisted he remain in his trade.

"We have no sons, Elijah," Mama had whispered through a ragged breath. "If we did, then one of them could take over the cooper business."

"Would you deny me the privilege of fighting for freedom?"

Silence permeated the house.

"My dear husband, I love you with all my heart. Is it so wrong for me to want you unharmed?" Mama's tears stabbed at Delight's heart. She understood her mother's sentiments and her father's longing.

"Freedom is always purchased with a price. I am not afraid to sacrifice my life so that our grandchildren will live without the tyranny of England."

"And deny our unborn child a father?"

Papa did not reply. The only sound came from Mama's muffled sobs. This baby was their eighth child, hopefully a boy for Papa.

Delight felt her own eyes sting. Frustration dug at her senses. At least in Boston she could do her part, possibly enough for Papa's share. When the war for independence was won, she would tell him of the many times she had relayed messages to the patriots.

One of their new neighbors, Abby Rutherford, had brought a loaf of bread and a cheery welcome when they first arrived. She and her husband had two sons the ages of Mercy and Hope and seemed cordial enough until Mistress Rutherford mentioned her intense dislike of the patriots.

"We are of the mind that liberty is the utmost course for our country," Mama had said with a smile.

Mistress Rutherford stiffened and moved toward the door. "I am dismayed at how you feel about King George. He is our established king. I certainly hope you soon come to your senses."

Mama wiped her hands on her apron and stepped ahead of the woman to the door. "Thank you for the bread, Mrs. Rutherford. If you think a pompous, selfish man across the Atlantic cares about anything other than lacing his pockets with our money, then you have lost *your* senses."

Mrs. Rutherford stomped out, red-faced. Mama whirled around and faced her daughters. "We women may not carry muskets and bayonets, but we can surely sear the Tories' hearts with the truth. Remember, the truth shall set us free."

⟨⟩

Henry fought loyally for the British. Not once did he regret his enlistment, knowing at the end of the rebellion, he would live out his days in the colonies. He spent the winter of 1776–77 in Canada, fighting bitter cold and hunger from rationed provisions. He didn't mind the vigorous training, for he acquired strength and a disciplined will about him. Pride and determination clothed him more securely than the white wool coat issued to keep him warm. He had made splendid friends. One in particular, Adam Bennett, had been drafted from a poverty-stricken area of London. In him, Henry found a kindred spirit.

On May 6, 1777, soon after the St. Lawrence River had thawed enough to allow passage, General John Burgoyne arrived in Quebec. Pleased with the training of his regular troops, Burgoyne set June 13 as the date to launch a massive campaign designed to free New York and the surrounding areas from the patriots.

"I heard the captain talking last night," Adam said. He polished a black powder smudge from his musket before continuing. "Quite admirable of us, I might say. The captain said military brilliance had emerged from the Canadian forces."

"Aye, Adam. I'm pleased. What else did he say?"

Adam leaned closer, staring down his long, pointed nose. "General Burgoyne said with the British right wing division under Major General Phillips and the German left wing division under Major General Baron von Riedesel, we are indeed an impressive and disciplined force."

"I'm proud. This war will soon be ended, and we can all go about our business."

On June 13, twenty-eight ships and several bateaux headed across Lake Champlain toward Fort Ticonderoga, where the hastily retreated Continental forces gave the British success. The campaign continued, and Henry's optimism that the war would be quickly won gave way to endless fighting, following a long, grueling overland wilderness trail to Fort Edward. Henry faced fatigue and discontent in a land he had once believed was his destiny. He despised the rebel movement and vowed they all should be shot or hung for defying King George.

Just north of Albany, New York, at Stillwater, the fighting grew steadily worse. The Americans were proving to be a fighting force of their own.

Henry heard the order to advance. Gripping his musket, he charged forward amid the blinding smoke. The cries of wounded men and the blasts of gunfire spiraled terror through his body.

"Henry!" Adam shouted.

He turned to see his friend fall into bush and thorns. *Dear God, no!* Henry rushed to Adam's side and pulled him into a clearing. Blood gushed from his friend's chest and onto his uniform. Henry covered the wound with his hand, staring in horror at the crimson river flowing between his fingers.

"Let me bandage you." He looked for help, but his compatriots were involved in heavy fire. He saw another soldier fall.

"Spare yourself," Adam whispered. "Thank. . ." He breathed his last.

Henry held his friend a moment longer, not certain what he should do. The idea of abandoning Adam seemed cruel. A moment later white-hot pain seared his upper leg. He grabbed the torn flesh and viewed the flow of blood oozing between his fingers. This time it belonged to him. A moan escaped his lips, and he fell beside the lifeless figure of his friend. Conscious of the battle going on around him, he continued to fire his weapon until blackness overtook him.

August 1777

"I saw Connor Randolph staring at you after worship yesterday," Charity said with a smile. "He is quite handsome."

"He's a Tory," Delight said. "I would rather cut off my right arm than look his way."

Charity's eyes widened, and the conversation seized the attention of Remember, Faith, and Patience.

"You should not say such things," sixteen-year-old Remember said. Known for her devotion to biblical teachings, she would most likely be reciting scripture in the next breath. "'But I say unto you which hear, Love your enemies, do good to them which hate you.'" She lowered her lashes in reverence.

Delight fought the anger rising inside her. Crossing her arms, she stiffened to do battle with her sister using a piece of scripture from the Psalms. "'I have pursued mine enemies, and destroyed them; and I turned not again until I consumed them. And I have consumed them, and wounded them, and that they could not arise; yea, they are fallen under my feet.'"

"How can you say such things when our Lord directed us to love our enemies?" Remember touched her heart.

"Watch me," Delight said. "I shall stitch those verses onto a sampler."

"Hush, you two." Charity's normally pale cheeks heightened in color.

Why did her sister even bother with peacemaking effort? After all, Charity had started the disagreement with her reference to a

Tory casting his hideous glances Delight's way.

I must calm down. Considering her position in the family, Delight fought her desire to produce more rebuttals. "Forgive me for upsetting you. I simply have decided opinions about those loyal to England."

"I agree with her," Patience said, a rarity, given her timid nature. "Here in Chesterfield, our lives are quiet, but do you remember the soldiers in Boston? Have you forgotten how they arrested our friends?" She smoothed her apron, then toyed with a wayward strand of hair.

Wise thinking, Patience. Delight hugged her sister's shoulders. "Let's not quarrel, sisters. We have seen and heard enough about the war. We all want it to cease. For me, I cannot fathom an end until we are free of the British." When she saw the dismayed look on Remember's face, she touched her cheek. "You have heard Papa say he wants to fight. I know your heart."

Remember wiped a tear from her cheek and nodded.

The idea of Papa enlisting frightened them all, and Delight understood that each of her sisters responded differently.

"Quarreling will not make things better," Charity said, her tone soft as a whisper.

"And I'm quick to argue and state how I feel," Delight said. "I am the oldest, and I need to set a better example."

"Is it so wrong to want everyone to live as Jesus wants?" Remember said.

"No, not at all," Delight said. "Unfortunately, it is impossible when we are all so sinful. And what of us? We are a loving, Christian family, and we constantly quarrel with each other." Delight glanced into each sister's face and silently prayed. *Oh Lord, please keep my family safe and help me to love them more.*

"I don't love the soldiers or the Tories," Patience said, her attention focused on the wooden floor of their home.

Charity reached for Remember's hand. "We will all try harder and pray more for each other and for the end of the war."

✌

A week later, Delight still pondered that day's conversation with her sisters. She punched down the bread she was kneading, added more flour, and worked it into the dough. Baking bread had a way of diminishing her problems and unanswered questions—especially when she slapped the dough against the table.

Just this past Sunday, the minister at their meetinghouse had spoken against the patriots. He even held a special prayer service for those loyalist lads who had enlisted to fight with the British—the detestable Connor Randolph included. Papa, Uncle Matthew, and a few other men vehemently protested, stating the same should be done for those enlisting in the Continental army, but the minister refused.

"My household will no longer be associated with this meetinghouse," Papa announced, his voice booming above the mild-natured minister.

"My wife and I included." Uncle Matthew stood beside Papa.

"You are speaking against the king," Connor Randolph's father said. He rose to his feet and clutched the pew in front of him. "You and your patriot friends will be punished for your treason."

"Anyone who shares in our beliefs that freedom is worth any price is welcome." With those words, Papa nodded to Mama, and all of the Butlers left the building.

As Delight considered these events, she remembered her determination to love her family more and help keep them safe. Often she reasoned God had made a mistake by not making her a boy. She prayed for God to use her for His purposes, and she could not stop entreating Him to give the patriots victory and freedom for their land.

As she divided the bread dough and shaped it into loaves, Mercy and Hope burst through the door with Bear right behind them. The two girls, ages nine and eight, were only thirteen months apart and looked very much alike, each with a splash of freckles across their noses.

"Where is Papa?" Hope said between breaths. "We have to tell him something important."

Delight smiled into their sweet faces. No doubt they had seen a snake or a fox while they took a break from their chores and rambled over the countryside. "He is due back any moment, girls. Can I help you with something?"

They both shook their heads and gulped for air. For the first time, Delight saw alarm in their eyes and immediately feared the British had arrived in Chesterfield. "Why? What is wrong?"

Mama emerged from her chair at the spinning wheel. Delight read the silent concern in her face, too.

"British soldiers are just outside of town. They're marching this way," Mercy said between gasps.

Delight hid her dismay. *Is Chesterfield going to be another Boston? Are we to once more cower to the redcoats' demands?*

"But some of them look hurt," Mercy continued.

Wounded. Oh my, I didn't want Mercy and Hope to be exposed to the ugliness of war. Wanting to reassure the girls, Delight formed her words. "I'm sure they are simply in a hurry to get somewhere. Would you like to help me with the bread?"

Before the girls had an opportunity to reply, Papa stepped inside. The two younger girls ran to each side of him.

"What goes on here, my angels?" Papa wrapped his arms around each girl.

"We saw British soldiers," Hope said, "and we're frightened."

"There is nothing to be afraid of. Those soldiers are merely passing by. I witnessed them myself." Papa spoke in the gentle tone he reserved for the women in his household. "Do not concern yourself. Take Bear outside and engage him in a game of sorts."

"But what if they come here?" Mercy's eyes pooled with tears.

"If you see a soldier draw near to our home, Bear will surely alert me immediately."

Once the door closed and the two girls disappeared, he shook his fist. "Dirty redcoats, scaring my girls." He kissed Mama on her cheek and smiled at Delight, but his gestures did not disguise the anger on his face. "I will be about my business." He exited through the doorway, but not without Delight hearing him mumble beneath his breath. "I'm ready to use my musket."

Twenty minutes later, Bear's barking grasped everyone's attention. Mercy and Hope shouted for Papa. Delight opened the door to see a small band of soldiers moving their way. A wounded soldier was slung between two compatriots, his white breeches stained red with blood from a wound to his upper leg. Papa met them as they plodded toward the house. Mercy and Hope lingered behind, holding onto Bear.

"Absolutely not!" Papa said. "Take him elsewhere."

A soldier pointed his musket at Papa's chest. The little girls screamed, and Delight rushed outside with Mama right behind her. All of her sisters had gathered in the front yard, staring in horror at the scene unfolding before them.

"Calm your dog, or it will be a dead animal," the soldier said.

Papa narrowed his eyes. "Bear, quiet."

"General Burgoyne has issued an order. You, Elijah Butler, are to keep this soldier until he is well and we return for him."

"And if I refuse?" Papa lifted his chin.

The soldier pricked the scarf tied about Papa's neck with his bayonet. "Would you like to face arrest?"

Chapter 3

Delight stood speechless and admired her father's proud stance in the face of the redcoats' demands.

"We will nurse him properly," Mama said. She had grown so large with the baby that she could scarcely walk.

Papa's gaze remained fixed on the soldier, and he ignored Mama. All the while, the bayonet rested within a hair span of his throat. "I have seven daughters and another child due any day. What do you expect from me?"

"You deal with his care," the soldier said. "I have my orders from General Burgoyne. Take your complaints to him." He thrust a piece of paper into Papa's hands.

"We will find a place for him." Mama stepped to Papa's side and lifted a defiant chin.

"He can have my bed," Delight said. Although it consisted of a small rope structure in a room shared with Charity and Remember, the bed could be moved into the hall downstairs, and she could make a pallet with her sisters.

The wounded soldier lifted his head, covered in a thick mass of auburn hair, most of which lay over his eyes. "Thank ye, lass." His words were spoken in a thick Irish brogue. "I'll not be troublesome to ye."

He looked ghastly pale, and she might have felt some sympathy if he hadn't worn the despised uniform. Two soldiers half-carried, half-dragged him inside, where Mama directed them to the hall. They eased him to the floor, being careful not to further injure his leg.

"Has a doctor tended to him?" Mama peered into the wounded soldier's face.

"Briefly. Too many others needed the doctor's attention," said the soldier who had previously aimed his musket at Papa. "Fortunate for him, the doctor did not see fit to amputate his leg. See to it he does not grow worse." He gave Papa his attention. "Or it will not go well with you."

Lobsterback pig! Delight thought. *How dare you talk to my father this way? I wish I owned a musket. I'd show you.*

She studied her mother's face. Earlier today she had experienced pains, and now she had the enemy to nurse. When Mama attempted to bend to the soldier's side, Delight stopped her. "I will take care of him to my utmost. There's no need to make more work for you." She stole a glance at the soldier's bandaged leg, soaked in fresh blood.

"I can assist," Remember said. "I don't mind, really."

"I can manage." Delight promised herself that none of her sisters would be subjected to the atrocities of the British. "It shan't be toilsome to change the dressings." She reached for Remember's hand. "You can help me bring my bed downstairs."

"I will find some fresh bandages." Charity disappeared with Faith behind her. Patience snatched up Mercy and Hope's hands and hurried toward the house.

A soldier who had helped carry the wounded man kneeled at his side. "We will be back for you soon, Henry. I'm sorry about all this—and Adam, too."

The man they called Henry nodded and closed his eyes, obviously in more agony than he cared to state.

Nearly an hour later, Delight dabbed at the soldier's brow. Huge droplets of sweat had beaded upon his face. She'd helped to lift him onto the bed, and once there, he fainted. She hated to admit that she had actually taken pleasure in his pain. Certainly God must be disappointed in her.

The time had come to change the man's bandage. She had a basin of water ready to cleanse the dried and fresh blood and a box of dried herbs that might be needed for a poultice. Not given to a squeamish stomach, Delight picked at the tear in the white breeches surrounding the wound to better examine the injury. As she pulled aside the bloodstained material, Charity, Remember, Faith, and Patience looked on.

"If you cannot watch this without becoming ill, I suggest you leave me be." She knew full well only Remember might remain— to pray for the man.

"You girls have chores," Mama said from the doorway. "If Delight needs assistance, she will summon you." She placed a mug of feverfew tea next to Delight.

Another concern crossed Delight's mind. "Is the baby coming today?" she said, remembering the look of pain that had swept over her mother's face earlier when Papa spoke with the soldiers.

Mama nodded and offered an endearing smile. "I believe so. Please pray for a boy—more so a healthy, whole child. Your father would be so pleased if he had a son."

"Of course. And perhaps you need to be in bed?"

Her mother turned from the doorway and moved into the kitchen without a reply. She appeared to forget Delight had questioned her.

I know where I get my stubbornness. She focused her attention on Henry, who appeared to be studying her curiously.

He drew in a quick breath as she slowly unwrapped the blood-soaked bandage, which looked more like a shirt ripped into strips. "I be a thanking ye again for the care."

So the redcoat knows a few manners when it is imperative, Delight grudgingly acknowledged to herself. She looked at him and said pointedly, "I don't recall having much of a choice."

He said nothing in response, so she began washing the area around the open wound. A musket ball had grazed the leg deeply enough to cause a lot of bleeding, but he would recover as long as infection didn't set in. The flesh around it showed no signs of reddening, a good sign. Yet a poultice of yarrow was in order.

"Aye, ye have a gentle touch," Henry managed to say through a ragged breath.

His comment amused her, especially when she could have been a sight more tender. "You will heal, if you take care."

"I will be talking to the Almighty about that. We've already held a few conversations." He dug his fingers into his palm. For a brief moment, compassion seized her, but she refused to let that show. After all, Henry was the enemy.

"What is your last name?" she said as she mixed the dried yarrow with some water and applied the herbal mixture to the wound.

"O'Neill. I'm from Ireland."

She smirked. "I can tell."

"But I intend to stay in the colonies after—"

"The patriots secure our freedom." She lifted a brow and met his attention without the least concern about hiding her agitation.

Henry scowled.

"We may not want the likes of those who contend with the king living here," she added.

"Your brashness might secure your family a wealth of trouble," Henry said.

She tightened the bandage around his upper leg a little rougher than necessary. Admirably, he did not complain or wince. "I daresay your wound may get infected, or you might eat something poisonous, or our dog might not like the way you converse with the members of this family and eat you."

He stiffened. "Aye, woman, ye don't frighten me."

Delight gathered up the soiled bandages and dropped them into the basin. "I am not about to be threatened by a pompous redcoat. Go tell that to your General Burgoyne!"

⸙

If Henry had been able to stand, he would have dragged himself from the Butler household and reported the whole lot of them to his captain. But since he had no choice, he was forced to endure the insults aimed at King George. The thought made him feel even more furious—and helpless.

His leg felt like someone had touched him with a hot poker. To be sure, the pain had not ceased for four days. At first he'd worried the doctor might amputate, then he'd worried infection might kill him. And now he had this! This insensitive rebel woman assigned to nurse him would rather see him dead.

He narrowed his eyes. Everything inside him wanted to explode, and she looked as though she felt the same. He'd met better company among Ireland's landowners than he now faced living with these disagreeable colonists. Delight was her name? Quite possibly the woman served as a handmaiden for the devil.

Taking a deep breath, he reached for the mug of tea while

Delight swished her skirts and left the room.

Lord, help me with these dire circumstances. The rebels here in the colonies are most difficult. And I know the woman assigned to nurse me regrets her position. I am imploring Ye to heal me quickly so I can rejoin my regiment.

He lay back on the bed. War was not at all what he had expected. Men died, men were wounded, and friendships ended in a half breath. But he hadn't been prepared for the passionate loathing of so many Americans.

Henry persuaded his thoughts to turn to other matters, so he studied the neatly kept room. What few furnishings the Butlers owned were simple and plain. Two straight-back chairs rested against one wall with a spinet setting between, a deep wine-colored sofa against another, and a mirror hung to reflect the light from the fireplace and candles. A far wall held the portraits of Elijah Butler and his wife in their earlier years. He noted the kitchen was connected to the rest of the house, not like some he had seen where the cooking was done separately. He imagined the second story to be as neatly kept. This family did better than most.

Hours later in the twilight, he heard a commotion.

"I'm going after your aunt Anne," Elijah Butler said. "Delight, Charity, tend to your mother until I return."

Ah, the mistress is in her confinement. He slowly tried to raise himself, but he found no strength for the task. The sounds of excited female voices filled the house.

"Hush," Delight said. "Mama does not need us scurrying about like a bunch of chickens. Come, let's pray for her and the unborn babe."

Henry strained to hear the woman who had vexed him so. Could she be a follower of the Lord and Master, Jesus Christ?

"Heavenly Father, we are gathered here in concern over our mother and the unborn child. We are asking Thee to guard her and keep the babe safe in the shelter of Thy wings. Papa wants a son in a powerful way, so we're asking Thee to bless him with a boy."

"And mend the leg of the soldier we are keeping here," another voice added.

"That is very thoughtful of you, Remember," Delight said a moment later. "Lord, help me to hold my temper with him so I shan't disappoint Thee. In Jesus' name, amen."

Henry chuckled. Some aspects of this family were a bit amusing.

He slept fitfully during the evening. The events of the impending birth had the Butler family bustling about, and they seemed to forget him in the excitement, which suited him just fine. When darkness settled, Elijah entered the hall. He towered over Henry, the expanse of his shoulders outlined by the firelight from the kitchen.

"Mr. O'Neill," he said with a slight edge to his tone.

Henry ached from the day's journey and the endless pain in his leg. "Yes sir."

Elijah bent beside him. "Let me give you a word of warning. Are you a family man?"

"No sir. I have never married."

"My family means more to me than you could ever imagine. If I find out that you have harmed one of them in any way, I will cut your other leg off myself. My wife and daughters are the reason God gives me breath. They come second only to God, and my beloved country is third. For those considerations, I would gladly give my life."

Henry heard more passion in this man's words than from many of his commanding officers. He didn't doubt for one minute that Elijah Butler would take an axe to his good leg if he upset his family. Visions of the man's daughters, especially Delight with her quick temper, raced across his mind. "I understand perfectly."

Elijah rose to stand over him again. His mood instantly brightened. "This is a fine night. A new birth is a blessing, and my sister-in-law says it shan't be too long." He turned and walked from the hall.

"Mr. Butler," Henry called out. "I will be praying for your wife and the babe. My mother birthed fifteen children, twelve living, and I well remember how we prayed for her."

The man spun around. "I've been lucky that all of my children have survived save a twin sister to young Mercy."

Henry watched the man disappear. Someday he wanted a wife and children, if God saw fit. And from what he had seen of the Butler family this day, they were a good Christian family, although he didn't know how they could reconcile their faith with their rebellion against the king.

Dozing off to sleep, he dreamed of his regiment and the constant drilling. Always the soldiers talked of breaking the will of the colonists who refused to obey King George. What did these people hope to gain by their rebellion? No finer life existed for those who fell under the jurisdiction of the crown. A twinge of something long-since past pierced his heart. He remembered the oppression of family and friends in Ireland, the starvation, and the endless work. He had elected to leave his homeland and make life better for himself. What price was freedom? For the first time, Henry wanted to know how these people viewed their circumstances— not that he intended to change his mind. After all, he'd made an allegiance to England, and he was an honorable man, willing to do whatever necessary in the service of His Majesty, noting Elijah had declared earlier the same about himself. Nothing more.

⟐

Much later, Henry awoke to Elijah's shouts of, "It's a boy!" Thrilled voices filled the house. "He is a fine-looking lad," Elijah continued. "Praise God."

"Oh Papa, this is wonderful," Delight said.

"What is his name?" a much younger daughter questioned. "Will it be the same as yours?"

"Of course, my sweet Mercy. Elijah Paxton Butler."

The man's words tugged at Henry. How often had he heard the same gratitude to God expressed by his own father? These people were enemies, but they all prayed to the same God. The thought confused Henry to the point he could not go back to sleep. *If we all pray to the heavenly Father for protection and victory over our enemies, how does God decide who is the victor? Who is really on the side of God?*

⟐

Delight's eyes burned from lack of sleep. She stirred eggs into the huge skillet laden with bacon grease. Biscuits baked, and the aroma teased her senses. How good they would taste with freshly churned butter and a generous helping of the berries Mercy and Hope had picked the day before.

For two nights, she had stayed up much later than her usual custom and talked with Papa, Charity, and Remember. Papa loved reminiscing about the birth of each of his children. But when the clock struck twelve, she and her sisters went to bed. Papa spent the remaining hours seated by Mama's bedside, holding little Elijah just as he'd done with her sisters.

The baby's birth had caused so much excitement in the Butler household. New friends in Chesterfield and Papa's brother, Matthew, and his wife, Anne, visited and brought their hearty congratulations along with a wooden rattle carved to look like a fish. Another neighbor brought a pudding cap for the baby, although it would be months before he would be toddling about and need the cap to cushion his fall.

The last time Delight had checked this morning, Papa had fallen asleep and Mama held the baby. What a true blessing for Mama and Papa. They loved their daughters and often exhibited a fierce protectiveness toward them, but now they had a dear son.

A smile spread across her face and a few tears of joy sprinkled over her cheeks at the thought of little Elijah. She knew God had blessed them despite the orders to house the redcoat.

Delight picked up the mug of chamomile tea she had brewed for Mama. The herbal liquid would help her get much-needed sleep. The other women in this family could take care of everything while Mama recuperated from childbirth. They would all be fussing over who would hold Elijah.

Much to her distaste, she needed to check on Henry. Secretly, she'd named him the prisoner. His bandages should be changed again, and surely the man was hungry. Papa said it would take several weeks before his leg healed. Not a day too soon.

Midmorning, she heard the pleasant sounds of Mercy's and Hope's laughter. They were nowhere to be seen, but she soon realized they were in the hall with the soldier. Angry that the girls had sought company with Henry, she stomped into the passageway, prepared to save her sisters from the enemy. Instead she found Mercy and Hope seated on the floor with their cornhusk dolls, conducting a tea party with the wounded soldier.

Chapter 4

"What are you doing?" Delight stared in disbelief at her younger sisters' wide-eyed innocence.

Henry lifted a walnut hull teacup to his lips. "We are enjoying a spot of tea." His thick Irish tongue sounded humorous with his English statement, but she was in no mood to be jovial.

"Yes, sister. We are also having our tea with sugar and cream and bread with apple butter." Hope lifted a piece of broken pottery that no doubt served as a saucer.

Mercy swiped a sprinkling of dirt from her indigo skirt and stared up with the gathered portion of her mobcap framing her face. "We're not doing anything wrong, Delight. Please do not be angry. Mr. O'Neill offered to play with us."

Delight crossed her arms over her chest and scrutinized the three before her. "You volunteered to play with two children?"

He offered a faint smile—the first she had seen or believed she would ever see cast in her direction by him. "Aye, the wee lasses were looking for a playmate. Since I am engaged in idle time and enduring the pain in my leg, well, I offered."

Since when do soldiers play with children? Suspicion inched through her thoughts. This must surely be a new ploy by the British, and Delight knew a devious act when she heard one.

"I'm the oldest of twelve back in Ireland," he continued. "Sometimes I miss me brothers and sisters." A rather sad look swept over his pale face as he peered at her through deep blue eyes.

Henry obviously desired sympathy, but he would not get it from her. Let him waste away his hours with children's games. She didn't care.

"Very well." She felt quite victorious in seeing through his words. She turned to leave, but another notion crossed her mind. "If you are going to have a tea party, why not the Boston Tea Party? Mercy and Hope could pretend to be the Sons of Liberty."

Henry dug his fingers into his palms. Oh, how Delight Butler vexed him. She twisted her remarks like a knife in a man's flesh. Why didn't she leave the affairs of war to men and the business of play to children? He found it no surprise that these rebels plagued the king. Anger brewed inside him and threatened to bubble over. If not for Mercy and Hope playing nearby and the threatening words of their father, he would lash out at this impertinent young woman without delay.

Instead he simply smiled. "Thank ye for the suggestion, Miss Butler, but if we conducted that party, we'd have to dress as Indians and steal away in the dead of night like criminals."

Delight's face reddened, and her large brown eyes appeared to ignite like a raging fire. Clenching her fists, she swallowed hard, no doubt to maintain her composure in the presence of her younger sisters.

"Girls, I could use your help in preparing the noon meal," Delight said with tenderness in her words.

How could one woman be so disagreeable in one breath and reflect an angel's smile in the next?

"Must we?" Hope offered a most dismal look.

"I believe so, but this afternoon you can visit Mama and the baby for a little while."

Mercy brightened and clapped her hands. "Dare we hold him?"

"It is quite possible." Delight bent to gather up a walnut cup and pottery saucer. "I believe there will be time today for us to have a tea party beneath the shade of the maple tree outside, with real milk and a biscuit."

"Will Mr. O'Neill join us?" Hope said. "He is quite lonely, you know."

Delight tilted her head and touched the cheek of the youngest sister. "Oh my sweet Hope, he cannot come outside until his leg heals."

"How sad." Hope rose to her feet and curtsied to him. "Perhaps another time. Thank you, Mr. O'Neill, for playing with us."

"Yes, indeed," Mercy echoed as she offered an identical curtsy.

"Thank ye for joining me, lasses. I appreciate your conversation." Henry did enjoy the little girls. Their delightful chatter eased the frustrations of war, the steady throbbing in his leg, and the memories of Adam's last moments.

Once alone in the hall, exhaustion and weakness embittered him. He clearly wanted to rejoin his regiment soon and put this captivity behind him. For a few hours he had indulged in children's play when in fact this was the home of the enemy.

A shadow grasped his attention. Delight stood in the doorway, carrying a huge knife and towering over him like an executioner.

Gracious, what is this woman intending to do now? Henry closed his eyes. "Miss Butler, did you have something to say?"

"You are to stay away from my sisters." Her voice stung with hatred.

"The young lasses sought me, and I merely obliged." *I am not afraid of this woman. Her father, perhaps, but not this snip of insolence.*

"I must ask you to discourage them in the future." She shook slightly.

"Is your weapon intended to add weight to your demands?" Henry had no regard for his safety at this point. With the burning agony in his leg, she could hasten his journey into the Eternal, and he would not mind the least. "For it means nothing to me."

She stared at the blade and turned it over in her hands. "It would make a fine tool to amputate your leg, although I dare say the process might take a sight longer for me than it would a doctor."

He laughed and forced himself onto one elbow. "I do not frighten easily, lass. I've experienced the horrors of war: the screams of the wounded, the sight of mangled bodies, and the death of a dear friend beside me. You are but a gray cloud in a vast storm."

Delight clutched the knife against her body.

Immediately Henry regretted his bitter statement. "I did not intend to shock your sentiments, of which I ask your humble pardon."

She nodded, but for once she had no reply. *She's a fair lass, too.* Henry noted the deep color of her pursed lips, the smoothness of her skin, and her wavy hair, the color reminding him of tea with cream.

"War is not a pleasant task, Miss Butler." Henry no longer felt compelled to punish Delight with words or jesting. Across his mind marched the memories of those he'd no longer see in this life. "Those whom we serve enlist us to do what they cannot comprehend alone. We train to kill, we march in honor, and we forget we are mortals who might not live to see the next sweet blue sky. For each battle, a certain number must die to attain victory, or we admit defeat."

She moistened her lips. "Nevertheless, it is a sad state of affairs, nothing to take lightly."

"Is your cause worth the deaths of good men like your father, who is celebrating the birth of his son?" Henry had not intended to sound morose. The words simply flowed from his heart, for he indeed ached with what he had seen and heard on the battlefront. He detested the rebels and the problems they caused in refusing to obey the king's and parliament's commands, but more so he hated the ravages of war.

Delight stared into his eyes. He saw her defiant stance coupled with determination, a look he'd quickly learned was a vital part of the young woman before him. "I believe, Mr. O'Neill, as my father says, freedom is worth any price. I only wish I could do more in the strife."

The incessant pain forced Henry to lie back. "What is this freedom you rebels seek to die for? Define it for me so that I might understand." He hoped she saw his seriousness. The matter had plagued him for months, especially since Adam's death.

She slowly anchored herself on the floor beside Henry. The faraway look and the moisture pooling in her eyes told him she believed wholeheartedly in the American cause.

"I would like to join this discussion." Elijah appeared in the hall with them. "If Delight does not mind." He sauntered into the hall and seated himself beside his daughter. Flashes of gray streaked through his hair, tied back with a piece of leather, and his eyes held the lines of age. But his body appeared lean and strong.

"I will tend to the noonday meal," Delight said, offering her father a smile.

"Your sisters are capable. I would prefer you remain with me. Your views are important, too." Elijah grasped his daughter's hand, his white blouson shirt brushing against her arm.

He truly loves his daughter, this man who more closely resembles their dog and yet exhibits the gentleness of a lamb, Henry thought. *What a strange fellow to value a woman's opinion. Is this another characteristic of the rebels?*

"Freedom is not a word to simply offer a definition, but a condition of the heart and mind so compelling it calls cowards to acts of heroism." Elijah spoke softly, reverently. "It is independence from oppression and a commitment to a way of life that knows no class or favoritism. It is a conviction of representation by all the people." He took a deep breath, his very countenance exhibiting pride. "A portion of the Declaration of Independence says, 'We hold these truths to be self-evident, that all men are created equal, that they are endowed by their Creator with certain unalienable Rights, that among them are Life, Liberty, and the pursuit of Happiness.'"

Henry could not quarrel with the claim, but he wasn't certain about the contents. The words sounded more like a child's dream, and it troubled him. "What is this Declaration of Independence?"

"A document signed on July 2, 1776, in which the thirteen united American states declared their separation from England."

Which is why I am fighting this war, Henry thought. "Have you no loyalty to the king?"

"None, neither do I have respect. He brought this on himself when he taxed us unfairly in order to pay for his war with France. We were not even consulted before they demanded we pull from our pockets that which we have earned on our own."

Henry felt his temper mount. "But King George and the parliament have the right to exercise power."

"Why?" Delight did not raise her voice, but her chin quivered. "Does the king or the prime minister really care about you, Henry O'Neill, wounded in his service far from England?"

Henry swallowed hard. He had always been given to contemplation on serious matters before expressing his views. Elijah spoke of political affairs of which he had little knowledge, and Delight asked a question he could not answer. He recalled the poverty in Ireland and Adam's stories of the poor conditions in London. The aristocrats ruled over the impoverished. They had the financial means to educate their children and purchase land. Henry needed time to deliberate this strange way of thinking, for to him it sounded like a dream. And if he conceded to their way of thought, then Adam died for naught.

"A country cannot stand without those versed in authority ruling over the people," Henry finally stated.

Elijah offered a grim smile. "This United States of America will have all the people electing those of their choice to make laws and carry them through."

Frustration agitated Henry. "Your ideas are foolishness. England is the most powerful nation in the world—more than any rebel colonies—and they have the Germans and many tribes of Indians to assist them. You will lose and beg King George to draw you into his fold."

"Not I," Elijah said with quiet conviction. "I will die first for my God-given rights."

"And I shall pick up a musket and follow after you." Delight's tears trickled down her cheeks. Never had Henry seen such radiance

Have these people gone mad?

Chapter 5

With her pale blue skirt wrapped around her ankles, Delight struggled to stand, but Papa lent a hand, righting her to her feet. He wrapped his arm around her waist and planted a light kiss on her forehead.

"Daughter, we need to pray again for this man's healing. Despite his beliefs being contrary to ours, he is loved by God, and we are wrong to hinder his healing by omitting prayers."

Oh Papa, I know you are right, but this is so hard when I know he defies your very soul. Looking up at her father, Delight said, "Of course, shall I gather the others?"

He nodded, and she slipped into the kitchen to summon them. A few moments later, all seven sisters and their father held hands and bowed their heads around Henry. She glanced at the soldier, and curiosity etched his brow. He blinked, and for a brief moment she viewed a solitary tear.

"Almighty Father, we are heartily sorry for not beseeching Thee more often about the condition of Henry O'Neill's leg." Papa's voice, his prayerful tone, thundered about the hall. "We implore Thee to heal him and make him whole again. We also ask that Thou wilt heal the differences between us. Show the errant their sins and increase Thy glory. In the midst of war, we forget Thy bounteous love knows no manner of men. May the world see the victory of liberty comes from Thee. In Thy Son's precious and holy name, amen."

For the first time, Delight felt the nudging of her heavenly Father to treat Henry with love. But her heart refused to sway. *Father God, I am so confused. Help me, above all things, to be a godly woman convinced of my purpose in Thee.*

During the following week, Delight chose to have a sister accompany her when she tended to Henry and prompted others to serve him his meals. The mere notion of being alone with him tugged at her conscience. She felt a peculiar mixture of anger and guilt in the presence of this man whom she wanted to hate but knew she should not.

"Your leg is healing properly," she said one morning while placing a clean bandage over the wound. Patience sat by her side, gathering up the soiled rags to wash.

Henry offered a faint smile. "Splendid. May I trouble ye to ask how much longer it will be before I am healed?"

Delight shrugged. "I daresay not as quickly as you might fancy. In a few days, you might try to stand, but even then it will be days before you can walk unassisted—or join your regiment."

"Aye, and I remember a few days ago when sitting up was an accomplishment." He released a sigh. "This wasting away of hours plagues my mind. If only I could toil at something."

"Soldiers are required to stay on their feet," she replied, not at all condemning, but truthful. "What can you do?"

"I'd settle to be working at my craft."

She lifted her gaze to meet his. *He does have kind eyes.* "And what is your craft?"

"I weave cloth, taught to me by my father."

"An honorable trade." Delight secured the bandage in place. No longer did she take comfort in his pain.

"I'm proud of my skill. I wanted to come to the colonies and set up my loom."

Understanding nestled into Delight's mind. "So you joined the British army?"

Henry nodded. " 'Twas the only way I could afford passage. Life in Ireland is quite difficult."

"So now you make life hard for us? If you want an easier way of life with more opportunities, then you are fighting for the wrong side."

Henry shifted. "I know you are convinced of my error, but I must be loyal to my king."

"Again, I ask why."

Henry said nothing, and Delight did not feel compelled to taunt him further with her convictions. He leaned back onto the pillow and clasped his hands behind his head. "I need to ask your father about the affairs of the war."

"Shall I fetch him?" Patience said.

"That is not necessary," Henry replied. "I shall inquire of him later."

Delight deliberated revealing what she knew. What harm would it do? She realized no good would come from her boasting and purposely spoke softly. "I hear your General Burgoyne is not faring well along the Hudson River."

Henry closed his eyes. "Would you mock my loyalties, lass?"

"Indeed not. I speak the truth clearly."

He moistened his lips. "What do you know?"

"At a place called Freeman's Farm on 19 September, a fierce battle took place in the afternoon." She paused. A wave of guilt swept over her at relaying the information.

"What else happened?"

She took a deep breath, realizing God did not relish any man losing his life. "Nearly six hundred of General Burgoyne's men were killed, wounded, or taken prisoner."

"So he surrendered?"

"No," she said sadly. "Americans withdrew at nightfall, but they did not have the casualties of the British. I expect there will be more fighting shortly."

A wave of sadness appeared to beset him by the way he sighed heavily and cast his gaze away from her. Delight knew not how to continue the conversation. "Come along, Patience. We are finished here."

"Thank ye, kindly," he said, obviously distracted.

Delight gathered up the basin. *My heart is softening toward Henry. How extraordinary. I might not have been so eager to report the conditions of war if the British had not lost so many men.*

♊

Late into the night of the third week of Henry's recovery, he lay awake while a hundred thoughts raced about in his head. Tonight, he had prayed until no more words would come. He felt dirty, a traitor to the king for the substance of his musings, but he could not rid himself of the rebels' beliefs.

I would be hanged or shot for these treasonous ideals. Still his mind continued to wander. He'd viewed enough of the Butler family to see and feel their passion for freedom. Henry shuddered. Had he no respect for Adam's death and the countless others who had fallen by the Americans' hands? Rather he had died than face this disillusion about himself.

All the talk of liberty had soured his mind to those values deemed important by the British. Yet a haunting recollection and a poignant memory of his life in Ireland nibbled at his soul. Hungry brothers and sisters, mounting taxes, no hope for a future with the rule of landowners—all these things seared his heart. If Ireland had been in revolt, he would have picked up a hoe or a stick for his homeland.

I know how these rebels feel. But in understanding them, do I dare side with their cause? If he confessed his true feelings, he admitted a kinship to them.

Shortly after Henry had succumbed to rest, he awoke to the low hum of voices. He recognized they belonged to Elijah, his wife, and Delight. Darkness prevailed except for the faint light of a candle, and he focused his attention on every word.

"Elijah, cannot someone else deliver this message?" Mistress Butler wept with her soft request.

"There is more fighting along the Hudson. Our troops need the information. I have no choice, my dear Elizabeth. My conscience gives me no rest."

"But the danger," his wife continued, "and you wish to take Delight?"

"No one will suspect a man and his daughter delivering goods. We shan't go far, and danger will be beyond us. Once I make the delivery, I will be home immediately."

"Mama, please understand. I want to help Papa. God will be with us. He will be our shield and protector." Delight's voice rang out true as always. If the young woman had any doubts about the dangers and risks of this rebellion, Henry had never heard them.

"What if soldiers arrive to question Henry? Most assuredly he has heard every word. What will become of us?" Mistress Butler reasoned.

Elijah drew in a heavy breath. "I believe he will honor our home. He is a God-fearing man, one who knows the way of the righteous. He wears a British uniform, but his heart strengthens to our cause."

Silence echoed around them. "Very well," Mistress Butler whispered. "Godspeed. I'll prepare a bundle of food while you hitch up the wagon and ready yourselves. How long will you be gone?"

Again no one spoke. Elijah must have motioned to his wife. "If all goes well," he said, "we will be spending the evenings in various homes along the way."

"Am I to suppose you have other duties along the way?"

Elijah's boots tromped across the floor. "Yes, my dear. Not a moment shall be wasted."

All of Henry's earlier thoughts resurfaced. A bit of relief washed over him in not knowing their destination. He felt no ill will toward Elijah and his mission. Quite the contrary, he rather envied and admired their courage. *Oh Lord, I cannot fathom having such faith in one's convictions. I am greatly troubled. In my pledge to serve the king, I should turn Elijah in. Even while I pray, my heart is twisted and turned in searching for the truth. But he is right. I could never report his workings to the British.*

⟡

In the dark of early morning with only the stars and a three-quarter moon lighting a white path, Delight rode with Papa in silence. They traveled along a solitary path toward the rendezvous point in New York with the rhythmic sound of the horses' hooves easing her mind like a lullaby. Tucked away in her left shoe was the precious information for General Gates. The warm evening and the lull of the wagon made for her half-awake, half-asleep state.

"Would you like to lie down in the wagon?" Papa's question broke the silence.

"I think not. I like riding here next to you."

"As though you were a little girl again?"

Delight smiled and linked her arm in his. "You have always been tree height to me, Papa."

"Someday, probably sooner than I desire, another man will

inspire you to those sentiments."

She laughed lightly. "He'd have to possess all of your fine attributes."

"All?" he teased. "Shall the poor man also have my faults?"

"Oh Papa, you have so few."

He roared, sending his mirth out into the night. "I believe you need to have this discussion with your mother. She might enlighten you."

Delight leaned on his strong shoulder. "You are going to enlist, aren't you?" She whispered the words as though Mama rode with them.

"I am anxious to do my share."

"Is that your second mission in New York?"

"Possibly."

"But you are contributing to the cause now."

He paused before continuing. "This is not the first time."

Guilt crept through her about not telling Papa what she had done when the redcoats occupied Boston. "Is it not enough?"

"Not when it plagues a man's heart and mind to do nothing less for the freedom of his family."

Tears stung her eyes. "You should be an orator."

"A cooper suits me fine."

"A man should always seek higher aspirations," Delight insisted.

"I am, daughter. It is my fondest wish for my children and grandchildren to proudly state their father and grandfather fought in the war for independence."

"But—"

"Not simply in the capacity of carrying information."

Delight felt a yoke of sadness. "I understand, for as a woman I have wanted to do so much more."

"Your mother and Aunt Anne are planning to melt down pewter next week and make musket cartridges."

"And I will help."

Papa hurried the pace on the horses. "Your soldier must not discover this."

"Who? Certainly you don't mean Henry. I would never reveal

patriot information."

"Your sisters might speak unawares. That is why your time with Mama and Aunt Anne must be in secret."

She nodded and closed her eyes, more weary than she'd originally believed.

"Henry is a good man," Papa said. "Our plight for freedom is not unknown to him."

Irritation clouded over her. "What do you mean?"

"Delight, remember how Henry told you he joined the British army for transportation here from Ireland? For a better way of life?"

"And he is a weaver of cloth by trade."

"Do you not see? Henry is no different than my father coming to America to establish his cooper trade or the thousands of others who braved the dangers of ocean travel to better themselves and their families."

Papa's words made sense. Although Delight distrusted Henry, he often displayed a likeable side. "I comprehend what you are saying, but how do you propose to convince him?"

"Through prayer and what he senses in our family. The longer he lives in our home, the more he sees our passion for liberty."

She sighed. "One afternoon Mercy and Hope were playing with their dolls in the hall. When I listened to their chatter, they were imitating you and Mother discussing your enlistment."

Elijah chuckled. "And what was the result?"

"With the girls, Mercy enlisted despite Hope's protests. Of course, Henry heard every word. At the time I merely found it all humorous, but his privy to the game is, as you say, an influence to our way of thinking."

"And you, Delight, are the biggest influence in his life."

"Papa, I'm afraid you are sadly mistaken. Neither of us is prone to pleasantries. We barely tolerate each other."

"Do you know why?"

She righted herself from his shoulder. "I have no notion whatsoever other than I have tended to him while he recovers."

"Ponder on this matter. You are a loyal patriot and a godly

woman. Of late, I have noticed you are kinder to him, but you have not relinquished one bit from our cause."

And I shall not deviate. "You would like for me to be gentle, but firm?"

He turned and smiled broadly. "A wise and beautiful daughter I have."

"For you, Papa, I can do what you ask. Sometimes he is not entirely intolerable."

Elijah's laughter rang around them. "Delight, I do believe the two of you would make a fine pair—providing he forsook his redcoat ways."

Delight bit back the remark she'd have eagerly passed to her sisters if they had mentioned such a ridiculous notion. "Papa, surely you don't mean such?"

"Indeed I do. I see the way the man looks at you and is thoroughly confused, and I see the way you are vexed with him."

"That is not an indication of love."

"Is it not? Perhaps this is another matter to discuss with your mother."

Out of respect, Delight chose not to reply. Never in a hundred years would she consider Henry O'Neill a proper suitor—not even if he enlisted in the Continental army and became a general overnight.

Chapter 6

Much to Henry's confusion, he sorely missed Delight. Her wit and clever mannerisms kept his mind occupied, although he could live without the sarcasm. She made him feel alive. By their battling of words over the war, he could once again imagine carrying his musket and exchanging conversation with his compatriots. Never, in all his days, did he think he would miss a lively discussion with an argumentative woman.

In moments like these, he recalled his time with Adam. His friend had said he'd been drafted into the British army along with many young men of poor means. Henry pushed Adam's memory aside. Neither unshed tears nor bitterness would bring back his friend. More so than ever, Henry felt guilt pricking him like a burr, for his sentiments leaned toward the rebels. He agreed with most of their complaints.

Eager to depart from this room he had come to regard as a prison, Henry inquired of Charity for a fallen limb. She and Faith secured one, and with a little effort, he trimmed and fashioned it into a crutch. His restless spirit yearned to be outside even if it meant more pain. The weather had grown slightly cooler, and he longed to linger on a grass blanket with Bear and enjoy the first whispers of autumn.

One aspect of his confinement embarrassed him. He earnestly desired the necessary room rather than have to endure one more day with the chamber pot. He cringed each time Delight lugged it from the room—and she was always quick to note her disgust. For that concession alone, he'd crawl from the Butler home. Once he secured his freedom, he would beg Mistress Butler for a set of Elijah's clothes while he mended the huge tear in his uniform breeches.

When Henry was ready to try out his crutch, Charity, Remember, Faith, and Patience offered aid, but he stubbornly refused their assistance and struggled to his feet. *Wish they would go about their*

business. This is difficult enough without women hovering over me.
Forcing his weight onto his hands, he leaned on his good leg and
pulled himself up far enough so that he could grab the crutch.
He sweated profusely but dared not give in to the pain. Once he
steadied himself, he glanced into the sisters' anxious faces and
grinned.

"Look here, lasses. I am ready for a race." He moved about the
hall until he mastered the technique, then set his sights on the
kitchen. From there he'd venture into the blessed outdoors.

As he hobbled across the wooden floor, he could hear the
birds and smell something pleasant, which was a sight better
than himself. Bear walked alongside him, seemingly offering
encouragement. Odd, the dog had become a constant companion
after Delight declared the beast might eat him. He stopped to
take a long look at the kitchen—the source of laughter, tantalizing
fragrances, and more than one quarrel among the sisters. From this
room came a world he had grown to admire and respect. During
his initial entry into the home, his suffering had blinded him to
almost everything. But now, spotless best described the Butler's
kitchen, with rising bread—another pleasant smell—and the tart
sweetness of a bowl of apples. He'd forgotten how wonderful life
could be. Henry vowed to always treasure his two legs and the
freedom to have them take him places.

Thank Thee, Lord.

Outside in the bright sunlight in the company of the young
misses, he trudged toward a maple tree. Already he required a rest
but felt too proud to confess his weakness. "I should like to sit in
the shade of this glorious tree and enjoy a most beautiful day."

Henry's gaze drank in the beauty of changing leaves in gold and
scarlet. The air was cooler, too, and refreshing. How much he had
missed in a few short weeks.

"Would you like something to read?" Remember folded her
hands primly in front of her. At times he wanted to laugh at her
pious habits, for most surely her sisters mocked her mercilessly. Yet
Miss Remember beset him with her servant's heart. Aye, he should
follow her example.

"A Bible would be fittin' and anything else ye might have." He dropped the crutch and eased onto the soft ground, relishing every blade of grass beneath him. He tugged at one and held it up to the sunlight splaying through the tree branches, examining every strand. "I believe I've found heaven," he announced to the young women surrounding him. Glancing about, he wondered where Mercy and Hope had gone. "The little lasses, are they not out and about?"

"They're with Aunt Anne," Charity said. "She has a little boy their age, and the three play together famously."

He nodded. "Children need those times before they spend their lives working." He recalled well the day when whimsical inspirations were put aside to help provide for his brothers and sisters.

Once Remember returned with a Bible and an additional pamphlet, the sisters left him alone to read. Bear curled up next to his side and laid his mammoth head on Henry's lap. He breathed in the wondrous earth. Always given to the spaciousness of God's creation and a driving need to be outside, the three weeks of recuperation had deprived his natural instincts. Even when weaving in Ireland, he had the loom beyond the confines of four walls, surrendering only when night fell or the elements of weather prohibited his craft. That is why he enjoyed the rigorous training of the army while others complained.

Henry grasped the pamphlet Remember had brought to him. He curiously read the title: *Common Sense* by Thomas Paine. How peculiar, he hadn't heard of this title before. Perhaps the reading would spin away his hours. Completely immersed in the curious topic, he read for the next hour. One portion in particular, in which the writer addressed the purpose of kings, resonated with him.

Paine wrote, "*Government by kings was first introduced into the world by the Heathens, from whom the children of Israel copied the custom. It was the most prosperous invention the Devil ever set on foot for the promotion of idolatry. The Heathens paid divine honors to their deceased kings, and the Christian world hath improved on the plan by doing the same to their living ones. How impious is the title of sacred majesty applied to a worm, who in the midst of his splendor is crumbling into dust."*

Had Mr. Paine written the truth or merely twisted it to suit his own purpose? Henry felt the conviction of the man's words sear his heart. God be his judge, every word of *Common Sense* spoke to the core of his being.

∽

Near dusk on the third day of their travels, a few miles inside New York, a man on horseback approached Delight and her father.

"Are you a stranger to this fair country?" The rider reined his stallion in close to the wagon. The horse was a fine one indeed, its coat a silky black. It pawed at the ground, indicating a desire to run with the wind. The animal's master offered an incredible smile, sinking deep dimples into the corners of his cheeks.

"A sojourner, my friend." Papa brought the horses to a halt.

An odd reply for Papa unless. . .

"Ah, we are all but travelers on this earth for as long as the Lord blesses us," the young man said. "Pray tell, where are you bound?"

"Where the soil breathes of liberty."

The young man smiled. "I'm honored to meet you, sir. I've heard courageous tales about your endeavors."

I was correct in my assumption. Pride soared through Delight at Papa's valiant stand for the patriots.

Her father reached out to shake the man's hand, then nodded at Delight. "This is my daughter."

The young man extended his hand to her. "A pleasure to meet you, miss. I shall be near your home two weeks hence, the Lord providing."

"Do honor us with your presence," Papa said.

"Thank you. I shall most certainly do so." He tipped his tri-corn hat.

"We look forward to seeing you again," Delight added. She felt a glimmer of warmth spread over her cheeks at his engaging smile. She must ask Papa his name, since they had not been properly introduced.

"Pardon my hasty departure, but I must be on my way," the young man said.

"Of course." Papa turned to her. "Your shoe."

She hurriedly removed it and produced the document for her father. In the next instant, the young man turned his steed and disappeared into the brush. A strange sensation flashed through her body.

"And who might that be?" Delight's cheeks grew hot at the realization of her interest in the dark-haired young man with the dimpled smile, and she hid her confusion by bending down to put on her shoe.

"James Daniels, the son of an influential patriot. Both have worked closely with Sam Adams and the Sons of Liberty," Papa said, picking up the reins. "He's not married."

Delight caught her breath. "I simply wondered what his name was." *First Papa mentioned the most absurd possibility with Henry, and now he indicates Mr. Daniels is not married. Is he anxious to marry me off?*

"I merely mention his marital status because he works diligently for the patriots, often transporting information through enemy lines. He's been beaten by loyalists, wounded by British soldiers, has witnessed his father's death at Bunker Hill, and watched while his home burned to the ground, yet still he refuses to settle for anything less than liberty."

Delight's heart pounded hard against her chest. Such valor! Such heroism! That was the sort of man she wanted to share a home with one day, not the likes of a redcoat named Henry O'Neill with his carrot-top hair and unbridled loyalty to the British.

The matter of Henry had better be laid to rest. She had given Papa her word to treat him as a friend and a guest in order for his Tory heart to soften, but nothing else. And what did Papa mean by referring to Henry: *"I see the way the man looks at you and is thoroughly confused"*? No mind, she didn't intend to explore it another minute. The thought repulsed her.

That night, Papa and Delight slept under the wagon. They were anxious to return home and had traversed long into the evening until exhaustion prevailed against them. Even then, Delight's mind reeled with the happenings of this cherished time with Papa.

She'd witnessed a side of him that brought tears to her eyes—a true patriot. One day, she would draw her children to her side and tell them about their grandfather. Sooner than those days, she'd reveal her own small part in the war, although she still desired to do more than make musket shells.

James Daniels existed as another matter: quite handsome, that man. His smile could charm the bark off a tree. In short, she wouldn't mind his visit at all.

Two days later they finally made it back to Chesterfield. The small village had become home, but Delight sorely missed the excitement of Boston. Mercy and Hope met them with enthusiastic affection as though they had been gone for months. Mama and the rest of Delight's sisters filed out one by one to offer their hearty welcome and share in Papa's and Delight's embraces.

"Did you have a pleasant journey?" Mama eyed him suspiciously. She knew Papa's designs.

He lifted baby Elijah from her arms and held him close. "Tremendous success, my sweet Elizabeth. I will share it all with you after dinner tonight." He sniffed the air. "Do I smell venison stew? All the while we were gone, I pondered your fine cooking. Nothing compares to it."

Mama shook her finger at him. Her large, brown eyes twinkled, giving away her feigned irritation. "Elijah Abraham Butler, you most assuredly have done something of which I shall disapprove. Is that where your compliments lie?"

Papa graced her cheek with a kiss. "And how is Henry faring?"

She released a sigh, then laughed before throwing her arms around his neck. "He is doing quite well." She pointed to the maple tree where Henry waved. "He has set up a loom and is weaving all sorts of marvelous things."

So now he captivates the heart of my mother? Delight could scarce believe her ears.

Charity nearly bubbled with excitement. "Come see, Papa. He has begun weaving diapers for Elijah."

"And he is able to weave black-gauze aprons, damask cloths, and a host of other wonderful things," Patience said.

"Wonderful!" Papa strode toward the maple tree, carrying Elijah, while Mercy and Hope nestled close to their father's sides. "Greetings, Henry."

"Aye, Elijah. We missed ye." Henry grinned. "And ye, too, Delight."

I fail to believe you missed me. She released a heavy sigh. His comment irritated her, since they rarely enjoyed each other's company.

"I have taken to repay ye for your kindness," Henry continued. "Mistress Butler states some of my goods are not available here."

"True," Papa said. "We have need of your fine services." He examined Henry's work and complimented his craftsmanship. "I'd like to keep you employed. The entire town could use your services."

"The British army would not agree with you, sir." Henry's blue eyes fairly danced, and a smile twisted at the corners of his mouth. Never had he talked so freely and acted so lively.

"We might be able to arrange something."

Papa, this daring invites trouble. You cannot trust the enemy.

Henry chuckled. "I do long for this war to be abated, for I miss my trade." He peered around Papa to where Delight stood. "See, your generous care has given me strength to spend me days outside."

"I see that," Delight said. The smile he offered made her uncomfortable. A vision of the helpless, wounded soldier who relied on her assistance strolled through her mind. Why did she suddenly prefer the hurting man to the one on his way to wholeness? Confusion needled at her. She disliked the man immensely, and once his leg healed, he would be gone. That thought should give her tremendous pleasure. But it didn't, and an inkling of validity in her father's words made her furious.

"Soon I will be running like a strapping lad," Henry said. "Already I'm leaning less and less on the crutch."

"In your haste, are you causing more harm to your leg?" Delight instantly regretted her question. She wished Papa had never indicated his observations about Henry.

Henry's gaze met hers, causing another flush of warmth to her cheeks. "Methinks the use makes me stronger, but I thank ye for the concern."

She felt the stares of her sisters like a sharp sword. No doubt, they would have thought little if she had returned his comments with a sharp retort. "I. . .I hope you understand your healing is of utmost importance to all of us."

"Come along." Papa's voice rang out above the silence. "I am famished, and I'm sure Delight is as well."

"Shall we call you when the meal is ready?" Mama said to Henry. "Or do you wish to join us now?"

"This is your family's time together," Henry said, already scrutinizing his weaving. "There is still more than an hour of daylight left, and I am eager to complete this piece. In fact, I should most enjoy eating here."

"Very well." Mama linked her arm into Papa's. "I will have one of the girls bring you a generous portion of venison stew."

"Please, ma'am, could Miss Delight bring it to me?"

I f Delight had set her mind to behave like a heathen, she'd been given the opportunity. Her first evening at home, and Henry wanted her to deliver his meal? If he could hobble about on his crutch, he could make his way to the kitchen when he finished his weaving.

As they strode toward the house, Papa stepped to her side and whispered, "Remember our conversation? This is an opportunity for you to extend Christian love and further instruct him in the way of patriots."

She obediently nodded but inwardly cringed. "Yes, Papa."

"When darkness settles, I'll invite him to a game of checkers and afterward chess. I feel merriment in my bones."

Delight knew the details of Papa's evening plans skirted around the war. He merely wished to postpone telling Mama he had enlisted in the Continental army. He had money stored away if times got lean before his return, and Uncle Matthew and Aunt Anne had already shared an abundance of vegetables and apples. All of the girls had been busy helping Mama preserve food for winter, from dried beans and squash to fruit preserves. Soon they would be cooking thick, dark apple butter flavored with sugar and cinnamon and pouring it into jars. Aunt Anne had given them rhubarb sauce from the spring and jelly from wild berries. Before Papa planned to leave, he'd help Uncle Matthew butcher pigs, sheep, and cows for the long winter ahead. Already, hams hung in the smokehouse.

Enduring cold weather without Papa sounded more dismal than the inches of snow that would drift against the sides of their house. At least they had the companionship of Uncle Matthew and Aunt Anne—and there were other dear folk in Chesterfield, too—but how she longed to return to Boston. Delight shook her head. Dwelling on her gloomy situation would not change the current circumstances.

Casting aside her contemplations, Delight took a pottery plate of the thick stew, a chunk of bread, and a pewter mug of milk to Henry. His request still irked her. Since when did she become his keeper?

Remember your word to Papa. He sees a patriot's spirit in the man, whether you do or not.

Henry obviously didn't see her approaching, for he stirred not a muscle while he attended the loom. His breeches had been mended in her absence, albeit the stitching looked a little less than even, but it did bind the tear sufficiently. He had definitely been busy, and in light of his weaving, she admired his industrious nature. Delight studied him, tilting her head slightly.

"You are gifted," she whispered.

"Thank you, lass. I wondered if ye intended to speak to me or possibly—"

"Douse you with the stew?" In truth the act had crossed her mind, teasing her hands until they tickled.

His blue eyes widened and he laughed, long and hearty. She liked this side of Henry, and he looked. . .well, rather pleasing. "You are blushing, Miss Delight. Methinks ye had the thought rummaging about your head. I'm glad I spoke of it before I wore my meal."

Best you not know the truth for I'd be redder than the jacket of your uniform. She handed him the food.

"Thank ye, lass. Sit down, please. Have you eaten?"

"Not yet."

"Would you care to join me?" Henry's tone indicated an earnest request, one that left her bewildered.

"I. . .I could fill a plate and sup with you." She wondered what the origin of her awkwardness might be. That strange sensation in the pit of her stomach assailed her again, as if she still traveled in the wagon and had hit a bump in the road.

"Splendid. I shall wait for ye and tidy up a bit around our spacious dining area."

Again that endearing smile. What had changed with him? She excused herself and returned a few moments later, but not without some jesting from her sisters about choosing to dine with Henry rather than her family.

"Never mind, daughters," Papa said. "She is conducting herself in a hospitable manner, and I find the trait commendable."

Delight relaxed in his defense of her. They had grown closer in the past few days, and she'd have been incredibly hurt if he'd allowed the teasing.

Once seated beneath the towering maple on a soft green blanket sprinkled with a few turning leaves of scarlet and gold, she noted the red color of Henry's hair blended with the early signs of autumn. She scurried through her mind for a topic of conversation. She didn't dare tell him about her and Papa's journey.

"Shall I give thanks?" Henry said.

Delight bowed her head respectfully, eager to hear how a redcoat asked God's blessings.

"Heavenly Father, thank Ye for bringing my friends home safely. I have missed them."

Missed them? Delight's fingers trembled.

"Thank Ye for the continued healing of me leg and the craft Ye have given me to repay the Butlers for their kindness. Bless this food and the hands that have prepared it. In Jesus' precious and holy name, amen."

He prays just like the rest of us. How strange, and he didn't mention the war.

Henry picked up his pewter fork, soon to be melted down into musket balls. "I smell the changing season in the air, and from your house, apples and cinnamon."

"Mama does make delectable apple dishes. I was thinking about it myself—and all the preparations for the coming months." She nibbled at a piece of bread, conscious of his gaze upon her. Her stomach growled, and she fought the urge to devour the entire piece of bread, but those were inappropriate manners for a lady. "The nights are growing cooler," she added. "A welcome respite from the hot summer."

"I spent two winters in Canada, frightfully cold."

She nodded. "I suspect that must have been a hard life."

He glanced up from his food and caught her watching him. "All soldiers struggle with difficulties, lass. The elements can be friend or foe."

She hastily looked away. This uneasiness between them must be attributed to only one thing. "Henry, we are not arguing."

He shrugged. "I gather it's because neither of us wishes to debate on our differences."

"I am too weary to contend about the war." Her admittance compounded the exhaustion pelting against her body.

"And I am too glad to see ye."

Her appetite immediately diminished. "Why did you say that?" She wanted to sound demanding, but instead she whispered the question.

He rubbed his chin with its weeks of growth. "I'm not certain, but it is the truth."

I cannot admit the same conclusion when I'm not convinced of my feelings. Oh Henry, I would rather be quarreling.

They finished eating in silence while Delight tried to remember all those things she appreciated about the handsome James Daniels. That's where her musings should rest, not on a redcoat.

"Delight, I would like to discuss something with ye," Henry began. "While ye and your father were gone, I made a decision."

Her head spun, not knowing if she wanted to hear his findings. Perhaps knowledge of his subject matter would put her heart at ease.

From the house, Mercy and Hope raced toward them, waving and calling their names. "Papa is ready to play checkers with us and chess with Mr. Henry!"

⬧

Henry waited patiently while Elijah pondered his next move. The master of the house had fallen under the luck of the Irish. The patriot was three moves short of losing his king. They played by firelight, with the Butler family seated around and nary sputtering a word. Henry felt the family's championing Elijah in the silence wafting about the room.

On Elijah's right, the mistress held a tight smile. Her gaze wandered to the crackling fire, where she stared intently. No doubt her husband's role in the war kept her attention from the chessboard. She alone did not take the game seriously. On his left, Delight's sights fell on the sadly missing pieces of her father's side.

Be glad the fate of the colonies has not been decided in this game of reason.

His gaze could have feasted on her comely face forever, but he dared not relinquish his thoughts to his stirring emotions. First the family needed to learn of his discoveries, then he must make necessary plans. Only the advanced healing of his leg slowed him from making declarations this very night. Out of respect for Elijah and Delight's return home, he must refrain from drawing attention to himself. Although, if not for the precipitous arrival of Mercy and Hope, he would have told Delight of his prayerful conclusions earlier in the evening.

A smile lingered on his lips, not for the game but for the peace enveloping his soul. He loved this family with all of their quirks and pleasantries. Ah, Elijah truly led his household in a worthy manner, and the mistress held a silent strength. Noticeably, each young woman not only possessed worthy inner qualities but also outward beauty.

Delight had captured his heart and mind. She must have a sprinkling of Irish to love a good debate and fear not any game. Her oval face and flawless skin would hold any man's attention, and he dearly loved her spirit.

Charity, a vision of sweetness with not near the hasty tongue of Delight, held the qualities of a devoted wife and mother. Sometimes he wondered if deep inside the lass a resolute spirit grappled to surface. She always looked a bit pale, and Henry prayed God would keep her healthy.

Remember shared her faith in every word and act. Benevolent best described her nature. One day, she'd be a prize for the man who won her heart. Aye, he must have a servant's heart as well to do her proper.

Faith and Charity were both very much alike. They even resembled each other, more so than the other sisters with their freckled noses and sparkling smiles. Faith liked to cook and did a fine job.

Patience, the shy one. He had seen her slip away to put her

thoughts into words. He viewed depth beneath those huge, brown eyes curtained in thick lashes like her mother and sisters. If he were not mistaken, quiet strength lived within her heart.

Mercy and Hope possessed the innocence that brought joy and laughter into each family member's life. They certainly had done so to Henry. When they lifted their angelic faces framed by a sea of lace in their mobcaps, he could refuse neither of them.

Again he stole another look at Delight. She must have sensed his scrutiny, for she met his quick look with a blush. If they were alone, he'd be hard pressed not to steal a kiss. Suppressing a chuckle, he could imagine her incensed reaction to such a bold act. When the time came to say good-bye, he would miss her sorely. How could a man lose his heart in so short a time? Even so, he'd found a higher purpose in the cause of freedom.

Finally Elijah moved his rook. "Henry, it is a powerful affliction to lose a game of chess in my own house, but I wouldn't want you to lessen your skill."

Henry chuckled. "Are ye sure ye want to move that piece, sir?"

Elijah looked up, his gray eyes peering into his opponent's. "Is that a strategy? I'm thinking you are pushing me to make a different move."

"Aye, I am." *God is my witness. I have a weak spot for those destined to lose.*

"The rook stays."

The women were silent as they huddled around Elijah.

Henry moved his knight and took the rook. Elijah groaned, left with only a bishop and king. His next move put his king in check. "I believe I'm a beaten man," he said. "My king is doomed."

"Such a sad state of affairs, but I have always favored this game, and ye played well, my friend," Henry said.

Elijah clasped his hand on his shoulder. "You are a good man, Henry O'Neill, no matter what color uniform you wear. You took my king in a befitting game."

Elijah took a deep breath. Courage nearly escaped him. "You should have won. Americans fare better without the rule of royalty." He rose from his chair. "Good night, dear people. May you sleep well."

Chapter 8

For a long moment, Delight believed she had misunderstood Henry. Wonder at what had transpired in her absence danced across her mind. She glanced about the room. Papa's mouth stood agape. He, too, must be evaluating Henry's words. Illuminated hope from her father's prayers, of which she had only half attended, lifted her spirits.

"Henry, would you care to elaborate?" Papa said, his tone befitting curiosity.

He turned and faced them all, lifting his chin with an air of pride. "Sir, I don't want to dampen your first night home with a matter about me self."

"Indeed, if I heard correctly, greater jubilation than our return has blessed this family."

Delight watched a myriad of emotions crease Henry's face. Even in the faint light, she could see his eyes mist. Was this what he wanted to tell her earlier? She braved forward, curiosity propelling her words. "I would like to hear what has transpired."

Only the sound of the clock ticking from the parlor graced her ears. Henry's gaze seemed to sweep from one person to the other, finally resting upon her.

"Perhaps Henry doesn't need such an audience," Papa said.

"I agree." Mama stood from her chair beside him. "Come along, girls. This has been an exhausting day, and I think it is time we join young Elijah in our own beds."

"I will accompany you," Papa offered. "In addition, my dear Elizabeth, you and I have a matter of our own to discuss."

"Aye," she said, her skirts bustling around the table. "I fear I may already know."

Poor Papa, but then again Mama might have steadied herself for the inevitable. Delight took her leave of the departing group in silence, certainly a trait uncommon to her. She smiled at each one, offering an embrace and words of love before they mounted the stairs. Not one teased or asked why she alone should be privy to Henry's words, although she hoped each thought her nursing position gave her the right to hear whatever tormented him.

Noting her clammy hands, she rubbed them on her apron and methodically placed the chess pieces back into an engraved wooden box.

"I was so distracted that I'm not sure how I defeated your father," Henry said softly.

She avoided his stare while a blundering loss for words added to her discomfort. Finally she spoke. "He rarely loses. You must be well versed in the game."

"Delight." His voice soft, laced with warmth and a spark of tenderness, sent chills to her toes.

Startled by the change he evoked in her, she lifted her gaze to meet his. Unable to speak, she listened to her heart pound furiously against her bosom.

"Could we converse outside? I know the evening's a bit cool, but if you don't mind—"

"The night is pleasant, but I shall take a shawl nevertheless."

Henry reached for his crutch just when she sought to hand it to him. Their fingers touched, and she hastily pulled back as though she had been burned. Perhaps she had.

They stepped into the chilly night air, and he closed the door. The creaking hinges and the singing insects sounded soothing in a strange way. Delight swallowed hard. *Help me, Lord, for I know not how to act or what to say.* The realization that Henry might no longer be her enemy both excited and alarmed her. The unknown, that is what she feared.

"A stroll would be pleasant," she said. Placing one foot in front of the other gave her something to do. Without movement, she would most assuredly dissolve into a pool of emotions she did not comprehend. Her anticipation closely resembled the cherished moments when her younger sisters accepted the Lord as their personal Savior, although nothing could compare to knowing a loved one embraced the Lord.

Bear joined them, loping along on the other side of Henry. She wished the dog had elected to separate them. At least she could have afforded herself some comfort with the animal between them.

"God has been speaking to me," Henry said. "I confess I may have made a tragic error."

"In what way?" If her heart beat any fiercer, it would surely burst.

"With the aspirations of this country, especially with the patriots' cause."

"Are you certain you want to be telling me rather than my father?"

"I believe he already has assessed my heart."

"Then, pray tell, what has God spoken to you?"

He clasped one hand behind his back and took a few more awkward steps before speaking. "Ye know my homeland in Ireland is poor. There is no hope for a man in me low estate to better himself or own land. Although me father has an honorable trade, he has never made enough to take care for all our needs. Always the taxes. Always the hard work."

Henry took a deep breath. "Here in America, I see a man's fondest dream of securing a bright future—hope of owning a prosperous business and feeling pride in his endeavors. I mistakenly believed the British had a right to make monetary demands—or any other mandate—on their colonies. But when I reflected upon me home, the poor drafted into the army, how one is born into a permanent station in life, I grew furious at the unfairness of it all. Here in America, I sense victory over oppression regardless of heritage."

Undoubtedly an answer to prayer, Delight silently acknowledged. She looked up at him and said, "Your words are true. Those are the things for which we strive."

"But I grew angry with me treacherous thoughts about Britain and wondered if me conclusions were simply unfaithful to the king. Indeed this poor man who hungered for liberty. . ." He paused. "Am I making sense, or am I rambling on?"

Still trembling, she admitted, "I understand you perfectly."

"The problem has been me friend Adam, who was killed just before I received my injury. I wanted the patriots to pay for his death, and I sincerely felt me sympathy for your cause meant he died in vain."

Delight sensed the grief he bore. It troubled her spirit, touching her heart as though God wanted her to feel Henry's intense pain. "I am so sorry. I've been guilty of thinking the British were all animals—hating them with no more provocation than seeing the uniform on their backs."

"And I've sinned with the same beliefs about patriots, but me mind has conformed to what I now believe is God's choice for me life."

She stopped in the middle of the road. "And how did this happen?"

"Sweet Remember acted as God's messenger, an angel in her own right." She heard the smile in his voice. "The first day I hobbled out to the maple tree, she asked if I wanted to read. She brought me a Bible and a curious pamphlet by the title of *Common Sense.*"

Delight giggled and covered her mouth. "Oh, my. How very much like me."

He joined in her laughter. "I thought she had brought me a novel, something in which to lose my worries. I began reading, and time slipped by. Everything I have ever secretly felt or desired was written within those pages, as though the diary of my longings had taken form."

"And did you struggle with what Mr. Paine recommended?" She considered how she would feel if a dear friend had fallen prey beside her and the enemies' beliefs had suddenly become her own.

In the darkness, she saw him nod. "Aye, and I still do, but God, in His mercy, has shown me that liberty and freedom are due all men. I sorely miss Adam, but he is in a better place where freedom is not a question that bleeds a man's soul. No longer are ye rebels in my eyes, but patriots worthy of God's blessings."

Delight's eyes moistened and a single tear trickled down her cheek as her throat constricted with the overwhelming stirrings in her heart. "Papa and I have prayed for this, but I've not been a good example of our Lord. I gloried in your pain and hated you for what you represented."

"Neither have I pleased Him, urging ye to quarrel with me."

She hesitated. *Lord, I know not what Thee intends in Thy great plan.* "What shall we do now?"

"Friendship, perhaps?"

"I would like a good friend."

"This is splendid, and I hope our days of bickering are finished. I promise to do me utmost to prove it so." His words were punctuated with sincerity.

"And I as well, although I shall miss our debates." She laughed, and he joined her.

"I met a neighbor in your absence, Mistress Rutherford."

Delight could not think of one compliment regarding the woman. "She's. . .she is an unusual woman."

"She enjoyed my company until she discovered me reading Mr. Paine's pamphlet."

"What did she say?"

"Well, lass, she was familiar with his writings and less than pleased with me."

Remembering Abby Rutherford's surly disposition, Delight imagined the woman's response. "Neither are we among her favorite people."

"I know with a certainty that if I ever desire a heated argument, I need only to knock on her door."

Again they shared a laugh, and it shattered the wall of past tensions between them. They walked farther, Henry limping along and Delight keeping pace beside him. Her thoughts raced with so many notions about this man. What would he do once his leg healed? And what of this new. . .friendship?

Logic gave her no peace. For once Henry's leg mended, he would be gone, but where?

Ↄ

Although the night had a crisp edge to it, Henry felt uncomfortably warm. He wanted to tell Delight first of his revelation, but now that he had, he didn't know what to expect from her. An air of foolishness swept over him. This woman had no concept of her effect on him, and she might make light of it if she did suspect his growing feelings.

Friendship, he'd suggested. And she had agreed. Rather he

continue voicing his plans for the future than speak too soon and face rejection.

"Once me leg heals completely, I will need a new uniform," he said.

The soft thud of his crutch against the road sounded as calming as the creak of a rocking chair against a wooden floor. "Blue is much more pleasing with your hair than red." She laughed, and her mirth eased his anxiety.

"My whole family, even my mother, has this color of hair! Dare you criticize it?" He couldn't hide the jesting in his voice.

"I shan't find fault in the substance, Henry. It is the unusual shade that I speak of." She brought her finger to her lip. "I believe Papa would gladly accept any color of hair, since he has nary a strand."

"Poor Elijah. I assumed living with eight women would cause any man to lose his hair."

She started to scold, but once again the two broke into laughter.

"I like the sound of your laugh," Henry said, "like the sound of a million fairies flutterin' about."

"You speak of fairies?"

"Little magical creatures from Ireland, lass. Not real of course, but I do know some who are not thoroughly versed in the Christian faith and believe folklore is true. They live and breathe leprechauns and such."

"Leprechauns?" She laughed again.

"Wee elves living in only me homeland, and if ye catch them, they will reveal hidden treasure." Whenever he spoke of Ireland, his brogue thickened.

"Do you miss home?"

"At times. I knew when I enlisted that I might never see me dear family again, but I'd love for them to see America."

"A pleasant thought. Perhaps someday they will."

"Perhaps they will. I would like to see the look on their faces at this wondrous land."

"Henry, are you sure about. . .changing sides?"

He heard the hesitation in her voice. "I would be a turncoat." He didn't feel remorseful. He merely stated a fact. "But rather a turncoat from the British than a man hindering the freedom of another."

"I am proud of you."

His heart seemed to swell. "Thank ye, lass. God gives every man a call on his life, and mine appears to be this one."

∕∕

The next two weeks found Henry growing stronger. Once a soldier stopped by to check on him, a friend who took the time to give him news about the war. He assured Henry that within weeks he would join up with the fighting again. Henry said nothing of his new allegiance. All would know the truth when his leg healed.

Every day he relied less on his crutch, until the morning arrived when at last he could cast it aside for a limp. Along with his healing came an enthusiasm for life—a vigor that gave him fresh hope for the days ahead. He abandoned his uniform for a tricorn hat, a white blouson shirt tied at the neck with leather pieces, brown breeches, and white woolen socks with his boots. Soon—much sooner than he desired—he must enlist in the Continental army. Not that he didn't want to fight for the cause. He simply loathed the thought of leaving Delight and her family.

He believed she didn't realize his true feelings, but her sisters whispered things that caused her to blush. Before he left their loving home, he must reveal his heart and take the chance of her rejection.

The people of Chesterfield learned of Henry's weaving and kept him constantly in their employ. He gave every bit of his earnings or barter to Elijah. After all, it was the least he could do.

The pattern of life became predictable. Predictable, that is, until Saturday, October 4, when a lone rider pulled a magnificent black stallion to a halt in front of the Butler home. Henry glanced up from his loom, taking in the noble stance of both horse and man.

"Good day, sir," the stranger called.

Henry returned the greeting and rose to meet the man. Elijah was off delivering a barrel, and the women were alone. "Can I help ye?"

The man tied his reins around a hitching post and sauntered

Henry's way. "I am James Daniels, looking for Elijah Butler. Is this his home?"

Henry extended his hand. "Aye sir, that it is. I'm Henry O'Neill. Elijah is due back shortly. He had goods to deliver."

The dark-haired man grinned broadly. "Mind if I sit and visit with you while I wait?"

Henry gestured for James to join him beneath the tree and offered a jug of water. He seemed a pleasant fellow.

"Did you receive an injury from the war?" James lifted the jug to his lips.

Henry touched his thigh. "Aye. Though it is nearly well."

"What battle?"

"Near Stillwater."

"Blasted redcoats. But we're turning them now. I hear tell there is a new battle brewing up along the Hudson now. We will whip them this time."

"The patriots need a victory to keep up their spirits."

James leaned closer and peered from side to side. "I hear Burgoyne has had his fill of deserters. He's offering ten and twelve dollars for the return of every missing soldier."

Chapter 9

Delight and Mama spent all morning behind Aunt Anne's house, melting down pewter and lead from dishes, kitchen utensils, and various other cups and candlesticks.

Aunt Anne, a quiet lady, small in stature, with flaxen-colored hair and sky blue eyes, was certainly not the picture of rebellion. She tossed a candlestick that once had belonged to a grandmother from Germany into the kettle. "I daresay my proper grandmother would have fainted dead away if she had seen me do this."

"Do you have any regrets?" Delight searched her aunt's placid face.

"Not at all. If I were forced to carry a torch from room to room, I'd still melt down my candlestick." Her words were spoken quietly but with the forcefulness of a lightning bolt.

"Here is my contribution." Mama's eight pewter goblets fell with a plop. "Mother gave me those as a wedding gift. Aye, she'd have disowned me, I fear." She stirred the contents with a heavy stick, then straightened her back. "I'd rather use them to supply a patriot's musket than to drink ale taxed by the British."

Delight laughed. Her mother had a way with words that she envied.

Aunt Anne poured another kettle of hot molten liquid into a musket ball mold, and while it cooled, Mama and Delight formed cartridges from the ones made the day before. Delight much preferred making the cartridges. She could see a finished product, ready to transport to the Continental army.

"Daughter, are you lining these up like soldiers in battle?"

"Precisely. I want to see how many of our men we are aiding." She pulled her sewing scissors from her apron pocket and cut several sections of paper to extend beyond a six-inch metal tube. Once they exhausted the paper, they would use fabric. "Every one of these I cut makes me feel as if I've increased our chances to win the war. It makes me proud—but in a satisfied way." The feeling was different than that which she'd had while running messages in Boston, but the work was a worthwhile endeavor, nonetheless.

Delight rolled the tube one inch beyond the paper's edge, then dropped in a musket ball on the end where the paper overlapped and tied it tightly with twine. Holding the paper and tube securely, she poured in an explosive powder, pulled out the tube, and tied that end.

"I wonder what the British soldiers would do if they found us melting metal into musket balls and assembling cartridges?" Aunt Anne studied what they had completed.

Mama chuckled while tying the powder charge on a cartridge. "They'd take them all for themselves and probably order us to make more."

"I would rather be shot by my own handiwork," Aunt Anne said. Hearing baby Elijah cry out in his sleep, she stepped over to the cradle once used by her children and nudged it into motion. "How soon must Elijah leave?"

Mama's mood instantly changed. and her facial expressions revealed the weight of her concern. "One more week to get the butchering completed. I cannot convince him otherwise, and sometimes I am not certain I should."

"Matthew is talking the same." Aunt Anne glanced up. "Joining the others in the fighting means so much to him. Like you, Elizabeth, I understand his longing, but I am still afraid. If only we didn't have to worry about their safety."

"Henry is anxious for his leg to heal so he can enlist in the Continental forces." Delight instantly regretted her words. They were talking about husbands. She and Henry were friends.

"And how do you feel about his decision?" Aunt Anne rejoined them as little Elijah drifted back to sleep.

Delight hesitated and took a deep breath. "I am proud for him. He is a good man, and I'm sure he will fight bravely."

"Is that all?" A half smile tweaked at Aunt Anne's mouth.

Delight ignored the implication and tended to the task of cartridge making. "We have begun a comradeship, and naturally I'm concerned about his welfare."

"Is that all?" Mama repeated Aunt Anne's question. When Delight's gaze flew to her face, no measure of teasing greeted her.

"What. . .what do you mean?"

Mama opened the musket ball mold and studied the metal to see if it had cooled sufficiently. She closed it abruptly, an obvious indication the contents needed to set awhile longer. "I see the way Henry looks at you, my dear. And although you may not be fully aware of your own sentiments, I see a spark of something more than admiration in your face."

Papa said nearly the same thing.

"Mama, I have nursed the man back to health, and we've come to know each other very well."

"Precisely."

"Friendship doesn't indicate anything more significant," Delight said.

"But it is a beginning. Need I remind you to whom he sought to reveal his decision to desert the British? While you were gone with Papa, he was like Bear without Mercy and Hope."

"I've noted the same behavior in the times I have visited," Aunt Anne added. "Matthew's remarked about you and Henry, too."

Warmth flew to Delight's face, and she shook her head. "You are sadly mistaken. Look at all the quarrels we've had—"

"Before he chose the side of the patriots," Mama said.

"In addition, I have my mind somewhat occupied with another."

Mama lifted a brow. "Daughter, it is not wrong to care for Henry."

But I don't know how I feel. If I did, this discussion would not be so difficult. She lowered her head and stuffed a musket ball into the paper form. "I understand." She paused, then added, "While with Papa, I did meet a pleasant man who said he planned to visit here soon."

Mama shrugged. "He captured your heart in one meeting?"

The conversation made her uncomfortable. "No, not at all. He's simply been in my thoughts."

"You are as stubborn as your father," Mama muttered. "Before we married, he told my sister his feelings for me were merely friendship and he could never imagine anything more. Three days later he spoke with my father about a possible marriage."

Aunt Anne laughed. "How well I remember. Although Matthew and I were young, we enjoyed the story."

But Henry and I are not you and Papa. We have said too many cruel things to each other to contemplate. . .consider. . .a mutual attraction.

But she'd seen the tenderness in Henry's eyes.

Mama hugged Delight's shoulders. "Forgive me for upsetting you. Affairs of the heart are never easy."

Henry conversed with James for almost an hour while they waited for Elijah. He continued to weave as they spoke about the war, the ongoing battle in Saratoga, the Continental Congress, and whatever other subjects the man fancied. James laughed easily— a good-natured lad in Henry's opinion. They commented about the pleasant weather and the fate of the troops in the winter months ahead.

"Under whom did you serve?" James finally said.

A nearly ill sensation inched around Henry's stomach. "Me references are not of the utmost."

James peered at him in obvious question. "In what manner?"

Henry ceased working and eyed the man squarely. "I was a member of the British forces—a redcoat, a lobsterback—until recently."

Not a trace of emotion crept across James's face. Neither did he utter a sound.

"The truth is, I got me self wounded at Stillwater, and soldiers brought me to the Butlers to mend. While here, I made some profound observations." He released a heavy sigh. "Me sympathies now belong to the American side. In short, I am a turncoat, and from what you said earlier, I have a price on me head."

James studied him for several long moments, as though search-ing for some mark of deceit—or so Henry surmised. "The British are combing the countryside, looking for their soldiers."

"I will be wary."

"May I ask what your plans might be once your leg is healed?"

The words were simple, the implication deadly.

Henry stiffened. "Me allegiance is to the Continental army. I will join and fight alongside the likes of ye."

"The likes of me?" James's voice rose. He clenched his fists and stood from the hard ground.

I am no match for a well man. If he desires a fight, I shan't be in worse condition than the day I arrived here.

A slow smile spread over James's face, and he stuck out his hand to grasp Henry's. "I would be proud to stand against the British with you. You have courage, Henry. It takes a brave man to admit he's wrong and do something about it."

"Then sit down, James. I am a bit uneasy with ye towering over me with your fists drawn."

James's laughter echoed around them, and once again he seated himself and talked on as before.

"Tell me, Henry, what do you know about Elijah's daughter? I met her two weeks ago and haven't been able to rid her face from my mind."

Not me Delight! Henry sought to resume his work, but his fingers refused to work together. *Could it be James and I are destined to be foes clamoring for Delight's affections instead of friends?* "The Butlers have seven daughters."

James shook his head. "I did not hear her name. She has light brown hair, large eyes—most likely brown, for it was dusk and some things I could not tell."

"Your description fits them all, and they are all quite comely."

From the two-story house came Mercy and Hope racing toward them. "There are the two youngest now." Henry beckoned to the girls and a moment later introduced them to James. The girls curtsied and politely greeted the man.

"My sisters, Charity, Remember, Faith, and Patience, have prepared a noonday meal," Mercy said. "Would you care to join us?"

"Thank you, I will indeed," James responded. "I'd like to meet all of your family."

But not me Delight if I can help it.

Hope offered a grin, displaying two missing teeth. "Papa will be home later, and Mama and Delight are at Aunt Anne's." She nodded, punctuating her words. "The baby is with Mama."

Henry awkwardly pulled himself up from the loom, his leg stiff from sitting all morning. If he had any luck at all, Elijah would return shortly, and James would venture on his way before Mistress Butler and Delight found their way home. Even better, perhaps James would find himself enamored with one of the other young women of the Butler household.

The moment Henry and James entered the kitchen, Charity began to blush, and James could only stare at the young woman.

James leaned over to whisper, "You were right, uh, about their pleasing appearance." He removed his hat, and Patience invited him to sit at the table while Faith set an extra plate, Remember added a mug, and Charity sliced a generous hunk of fresh-baked bread. Viewing all that transpired, the guest wore a constant smile.

An inward chuckle threatened to surface in Henry. With a stroke of God's mercy, his Delight would not move James in the slightest.

Elijah arrived shortly after Henry pronounced grace and took over the duties of entertaining the guest. Between Elijah and James, Henry heard quite a bit of news about the successes at Saratoga.

"General Arnold did an outstanding job," James said. "But there is a rift there with General Gage. Undoubtedly, if Arnold had received the reinforcements he needed, we would not have had to withdraw and instead would have given the British a good whipping."

"The battle is not over," Elijah said, "and with a taste of victory, we will run those redcoats back across the Atlantic."

"A good many of them are homesick and disillusioned," Henry said. "The situation here is not what we expected."

James looked at him with an air of appreciation. "You, Henry, know better than most the morale of the troops."

"Many of us thought we'd get here and the rebellion would be put down in a few months. We also believed there were very few patriots, and the loyalists were eager to join our forces."

"I fear it will be a long while before America finds its freedom." Elijah set his mug on the table. "Fine meal, my daughters. The cottage cheese and bread were quite tasty."

"I agree," Henry said.

James echoed his praises, and once more Charity blushed scarlet.

"James, will you be staying with us this night?" Elijah said.

"No sir. I need to ride on to Rutland before the afternoon is done."

"I would like for you to meet my wife. Are you of the mind to take a walk to my brother's home?"

Henry held his breath, wishing most intently that James would refuse Elijah's offer. Albeit good manners prevailed and the guest agreed. "And your other daughter is there also? The young woman I met two weeks past?"

"Most assuredly." Elijah winked at Henry. "Would you care to join us, Henry?"

He knows precisely what is happening here. Elijah Butler enjoys the game of matchmaking—too much. I fear James and I will be a source of amusement for him.

"Indeed, sir. This leg needs a bit of stretching out, and the walk will be refreshing."

Chapter 10

Delight counted the number of musket balls remaining and proceeded to cut fabric to form the cartridges. She had used all of their paper earlier and now resorted to the scraps before her. Holding up a strip of cloth, she turned to Aunt Anne. "I remember the dress you made from this."

Her aunt smiled and reached out to touch the pale green fabric. "The remnant still serves a good purpose, although I never fashioned it as a covering for a cartridge." She stared at the other pieces spread out on the ground. "Neither did I consider the cloth used for Matthew's shirts or my children's nightshirts."

Mama planted her hands on her hips. "I daresay, we never thought we'd be melting down our pewter and iron for musket balls either." She reached down to stroke baby Elijah's cheek with her finger. "But freedom requires a large toll."

Delight sensed her mother's sadness in Papa's approaching departure. For Mama, that knowledge must stand foremost in her thoughts. Delight wondered how she would feel if the man she loved intended to leave for war. Understanding Papa's not-so-distant journey to the Continental army saddened her enough.

The sound of men's voices alerted her. She quickly glanced at what they'd been doing and deemed it impossible to hide their workings.

It cannot be loyalists or British soldiers!

"I believe it's Elijah's voice I hear, but I cannot distinguish the other man." Mama released a ragged breath. Her face had turned a ghastly shade of white. "We should have devised a way to conceal what we have been doing."

Aunt Anne nodded, and she trembled. Delight's aunt seldom raised her voice or spoke openly in a crowd. Delight searched for something soothing to say, but with her ears strained to listen and a myriad of fears sweeping through her mind, she could only place an arm around Aunt Anne's thin shoulders. Suddenly Delight remembered the night she'd delivered information to Cavin Sullivan when the British soldiers pounded on the door of his tavern. She'd had nightmares for weeks following that frightful evening. Glancing about, she saw this fear now filled Mama and Aunt Anne.

"Elizabeth!" Papa called out.

Unaware of holding her breath, Delight let out a sigh of relief. *Thank Thee, merciful Father.*

"We are back here," Mama called.

Delight saw Papa move alongside the house with Henry behind him. He maneuvered fairly well without his crutch, his limp gradually becoming less profound. Then she saw him: James Daniels. Her knees grew weak, and she felt her face grow warm. The man indeed struck a fine pose.

"My dear Elizabeth." Papa waved at the fire heating the kettle full of metal and the other signs of what they were doing. "In the future, please use some discretion. We could have been the British." He shook his head, then offered her a light kiss to her cheek.

"The thought occurred to us too late," Mama replied. "Forgive me for alarming you."

Silent concern passed from Papa to Mama. He turned to greet Aunt Anne. "Good afternoon. You three have done well this day." He lifted Delight's chin and for a terrifying moment, she thought he might comment on her reddened face. "You above all should have used caution."

Why me? Sometimes Papa confused her.

"Elizabeth, I would like for you to meet a fine man here, James Daniels."

Mama curtsied and offered a welcome.

"Thank you, ma'am. Your daughters prepared an admirable noonday meal, and I am beholden to their kindness."

Was it her imagination, or did he cast a sideways glance at her? If anyone could paint the portrait of the most handsome man in America, surely James would be the subject.

"I'll be certain to tell them so." Mama looked obviously pleased. Had she been smitten by James's charms as well?

"This is my sister-in-law, Anne Butler."

Aunt Anne appeared to be calmer than Mama, but shy nevertheless. She curtsied and offered a faint smile.

"And this little one is my son," Papa continued, "another Elijah."

James peered into the cradle at the sleeping baby. "A fine young man, sir."

"And do you remember my daughter, Delight?" Papa grinned broadly, and again she felt her color mount.

"I remember the lovely woman I met two weeks ago, but I did not know her name. It is indeed a pleasure to see you again, Miss Butler."

She curtsied, feeling extremely awkward. "Thank you, sir." Sensing someone staring at her, she stole a look at Henry. He did not look pleased. *We are simply friends. He should be happy for me.* But the voice in her heart revealed Henry's true feelings.

"James must be leaving soon, but I wanted him to meet you." Papa wrapped his arm around Mama's waist and laughed. "Thankfully, all of my daughters resemble their beautiful mother."

"Indeed they do," James said. "How fortunate for them."

Papa and James shared a hearty laugh, but Delight cringed and Henry gave a tight smile. She caught James's gaze, hoping she did not faint away with him before her.

"It has been an honor spending these hours with you and your family," James said, "but I must be getting along. I have a lengthy ride ahead of me and business to attend."

"Do come back," Mama invited.

"I shall, and I will look forward to visiting with all of you soon." He made pleasantries to Aunt Anne and then to Delight. "Seeing you again has been most delightful." He suddenly reddened, no doubt embarrassed at his choice of words, given her name.

She nodded and bid him good day.

"Are you ready, Henry?" Papa said. "Can you manage another walk?"

"I believe I'll stay and help the ladies finish their work." Henry leaned against an oak tree. "I would like to see this completed and the evidence removed."

"Excellent idea."

Henry shook James's hand. "Thank you for the lively conversation. I look forward to many more."

Henry and James are friends?

James grasped his shoulder. "You are a fine fellow. I enjoyed your story, especially the ending. I'm glad you are on our side."

The guest walked away with Papa, then whirled around to Henry. "Do not forget what I warned you about. Ten to twelve dollars is a great deal of money."

James is a pleasing man to look upon, but I don't know his nature. Could he possess Henry's wit and compassion? Delight wrestled with her thoughts. She had been drawn to James since their first meeting two weeks earlier, or was she drawn to his handsome appearance and the adventurous and dangerous life he led for the patriots? Surely all the women who were blessed by his presence felt the lure of his charm.

But what happens when the glow of adoration wears thin? She had no answers, for Henry held so many admirable traits that she found it difficult not to compare the two.

Delight wanted to understand what James had referred to in his closing words with Henry. Impatience wrapped its cloak around her while James and Papa slowly ambled toward the road. A leaf floating from the highest branches of a tree could not have moved more slowly. Finally they moved far enough away so that they could not overhear her question.

"What did James mean?" She picked up several pieces of fabric to show Henry how to form a cartridge. No point in exhibiting any more concern than she already felt.

Henry shrugged. "Nothing of importance."

She knew by the way he avoided her that a matter of great importance plagued him. "Henry!"

"Delight," Mama scolded, "remember your manners."

"But he is concealing information from me." Irritation settled on her shoulders like a heavy yoke.

Mama cleared her throat. "In defense of him, I believe you are interfering with his private affairs."

Stunned, Delight could only stare at her mother. She had been disrespectful. Taking in a deep breath, she forced herself to face Henry. "I. . .apologize."

Instead of seeing condemnation in his blue eyes, she saw compassion and the clear distinction of something else. She shivered, captured by the tenderness in his gaze.

"I am not offended," he said. "I will tell ye what James referred to, and we can talk further about it on our walk home."

She nodded and blinked back an inkling of tears, of which she knew not the origin—nor was she certain she wanted to know.

"General Burgoyne is offering ten to twelve dollars for each British soldier brought in. Desertion has become a significant problem, and the general seeks to increase his troops."

Delight gasped, and her hand instinctively covered her mouth. "But they placed you here in Chesterfield until you healed."

Henry patted his leg. "This is healing much faster than I originally imagined. Very shortly, I will be able to do all the things I did before. The problem is. . ." His voice trailed off, and he picked up a few musket balls, toying with them as if they belonged to a child. He dropped one of the balls into the cloth form and picked up the gunpowder. "Of course ye already know my convictions on that matter. I need to enlist in the Continental army before the British lay claim to me."

"But—"

Henry raised his hand in protest. "We will continue this discussion later."

At times she wondered if Henry could be more stubborn than she. And she truthfully didn't mind when he took the upper hand—not of late, in any event.

❦

Papa prepared to leave for the war on October 24, 1777, seven days after Burgoyne surrendered to Gates at Saratoga. Delight's father was determined to serve under the general who had forced the British to drop their arms. They heard the news from James Daniels, who happened to pass by Chesterfield late one evening.

His handsome face and proud carriage still took Delight's breath away. Sitting in front of the fireplace, he struck an overwhelming pose with the light from the rising flames framing his head. When she turned so he wouldn't see her face, she caught a glimpse of Charity, whose cheeks blushed brighter than a shiny apple. *My sister is taken with James, too?* She stole a glance at James. For a moment she thought he held Charity's gaze in his sights. *How dare you, Charity, turn this man's head when I had not decided whether to set my cap for him?* Frustrated, she attempted to listen to Papa's and James's conversation.

"I'd like to think we are going to end this war soon," James said. "The redcoats got a taste of real fighting in Saratoga and now know what it feels like to surrender."

Papa laughed heartily. "I might not get to fire Brown Bess before all of Britain leaves American soil."

I hope so, Papa, for then none of us would have cause to worry.

James left soon after Mama insisted he eat a heaping plate of ham and beans. As usual, he thanked Mama and Papa for their hospitality. He neither spoke to Delight nor looked her way, which angered her immensely. But did she see something pass between James and Charity?

≈

The day before Papa left for the war, he drew each family member aside to tell of his love and to insure encouragement for the days ahead. His visiting took most of the day and into the evening.

After rocking little Elijah, he lifted his gaze to Delight. "We have not yet spoken. I'd like to take a walk." He settled the baby into Mama's arms and kissed the top of his forehead. Mama whisked away a tear, and Delight pretended she did not see.

Silently they moved into the evening and ambled toward the road winding from the town.

"Delight, I am leaving a tremendous responsibility for you as the oldest. You've always excelled in taking care of the younger ones and assisting your mother, but I am afraid this will be the hardest time of all."

"God will help me." *I will not cry. I'll be stalwart.*

"Allow Henry to share the burden while he is still here."

"Yes, Papa."

"He is a good man, daughter."

"Yes, Papa." Hadn't they discussed Henry's merits enough?

"Delight, is your heart torn between Henry and James?"

"I haven't given the matter enough consideration to be able to answer your question."

"Let me suggest you speak with God about the matter. I have a preference for you, but I would rather you hear it from Him."

"I'll devote more time to prayer and reading the scripture," she said. "Perhaps it is neither man."

Papa chuckled, his voice musical with the sounds of the evening insects. "Whoever steals your heart must first give his own."

"Yes, Papa." She leaned her head on his shoulder, longing to listen to his words until the sun rose.

A few moments later, he cleared his throat and slowed his pace. "Another matter needs to be remedied."

Her pulse quickened. "And what is that?"

"I want you to promise that you will not endeavor upon anything foolish or dangerous during my absence."

Her heart pounded furiously. "What do you mean, Papa?"

He shook his head and released a deep sigh. "I know about your activities in Boston—the things you did for the patriots."

She felt her strength drain away. "How. . .how long were you privy?"

"Since the beginning."

She feared her weakened knees would force her to the ground. "Oh Papa, I am so sorry, but I could not tell you about carrying the messages." The realization he knew about her activities all along both alarmed and relieved her. Shame for the deceit plagued at her heart.

"Daughter, I lived in fear of your being caught. What were you thinking the night you crept out to Cavin Sullivan's tavern?"

Speechless, Delight could only wring her hands.

"I nearly killed those soldiers when they pounded on Cavin's door in search of rum." His voice rose with each word. "My daughter at a tavern in the wee hours of the morning?"

"You were there?" she said.

"Child, I followed you when I couldn't find the message myself!" Papa grabbed her shoulders and swung her around to face him. She gasped. His tone softened. "I admire and respect your courage, but you were taking too many chances."

But I did it for our country! She swallowed hard, remembering the times when she'd sensed someone stood in the shadows watching her as she skirted about Boston. "Why didn't you reveal your knowledge?"

"Because I was involved more deeply than you, and I saw that you could get past the British when the rest of us would have been detained." He broke into a sob. "I am a selfish man to allow my own flesh and blood to face insurmountable odds."

Her heart nearly melted in a pool of tears. "You are not selfish. You love your country and seek its freedom."

He wrapped his arm around her waist, and the two walked a bit farther. "I saw in you a sense of pride in your country, and I realized you would do whatever you could to aid the patriots. Unfortunately, my love of freedom blinded me to making sure you were free from danger. I should have forbidden you to continue your work. Will you forgive me?"

Her heart seemed to wrench from her chest. "Papa, there is nothing to forgive. If we did not come first in your prayers, you would not have volunteered to help."

He leaned his head upon the top of hers. "I had been involved with the Sons of Liberty since the very first. I've debated with Sam Adams, Hancock, and the others, helped unload those three ships loaded with tea in Boston Harbor, and smuggled muskets and supplies to our troops."

His confession brought a surge of deep pride to Delight, but then a thought needled at her, one she could not dispel. "Am I the reason we fled from Boston?"

Silence prevailed until Papa spoke. "Indeed you are. Your mother knew about me, but I did not tell her about your daring work until we moved to Chesterfield. I have continued my responsibilities here, but fortunately your work has been curtailed."

"I wish I could do more." Her regrets riddled through her body. "Making musket cartridges doesn't give me the satisfaction that running messages offered."

Papa squeezed her lightly. "It will have to do, because I want your word you will not venture into anything dangerous during my absence."

Given the opportunity, she would do anything for the cause, but Papa demanded an answer. "What do you mean by dangerous?"

He stopped in the road. "Any act that threatens your safety."

She groped for words.

"Delight."

"I promise to do my utmost not to involve myself in anything... dangerous."

Chapter 11

At dawn, the family rose to properly send Papa off to war. Mama kissed him lightly and gave him a miniature of herself. He laced a piece of leather through the top and tied it around his neck. Charity packed his knapsack full of biscuits, hard cheese, and dried beef. A wooden canteen swung over his saddle.

"I am so lucky to have such a fine family to see me off. Many soldiers don't have a horse either. God is blessing us indeed."

Remember gave him her Bible so Mama could keep the family Bible with all their family history. Patience slipped a piece of paper inside, most likely a poem or possibly a letter. Faith made certain he had a mug, a few cooking utensils, and a pewter plate—Mama had saved it from being melted into musket balls. Mercy and Hope stroked the horse, obviously unsure of what to do to keep their tears at bay.

"Here is a powder horn. It belonged to me friend who was killed. I'd like for ye to have it." Henry shook Papa's hand and they hugged.

Delight knew the two men had discussed matters long into the previous night. They'd become fast friends, and Henry wouldn't be with them much longer either.

Delight had shined Papa's boots with her tears and polished his musket until it glistened. All the talk about liberty and separation from Britain seemed to lessen in meaning in the face of Papa's leaving. The British occupation in Boston, Henry's abrupt arrival, and even the making of musket balls and cartridges had kept the war on the surface of her heart, the part ravaged with anger. But this event tugged at her very being. This was Papa who rode off in defense of his country and his beliefs, Papa who might not survive the ordeal. Suddenly the war became more than a challenge. The mutual struggle had snatched her spirit and left her vulnerable and afraid.

Biting back a fresh sprinkling of tears, she forced a smile and handed Papa his musket. He kissed her forehead and met her smile with one of hope and a special look meant just for her—be strong and courageous.

He held Mama close while she silently wept against his chest. "Soon, it will all be over, my dear Elizabeth, and then I shall be home."

"God be with you." Mama touched his cheek as if memorizing every beloved portion of his face.

Delight repeated the blessing with her sisters, blinking back the stinging wetness blinding her vision. "Hurry home, Papa."

He swung up onto the saddle and nodded toward Henry. "I thank you for last night's conversation. We have a kindred spirit, and I am appreciative of your friendship."

"We have much to do once the war is won," Henry replied. "And I will be lookin' after things until it's time for me to go."

A feeling similar to the time when she was a child and fell out of a tree rose in Delight. The jolt had knocked the wind out of her, just as now she was left breathless at the realization of the sacrifice required to win this war. The battles would not be won by those carrying messages through enemy lines, melting pewter and iron into musket balls, or nursing British soldiers to health, but by the blood of those emptying themselves for America's right to liberty. Delight had mastered the simple maneuvers, but Papa had volunteered his life.

Papa waved, and his horse trotted down the road. Oh, that he might never need to fire his musket, but Delight knew better. Oh, that he might not be cold, wet, and go without food and water, but Delight knew better. Oh, that he might never see his friends and fellow soldiers perish, but Delight knew better. *Father God, bring him back to us unharmed. I beg of Thee.*

Once he disappeared from view, she gathered up her skirts and hurried across the field behind their house. She had to flee the dismal scene of Mama and the girls weeping. Scurrying up a little hill, she swept down across a tiny, gurgling stream, up another grassy bank, and under a grove of elms, where she sank to the hard earth in a heap of liquid emotion. Mama had always said she and Papa shared liked temperaments. As a little girl, she had tagged along behind him wherever he went. This time she'd been forced to stay behind. . .and wait. . .and pray.

"Delight."

Unaware of another mortal nearby, she lifted her head from whence the sound came. Henry stood before her, his face filled with compassion.

"May I join ye, lass?" he whispered.

Too spent to argue or agree, she said nothing. He eased down beside her, favoring his leg and allowing it to stretch out before him.

"You shouldn't have followed me," she said with a sniff. "Your leg is not mended enough."

"It grows stronger every day." He handed her a handkerchief. "I stopped for this."

"Thank you." *Soon you'll be gone as well.* The thought made her nearly as miserable, but she shoved away its confusion. "Why did you come?"

Henry picked up a golden leaf and appeared to study its veins. "Thought ye might need to talk."

She lifted her head and met his blue gaze. "I don't know what to say about anything."

" 'Tis nothing wrong about grieving your father's departure."

His words served to open the floodgates of her soul again. She attempted to swallow the tears, but her efforts failed.

Henry drew her into his arms and held her close against his chest. "Go ahead and cry. It will make ye feel better." His embrace comforted her while she soaked his shirt with her weeping. After several long minutes, she became aware of his chin resting atop her head and his hand stroking her back as if she were a small child. Humiliation overcame her at the thought of allowing Henry to witness her sorrow. She pulled back, not certain what to say, if anything at all.

"Forgive me," she said. "I do not like others to see me distraught."

"There is no reason for an apology. I am your friend, remember?"

His words coaxed a smile from her. "I rather others not see my weaknesses."

He nodded to punctuate his words. "The last thing ye are is weak, lass. At the very least, you are the strongest woman I've ever seen—and the most stubborn."

Delight found another smile curving her lips. "Like my papa."

"Aye, I believe so." He leaned back against the elm and pulled her next to the hollow of his shoulder. *Do not be refusing me this wee bit of holding ye. It may be all I have to cherish in the days to come when I can't see your face or hear your sweet voice.*

Her back remained stiff, but she did not pull away.

"Tell me about Elijah. In your eyes, what best describes him?"

She entwined her fingers and pressed them beneath her chin as though she planned a lengthy prayer. "He is a proud man, my papa. Decidedly stubborn and determined all of us should have the best of things—not wealth, but love and a sense of purpose in our lives. He never complained of so many daughters and not having a son but always claimed God gave him the utmost of everything."

Henry chuckled. *Indeed He has.* "I hope to have many of his fine attributes someday."

"You have many now," she whispered. A moment later she rubbed her palms together vigorously, no doubt embarrassed of her assessment of him.

"What is your fondest memory of Elijah, the one standing foremost in your mind?"

Delight tilted her head. "Without a doubt, I remember the occasion." She smiled faintly. "Albeit I'm a little reluctant to tell you the story."

He afforded himself a light pat of her shoulder. "Tell me, please. I promise ye will feel better."

She clasped her hands together as though ready to offer a prayer. "And you promise not to laugh?"

He heard the hint of a threat, but he had been the target of her temper before and had lived through it. "I'll do me utmost."

She settled back against him. *Aye, the touch of her is heaven.*

"What I best recall is a time before Mercy or Hope was born, so I must have been about five years old. Mama had asked me to feed our dog—Bear's mother—but I was afraid of her. The animal stood as tall as my head, and I thought she might devour me if I didn't give her enough food. I hadn't told Mama or Papa about my fears because I didn't want to disappoint them."

I can see ye then as ye are now, always wanting to take care of things yourself, just like ye nursed me to spare your mother during her confinement.

"I wanted to ask Charity to go with me, but the fear of her being eaten stopped my invitation. I knew if Charity were lost, Mama and Papa would be very angry." She glanced up at him. "Charity did perplex me so, crying whenever she couldn't have her own way, so the thought did enter my mind."

Considering the two girls were often at odds, Henry didn't doubt her statement in the least. A smile tugged at the corners of his mouth. "Did the dog have a name?"

She nodded. "Grace."

Henry couldn't stop the mirth rising within him. "Do go on, lass. I'm not teasing you. It is the dog's name that amuses me."

She sighed and moistened her lips, those lips he longed to kiss. "Mama had the bowl filled with milk and dried bread, and I nearly sloshed it over while I carried it outside. I kept hoping the dog would be gone, and all I'd need to do was set the food down and hurry back inside to Mama, but that didn't occur. When Grace spotted me, she came bounding over. She looked like a huge creature ready to consume me. I screamed and dropped the bowl. Grace kept running, but I stood frozen to the ground."

Henry envisioned the frightened little girl, convinced she would be the huge dog's dinner.

Delight sighed. "All of a sudden, I felt Papa's strong arms scoop me up into his. I clung to him sobbing and would not let go. Tenderly, he asked me why I feared Grace, and I told him."

"What did he say?"

"He told me I was more important to him than Grace, and if I wanted, he would get rid of the dog. Grace simply wanted to play. Of course, I didn't believe him. So while he held me with one hand, he petted Grace with the other. Finally I lifted my head from his shoulder and saw the dog licking his hand and wagging her tail. Papa coaxed me to pet her, too. Finally, with my hand overtop his, I stroked her head. Every day after that, Papa and I went outside to visit Grace. After a few weeks, I learned the dog was not going to eat me at all, and she really did want to play. The first few times she licked my face, I panicked, but Papa called her wet splashes against my skin kisses, and somehow I managed not to mind those either." Delight looked up at Henry. "Sounds rather silly doesn't it?"

"Not at all."

"Grace and I became fast friends."

"I am not in the least surprised."

She glanced down into her lap. "I have a habit of fearing those things that mean no harm and ignoring real danger."

"I have never meant to harm you," he whispered. With more courage than he ever imagined, he lifted her chin with his finger. Surprise illuminated her gaze, but he refused to back down. Slowly he descended upon the softness of her mouth, drinking in a light kiss and praying she would not find him repugnant.

"Delight!"

Chapter 12

Startled, Delight peered up into Charity's astonished face. "You should be ashamed." Her sister's tone was laced with indignation.

Delight stammered for words. Up until a few weeks ago, she had never had a problem speaking her mind clearly—and quickly—with words that cut deeper than a sharp hunting knife.

"Papa hasn't been gone two hours and already you are behaving indecently. You are a disgrace." Charity wagged a finger in front of Delight's face. Judgment seeped from the pores of her skin. "You should have lingered for Mama. Abby Rutherford stopped by to tell her Papa was bound for eternal punishment for joining the patriots."

Shaking her head to dispel the accusations and the neighbor's judgmental words, Delight fought the urge to tell her sister to mind her own affairs.

"And I thought you felt something for James. Now I see you are fickle. . .or are you toying with both men's affections?" Charity lifted her chin. "We all are going to church to pray with Mama. Looks like you need to be on your face repenting for your sordid actions." She crossed her arms over her chest as if to punctuate her declaration.

"I have done nothing to dishonor God or shame my family. You, sweet sister, are the one who is viewing matters as evil when I am innocent."

Henry rose to his feet. He appeared impassive, as though the hostility between the two sisters was nothing more than an exchange of pleasantries over a cup of tea. "Charity." The low timbre of his voice issued confidence and control.

I don't need him to defend me, Delight thought. "Henry—"

His look stopped any further utterances. It reminded her of Papa when he expected her to cease everything immediately and do his bidding.

90

"Delight longed for a solitary place where she could grieve your father's departure and the impending danger of war. I sensed her sorrow and followed for the sole purpose of offering comfort, which is exactly what happened here."

"But. . .you exchanged a kiss!"

"Precisely so. I initiated it, taking advantage of her weakened state, an action for which I sincerely apologize."

"Henry," Delight interrupted, "you must not shelter all the blame." She stared into his eyes and saw the tenderness she'd seen previously. A fluttering sensation jolted across her stomach. "I did not attempt to stop you."

"Nonsense, Delight. I am sorry for me bold actions."

Do you regret the kiss?

"Please." Charity's eyes brimmed with tears. "I shouldn't have lashed out at you. Mistress Rutherford acted so cruelly and was so self-righteous. Then you two looked. . .I thought—"

Henry stepped forward and touched her arm. "Ye are hurting, too. 'Tis nothing wrong with feeling as ye do with your father leaving."

Charity nodded, unable to speak for the tears rolling over her cheeks. Compassion overtook Delight, and she gathered up her sister into her arms.

"Forgive me," Charity said between sobs.

"I am not offended. We all are suffering from the reality of Papa joining the war, but quarreling is not the answer, and I can be the worst offender in that regard. I believe we must show our love for him by extending it to each other. Imagine Mama's torment." Delight's gaze fell on Henry, who seemed to be studying her. A smile passed between them. This time she felt no fluttering in the pit of her stomach. Instead a strange and lovely warmth filled her. In one brief moment, all thoughts of James Daniels vanished in a light that could never measure up to Henry O'Neill. *I love him. I sincerely do.*

"Shall we join Mistress Butler and the others for prayer?" he said.

Charity lifted her head from Delight's shoulder and took the handkerchief her sister offered.

"It is a little damp," Delight said. "Henry gave it to me earlier, and I soaked it thoroughly."

"I shall merely find a dry spot." Her sister attempted a trembling half smile. "I can always use my petticoat as we did when we were children."

"Excuse me, ladies. If ye are considering such actions, then I will go on ahead." Henry chuckled, breaking the tension in the air.

"Oh no." Delight raised a brow. "We need an escort." In the midst of laughter, she realized her affections did include Charity, the sister who had always vexed her so. She brushed the curly wisps of damp hair away from Charity's face and kissed her forehead. Just as Papa always did.

✒

Henry spent the next few days with one eye on the road and one ear listening for British soldiers. If caught, he'd be forced back into the uniform of the enemy, and be required to wield a bayonet in front of those he'd come to respect. He told himself on more than one occasion that he'd fall to his demise before raising a hand to stifle the patriot cause.

Soon James would arrive. Henry planned to ask him about enlisting in the Continental army as soon as possible. His leg needed only a few more days to heal properly. In the meantime, he would pass his time weaving for the people of Chesterfield and treasuring every moment spent with Delight.

Dare I reveal the depth of my feelings before I leave? He believed she felt the same, because he'd seen it in her eyes. During those times when he sat weaving outside beneath the maple, he dreamed of living out his days in America with Delight beside him. *Oh God, by all Ye deem holy, am I wrong to ask for this fair lass? I want to love her as Ye have instructed in Your own Word—as Christ cherishes the Church. Hear me cry, Holy God.*

Henry prayed God did not regard his plea as selfish, although he knew desiring something for himself held all those qualities. He prayed for this wondrous land, destined to one day be the greatest in all the world. With the ideals of the brave patriots, America's destiny could be no less. Here, God willing, he would live out his life and one day raise a fine family.

"Henry?"

He raised his sights, knowing the sound of Delight's voice. Her tone held a soft repose when she talked to him, just as he envisioned the sounds of the choirs of heaven echoed through the universe.

"Am I interrupting you?"

"Nay, lass."

"You looked so faraway, as though you held private sanctuary with God, and I surely did not wish to interfere."

"Truthfully, my thoughts were on the things of God." He rested his hands on his knee. "But I am finished for now. What can I do for ye?"

She slipped down to the leaf-covered earth beside him. A brisk breeze obviously coaxed a gasp from her, for she massaged her arms lightly. "Winter is coming." She wrapped her woolen shawl tightly about her. "Henry, you need an outer garment."

He laughed. "My coat is the British uniform. I believe I would rather be cold."

She glanced away, and he saw the visible traces of sadness etching her face. "I believe Uncle Matthew has an extra outer garment. I will fetch it today for you."

"How generous of you. But I don't have money to pay."

"He offered when you wove aprons for Aunt Anne."

He hesitated. "It is time I enlisted."

"I know," she whispered.

Is now the time to speak to her, Lord?

"Not yet, My son. Wait for Me."

The clear direction caused him to bridle his tongue.

"See, you are chilled," Delight said. "I will get a blanket from inside to wrap about your shoulders until I return with a coat." When he protested, she raised her chin. "You can't do the patriots a bit of good if you are ill. I nursed you once, and I daresay you remember how difficult I can be."

"Nay, I remember an angel's touch." He could not stop a teasing grin. "One with eyes of fire."

She instantly sobered. "I am sorry for the way I treated you."

"Are ye now?" He forced a jovial disposition, sensing her melancholia.

"Yes, and do not make light of me. I will sorely miss you, Henry O'Neill." She anchored her hands onto her hips.

He wanted to pull her close to him and kiss her soundly. But he restrained his emotions, wondering if another impetuous act might displease God or anger her. "I will miss ye, too—everything about ye."

Silence invaded their small place. In the distance a dog barked, and birds sang above them as though everything about the world rested secure. Reality spoke otherwise. *Thank Thee, Lord, for moments of reprieve when the rest of the world moans and shudders.*

"Promise me you won't get hurt." She lifted her hands from her hips and let them dangle at her side.

Heaviness settled upon his shoulders. "That is impossible, lass. Only the heavenly Father knows the future."

She drew in a breath and blinked hastily.

"But I will promise to heed caution and to serve the Continental army to me utmost."

"I expect you to exceed even those expectations."

"I am only a man guided by God."

"Then I pray He keeps you in the shelter of His wings."

Will ye prayers always include me? Dare I hope so? Henry swallowed the endearing words he yearned to speak. Silently he proclaimed his devotion until God willed him to make his declaration of love. He recalled the late-night conversation he'd shared with Elijah before his friend's departure.

"You have my permission to wed Delight," Elijah had said. *"I can't think of a finer husband for my daughter or son-in-law for Elizabeth and me. My blessings, Henry. Aye, she can be a handful, but you will never find greater devotion."*

"Thank ye, Elijah. I admit I don't know how she feels, but I know my heart."

Elijah laughed heartily. "Delight may not understand her own sentiments, but I do see your favor in her eyes."

Since then, Henry had looked intently into his beloved's eyes at every opportunity, hoping for a glimpse of love. At times he felt certain. Other times he doubted she felt anything at all. Perhaps he merely read words into her silent messages or the tone of her voice.

"I did come to tell you something." Delight's voice broke into his pondering. "Mama said James will be arriving by nightfall tomorrow."

≈

Delight left Henry in the cold air and walked back into the house to tell Mama about hurrying to Aunt Anne's for the promised coat. Taking a deep breath, she wished she could muster the courage to tell Henry that James meant nothing to her. But if she made the claim, then he would surely see her growing feelings for him. The idea of Henry not sharing the same affections sounded more devastating than not knowing his feelings at all.

Charity had admitted her fondness for James, and Delight had wished her God's blessing. How odd and yet wonderful that it took a misunderstanding to bring the two sisters closer together. All these years they had quarreled with and avoided each other, and now they were inseparable. Indeed they giggled and talked late into the night like dear companions.

"Henry does care for you," Charity had whispered just last evening while the rest of the house slept.

"Are you certain?" Delight's pulse quickened at the thought.

"Absolutely, without a doubt. He has eyes only for you, as though you hung the stars in the sky."

"Is that blasphemy?"

Charity sighed. "I pray not, for he is a godly man, and I sense his great love."

"Oh Charity, if only he would speak to me about his feelings. I ache to hear any words of endearment." She shivered with the truth echoing through her. "Yet I am fearful if something should happen to him."

"What if he should leave without telling you?"

Delight felt her spirits sink. "Pray he speaks his mind before he departs."

"I will, sister. I will with all the fervency in my very being. He would not have kissed you if he did not care."

"Thank you." Delight felt her eyes moisten. "I wish we could have become close long before this very moment."

"Aye, we've missed so very much. I always loved you, but our closeness now is beyond my deepest dream."

Delight's eyes moistened with the confession. "And I love you, Charity. Just like your name, you give in abundance. I will pray James sees your goodness."

Delight smiled at the remembrance of the sweet times lately with all of her sisters. Adversity had a way of ushering in God's grace.

Glancing at the huge piles of wood Henry had chopped in preparation for winter gave Delight a sense of relief. Her family would not go hungry. Neither would they freeze in the cold. They'd have the company of each other to sustain them through the hard times until Papa—and Henry—returned. If only she had some type of assurance that Papa and Henry might fare as easily. She wanted to do something to help, but what? Helplessness wove its web of inadequacy, leaving her heavyhearted and frustrated.

She could not carry a musket, although she had heard stories of wives who followed the troops to cook and tend to the soldiers. Some, when they saw their husbands fall in battle, picked up their weapons and continued the fight.

She'd promised Papa not to indulge in dangerous activities, which meant in her estimation that she could do little of any value for the cause.

"Where is your faith?"

The whispers from a place neither her heart nor her mind could claim spoke with a truth she could not deny.

"You believe in Me for eternity. Why can't you trust Me with the present?"

Chapter 13

The next evening, Henry waited with tumultuous feelings for James's arrival. The man had become a good, respected friend, and he valued their relationship. But what of the man's interest in Delight?

Loving her meant Henry desired the utmost for her, God's richest blessings. *I need to fade into the background and allow them to grow closer. I give her to Thee, Lord. My wish for her happiness exceeds my selfish ambitions.*

The afternoon came and went. Henry delivered woven goods to three families and took an order for one more. All the while he harbored mixed emotions about James's tardiness. Mistress Butler waited the evening meal in anticipation of their guest joining them, but at last they partook of the food. James was a man of his word. He lived a daring life. He would walk through Satan's fire if it furthered the cause of the patriots. His delay sent an uncomfortable sensation up Henry's spine. Surely the British soldiers and loyalists sought to end his life—a possibility Henry tried without success to push from his thoughts.

"James must have been detained," Mistress Butler said during the meal. A silence had befallen them. Even Mercy and Hope were unusually quiet. In their young minds, a word from their guest might be a word from Papa. "Shall we pray for him? Perhaps Henry would do us the honor."

What a blessing for me to lead this family in prayer, Henry thought as he bowed his head. *Thank Ye, Lord.* "Heavenly Father, we welcome Your presence into our lives, and bless Your name for these bounteous gifts. We humbly ask Ye keep careful watch on our dear friend, James. Protect him from harm's way and sustain him in the shadow of Your blessings. Lord, also remember Elijah. Bring him through this war without injury and back to all of us who care for him. In Jesus' name, amen."

Once the firelight cast its shadows, the sisters closed the shutters and latched them. Mistress Butler fed the baby and rocked him to sleep, nearly drifting off herself before gathering up a basket of mending. An hour later after reading the scripture aloud and practicing their writing, Mercy and Hope made the trek upstairs to bed. Some of the young women busied themselves with knitting or their samplers, while Patience wrote a letter to her father, and Charity kept one eye on the door. Delight said little, no doubt fretting with Charity over James's absence. She held a book in her hand, but not once did he see her glance at a page. Henry listened for every sound, anxious to hear Bear's bark, announcing a caller.

"I am certain James will be here soon," Henry said, long after the hour grew late. "Only his loyalty to the cause would hinder his presence."

"I agree." Mama put aside her mending. "I believe we should not tarry in obtaining our rest. If he arrives, we shall hear him."

Henry knew he wouldn't be able to sleep. The gnawing in his spirit had lingered after his prayer. "I believe I will resume the watch a wee bit longer."

"I should like to keep you company." Charity spoke from a corner chair where she had long since set her basket of yarn at her feet. "Delight, I would appreciate your presence."

"Of course. We can talk or read."

"Do not stay up too late, girls," Mama said. "Tomorrow is another day."

Henry noted the gentle smiles and compassion exchanged between Delight and Charity. His beloved had told him of their renewed dedication to each other, and he'd seen the change since the day of Elijah's departure. He wondered about their common attraction to James and how they could ignore their emotions. Rather than deliberate the matter, he quickly discarded it. After giving the worrisome problem to God, he shouldn't keep calling it to mind. Tonight his concerns belonged to James.

His friend had mentioned running provisions and ammunition under the guise of shelled corn in barrels that Elijah had constructed. If the British searched the contents of James's wagon, they would find more than corn to grind into flour and certainly end his friend's quest for liberty—and his life. None of those possibilities needed to be communicated to the fair women of the Butler household. He believed they should be sheltered from whatever unpleasantness possible, with the exception of Delight. Henry had a feeling she could see her way through just about anything.

Another reason why he loved her.

"What do you suppose has detained him?" Charity said. In the next breath, she stood and paced in front of the fireplace.

"A number of things could delay his arrival." Henry purposely kept his voice calm and quiet. "With his activity among the Continental forces, he is probably on a special mission." His answer held more truth than he cared to admit.

Charity nodded and forced a grim smile. "Of course. Tomorrow we shall be exhausted because we tarried into such a late hour."

She obviously cares for James. He glanced at Delight. Worry lines creased her forehead. How he longed to comfort the burden resting on her mind.

"James is self-sufficient. It is wrong for us to agonize over his absence. He would not want any of us to fret over this." Delight stood and placed a hand on Charity's arm. "Let's go on to bed. Bear will alert us."

Charity's shoulders rose and fell as if a heavy sigh had drawn her strength. "Aye, you are correct in your assessment." Her gaze lifted to her sister's face. "Come along then."

The two bid Henry good night and encouraged him to seek his rest.

"I shall, lasses." He avoided Delight's face, knowing her heart was with another. "Sleep well."

After the women ascended the stairs, Henry allowed his own thoughts to wander. James was not blind to the uncertainties of his position. He had a clever side to him that had kept him a step ahead of the enemy. Still, danger loomed in these perilous times, and Henry could not help but think of Adam and his other compatriots who had perished in the fighting. Henry wasn't ready to lose another friend, albeit he realized many fine men on both sides held death as their destiny before the war ended. He could be one of those, too.

Henry had given himself four more days before enlisting. In truth, he and James planned to travel together to the nearest camp, where his friend assured him of a proper introduction to General Gates. Regardless of where James might be at the end of the allotted time, Henry planned to venture on himself. They had spoken about a great number of things from their boyhood days to their understanding of God's salvation to war stories, but nothing about Delight. He assumed she was a subject neither of them wanted to broach.

Repeatedly Henry told himself God had a special woman intended for his life, and if not Delight then surely someone better. But he could think of no one finer than the woman who had stolen his heart.

"Henry?" the one holding his thoughts whispered behind him. "Do you mind if I keep you company?"

Warmth flowed through him. "Of course not. Ye cannot sleep?"

She shook her head. "Charity is resting, though, and for that I am grateful."

Poor Delight. I know the pain of a heart wounded by love.

With the flames licking at the log he had just added, she eased down to share his bench. "I thought we might talk since. . ."

He quickly captured her gaze and held it for as long as she permitted. "Since we are waiting for James," he said, finishing her sentence.

Silence permeated the air, and she stared into the fire. "Yes, that, too. But I meant we could converse since you planned to enlist soon."

How sweet to concern herself with me in light of her feelings toward James, he thought. "In less than a week, I will be serving under General Gates."

"Perhaps you shall see Papa."

"I'd like nothing better than to fight with him."

She toyed with the cuff of her frock. "I would be most grateful if you'd tell him of our love and prayers."

"Aye, lass, I will. There's no need to ask."

"What do you intend to do after the war?" She peered into his face, her large eyes innocent and. . .did he see fear? "I assume you will want to continue your weaving."

"My loom is me livelihood, but I have a desire to live among the dear people of Chesterfield. Your father requested I return here."

She smiled. "We would all like for you to make your home near us."

He chuckled. "Delight, I remember when ye detested the sight of me, and now ye want me near your family?"

In the firelight, she blushed. "I remember, too. I am so glad those days are gone."

He memorized every inch of her lovely features. "Are there things you wish for me to do before I leave?"

"I think not. We are ready for winter, thanks to your and Papa's provision."

A strange, yet comforting silence fell upon them. He relished in it, promising himself these memories would warm the bitter winter days and nights ahead.

"I'd like to ask you something, Henry."

He raised a brow. "By all means."

Her gaze darted about, and she appeared to have difficulty forming her words.

✑

Why did I initiate this conversation? Delight cringed with what she so desperately wanted to ask, troubled over what Henry might reply. She had contemplated this for too long. The thought plagued her worse than enduring baby Elijah's cries when Mama forbid anyone to pick him up. She could not go on another day without knowing. Henry had acted so indifferently since the day Papa left. His impassiveness led her to believe he regretted his kiss. The notion of their brief embrace meaning little should have angered her, but instead the thought filled her with sadness.

"Delight?"

Oh, how I wish I had not pursued this matter. My mind should be on James and prayers for his safety, not myself.

"What is tormenting ye? I can see the anguish in your face."

The fire crackled, sounding like musket fire, and it caused her to gasp.

"Lass, it is only the fire."

"I know. Henry." She rubbed her clammy palms together. "Remember the day Papa left, when you followed me to the far field?"

He nodded.

"And Charity came looking for us?"

"I clearly recall every moment."

With a deep breath, she spoke the penetrating question. "Did you have any affections in your kiss?"

Henry leaned forward, his words spoken in a whisper. "Did ye?"

How can I answer without looking foolish? Dear Lord, this is difficult beyond measure.

Bear rose on his haunches and stared at the door. A growl rumbled in his throat.

"Easy." He stroked the dog's back. When the animal moved forward, Henry reached for the musket hanging above the fireplace.

Bear knows James. He'd never growl at him. The dog barked, and Delight jumped.

"Delight, go upstairs with your family," Henry ordered. "Do not come down until I tell ye everything is safe."

She started to object, but the commanding tone in his voice stopped her from protesting. Still she did not move.

"Now! This is not a time to argue."

"You might need assistance."

Henry raised an angry brow, and she hurried up the stairs. Someone other than James approached the house.

Henry heard Delight's light footsteps upon the stairs, but his sights remained on the door. The feel of the weapon in his hands gave him little reassurance. Those who roamed the night in search of mischief rarely came unarmed.

With one hand on Bear in hopes of keeping the dog quiet, Henry stepped to the window and slipped his fingers between the shutters, easing one side open to see outside. The culprit might simply be another animal roaming beyond the door, but Henry had a feeling this was not the case.

In the faint light of a half moon, he saw the outline of a wagon. The driver, wearing neither the uniform of a British soldier nor the varied garments of a patriot, leaned precariously to the side, as if inebriated or injured. Rather than open the door and possibly face trouble, Henry left Bear inside to protect the women. Releasing a heavy sigh, he stole out the back of the house.

Moving slowly around the rear to the corner, he considered how darkness often masked the sounds of night. The noises seemed to come from the distance—the singing insects and an owl's call. While he crept toward the front of the house, he strained to hear something revealing the wagon driver's identity. Nothing met his painstaking gaze. When he reached the front, he studied the wagon's outline. Not a soul loomed nearby, save the man, who looked ready to tumble to the ground.

Henry scrutinized the wagon bed and focused on the peculiar shapes filling the entire area. Barrels. The driver must be James, and indeed he must have been badly injured not to cry out. Bear must have sensed the calamity.

He moved to the wagon and worked his way around to the seat. Caution preceded his every breath for he knew not what might await him. "James?" A groan met his ears. The chap needed care, no matter who he was. Henry attempted to lift him in his arms while leaning against the wagon on his good leg. He feared dropping him, and with the man uttering nothing more than a whimper, the fall might kill him.

Help me, Lord. I need to get him inside.

Henry reached beneath the limp man and pulled him against his chest. He took a staggering step, determined to place one foot in front of the other until he could lay the man down within the house.

The door opened and captured his attention. Delight, carrying a lantern, rushed out with Charity. Instantly the two young women were at his side. Delight assisted with the man's legs and Charity held his shoulders and head.

"You are an answer to prayer," Henry said, "although I distinctly remember asking ye to stay inside."

"I watched from the window and assumed all was safe," Delight said. "And I saw you needed help."

"Is it James?" Charity whispered.

"I do not know, lass, but it most likely is. He's injured, but I don't know where."

"He looks like James." She caught her breath, no doubt halting her tears. "Delight, please shine the lantern."

Charity gasped at the sight of their friend, his face smeared with dirt and blood. A gash from his head oozed fresh blood.

"We'll tend to him and offer prayers." Delight's compassion sounded tender against the stifled sobs of her sister. "Don't worry, Charity. If he made the journey here, then he is strong."

Once inside, they carried him into the hall and placed him on Henry's mattress.

"Stay here with James," Delight said to her sister. "I will get a basin of water and see to bandages and herbs."

"Should we wake your mother?" Henry eased James's arm from his waistcoat to make certain there were no other injuries. Charity knelt at his side and helped pull the coat under him while Henry lifted.

"Let's see the extent of his wounds first," Charity said. She first saw the profuse bleeding from James's side when she pulled his arm from the other sleeve. "Oh dear Lord, please spare him." She peered into Henry's face. "Mama will know what to do." Rising to her feet, she disappeared up the stairs, the wisp of her skirts reminding him of a hummingbird's wings.

While Henry sought to make James comfortable, Delight returned with water and a cloth. She knelt in the same spot where she had once dressed Henry's wounds. "How serious is he?"

Henry hadn't had ample time to assess his friend's condition, but he did know the bleeding from his side needed to stop. "I have to find the source of this blood—either a knife or musket ball."

Delight held the lantern, neither flinching nor commenting about the open flesh.

"A knife, lass. His head, too. These need to be sewn or the wounds will not heal properly."

"Either Mama or I can do it," she said. "Blood usually makes Charity ill, but she may amaze us." Delight pressed the cloth to James's side to halt the profuse bleeding. Even so, red soon tinged her fingers.

Father, he is far worse than I imagined. "How could Charity's reaction vary from her disposition?"

Delight smiled sadly. "She loves James, and I'm sure she would do anything to help him."

Henry tore the remains of his friend's shirt away from the wound. *How can both of these women love the same man without quarreling? I don't understand their behavior, no, not at all.* It occurred to him that he and James probably cared for Delight. He thought of James as a brother. Perhaps there rested the similarities.

"Would you hold this for me, please?" Delight said.

He held the cloth against the open flesh while she gingerly washed the area around it. Tiny lines etched around her eyes while she concentrated on cleaning a small portion of the surrounding area.

"Thank you. I am afraid this isn't as simple as when you were injured."

"Aye, but I had a fine nurse." He refused to dwell on James's serious condition. As a soldier, he had learned the value of a clear mind.

"A surly one." She smiled faintly.

"She had a disagreeable patient."

Delight glanced behind them at the creaking stairs announcing Mama's and Charity's descent. The hum of their anxious voices intensified the critical situation.

"Mama, I have water and bandages along with yarrow, but one of us will need to sew his wounds," Delight said.

At the sight of the seared flesh illuminated by the lantern light, Charity covered her mouth. In the next breath, she righted herself and offered to retrieve Mama's sewing basket.

"Aye, I will need it," Mama said. Henry helped her kneel at James's side.

Charity swallowed hard while tears rolled unchecked down her cheeks. With a quick breath, she whirled around to fetch the basket.

"We must make haste," Mama said. "Is he conscious?"

"I think he's drifting in and out," Henry said. "Only moans, and scant few of them."

"That is a blessing for now." Mistress Butler brushed her long, gray mottled hair back behind her ears. Normally, she wore it in a bun at her nape. "From the looks of James, he must have rolled in the dirt during some scuffle."

Mixed with blood, the debris caused the open flesh to appear even more gruesome. Mama took nearly an hour to stitch up James's head and left side. Her stitches were neat, whereas Delight knew hers would have been jagged and uneven. More than once, Delight stole a glimpse at Charity's face, but her sister did remarkably well. She held James's hand as if the man were conscious of her touch. Thankfully his state masked the painful sensations certainly raging through his body.

"'Tis all I can do." Mama wiped her brow with the back of her hand upon completion of the task. "James's wounds will close and heal properly as long as fever and corruption don't claim him."

Charity stroked his forehead. Even in the dim light, he looked fearfully white. "We must pray."

"I will," Henry said. "Lord, we are all concerned about Your child here. He's hurt bad and needs Your help. Guide us in how we can help him. And Father, we pray no corruption shall plague James's body, but that Your power will touch him with divine healing."

He wondered what ill fate had befallen their friend. A thought occurred to him, and he mulled it over in his mind. What if James had been followed? Loyalists and redcoats alike did unspeakable things to patriots, especially those apprehended with messages and supplies. No one dare find any trace of James at the Butler home.

Chapter 14

I will take care of the horses and wagon." Henry rose stiffly to his feet.

"I'll help," Delight said, "as long as Charity will sit with James so Mama can rest." She needed fresh air and time to ponder James's ill fate.

"Of course." Charity reached to take Mama's hand. "Go on back to bed, Mama. Morning will come soon enough, and little Elijah will be demanding his breakfast."

Their mother studied James a bit longer. "Do you promise to waken me if he grows worse?"

"I give you my solemn word," Charity said.

Henry assisted Mama to her feet and did the same for Delight.

"Would you like a cup of chamomile tea before retiring?" Delight said.

Mama smiled wearily. "I think not. Once you and Henry are finished outside, perhaps you three would sleep intermittently in your vigil. Who knows what tomorrow will bring?"

"I'll see to it, Mistress Butler," Henry said. "Do not concern yourself with their welfare. I will make sure they rest."

And who will urge you to do the same? Delight grabbed her shawl and wrapped it around her shoulders before grasping the lantern.

Once outside, Henry drove the wagon to the back of the house, where he could hide both it and the horses inside the barn. He pulled the barn door shut, and with Delight's aid, he fed and groomed the horses.

Delight leaned against the side of a stall. "Henry, you never answered my question earlier."

"I believe I posed the same to ye."

Her thin shoulders rose and fell. "Must you torment me so?"

Me dear Delight. It is I who is tormented. Henry looked at her

107

steadily. "That is not my intent."

"Then were you trifling with me the day Papa went off to the army?"

Henry knew he must respond, and he dared not lie. "I am leaving shortly, Delight. I don't know when I shall return, but I assure you my kiss was with the utmost of affections."

Delight realized her desire for Henry's reply was selfish in light of James's grave wounds, but nevertheless she warmed with the sweet words. "Thank you, Henry. No one has ever given me such a lavish compliment."

"After tonight, perhaps we might talk?" His tone sounded wistful. "I mean once we are certain James is on the mend. I'm ashamed of myself for concentrating on my sentiments instead of placing my heart and mind into our friend's care."

She glanced up and nodded. "I understand how you feel, but God does not expect us to grieve continuously."

A brief silence followed when she could think of nothing to say.

"I want to see what's in the barrels," Henry said. "I know James has been smuggling supplies and provisions to the troops for some time. My guess is someone wanted what he carried."

He climbed onto the wagon and pried open one of the barrels with a crowbar. Delight held the lantern high, anxious to see the contents.

"Corn," she whispered as Henry allowed the kernels to flow between his fingers. The sight somewhat disappointed her.

"Quite possibly there is something else in the bottom." Henry dug his hand deeper, nearly to his elbow. "Ah, lass. We may have a treasure here. Do you mind fetching me a bucket?"

Once the desired item was obtained, she climbed onto the wagon bed beside him. Quickly he scooped the corn until his knuckles rapped onto a hard surface with a dull thud.

"What do you think it is?" She glanced about as though they were being spied upon.

"I think I know what we have here." He pulled a wooden insert from the barrel. "Hold back the lantern, Delight. It's gunpowder."

She stepped away from the wagon and drew in a deep breath.

So this was why James had been attacked. "Henry, this needs to be delivered somewhere."

"Indeed, but until James regains consciousness, we can only speculate where. I searched him but found nothing. Didn't really expect to. James is too sly to carry vital information on his person."

Delight well understood that precaution, which was one of the reasons she had assisted the patriots. Papa said James could read an item once and memorize it, definitely an asset to their cause. "I would gladly drive this wagon to its destination."

Henry replaced the wooden insert and picked up the bucket of corn. "I thought Elijah made you promise you wouldn't involve yourself in any dangerous activities."

Irritation piqued her, although truth be told, she had momentarily forgotten her promise. "How did you know about that?"

He poured the corn back into the barrel before replying. "He sensed you might have a difficult time keeping your word."

"I believe he would make an exception in this case."

"I think not." Henry replaced the barrel's lid and climbed down from the wagon. "If he had not felt concern for you, then he might not have alerted me to your promise."

She tapped her foot against the hard ground. "How else will it be transported?"

"I believe I'm quite capable."

"But your leg?"

He moved closer to her and took the lantern. "Is the question my leg or my loyalties?"

Stunned, Delight wrapped her arms about her. "I don't doubt your commitment to the patriots, but I had not considered you—"

"Risking my life for the American cause?"

The conversation vexed her, forcing her to consider things she hadn't mulled in her mind before. "Forgive me, Henry, but this is all new to me. First you tell me what Papa made me promise, then you announce your willingness to continue James's work."

"And you are confused?" His inquiry sounded condescending, his words jesting.

"Please do not laugh at me." Delight released an exasperated sigh. "Truthfully, the danger is not a blithe subject."

"Won't I face more peril as a part of the Continental army?"

"It appears so." How wrong she'd been in her evaluation of him, and it filled her with guilt.

He rested the lantern on the buckboard and grasped her shoulders. Peering into her face, he shook his head. "Ye can't rescue the whole world. Permit some of the rest of us to take on the responsibilities."

She didn't know where the tears came from, only that they flowed swiftly over her cheeks. "You are toying with me."

"Not at all, lass. Ye desire this war to be ended, the British sent back across the Atlantic, no blood shed, and no one to suffer pain."

She nodded, unable to respond. Her musings were foolish.

"It's an impossibility," he continued. "James is a perfect example."

Swallowing hard, she managed to control her tears. "In some respects, I—I have never really grown up. For me to view our lives as a fairy tale is imprudent."

"Oh, ye are quite grown up, Delight." He gathered her into his arms. "Sometimes I think ye were robbed of your childhood with all your preoccupation in caring for others."

"My sisters say I'm domineering." She attempted a smile.

"That ye are." Henry met her smile. "'Tis because ye love them and want their lives unfettered by life's problems."

How well you know me. It feels soothing and yet frightening. Oh Lord, Thou knowest my stubbornness and my struggles to keep from being overbearing.

"Delight, what are ye thinking?"

"That you know me all too well."

"Aye, I have a reason, a very selfish one." Henry gathered her up in his arms, and she welcomed his embrace, yet perplexity over the future still reigned in her heart.

"What rules your motives?"

He caressed her cheek and slowly descended upon her lips. "The lovely woman in me arms, the one who has given me reason to wake each morning and dream about the future." He sealed his words with a feathery light kiss, then deepened it when she slipped her arms around his neck.

My dear Henry, I long to tell you how you have captured my heart, but I'm fearful. With the thought of your leaving in a few days and possibly not returning, I cannot muster the courage to tell you of my love.

When the sweet kiss ended, she found the strength to say but little. "I pray God guards you and keeps you safe."

"Thank ye," he whispered.

She sought release from his arms. Another moment, and she would reveal the insurmountable love building in her heart. For now, it was enough to relay her feelings in a kiss. Stepping back, she took a deep breath. "Perhaps we should see how Charity fares with James."

A frown crossed his face, and in the faint light of the lantern, his hair looked to be on fire.

"Are you angry with me?" she said.

Quickly a smile met her gaze. "How can I be? I'm overwhelming you, and I do apologize."

Must you read my thoughts so perfectly? If you do, then surely you know my innermost secrets.

"I want to look about the wagon a little more. If James awakens before I return, please summon me so I can find out where to make this delivery."

She took a few steps, not sure she wanted their time to end but insecure about their uncertain future: James's injury, Papa's absence, Henry's enlistment, and her inadequacies. A thought occurred to her, and she whirled around to find Henry watching her. "What else did Papa and you discuss about me?"

He offered a broad smile. "I am not at liberty to relay our every word, at least not at the present."

⬲

Delight found Charity still holding James's hand. Her sister hadn't moved since she'd left her an hour earlier. Charity's tear-stained face glistened in the candlelight. No doubt, her every breath was a prayer.

Compassion overwhelmed Delight. *Oh Lord, please touch James's body with Thy healing.*

His face looked placid yet pale, despite the stitched flesh beneath the bandages.

"Charity, I can sit with him now. Why don't you rest?"

She lifted her gaze and pressed her lips firmly together as though she hadn't heard a single word. Opening her mouth, she attempted to speak, but instead, she merely shook her head.

"You cannot nurse him back to health if you are exhausted." When her sister failed to respond, she kneeled down and wrapped her arms around Charity's shoulders.

"I. . .need to be here in case he needs me."

"I understand." Delight touched their friend's forehead. Thankfully, he did not feel hot. "Praise God, no fever. Has he given any indication of awakening?"

"Not yet. Why don't you sleep?"

Delight smiled. "Do you honestly think I could with all this activity?"

Her sister offered a slight smile in response. "Not any more than I." Her frail shoulders sunk with a heavy sigh. "Where is Henry?"

"Tending to a few things in the barn."

"What did the barrels contain?"

"Gunpowder."

Charity gave no indication of surprise. "I thought as much. He has told me little about his business, but I suspected his endeavors were serious."

Delight braved forward. "Do you happen to know his destination?"

"Nay." She glanced into James's face and touched his cheek, as if his unconscious state allowed her such liberties. "We need to know soon, don't we?"

"Most assuredly." *Before good soldiers are killed for the lack of it.*

Chapter 15

Henry searched up and down the dark road for any signs of soldiers. He studied the brush and the slightest movements around him. Every shadow became suspicious, every sound a faceless man stealing across the night terrain. Bear remained inside and the house silent, yet Henry hesitated with every breath. Not only had someone attempted to kill his friend, but Henry also had the Butler household to consider. Evil men lay in wait somewhere.

How did James escape death and still keep the gunpowder intact? Why didn't the attackers steal the wagon while he lay in his weakened condition? Where and when did all of this occur? The questions ran repeatedly through Henry's mind, plaguing him like an army of rats. None of them could be answered until his friend gained consciousness.

Only when he decided to enter the house did he remember Delight's tender words. He knew without reservation she cared for him and not James. Although she did not convey her feelings with words, the truth glistened in her eyes and radiated from her face.

She had allowed him another kiss and responded shyly at first, then more fervently before pulling away. Delight Butler was not the type of woman to be frivolous with her affections, but he must proceed slowly.

Once he entered the hall, he watched the two sisters embrace. The sight warmed his heart as he recalled his own family left behind in Ireland. With a strange mix of awe, envy, and love, he realized the Butlers were his family now.

"You two can rest. I am here to keep a watchful eye on James," he said.

Delight laughed lightly. "I said similar words to Charity upon my arrival, but she would not hear of it."

"Is that what ye are telling me?"

"Indeed," she said. "Neither of us wants to relinquish one hour's sleep until we know James will be well."

"Aye, we are a strange threesome. . .but loyal ones." Henry studied James's face before easing down beside him. Deathly pale. *He does not look like he'll last the night.* From the corner of his eye, he saw Charity's tears. A selfish thread wove its way through his heart. In speaking his mind about his love for Delight, did he invite the same agony for her?

Henry waited through the night with Delight and Charity. They were all exhausted, but none would give in to more than a brief nodding off to sleep. James did not acquire a fever, surely a blessing, but the danger of infection had not yet passed.

Just before daybreak, Henry stood to stretch his legs. His friend's color looked better. Hopefully it was not wishful thinking on his part, but a step toward healing.

"I should start breakfast," Delight said.

"And I should do the milking and the morning chores." He smiled into her weary face.

Charity brushed a wayward lock of dark hair from James's forehead. "I'm afraid to move for fear he will waken, and no one will be here to tend to him."

"Then you must stay," Delight said.

"But I shouldn't shirk my responsibilities," Charity said. "I always begin the preparations for the morning meal."

Delight patted her sister's arm. "I believe Remember or Patience will do quite well this morning without you. Here lies your responsibility."

"Mistress Butler will be disappointed in me, I am afraid," Henry said. "Neither of you rested during the night."

"Mama knew we would not adhere." Delight shrugged. "I'm sure of it."

"It appears that I am the only one who had sense enough to sleep." James spoke hoarsely and didn't open his eyes, but his humor broke the chill of the dismal night.

Charity instantly dropped his hand. "Oh James, 'tis splendid to see you alive."

"Don't. . .you dare release my. . .my hand. Your touch kept me breathing." His words were slow and labored, but undoubtedly their lighthearted James was with them again.

Charity blushed scarlet but wrapped her fingers around his nevertheless.

"You gave us quite a scare." Delight sighed.

He forced a weak chuckle. "I scared myself, and I hurt in places I didn't know existed."

"You need your rest," Charity said. "Please, do not waste your strength by talking."

"First. . .first, I need to tell you about the wagon."

"I already found the contents," Henry said. "Corn, among other things. Where were you bound? That's all I want to know, so I can deliver it."

James closed his eyes. Excruciating pain passed over his features, and he drew in a shaky breath before continuing. "To Philadelphia. It is not much, but 'twill help. Thank. . ."

"Hush, James," Henry said. "Save yourself for healing."

He raised his hand, then dropped it. "A friend, Cavin Sullivan—" He swallowed hard and moistened his lips. "Was to meet me east of the city."

"No more, friend, lest you do more damage to your old body than already has been done."

The injured man nodded and appeared to drift back to sleep.

Henry paced the floor. He wanted to take the wagon to Philadelphia, but he didn't know a Cavin Sullivan. The mystery of how he'd locate this man pounded at his brain. Asking the man's whereabouts once he arrived invited a wee bit of trouble. With a heavy sigh, he realized he needed to leave shortly, but he had not a destination. Perhaps a few hours' sleep was in order, or else he'd tumble to the ground while driving the wagon.

"I know Mr. Sullivan," Delight said. "He used to live in Boston."

"Could you describe him to me?"

She tilted her head. "He's Irish and has a thick mass of red hair."

"That describes me!" Henry felt trapped with exasperation.

"Well, he's Papa's age and has a rounded middle." She glanced at Charity, then back to Henry. "He owns a tavern and drinks more than tolerable."

"Too many good men in this day and age drink too much." Henry shook his head, frustrated and not knowing which way to turn.

Delight smoothed her skirt. "I have no choice but to go with you."

"Absolutely not. I will not risk your life, nor will I go back on me word to Elijah."

"I promised Papa to watch your doings," Charity added.

"Did Papa speak to the entire family?" Delight's face reddened in anger, but her voice stayed low.

"Just Charity and me self," Henry said.

Delight folded her hands in her lap. "Your promises make little difference, since I am the only one who knows Mr. Sullivan."

"Sister, consider the inappropriateness of traveling with Henry alone. It will be such a scandal."

"I must go. There's no other way."

Charity rubbed her cheeks, fatigue clearly written on her delicate features. "Then I will accompany you, for I couldn't live with myself if something happened to you."

"But what of James? You can't leave him unattended."

Her sister stared into James's face, then lifted her gaze to Henry. "Would you consider waiting one more day so I can be assured of his recovery?"

Oh dear Lord, I promised Elijah to keep Delight safe and look after his family. Now what am I to do?

"It is nearly two hundred and eighty miles to Philadelphia," Henry said. "That is a good fourteen to fifteen days' travel with both of ye along."

"Are you saying you could make it in less time without us?" Delight raised a challenging brow.

"Precisely."

"Then we will make faster time with Charity and myself, for we both know how to drive a wagon."

"And pray tell, lass, where do ye intend to sleep or even ride for that matter? Have ye forgotten the wagon bed is loaded with barrels?"

She touched a finger to her pretty wee chin, as he had seen her do so many times before. "We will all take turns driving, sharing a seat with the driver, and making do amongst the precious cargo."

"Delight Butler, ye are a stubborn one." How ever did Elijah get her to listen to reason?

"I'm not stubborn, but steadfast."

"Steadfast?"

"Being stubborn is a sin. Steadfast is in the scripture as an admirable trait."

He laughed despite his frustration.

"You give me no other choice." Charity clenched her fists. "I shall leave James's care to our sisters and ride along as a chaperone."

Henry thought he'd be ill.

⟨⟩

Delight slept with Charity curled beside her, since her sister refused to leave James's side. The extra day had strengthened him and given Charity peace of mind about his condition. Remember offered to tend to him, and Faith and Patience also volunteered their aid.

Henry, too, rested for the journey ahead. Due to the serious nature of the wagon's contents, they would be spending their nights under the wagon. A threesome, Henry had called them yesterday. Delight wasn't sure how she felt about the many miles that lay ahead. In one breath, she looked forward to his company, and in the next she feared the topic of their conversation. Love didn't choose who became tangled in its web, and for now, knowing Henry cared would help her through the war. In truth, she neither was ready for discussions about the future nor wanted them.

Her thoughts drifted back to Henry's kiss and his growing affections. Odd, she had thought of little else except him declaring his feelings, and now that he had, she quaked in her shoes.

Delight couldn't depend upon Charity to lead many discussions. She tended to shyness, although she did speak out earlier about the journey to Philadelphia—considerable gumption from a sister who whined and carried on about the slightest variance in her life. Charity obviously had matured into adulthood with a few new observations and surprises of her own.

As she considered the matter, Delight concluded that delivering several barrels of gunpowder while pursued by an unknown agent sounded considerably less risky than having Henry realize her immense love.

Moments before the departure, the three checked on James. He opened his eyes.

"You have a wonderful knack of waking at the most opportune moments." Charity bent to his side. "Henry, Delight, and I are leaving."

"For. . .where?" he managed to say. "Not Philadelphia?"

She nodded and offered a shy smile. "Aye, James. Delight knows Mr. Sullivan, and I am going along to chaperone."

James attempted to raise himself but could not lift his head. Charity gently eased him back onto the pillow. He blinked and cast his gaze around the room. "I see I'm in Henry's quarters."

"Right you are," Henry said. "But I shan't be needing them for a few days. How are you feeling?"

"Like somebody tried to kill me and nearly succeeded, but I survived their attempt."

"From the looks of you, surviving is debatable," Delight said. "You need to rest. By the time we return, you will be riding bareback."

"Seriously," Henry began, "do ye feel well enough to state what happened? I am thinking I need to be prepared."

James nodded. "I suspected I was being followed about. . . ten miles out of Chesterfield." He breathed in deeply, obviously fighting pain.

"Take your time," Henry said.

"Once dusk set in, I. . .left the wagon in a thicket and backtracked. I came upon two men. . .on horseback—loyalists by the sound of 'em—who were bragging about what they were going to do to me."

James closed his eyes and took several deep breaths before resuming. "I surprised them. . .took their weapons, and tied them to a tree, but I wasn't expecting a third. He came from behind. We. . .struggled, and he knifed me before I got the utmost of him."

Delight cringed at what James implied. She knew better than to glance Charity's way, knowing her sister's weak stomach.

"I made it back to. . .to the wagon and set my sights on Chesterfield. Not sure how I got here. . .save by the grace of God."

"That is also why you're still alive," Charity said.

Little sister, you continue to amaze me, Delight thought.

"I know ye are in pain, but is there anything you can tell me about the men before we venture toward Philadelphia?" Henry said.

James swallowed hard. "Two things you need to know. One. . . has been branded a thief. I saw a *T* burned into the flesh of his right hand. . .below his thumb. The other matter is the far barrel . . .on the left side of the wagon is filled with corn. . .just in case someone searches it."

"Thank you, friend. I'll be heading outside while ye tell the women good-bye."

Delight had no intention of lingering behind. Charity and James deserved a few moments alone. "Farewell, James. I will be praying for your good health." She stood, then turned to her sister. "Charity, don't persist in tasking James's health. You will have ample time to visit when we return." She tossed a smile over her shoulder and hurried to the doorway behind Henry.

❧

Hours later, the wagon ambled on in a southwesterly direction. Plenty of food lay packed around the barrels, and true to Henry's assessment, both girls had a difficult time lying on the wagon bed. Sleeping would be done in an upright position. Thankfully, Mama had packed ample blankets for the cold nights and chilly days ahead. Delight refused to think of the explosion that could occur with a single musket blast in the right direction.

"What's in the barrels that is so important to the soldiers?" Mama had said.

Delight decided to say nothing rather than lie to her mother.

"I took the lid off one and saw corn." Henry skirted around the real topic.

Mama placed her hands on her hips. "Henry O'Neill, must I question you like Mercy and Hope—or Elijah?"

"Indeed, ye might, Mistress Butler." He leaned against the wagon,

tugging at this and pulling at that.

"What is below the corn?"

"Ma'am, if there is anything beneath it, the Continental army has need of it."

Mama said nothing, only stared into Henry's face as the color rose up his neck in sharp contrast to his coppery red hair. "Perhaps I don't want to know what's in those barrels."

"A wise decision, Mistress Butler."

She wagged a finger at him. "You learned too many of Elijah's tricks while you two were together. Now you take good care of my girls, or I will skin you alive!"

"Of course. I would prefer a firing squad to facing you if something happened to one of them."

"Precisely. You'd best be leaving before I change my mind about allowing them on this mission. I already feel I've lost my good senses by going along with this. . .trickery."

A few moments later, Henry took the first turn at driving, and Charity volunteered to sit among the barrels. Despite the uncomfortable position, she eventually slept, which in Delight's mind was impossible in the excitement.

She glanced up at the sky with its graying clouds. Although it could snow, she prayed it would wait until they returned. On the other hand, rain had a way of chilling one to the bone. "Do you think those two men will follow us?"

"Lass, they'd have to find us first."

She shivered. "My thoughts are they'd be very angry."

"And out for blood. Again, I say this venture is not for the fainthearted. I could still make arrangements to send ye and Charity back to Chesterfield."

She straightened on the seat despite the fact her back ached and walking looked more agreeable. "You are afraid of Papa?"

"And rightfully so. He once threatened to cut off my good leg if anything happened to one of his family."

"But my company is worth any risk."

He laughed heartily. "Are ye asking me to choose between my good leg and you?"

Teasing eased her heavy heart. "'Tis a small price to pay for a lady's company, don't you agree?"

"Are ye worth the trouble?"

"Papa thinks so." *Do you, dear Henry?*

He nodded and pressed his lips together. "Me Delight thinks highly of herself. Pride cometh before destruction, lass."

"A woman that feareth the Lord shall be praised."

Henry shifted his healing leg, and she sensed it stiffened. "I would like very much to drive now," Delight said. "Your leg needs a rest."

"I think not. It is fine," he said. "Although we could quote scripture all the way to Philadelphia to pass the hours."

"I am sure that would make Charity and Mama very happy. Remember is most likely praying for that very ideal."

"Why don't we recite the Song of Solomon?" His voice rang with laughter.

"Henry, what a shameful suggestion." *Those thoughts traverse through my mind enough without reminders.* She crossed her arms across her chest in feigned annoyance. "Perhaps I shan't speak to you at all until we return home."

"Then ye can listen, for I have much to discuss about us."

Chapter 16

Henry couldn't believe his daring, but he had experienced God's prompting to talk with Delight about their relationship. He sincerely doubted if she would jump from the wagon and walk home. She was far too committed to the patriot cause. And if she refused to listen, then obviously he'd misunderstood God's leading regarding their future together. His heart might be broken at the end of the journey and the rendezvous with Cavin Sullivan, but the Father had promised His abiding grace in times of adversity.

Delight perplexed Henry. She appeared to enjoy his conversation and they shared teasing readily, but her physical response to him fluctuated like the changing tides. She seemed to enjoy his embraces, then would pull away as if suddenly assaulted by guilt or remorse. . .or something. She might still have feelings for James, or perhaps she bore no strong feelings toward Henry other than friendship. In any event, he needed to have the answers.

"Delight, if not for this journey, I would be enlisting. I have no doubt that God placed me in your home for the purpose of understanding true liberty in Him and true freedom for men to govern themselves." He glanced at her pale face. Did his topic disturb her this greatly?

"I am pleased we were used for this noble purpose."

With only the sound of nature around them and the steady plop of the horses' hooves on the road, he continued. "Until I joined your family, I believed God intended the aristocrats to rule and the poorer classes to adhere to their mandates. I was convinced of this, even with the suffering of my own family in Ireland and the testimony of my friend Adam about his meager life in the slums of London."

"I'm sorry for all you have experienced." The earnestness in her voice showed her compassion. "Previously the war felt like an adventure or a diversion, a topic to debate. I saw soldiers in

British-occupied Boston, with all of their pomp and circumstance, arrest men and escort them away. I heard men and women shout of the unfairness and ministers speak against the British from the pulpit, but the situation angered rather than frightened me. Even when I carried messages in Boston—"

"Ye what?" Henry must have heard incorrectly.

She massaged her arms. "Papa did not tell you?"

"Tell me what?"

Delight moistened her lips. "I passed messages for the patriots while we lived in Boston."

Henry exhaled heavily into the chilly air. "I am not surprised, knowing your resolve in such matters. Did ye not consider the danger?"

"Not exactly. It exhilarated me. Of course, my illegal activities are why Papa moved us to Chesterfield."

"Wise man." *I wonder if I can handle the trouble involved in loving and marrying ye, Delight Butler.*

"As I was saying, that used to be my attitude. When you came, I saw the cruelty of war from a different perspective. I truly wanted to hate you, but I couldn't. As a result I was constantly angry. At times, I actually considered that there were good, Christian men in the British flanks, too. Now I realize you could have chosen to keep your views about the patriots to yourself, and our friendship might never have taken place." She cast him a sideways glance. "For selfish reasons, I am glad you are now a man of true liberty."

"I am delighted, too, Miss Delight."

She smiled before a wistful look passed over her face. "Papa's leaving awakened me to the atrocities involved in this struggle." She gazed into his face, her large eyes reflecting sadness. "Finding James in such a mangled, bloody condition did not help either. Of course, you have seen more injured and fatally wounded men than you care to remember."

"True, and I will see it again."

She shuddered, and he did not think her reaction was due to the cold, and began again. "Forgive me, you were talking, and I should have been listening instead of voicing my own thoughts."

"Nonsense, I value your words. Every comment helps me to know ye better. In addition, what I have to say involves your own thoughts and sentiments."

"Do continue, Henry. I won't interrupt."

Suddenly, all his carefully prepared statements escaped his mind. He didn't know why he'd initiated the conversation or what he planned to say. Stammering and feeling ridiculous, Henry chose to abandon the subject and try again another time—once he remembered what he wanted to tell her about his love and the future. Humiliation warmed him to the bone, and foolishness cast an accusing finger in his face.

An hour later he recalled the purpose of his initial discussion—the future—but courage failed him. He couldn't tell Delight he loved her or ask her to wait for him until the war ended. In all honesty, he wanted to marry her before he enlisted.

❦

Five days passed, five weary days that extended into the night. Delight endured the uncomfortable wagon and persisted through each hour with less and less sleep. Henry often refused her offers to drive, as well as Charity's. And he always waited until complete darkness before stopping for the evening.

The wagon held a heavy load, and despite the urgency, the animals required rest. Often Delight and Charity strolled alongside it, but in those rare moments when Henry allowed them to drive, he slept. His limp had all but disappeared, yet Delight noted the way his leg stiffened after long periods in the wagon. He must be exhausted, but he never complained.

Henry traversed away from settlements. No point in arousing suspicion about the barrels or having thieves steal their corn. Sleeping under the wagon on cold, hard ground bruised her bones and threatened her disposition. Delight noted Charity grumbled not once, a rarity for her sister and an obvious improvement in her temperament. But of course, Delight herself had found patience in dealing with others of late. Perhaps both she and her sister were showing the signs of reaching maturity.

The past few days, Delight had wakened with a pounding

headache that plagued her until nightfall. Stubbornly she refused to tell Charity or Henry, knowing they could do nothing about the growing pain. Her throat felt as though someone had sliced it raw. This was not the time to be ill, so she prayed.

Delight wondered time and time again what Henry had planned to say on the first day of their journey, but she hesitated to inquire. Deep down she understood his sincere feelings for her as readily as she knew her own. Something always held her back from initiating a conversation on the subject. Cowardice disgusted her, so she elected to term her reluctance to another cause, but what? She felt the pangs of fear every time she gazed into his blue eyes.

Several days out on their journey, the weather turned nippy. One morning they woke to a dusting of snow coating their blankets. Although it quickly melted, the threat of a heavy falling needled at her mind. Along with her other afflictions, she had noticed a slight cough. Delight concentrated on swallowing the annoyance so as not to alarm Henry or Charity.

By avoiding the more heavily traveled roads, they saw few people except during those occasions when they needed to gather directions. The three conversed freely as their journey lengthened. The topics covered everything from Henry's boyhood memories, his friend's recollections of London, Bible passages, and a mound of stories that Delight and Charity told of their childhood.

Delight loved Henry's teasing. His wit and charm increased her feelings for him. Talking with him reminded her of Papa, as though he sat in their midst instead of marching off to war. Many of Henry's admirable traits were the same characteristics she valued for a husband. Of course, considering him in the future sounded easier than approaching the subject at the present.

"Henry, do you sincerely intend to live in Chesterfield after the war?" Delight said one late afternoon as the sun made its fiery descent and she rode in the wagon bed. "I know you have stated as such, but this country is vast."

"I believe so, lass. In me heart, I want to settle down with a family and resume me weaving. Remember, it's why I purposed to come to this fair country."

She nodded. "I remember you telling me that very thing."

"Where do you plan to obtain this family?" Charity said from the bench beside him.

Sister, do not force his reply. I'm not ready for this discussion—at least not now and certainly not in your presence.

Henry chuckled, a trait she had learned to recognize when he hesitated speaking about an uncomfortable issue. "It is all in God's providence. I believe I can provide for a family with my trade, but I do require a wife."

"And what are your requirements for a suitable spouse?" Charity continued.

Delight jabbed her finger into her sister's right side, but Charity ignored the touch.

"Are ye applying?" Henry's voice rang with merriment.

"Nay, but I thought I could recommend someone if I knew what you deemed important."

Henry urged the horses down the road. Soon they would need to stop for the night, and all of them wanted as many miles behind them as they could obtain. "A godly woman is essential. A woman with a sharp mind and who has convictions of her own appeals to me. Friendship is vital, and with that comes respect and admiration for each other."

"And what of beauty?"

Henry's laughter rang over the treetops. "Oh Charity, I am not a comely man, so how can I ask God for loveliness in a wife? Although the idea does have merit."

"Henry, I think you are most dashing. Don't you, Delight?"

Charity, if we were at home, you and I would toss words like puppies tugging at a bone. In fact, I would tease you unmercifully in front of James until you begged for release.

"Don't you think Henry is handsome?" her sister repeated.

Delight fumed. Later she'd tell Charity to tend to her own match-making. "He is pleasing to look at, if one appreciates red hair."

"His hair is what distinguishes him from other men."

"It reminds me of a rooster's comb." Delight uttered the words before considering their content.

"Sister, dare you be unkind to our Henry?" Charity sounded appalled.

Properly chagrined, Delight sought to remedy the situation. "I didn't mean to be derogatory. The color is simply unusual."

Henry cleared his throat. "Ladies, I'd welcome it if ye could talk about matters other than me appearance."

"Certainly." Charity's honeyed words irked Delight. She glanced back at Delight and offered a sweet smile before turning her attention to the road. "Now, what were we discussing? Oh, now I remember, what Henry prefers in a wife."

"I completed my thoughts," he quickly said.

"Wonderful. Commendable, too. I have another challenge. This time it is Delight's turn."

Oh no!

"What do you desire in a husband?" Charity said.

"Must we persist in this topic?" Delight envisioned her sister's neck as one of Mama's chickens in line for dinner.

"Aye. You are next, then I will give my desires."

Delight attempted to remember the items Henry had listed so she would not repeat them. If she did, she had no doubt that Charity would make pointed comments about the similarities. "Henry must surely be bored with this game."

"Nay, lass. I am finding this portion enjoyable."

Trapped, she must endure her sister's folly. "A man who honors God above all things."

Silence.

"Nothing else, Delight?"

"Unselfish, loving, intelligent, capable of courage and strength."

Charity sighed. "Forgive me for my observation, but your description sounds like Henry."

You will be at my mercy this night, Delight promised her sister silently, then quickly added, "I believe I spoke in generalities. All Christian women want those qualities in a husband. This is the essence of a true gentleman."

"You are most insightful. And I do believe you are quite intelligent, sister, with an apt mind and the qualities of a true friend. I only wish I had your beauty."

Red-faced, Delight chose not to respond. She'd lost in Charity's little amusement. Thankfully, dusk had replaced the light, for she could not look into Henry's face without sinking into a puddle of humiliation.

A few moments later she gathered her courage. "Charity, this is not the end of this matter."

"I certainly hope not. Such a pity for me to marry before you." Charity laughed until Henry joined in. At first Delight scrambled for the right words to express her anger, then she, too, broke into a fit of laughter. "Charity, I will get even. Then we will see who shares the mirth."

"I don't doubt your merciless spirit for an instant." Her sister giggled. "But it was such fun."

"Henry, are you going to allow this infraction into your private affairs without revenge?" Delight desperately attempted to disguise the smile on her face.

"Your sister is a worthy opponent. I am afraid King George's army has met their match. As for me, I am going to get some rest before morning arrives."

"I, too, shall sleep, but my mind will be spinning ways to defend my honor," Delight said. *Sweet Charity, this deed will be avenged one day. If not by me, surely one of our sisters will catch you unaware.*

Chapter 17

Another day passed, and Henry still laughed over Charity's blatant questioning about what he looked for in a wife and what Delight sought in a husband. Now, as he hitched the team to the wagon with the cold whipping around his neck, he resolved to speak to his beloved before the sun set that day. By nightfall, he would know if he had a future wife.

A twig snap behind him. The skin on the back of his neck tingled. The sound couldn't be from the women. They had ventured in the opposite direction, and he would have heard their arrival. His gaze flew to his musket, lying across the wagon seat.

"Don't be considering a step near that gun," a male voice said. "Just be standing there nice and quiet and don't be turning around."

An Irishman. "What can I do for ye?" Henry said, forcing kindness into his words.

"Aye, answer a few questions, like what are ye doing with this wagon?"

Is this one of the men who attacked James? "I am transporting corn."

"Is it your own wagon?"

"It belongs to a friend." James had said that one of the men who attacked him had a *T* branded into the fleshy portion of his thumb. *I dare not anger this man for fear of endangering Delight and Charity.*

"Where is your friend?"

"He is nearly a week's ride from here. Why do ye ask?"

The musket barrel rested against his lower back. "I'm asking the questions. Methinks this wagon is stolen. What do ye have to say about that?"

Henry wished he knew to which side of the war the man held his allegiance. "As soon as I deliver the corn, I am returning his wagon."

"Your name?"

"Henry O'Neill."

129

"Do ye mind if I examine the contents of those barrels?"

"Corn is corn, sir, but ye may look. The last one on the left is open."

"I well know!" the man said. "Tell me what happened to the driver of this wagon before I send a musket ball into your back and spill your blood over this hard ground."

Henry needed to get the advantage of this situation before Delight and Charity returned. "I am not at liberty to say."

"Then ye will forfeit your pitiful life."

The gravity of the man's words settled like black smoke on the field of battle. "Dead men cannot provide information."

"Neither can they steal goods."

Henry searched for a weapon within his grasp. "I have not stolen anything. I am making a delivery of corn."

"Perhaps I haven't made me self clear."

From the sound of the man's voice, Henry realized he was about to draw his final breath. Meeting God face-to-face held indescribable merits, but his departure would leave Delight and Charity at the mercy of an unscrupulous man. He whirled about to shove the musket from the man's hands. It fired, piercing the air, piercing the violence of a man's soul.

As he struggled against the Irishman, Henry heard Delight scream. He'd attempt any feat to protect her and Charity—aye, shed the blood from his veins. The gun barrel slammed against the side of his head. Blinding pain spun him into anger. Blood trickled over his forehead and into his eyes, blurring his vision.

"Stop! Please stop!" Delight's voice echoed around him. "Cavin Sullivan, he is one of us."

The man hesitated long enough for Henry to send a blow to the side of his face. He fell, and Henry sprawled on top of him.

"Stop! Henry, Cavin!" Delight pulled on his shoulders. "This is not the enemy."

Henry, no longer numb to her words, ceased his pounding and posed the question, "Are ye a patriot?"

"By all that's right and holy!" A purplish-blue bruise already colored the Irishman's cheek. "This is James Daniels's wagon!" He peered up. "Delight Butler, is it ye, lass?"

"Aye, Mr. Sullivan."

"I have made a terrible mistake," Cavin sputtered.

Henry still felt rage surge through every part of him. He trembled and wiped the blood from his face and head with his arm. "Indeed, ye have."

Delight helped him to his feet while Charity assisted Mr. Sullivan. "James has been badly injured. We are transporting the barrels for him."

Cavin Sullivan gripped the side of the wagon and fought for his breath. "You throw a hard punch," he said.

"I don't take too kindly to a man sticking a gun in me back."

"I thought ye had stolen the wagon."

"Ye should've listened to me." Henry found his temper rising again. *Help me, Lord, to gain control.* He drew in a ragged breath. "Tell the story while I calm me self."

The older man eyed him suspiciously. "James was late to our meeting place, and I went in search of him. I'd heard the story about a branded thief and two other loyalists searching for him and the wagon. I thought ye were one of them."

"'Tis true. I'd have done the same thing." Henry's words appeared to soothe the man. "Hope I didn't hurt ye too much."

Mr. Sullivan offered a grim smile and stuck out his hand. "Glad to meet a good Irishman, even if I am on the opposite end of his fist. I imagine your head is a wee bit throbbin'."

"Indeed it is." The man's missing front tooth told Henry that he held the infamous Irish temper. He extended his hand and the two shook. "Whereabouts ye from?"

"Near Dublin. And ye?"

"County of Londonderry, province of Ulster."

Delight handed Henry a wet cloth, and Charity did the same for Mr. Sullivan. "Ye lasses are a gift from God," the older man said. "Ye certainly saved two Irishmen from killing each other." He wiped his bruised face and turned to Delight. "I see ye are still aiding the patriots. And what of Elijah?"

"He enlisted."

The Irishman's eyes sparkled. "Couldn't stop that man."

A twinge of jealousy about the man's familiarity with Delight pulled at Henry, but he refused to let it show. *Forgive me, Lord. Ye hast given me a new friend, and I am behaving shamefully.* "How can we help ye?"

"Oh, 'tis me to lend a hand. I have a wagon back in the woods to carry the barrels. I will take them on to Philadelphia."

"Praises to God," Henry said. "I'll help you load, then we can journey back to Chesterfield." He studied his recent opponent's face. "You might need a bit of rest and nourishment before setting out alone."

"I brought a bit of rum—" He stopped and cringed. "Pardon me, lasses, I know how your father feels about the spirits, but it does numb the pain."

"And your mind to clear thinking. Our Lord taught us about the dangers of drunkenness," Delight said with a lift of her chin.

That's my sweet Delight. She never hesitates to tell one the truth— except when it comes to her heart.

The road home. The words alone sounded like manna to Delight. Weariness tugged at her whole being. She had offered to sit on the wagon bed. With the extra room available now that the barrels had been unloaded, she lay down and instantly fell asleep. Strange and terrifying dreams plagued her, so strange she believed she was awake only to realize otherwise.

"Delight. Delight."

She knew Charity shook her, but she couldn't awaken. Her head pounded like a soldier's drum. "Let me sleep. I am so tired."

Am I dreaming again or is Charity still talking?

"Henry, her head is so hot. We must do something."

Delight's thoughts drifted back to a dream where Papa and Henry rode down the road toward their house in Chesterfield shouting, "The war is over! The British are defeated!" A hand touched her forehead, then caressed her cheek. It did not belong to Charity.

"Delight, can ye answer me?" His voice rang tender to her ears.

She attempted to stir and reply, but her throat felt as though a hot poker had seared it. The words failed to form. Only the semblance of a moan met her ears. Blissful sleep caught her like the waves that used to slap against Boston Harbor, and she felt herself sweeping out to sea.

Henry had realized helplessness in his days, but nothing like the overwhelming despair of watching Delight suffer with fever and delirium. She fought the blankets Charity tucked in around her, while a swirl of new-fallen snow quietly covered her body.

"We need shelter." He urged the horses down the road. "I remember a village a few miles ahead. We will seek a place to stay and medicine for Delight."

Charity sat at her sister's side, continually dabbing her flushed face. "Perhaps we can find some broth and a warm place for her to sleep. I care not for myself, but this fever must be broken."

Henry ached at the thought of his beloved's illness. "I should never have allowed ye to come. Being exposed to the elements has made Delight ill, and ye may possibly be next."

"Nonsense, I feel perfectly fine. The truth be known, I noticed Delight had a slight cough before we met up with Mr. Sullivan."

Henry tightened his hold on the reins. "Why didn't she say something?"

"Delight? She never admits to feeling poorly for fear someone else may need tending."

"I understand exactly what ye are describing. At times she reminds me of a hen fussing over her chicks, the way she treats ye and your sisters." The longer he considered the matter, the more irritated he grew with himself. "It's time she allowed someone to take care of her."

"That will take a few hundred prayers."

"I have another idea." Henry glanced up at an angry sky. It matched his mood. If they did not find a hospitable home, they would be covered in snow. Delight desperately needed a roof over her head.

"So do I," Charity said. "Marry her, and none of us will have to fret over whether she is taken care of properly."

"Aye." His voice saddened. "I would most gladly oblige, but I fear she doesn't hold the same affections as I do."

"Henry O'Neill. How can you be so clever and still not understand what Delight feels for you?"

Curiosity mixed with frustration assaulted him. "She's had opportunities to reveal more of her feelings but has chosen not to. I know she cares for me, but is it enough to withstand the future?"

"Love does peculiar things to a woman," Charity said. "You may want that very thing until you find it, then you are afraid. Has she welcomed tenderness in one breath and shied from it in another?"

"You know 'tis true. What can I do?"

Snow began to trickle down in huge flakes. "Make her think exposing her heart is her idea. She's too stubborn to do so otherwise. For the present. . ." Charity faltered. "We must pray, for her fever is rising."

Henry caught his breath and glanced behind him where Charity held a blanket over Delight's face to keep the wind and snow away. "Does she have a rash or is her breathing irregular?"

"Nay. For that we must be grateful."

"Father God," Henry began, "I know I have been amiss in allowing Delight and Charity to join me on this ominous journey, and I am truly sorry. But it seems my errant ways have contributed to Delight's illness. Please touch her with Your healing power and break the fever raging through her body. In Your holy Son's name, amen."

He looked ahead into a swirling mass of white and saw the outline of a house and barn. *Thank Thee, Father. May these people be good Christian folk.* "I see help ahead."

Within minutes, Henry pulled the horses to a halt and braked the wagon. He stepped down onto his bad leg, and it nearly collapsed. Righting himself, he faced a snarling dog that had no intentions of allowing him to pass.

"What do you want?" a male voice called from the door.

The dog stepped closer. "Shelter and possibly broth for an ill woman in my wagon. I can pay."

"Ill, ya say?" the man said in a raspy tone.

Henry couldn't turn to face him for fear the dog would sink his teeth into his uninjured leg. "Yes sir. She has a fever."

"Is it pox? We don't want any sickness here."

Henry had feared the same thing. He knew well the deadly effects of smallpox. "She does not have a rash. I believe it's from exposure to the weather. We have been traveling awhile."

The dog growled. "Can you call off your dog?"

"Not until I'm ready. Besides, my wife and I don't want sickness at our door."

Obviously you aren't generous in spirit. Henry cringed and clenched his fists. "Perhaps some broth then?"

"I will ask the wife, but you cannot come inside."

Henry glanced at the barn. "May we rest in your barn?"

The man said nothing, and since Henry couldn't see him, he waited. "I'll pay for the use of it."

Silence echoed around the wagon.

"All right, you can use the barn. Don't want no money except for hay, and you can feed my animals while you are taking up room."

Is there no end to his rudeness? "I agree, sir. Now will ye call the dog?"

"King George come here, I say." The mangy animal skirted around the front of the wagon. Henry whirled around and saw it leap onto the porch beside the old man, who closely resembled the dog. "I'll ask my wife if there is food inside, but I can't promise anything."

"Thank ye. Any herbs for tea would be appreciated."

"You keep asking for more and I detest it. And don't be starting a fire or coming outside when it is dark. The dog guards things real well."

Chapter 18

Henry carried Delight inside the barn and placed her on a makeshift mattress of hay covered with a blanket. Once the door closed, the draft vanished. Still she needed to be kept warm—Charity, too. In this structure, they had little more than shelter, and all he could offer Charity to eat was soldiers' provisions of hard biscuits and dried beef, unless the farmer and his wife found food to spare. At least they had a lantern.

The owner did not complain when Henry led the horses inside. "I'll be expecting good payment for the hay," he'd shouted.

Oh, me Delight. I never wanted this for ye. But I will get warm food for ye and Charity and herbs no matter what the cost. He would wait a moment more before he ventured outside to the house and faced the nasty temperament of the owner and his mongrel.

King George, what a fitting name.

With twilight fast approaching, Henry looked for a tool to keep distance between him and the dog. Oddly enough, the barn was well maintained and neat. Various tools hung on pegs or leaned against a wall according to size. He had expected the contents to be in disarray to match the old man's disposition. Snatching up a hoe, he headed for the door.

"Henry, do be careful." Charity wrapped a spare blanket around her shoulders.

"I will, lass. No matter what ye hear, stay put. I have a feeling the dog and I might have a skirmish." He grinned for her sake. "Pray the man's wife is friendlier than he."

She nodded. Her obligatory smile soon faded when Delight moaned.

Without another word, Henry slid open the barn door. As expected, the dog approached him in a fury.

"King George, get out of me way." Henry raised the hoe. "I aim to converse with those people, and the likes of ye will not stop me."

The door of the house opened, and the old man stepped out, his hand grasping a musket.

"What are you doing with my hoe?"

Henry kept one eye on the dog and shouted back, "I'm protecting me self from your dog. I need to purchase warm food for the women and possibly something for fever."

"I heard you before," the old man said.

From behind him, a plump woman with snow-white hair pushed by the old man. "King George, get into the house this minute!"

Immediately the dog obeyed.

"The lady is ill?" she said, moving toward Henry. "And you need food and herbs for a fever?"

"Aye ma'am."

"Rachel, you don't know what that woman has. Could be we might get sick and die," the old man spat.

"I am already old and ready to meet my Maker, Horace, and I intend to help." She neared Henry and smiled. "I'm Rachel Henderson. You bring those women inside. I have beef stew and medicine to help break the fever."

Thanks be to God.

Henry refused to sleep that night. He sat by Delight's side near the fireplace just as she had done for him. Charity stretched out on the other side of Delight, finally succumbing to sleep. The Hendersons were hospitable after all, simply cautious about loyalists, although the dog's temperament could not be disguised. Mistress Henderson had brewed some feverfew tea, and Henry had helped Charity administer it. Now he waited and prayed.

Mistress Henderson declared herself a believer, but her husband had no use for God. Henry could not imagine the misery of people who did not know Jesus as their Savior. How wretched they must feel with the uncertainty of life. It was difficult enough to face sickness, death, and the struggle to survive during these war-torn days, but to have no hope must be the epitome of despair.

Delight's face tinted pink with the fever looked peaceful, but the color veiled her ill health. Her lips, normally a deep wine, were now purple. He bent and brushed a kiss across her forehead.

"Me sweet lady," he whispered. "I pray the fever breaks tonight with God's healing. I want to see the light in your eyes, the sparkle that reminds me of heaven's gate. I love ye, Delight, with an affection I never thought possible."

Henry continued to watch her, wiping her forehead with a cool, damp cloth and praying. She was strong and healthy. She could recover in a few days with rest and proper food. His mind wandered back to special moments with her. Even their initial quarreling reigned as cherished moments. A strong woman, his Delight. Psalm 37:4 rang through his mind, as it had done so many times before: *"Delight thyself also in the Lord; and he shall give thee the desires of thine heart."*

Aye, I'm sure the Lord is pleased with ye. Always I see ye strive to serve Him. What a worthy mother ye will make someday. I pray He allows ye to be the mother of our children.

✍

Shortly after midnight, Henry added another log to the fire and studied Delight's face. No longer did color tinge her cheeks and perspiration bead upon her forehead. Elated, he touched her cheek. Coolness met his fingertips.

"Praise God," he whispered. He stared into her lovely features. "Charity, wake up. The fever's broken."

Immediately Delight's sister sat upright and confirmed Henry's words. "It is a blessing," she whispered, "a real blessing."

Delight opened her eyes and glanced about, obviously confused by her whereabouts.

"We're in a farmhouse, lass," he said. "How are ye feeling?"

She took a deep breath. "I was having the most beautiful dream, then voices woke me." She attempted a smile. "I gather I've been ill."

"Not for too long," Henry reported. "But long enough to cause us a scare."

"Forgive me." She swallowed with difficulty. "My throat aches, and I have a horrible taste in my mouth."

"The taste is the herbs," Charity said. "And tea will help soothe the pain in your throat."

Delight stared into Henry's face with a tender smile. "Someday

I'll tell you about my dream. . . . For now, I'd like to sleep."

Two days later, Henry, Charity, and Delight climbed into the wagon and said good-bye to Rachel and Horace Henderson. Henry wanted Delight to rest another day, but she insisted on traveling home.

"I can rest in the back of the wagon as easily as I can here." Nothing could convince her otherwise, and she used her stubborn nature to its fullest.

Rachel hugged her tightly. "I pray you will be stronger than ever before."

Delight felt tears well up in her eyes. "Thank you. Thank you for everything you have done."

"It was a true blessing," the old woman said. She leaned to whisper in Delight's ear. "Henry is a good man. You might consider marriage. He is quite devoted."

Warmth spread through her. "I promise."

The wagon wheels crunched into a fairly heavy coating of snow as the horses ambled down the road. The whitewashed countryside and ice-laden trees painted an air of serenity against the stark blue sky. If the weather stayed crisp and not bitter cold, they could very well be home before the next snowfall. Delight felt exhilarated, ignoring her weakened condition and a dull headache that plagued her like a pesky fly in the heat of August.

Gratefulness to be alive soared through her veins, or did her renewed spirit extend from her love for Henry? In any event, she was eager to resume their journey home. Yet in the same breath, she knew home also represented the growing nearness of Henry's departure. Sadness descended upon her. She refused to think of life without him. She would cling to the memory of her fevered dreams.

In them, she and Henry had a home of their own in a rolling countryside filled with green pastures and pastel wildflowers. The two walked through the fields hand in hand while in the distance children squealed with laughter and called to "Mama" and "Papa." What a lovely, sweet dream. She and Henry, a part of God's divine plan.

"Horace shook me hand," Henry said, glancing back at her with a smile wider than the Atlantic.

"Did he say any parting words?" Charity said.

"Only to stop for a visit if we were in this area again."

Charity shook her head. "Delight, his treatment of us when we first arrived was appalling. And I thought King George would tear Henry to pieces."

"Glad I slept through it, but I am so sorry you two were exposed to his bad manners and his monster dog on my account."

"I'd do it again." Henry lifted the reins and coaxed the horses a little faster down the road.

"Why is that?" Charity said in her familiar lilt.

Charity, will you ever cease wrapping every statement you utter around Henry and me?

He chuckled. "My good leg of course. I don't want to face Elijah and Mistress Butler's wrath."

They shared a good bit of teasing all morning long. The weather warmed, and the snow melted. Deer bounded across the road, their grace and spirit reminding Delight of Mercy and Hope at play. She missed her sisters and wanted to be home. There was no doubt that only the push of God would cause her to endeavor a lengthy wagon journey again. She felt a burst of energy.

"I am strong enough to drive," Delight said the second morning after leaving the Hendersons. With the provisions Rachel had given them, they'd had a filling breakfast and felt an eagerness to put miles behind them.

"I think not," Henry said. "When ye drove before your illness, ye hit so many ruts I feared the gunpowder would explode."

"I believe Charity drove then."

Charity tossed her a knowing look. "You are mistaken, Delight. I remember how I attempted to sleep between the barrels and realized I had either broken all my bones or my body was permanently bruised."

Delight did not recall their reporting the incidents quite the same way at the time, but it made for lively conversation. Anything to keep her mind diverted from the nearness of the moment when Henry would leave for the war. In the deep recesses of her mind, while she battled the fever, she thought he'd sat by her side and told her of his love. She sought to mention it to Charity and inquire as to the authenticity of her memory. The risk of appearing foolish always stopped her. During the time of the fever, she had experienced difficulty differentiating between her dreams and what truly happened, although her sister would not make light of it at all.

"Nevertheless, I'm so tired of this wagon. Can I please ride on the bench for a while?"

Charity wiggled her shoulders, and Delight knew she had conjured the perfect reply. "Henry, do you mind if I drive?" She whirled around to her sister. "Do forgive me, I misunderstood. You must want to ride beside Henry, not me."

When we are home again, I will not be revengeful, Delight thought, *but I will find ways to torment you out of love.* "Charity, you plague me worse than a nest of angry bees."

"I learned well from my older sister. Henry, I do hope you don't mind. Delight wants to be near you for a change of landscape."

Most assuredly you speak the truth, but Charity, please, you do not have to inform him of the matter.

Henry brought the horses to a halt. He helped Charity into the wagon bed and extended his assistance to Delight. As soon as his fingers touched hers and grasped her hand, she caught the familiar tenderness in his gaze and the smile he offered only to her. Suddenly the first and then the second time he kissed her danced across her mind, leaving her weak in the knees and trembling to the touch.

"Aye, lass, ye are still not well. I feel ye trembling." His hands seized her waist and lifted her to the wagon bench.

"Nonsense, I am quite strong."

Once they were on the road again, she did note her spirit felt exhilarated at sitting next to him.

"Do you think we could discuss a few important matters?" he said.

How can we with Charity straining to hear every whisper? She stole a glance and saw he peered down the road as if concentrating on every melting flake of snow. "Of course. Before you begin, I am most grateful for your kind care during my illness."

"Ye are most welcome, lass. Charity's and your safekeeping had been entrusted to me, and I gave me word to your parents."

Did his voice crack or was it her imagination? "What are the pressing matters you speak of?"

He sighed. "I believe you already know." He glanced at Charity, and she slid to the back of the wagon and allowed her feet to dangle over the side.

Thank you, sister. This may be our only opportunity to. . .to converse about private matters. Delight clasped her hands in an effort to hide her nervousness. "Continue, Henry."

From the corner of her eye, she saw his chest and shoulders rise with a deep breath. "I've thought about this at great length." His gaze swung to her. "Do. . .do ye have affections for me that are strong enough to last. . .until the Lord calls us home?"

Chapter 19

The illumination in Henry's eyes must have marveled the gates of heaven. Delight had dreamed, even seen a glimpse of that special radiance, but this brilliance far surpassed her deepest wishes.

"Do you not know?" she managed through a ragged breath.

"I've hoped and prayed for that very thing."

"I care for you. I care very much." Her heart beat fiercely. Her stomach fluttered as though a myriad of butterflies had suddenly taken flight.

"Dare it be love?" His face grew ghastly pale, and he dragged his tongue over his lips. "Delight, I do love ye."

A small cry escaped her lips, and her eyes filled with joyous tears. "And I love you."

He pulled in the reins and set the brake. His hands shook so he could barely complete the task. In the next instant he drew her into his arms. "It seems I've waited a lifetime to hear ye repeat those words—words sweeter than honey."

She lifted her face to meet his, silently begging for a kiss to seal the love bubbling inside her. He did not disappoint. Henry's lips claimed hers lightly. But with the fervency of the moment, the kiss deepened, and she eagerly responded. Her hands reached for his neck, and she raked her fingers through the mass of copper-colored hair.

He finally pulled himself from her. "Thank ye for letting me speak me heart."

Delight knew she had to be completely honest. "I am afraid, Henry. I'm fearful of the war and of your not returning. I could not bear living without you."

He touched his finger to her cheek. "I know, me Delight. But God has a span of time for each of us. He's marked our days, and there is nothing we can do to alter His plan. I promise I will do what is noble and right for our country and, God willing, return to you."

Oh Father, this apprehension of mine has kept me from loving Henry totally in my heart. Guard him, I beg of Thee. "I sense my trust in God faltering each time I think of you. I am so sorry."

He offered a slight smile. "I've read it in your eyes, and I will continue to pray for our Father's peace."

"Are you two finished with all your whisperings?" Charity called from the rear of the wagon.

Startled, Delight realized she had momentarily forgotten her sister's presence. "Probably not." She laughed.

"From the lack of conversation, I am assuming you two are engaged once more in a kiss," Charity continued. "I refuse to look for fear I might be embarrassed."

"Most assuredly." Henry chuckled. He took Delight's hand into his and kissed it.

"Papa and Mama will hear of this." Charity giggled. "After all, I am the chaperone."

"I shall be the first to tell." Henry's familiar wide smile broke across his rugged features. "In fact, I will shout it to all the world." He winked at Delight. "I love Delight Butler," he shouted. "I love the most fair lass in the whole world, and she loves me!"

Hours later they still chatted away, their conversation floating from one topic to another, but always with enthusiasm.

"When we have some privacy, I will ask ye to marry me," Henry whispered.

"And what if I should ask you?" Delight tingled from head to toe from his attentions. She attempted to look serious, yet a smile tugged at the corners of her mouth.

"Oh, ye are a modern lass," he said. "Shall I beware of finding us alone?"

"You two are properly suited," Charity called from the wagon bed. "I can recall a time not so long ago when you loathed each other."

"'Twas a mere disguise of love," Henry said.

"I think you should wed the same day we return to Chester-field," her sister said.

Delight felt her heart slam against her chest. As elated as she felt, a wedding could not take place until the war had ended. She refused to be a widow. Nay, they should wait until peace blanketed the land. Lifting her gaze, she saw Henry studying her curiously.

Henry, do not take Charity seriously. It is. . .impossible. "We cannot wed until after the war," she said softly.

A grim sadness captured her. In a moment, his happiness seemed to vanish. *I've hurt him, but surely he can see how foolhardy it would be to do otherwise.*

✐

Henry kept both hands on the reins and gripped them hard. Masking this disappointment was one of the hardest feats he'd ever attempted. Like a giddy young man, he had assumed Delight felt the same commitment as he and would marry him this very day if possible, but her vision of marriage lay in the future. The thought pained him greatly, and he fought hard to recover his former enthusiasm.

I'm being selfish. If I were killed, she'd be a widow. I don't want a lonely life for her.

"Of course, that would be utmost, lass. We can have a wonderful wedding with all of your family after the war."

"Splendid." She snuggled close to him and linked her arm in his. "For a moment, I feared you to be unhappy with me."

"The war could last a very long time. Perhaps another year," Charity called from the back.

Even longer, and every day would be miserable without my beloved to come home to. I'd agree to anything to keep her.

Delight abruptly straightened. "Surely not, sister. With the British defeated at the Battle of Saratoga, we must be facing mere months."

"What do you think, Henry?" Charity said. "Could you and Papa be home in so short a time?"

He carefully formed his words, not wanting to dishearten the women but believing there were many battles yet to fight before the British granted freedom to America. "Lasses, Saratoga is in New York. What of the South? Thirteen colonies exist where other British and American soldiers will battle. General Washington has a grand plan, I am sure, but things of this nature take time."

Silence echoed around him. Guilt assailed him for forcing reality into their tender hearts. "I did not mean to upset you," he finally said.

"You spoke the truth," Charity said. "James, with all of his zeal and enthusiasm, says the same."

"I do not agree with you." Delight slung the words as though pitching soiled straw from a barn. "We may not have fancy uniforms or generals of nobility, but we have the cloak of truth."

"Truth is certain," Henry said. "But the cause takes time, effort— and the blood of men to lead it to victory."

Defiance etched her face. "Perhaps you do not truly harbor freedom and liberty in your soul."

"And perhaps ye do not really know me at all."

Four days more, and the wagon rumbled over the outskirts of Chesterfield. Delight no longer felt exhilarated in the return, for she and Henry had not spoken since their disagreement. Anything she wished to convey to him was spoken through Charity. To her frustration, Henry acted as though nothing uncomfortable existed between them. Delight knew her childish behavior needed to stop, but her pride interfered. She wanted to apologize sincerely, but the words refused to come.

When she looked back on it, she realized she'd hurt him twice—first in her refusal to marry him before he enlisted and second in questioning his allegiance. Charity had scolded her severely, then hugged her and told her she loved her. Her sister was disappointed, and rightfully so. Henry was distressed and Delight shouldered all the blame.

Why can't I simply say I was wrong? Have I not learned anything from scripture?

A horrible thought sickened her. What if Henry should be hurt or killed in the days ahead, and she had not mended the problem between them? What if he became so disillusioned with her argumentative spirit that he found another woman to ease his wounded heart? She resolved to wait not a moment longer.

Already the last house in Chesterfield came into view. From there, they would soon reach home, and from there would come his enlistment.

"Henry," she said meekly from the back of the wagon.

"Aye." His tone balanced between cordial and impersonal.

"I want to say—"

Charity gasped. "Are those British soldiers in the distance?"

He pulled the wagon to a halt. "Lass, I believe ye are right."

Delight rose to her feet as the sum of her nightmares came within her view. Redcoated uniforms glittered in the afternoon sun, reminding her of blood shed for the cause of liberty. "Henry, you must run before they find you."

Charity grabbed the reins from him. "Yes, don't let them see you."

He whirled his gaze to Delight, his look filled with the love he had hidden for the past four days.

"Please, go." Delight reached to touch his shoulder, but the horses took a step and jolted the wagon. He steadied her, his touch scorching her flesh.

"Go with him," Charity said. "Now, before they see how many of us are in the wagon. I can take care of myself."

Delight needed no more urging and swung her leg over the side while Henry jumped to the ground. Grabbing his musket, Henry grasped Delight's hand, and the two raced toward the woods. She wondered about his injured leg, but for the present it didn't slow him.

God help us!

"Do you see them?" she said breathlessly, afraid to peer behind. One hand clung to Henry's, and the other held her skirts. Desperation and fear riddled her senses.

"Nay, but they will surely inquire of Charity. I believe they are looking for me."

Alarm seized her. "Will they harm her?" They raced into thick underbrush, where she stopped to gain her breath. Henry studied the wagon and soldiers.

"I think not. They have no reason to suspect anything amiss." He paused. "She has just met up with them."

Delight scurried to view the scene. "I am sorely worried about her."

"Do not worry about your sister. She is stronger than she appears."

A remembrance of the past weeks danced across her mind. Charity had amazed her on more than one occasion with her cleverness and gumption. "I comprehend what you are saying. I've seen and felt an inner strength that I greatly admire."

He sighed. "I don't like the fact that she is the one who must endure the soldiers' questioning. At the moment, selfishness is creeping all over me. I shouldn't have left her alone, fleeing like a scared boy."

"If you had stayed, you would be on your way back to fighting for the wrong side."

He nodded and continued to study the British, who had turned their horses around and trailed after Charity and the wagon.

Another stab of alarm snatched at her heart. "Why do you suppose they are following her?"

Henry stared at the small parade as though he were reluctant to speak his mind. "Possibly Abby Rutherford is hosting them for tea."

She heard the bitterness in his voice. "Are you thinking she may have alerted them to your whereabouts?"

"And those of James."

Oh no, poor Charity. "They would not be kind to him, would they?"

"Nay, lass. If they have him, he faces serious trouble."

"What shall we do?"

He turned and offered a smile. "Always we. Must you continually become involved with the perilous aspects of life?"

His infectious grin subdued her irritation. How many times had she questioned the same thing? "I know I am independent."

"But are ye totally dependent on God?"

Henry's inquiry burned to the core of her being. *How could he ask such a despicable thing, especially at a time like this?* "Of course I am."

"Are you, Delight? Completely? Without hesitation?"

An inner voice stirred her being. *Could Henry be correct in his assessment?*

I don't think so. I am the oldest. It is my nature to look after others.

"But in doing so, are you trusting Me?"

Delight trembled. The truth assaulted her. She did trust more in herself than in the Creator. Oh, she prayed, but too many times when circumstances required immediate attention, she acted before relying on God. Deep down, she knew He didn't need her assistance. God simply asked for her loving obedience.

She blinked and stared up at Henry, feeling his gaze upon her. He showed no condemnation, only an earnest desire for her to respond to his concerns.

Perhaps my weakness has changed his heart for me. Even worse, perhaps God may no longer feel I'm worthy of His favor.

Again the inner voice pricked her spirit. *"I will never leave thee, nor forsake thee."*

Oh Father, I am so sorry. Please forgive me and lead me in the right paths.

A tear slid down her cheek, and she shook her head to dispel the host of emotions flowing through her: remorse, regret, guilt. She prayed God's incredible love would ease the pain she had caused.

"What is it, darlin'?" Henry brushed the tear from her face. "I didn't mean to inflict the pain I see in your eyes. I had no right to ask ye about your own relationship with the Lord."

She swallowed her tumultuous mental anguish, wanting to speak clearly. "But you had every right, for I know your inquiry arose from love for me. I am sorry for what I said to you earlier. I—I despise my stubborn nature. Far too often, I believe I have the correct answers and must be in control of my destiny."

His demeanor softened, revealing a contrite man. "Me Delight, ye are in the presence of a self-righteous man. God must forever be humbling me."

She paused, wondering how much she could speak her mind without risking Henry's possible rejection.

"Go ahead, My child. Tell him your heart."

"I want to be your wife," she said. "I was afraid before. I thought if I lost you in the war, it wouldn't hurt as badly. I despise my harsh words. They were all lies. Please forgive me."

He opened his mouth, but she covered it with her fingertips. "You are so good and kind to me, more than I deserve. Aye, perhaps a little self-righteous at times." She smiled and bit her lip to keep from weeping. "But, if you will have me, I will marry you this very hour."

He gathered up the fingers caressing his lips and kissed them lightly. "I accept your humble proposal." He slipped his hand around her waist to the small of her back and drew her close. "I love your free spirit, and I love your determination. With God's help, we will have a beautiful life together. Ye are my delight from the Lord. With ye beside me, God has given me the desires of me heart."

She whisked away a tear. "But I can be bitter and relentless."

"Aye, so can I, but we are sweet as honey together." His lips were but a hair span from hers, and in the next instant he sealed his words. When at last he pulled from her, he held her close, so close she could hear his heartbeat. He released a heavy sigh. "Indeed I'm a self-centered man, basking in the presence of my beloved when Charity and James may be in grave danger."

"What are you going to do?" She carefully chose her words to separate herself from the solution.

He smiled and kissed the top of her head. "I think we should move around the trees and the town to your home. Once everything looks clear and dusk has set in, I will send ye to your mother so she can see ye are well and safe."

"And James?"

"Let us pray he is in seclusion and that God will protect him."

Hand in hand, they moved just inside the thicket of trees, wary of the sights and sounds around them and coaxing the sun to set. Speaking in whispers and only when necessary, they edged around Chesterfield, ever mindful of the soldiers in their red coats. From all appearances, the British looked to search every house in the small town.

"Are ye praying?" Henry said as they watched soldiers dismount at a home across the way from Uncle Matthew and Aunt Anne's whitewashed two-story.

"With all my might."

"I wish I could do something instead of observe. This is a helpless feeling."

"What is God telling you?"

He squeezed her hand. "He is in control. I believe I'm proceeding as He desires."

Chapter 20

Twilight painted the sky in colors of rich amber fading into deep blue. Another day finished, yet tasks haunted Henry with their lack of completion. Delight and he rested beneath a knoll on the hard, cold ground while waiting for darkness to completely settle. Twice they had observed soldiers coming and going at the Butler household. Neither time did the redcoats bring anyone out, leading Henry to believe James had secured safety. Charity either remained in the home or had fled with him. He preferred the latter possibility, since his friend had received serious injuries and could not yet be fully recovered.

He glanced at Delight, her face etched with exhaustion and her recent recovery from the fever. She needed to be sitting beside a warm fire and out of the cold air before she fell prey to the illness again. He wrapped his arms around her in hopes of keeping her warm.

Oh Father God, please heal those around me who are fighting disease and injury. Give us all strength and courage in these difficult times.

"I'd like for you to enter your home from the front," he said, hating to be apart from her but knowing her health came foremost. "I doubt if the soldiers plan to return this evening."

She snuggled into the hollow of his shoulder. "I would rather be here with you, but those inside might need a helping hand. And certainly Mama and Charity share worrisome thoughts about us." She did not say a word about his possible imprisonment if captured, and neither did he. "Charity may need comfort, too."

"Quite possibly. If I will not endanger your family or James with my presence, pass a candle three times at the rear. I'll arrive shortly. If there is trouble—"

"There shan't be." She rose from her crouched position and massaged the small of her back.

Henry tugged on her arm, pulling her back down beside him. He stole a kiss, then grinned. "So ye won't forget me."

"There is no likelihood of that happening." Her face sobered, and for a moment he thought she would weep. "Be wary."

"'Tis my true name, Wary O'Neill." He chuckled with his teasing.

She tilted her head. "Aye, your mother named you properly."

With those words, she moved across the field at a brisk pace. "You take heed," he whispered after her. Henry scrutinized the surroundings, ready to defend his beloved if necessary. One day they would have a delightful life together. He smiled at his word choice.

⁂

The windows were already shuttered, barring Delight any view of the goings-on inside her home. Although she wanted to believe nothing was amiss, caution guided her steps. A peculiar sensation played with her mind, as though danger lurked about. She shrugged away the feeling, attributing it to her recent fever.

I promised Papa I would avoid dangerous situations, but dire straits seem to follow me wherever I go. As Papa protected me from Grace years ago, my heavenly Father will protect me and my loved ones now.

Every step became a prayer. She hesitated, listening intently for God's voice warning her to return to Henry. But she heard nothing, only felt the eerie chill at her nape.

Delight lifted the latch and slipped inside the front door as Henry had instructed. She heard the low hum of voices, not the expected laughter from her sisters. Normally Mercy and Hope would be playing. Of course they could be reading scripture or praying or practicing their letters. Or the uneasiness racing through her might mean something truly frightening.

From the darkness a hand seized her upper arm. "You must be the one we've been waiting for."

She gasped and struggled to free herself. "Sir, let me go!"

"Not until you answer a few questions." He gripped her tightly and squeezed, but she refused to cry out. "I believe we have our prize," he called out. Intensifying his hold, he pulled her toward the kitchen and a crackling fire.

At the sight of her mother's anguish-ridden face and the protective way she cradled Elijah, Delight experienced a mixture of anger and compassion unlike anything she'd ever known. "Mama." The word fell from her lips without thought.

"There is no need to treat her cruelly," Mama said, rising to her feet and cradling baby Elijah in her arms. Her carriage would have rivaled that of the king.

The soldier holding Delight, a pasty-looking fellow, sneered at her mother and intensified his hold. "I will consider letting her go when she responds properly to my questions."

Delight winced. "I am fine, Mama. Do not worry." She quickly glanced about the room. One other soldier and two men sat about the room. Their muskets and bayonets lay within easy reach, stacking the odds against Henry. Her sisters huddled together, frightened and pale, while indignation soared through Delight. But Charity, where was she?

Her gaze flew to a corner. James was propped against a wall with Charity beside him. In the next breath, she saw he'd been gagged. No doubt, he had been quite verbal.

"We're looking for Henry O'Neill," the pasty soldier spat out. "The deserter has our gunpowder."

"And you think I know where he is?"

"Your kind neighbor, Mistress Rutherford, said you left with him. Lass, do your family and your country a valued service and tell us where to find him."

That insufferable woman! To think I once sat beside her at the meetinghouse, believing she could be won over with Christian kindness. Delight stiffened. "If I did know his whereabouts, I would not tell the likes of you." For a moment, she thought the soldier would strike her.

"There is a reward, you know," another soldier said.

Fury burned across her heart. "I have no need of your money."

The soldier who appeared to be in charge pushed her toward her mother. "Then wait with the others. He will return, and we're sure of it. He'd not leave a lass as pretty as you without a farewell."

She caught her balance and seated herself by Remember and Faith. Patience looked to be on the verge of fainting. Delight offered a reassuring smile to her sisters before replying to the soldier. "He is most certainly miles from here by now."

"We will soon know for sure," the soldier said. "I've been enjoying the fair lasses of this household. No wonder O'Neill sought to ignore his duty."

Disgusting pig. Don't you dare touch one of my sisters. Oh God, forgive me. I know that Thy presence is here—and that Thou art in control. I am trusting Thee in this. Please tell me how to proceed.

A man shifted nearby to stare at her. He smelled of dirt and sweat, and his malevolent smile sickened her. As he rubbed the side of his jaw, she saw it: the brand of a thief.

The wicked men who had tried to kill James had found him again. Not only did revenge rule their motives, but also the deserter's fee from the British. God help them all against their enemies.

She peered at Charity and James. From what she could see, he looked considerably better than at their parting, and Charity appeared well. What ideas were rumbling through their heads?

Several long minutes passed. A plan began to emerge from Delight's frenzied mind. She prayed it came from God and not from her driving passion to take care of her loved ones.

"This is all your doing." She turned to Charity.

Her sister blinked, obviously confused. *Please, Charity, this is a game. Henry will not stay away from the house forever. He will sense the trouble within and try to help. Hopefully, he can hear my voice and be alerted to what awaits him inside.*

"Do you have nothing to say for yourself?" Delight flung at her sister.

"Whatever do you mean?" Charity stiffened.

"Hush," Mama said. "You will wake the baby."

"The baby is not my concern." Delight hoped her insincere remark—a long measure from her deep love for the wee babe—revealed her intentions. "She," and she pointed to the figure snuggled next to James, "played me for a fool."

"This is not the time to discuss such matters," Mama said, flashing her a bewildered look.

"I demand quiet," the soldier who had pained Delight said. His brow wrinkled in annoyance.

"Oh, you do?" She peered into the face of the disgusting, pasty-faced soldier. "None of us would be here against our will if not for my shameless sister."

One of the other redcoats chuckled. Well, he would surely be entertained this evening.

"You are merely angry because I outwitted you," Charity said, louder than Delight had ever heard her sister speak.

Her sister's twist encouraged Delight. "I took you at your word. Why are you there with James after all you've done?"

Charity lifted her nose and linked her arm with James's. "He is hurt, and I am making certain he is nursed properly."

"Nursed? Like you did poor Henry, filling him full of lies about your affections for him?"

"'Tis not Henry's fault he found me more desirable than you."

I love you, sister. Help me continue this charade.

"Enough," the lead soldier said, "or I will gag the both of you."

"How dare you threaten me?" Delight attempted to stand, but Patience and Faith held to her arms. Remember clasped her hands together, no doubt in prayer for the scene unfolding before her.

"Calm yourself. You can deal with Charity's fickle behavior later," Patience said, overcoming her innate shyness. "You should not be surprised by Charity since she vexes us all."

Good girl. If we stall for time and deter the soldiers' attention, Henry may be able to overtake them.

"Leave Charity alone," Faith said. "If you were fool enough to believe Henry preferred you to her, then so be it. You are simply jealous."

If not for the danger besetting them, Delight would have burst into laughter at the preposterous conversation. She took a quick breath and glanced at Mama. In the firelight, she had paled. Poor Mama, but the sisters were on a mission and Delight could explain later. "Envious. I dare say not. She has no conscience or loyalties."

Charity laughed. Elijah woke with a howl.

"See what your quarreling has done." Mama shifted the baby to her shoulder and patted his back.

"Henry simply wanted a diversion during his days of recovering." Charity smirked. Even in the shadows, her facial expressions conveyed the manner of a haughty young woman. "You amused and bored him, but I held his attention. Now he is gone and made quite the twit of you."

Patience raised her fist. "Have you no decency? He broke Delight's heart. And what of James? Did you not steal his affections, too?"

Mercy and Hope began to sob as Elijah broke into an ear-piercing scream.

Patience, you are a jewel. And Charity, I forgive all of your teasing from these past weeks. "Have you cast your charms upon these men as well?" Delight detected a movement in the shadows from where she'd entered the house. She must act hastily.

"Delight, you will stop at nothing." Charity shook her fist. "I feel sorry for you, yet intelligence never was your strength."

Delight shook off Faith's and Patience's holds, scurried to her feet, and raced across the room toward her sister. She masked her fear with an incensed look, as though led by blind rage. Holding the captors' attention became foremost in her mind. The pasty-faced soldier seized her arm, and she pretended to stumble, knocking the musket from his hands and sending it crashing to the floor.

"That's about enough, chaps," Henry called from the doorway.

The other men reached for their weapons, but a second voice emerged from the shadows. "I would not be too hasty to put your hands on those guns," Uncle Matthew said.

The one soldier still held on to Delight, but she used her foot to maneuver the musket in Charity's direction. Her sister snatched it up. "Let go of my sister, or I will spill your blood over that fancy red jacket."

Charity, from whence did such gumption arise?

The soldier's hand rose to Delight's throat. An icy sensation awakened fresh fear in her. "The hole will have to go through her first."

Panic creased Charity's face. Their game was over. Before Delight could struggle against her captor, Henry strode across the room and laid a fist into the soldier's jaw, forcing him to release her. Another punch left the man sprawling on the floor.

"Did he hurt ye?" Henry said to Delight, holding down the belligerent soldier.

Delight shook her head and demanded her trembling body to cease quaking.

Henry bent to tie the soldier's hands behind his back. "I should not have sent you inside without me."

"We did not have any idea what had happened," she said through a ragged breath. "I trusted God, and He did not fail us."

She saw the soft glow of love emitting from his eyes before he reverted his attention to the soldier and the men Uncle Matthew held at gunpoint. Suddenly it occurred to her that her uncle had jeopardized his life and his home by helping Henry.

"Uncle Matthew, what will you do after this?" Delight said.

"I'm enlisting with Henry," he grinned, looking so much like Papa. "Rather than hide from the redcoats, I plan to defend my country."

"You will meet your death," the branded thief said.

"Rather a noble grave than live under the tyranny of the king," Uncle Matthew said. "You think about those things while you are in chains."

Charity quickly untied the knots binding James's mouth, then whirled and fell into Delight's arms. "I was so frightened for you."

"You were magnificent." Delight twirled her sister around the kitchen. "And so are our sisters. More so, our diversion worked."

In that instant, Elijah quieted while Mercy and Hope clung to their mother's skirts.

Charity smiled weakly before turning back to James.

"Remind me to never make the Butler women angry," he said. "I would not survive. What I just witnessed would shake any man's resolve." He clasped Charity's hand in his. "And you are full of surprises."

"I believe she had a good teacher," Henry said, urging the soldier to his feet. "In truth, my Delight is the epitome of a woman in love with her God, her country—"

"And her soon-to-be husband," Delight said.

Chapter 21

Delight shivered as she wriggled into her Sunday dress of indigo and white lace. Although the room had a distinct chill, she knew her shaking was due to anticipation of the wedding ceremony about to proceed. Nervous and excited best described her—and filled with a mountain of love for Henry.

Had it been only yesterday morning when she had fretted about her disobedience to God and her feelings for Henry? So much had occurred since then, and she had had so little time with him before he left with Uncle Matthew and James with the captured men. She prayed for an uneventful journey. Life certainly looked less perilous when she trusted God completely. Perhaps this way of thinking was what Papa meant all along. Not trusting God held more danger than anything man could conjure.

She wished he could be here this day to see her wed Henry, but he'd already given his blessing. When Papa received the news, he'd be pleased, and he'd have plenty of other weddings to attend once the war ended.

The war. She refused to let that reality darken her day. She must trust God, not simply today, but on every day of her life.

"Delight, are you ready?" Charity said from the doorway. "Mama started to come, but then Elijah demanded to be fed."

"Almost. Would you straighten my hair? It has a willful mind today."

Charity picked up a brush and in a few quick strokes had Delight's locks secured into a bouquet of loops and curls.

"Perfect." Delight turned to give her sister a hug.

"I am so happy for you," Charity said through a sprinkling of tears.

"Oh, you are not rid of me. I will be around for a while to make your life interesting."

Her sister giggled. "Henry's life will never be boring."

"Oh, but I love him so much."

159

"And he loves you."

"Thank you for everything you have done," Delight whispered. "I will never forget your goodness."

"We shall see. I imagine I can think of several things to tease you about once Henry leaves in the morning."

A few moments later, Delight stood by Henry's side, his hand firmly clasped around hers. Devotion flowed from his fingertips to her heart and back again. She felt his gaze upon her, and she smiled into those blue pools of tenderness. Never had she been so certain of the life before her. The uncertainties of the days ahead lessened in her understanding of God's provision, the dreams of this wondrous country, and her love for Henry, her beloved turncoat.

DiAnn Mills is a bestselling author who believes her readers should expect an adventure. She combines unforgettable characters with unpredictable plots to create action-packed, suspense-filled novels.

Her titles have appeared on the CBA and ECPA bestseller lists; won two Christy Awards; and been finalists for the RITA, Daphne Du Maurier, Inspirational Readers' Choice, and Carol award contests. Library Journal presented her with a Best Books 2014: Genre Fiction award in the Christian Fiction category for Firewall.

DiAnn is a founding board member of the American Christian Fiction Writers; the 2015 president of the Romance Writers of America's Faith, Hope & Love chapter; and a member of Advanced Writers and Speakers Association and International Thriller Writers. She speaks to various groups and teaches writing workshops around the country. She and her husband live in sunny Houston, Texas.

DiAnn is very active online and would love to connect with readers on any of the social media platforms listed at www.diannmills.com.

Faithful Traitor

by Jill Stengl

Enjoy Your
Bonus Story

Chapter 1

A good name is rather to be chosen than great riches,
and loving favour rather than silver and gold.
PROVERBS 22:1

October 1774

How does it look, Mummy?" Georgette Talbot turned before her mirror and touched the strand of matched pearls adorning her throat. The snowy skirt drifted about her slippers. "I hardly recognize myself. Are you certain the bodice is not too daring? I should hate to be the subject of gossip tomorrow. You know how Marianne's mother is."

"Victoria Grenville can only dream of having a daughter as fair as either of my two treasures. Should anyone criticize your attire, 'twould be a matter of sour grapes. You have superb shoulders and flawless skin—we must emphasize them."

"Since my face is plain," Georgette completed the thought. "If only I were beautiful like you." She covered her mouth with one hand, holding up her elbow with the other.

"Bosh." Her mother studied her with a critical eye. "Stop covering your lips; it appears ill-bred. You are far from plain, as I have told you countless times. A discerning man will admire your excellent teeth, shapely figure, and golden hair."

"If that is true, my world is bereft of discerning men. They take one look at my colossal mouth and back away."

"It is not the *size* of your mouth that frightens men away, Georgette." Her mother's blue eyes held a warning. "Perhaps a touch more powder, Agnes. Her cheeks are too red. Is that as tight as you can make her stays?"

"Yes, madam," the maid said.

"Any tighter and I should swoon during the first dance." Georgette felt like a feather pillow with a cord tied about its middle. Her inward parts must be entirely disarranged.

But at least her waist was tiny.

Georgette's mother huffed. "You must trust your mother with these things, Georgette. Remember how successful your sister was in her debut—she had Mr. Honeywell enthralled almost from the moment she entered the ballroom, and now look at her, happily wedded to a rising barrister."

"But I am twenty now and no debutante, Mummy. There are no Mr. Honeywells here in New York. If ever I am to have opportunity to wed, we must return to England soon." She gazed through her dormer window at the tall merchant ships anchored in the river. "Please, can we not sail on one of those ships? I should die if we were to spend another summer in this hot, stinking village that calls itself a city!"

Her mother directed the maid to rearrange her skirts, then stood back to judge the effect. "You will marry whomever your parents approve for you, Georgette. You must allow that Juliette is happy, and she scarcely knew Mr. Honeywell on their wedding day. I had not intended to tell you this yet, but your papa has already selected a suitor—a discerning man—who can support you in a manner even superior to the one you now enjoy." She adjusted her own golden cloud of hair while looking into Georgette's mirror.

"Surely you do not mean that Mr. LaTournay he constantly talks about." Georgette lifted one brow.

"I do. The man is charming, influential in city politics, and wealthy enough to make him the target of every matchmaking mother in town."

"Ha! As if such a man would form an attachment to me."

"Indeed, Mr. LaTournay craves an introduction, and your father is of the opinion that the man has admired you for some time."

Mr. LaTournay had been watching her? Georgette reached for her throat and struggled to swallow. "But Mother, his reputation!"

"I would discount much of the gossip you hear. Every man worth his salt sows a few wild oats before he settles down. You must not hold that against Mr. LaTournay. Is he not exceedingly handsome?"

"I have never met the man, Mummy, and I never wish to."

Her mother turned with a sweep of her skirts. "Come now. Your father has the carriage waiting."

Georgette drifted down the steep staircase with her gloved fingers skimming the handrail. Her anticipation of the dance had all but vanished. How often had she seen young women whisper behind their fans, cast fatuous glances at Mr. LaTournay's elegant figure, and burst into giggles?

"Georgette, do hurry!" Her father's call rattled the rafters.

❧

From their vantage point near the punch bowl, Georgette and her friend watched dancers spin and promenade across the floor. "I dislike sounding critical, but I believe the Harrisons invited too many ladies for the number of men tonight." To Georgette's relief, Mr. LaTournay seemed to be absent. Once when she spotted a tall man amid the throng, her heart had leaped to her throat, but the alarm proved false.

"There are few eligible men in town since this dreadful rebellion." Marianne Grenville fanned herself. "We must keep praying that the governor will return to the province and set things right. He has been away for months."

"Politics! I despise them. All this talk about the onset of anarchy. I should think any man of courage would refuse to put up with such nonsense." Georgette fluffed her skirts. "And as long as gaming tables remain open, my father is unlikely to take Mother and me back home to England. He says it is business that keeps him in town, but I know better. Marianne, if ever I am tempted to wed a gamester, please kick me."

"Surely it is not so bad as that."

"Surely it is. You may wish to believe ill of no one, my dear, but in this case thinking the worst is warranted." Georgette tried to sound indifferent. "My mother prattles about the importance of my making a brilliant match. As though any man would notice me when there are many local beauties of family and fortune for the asking. Such as you, for instance." She tapped her friend on the arm, smiling lest Marianne take offense.

"You are beautiful, Gigi, though not in the conventional way."

"So my mother tells me. And what precisely does that mean? Never mind; I think I should rather not know. It is certain that my style of beauty is not one to inspire sonnets and duels." She paused. "Not that I care for either."

Marianne blinked and attempted a smile. Dearly though Georgette loved her, Marianne would benefit from a dash more humor and romance amid her charms. "Someday, somewhere, you will meet the man you should marry, Gigi."

"Oh Marianne, I fear that the man of my dreams does not exist. Is there a man yet living in this world who will love only one woman all his life?" Closing her eyes, Georgette clutched her fan to her chest and inhaled deeply, releasing her breath in a sigh. "I would make that man happier than he could imagine, if only he would love me for myself. Do you never dream of such love?"

Marianne's blue eyes expressed shock. "I try not to dwell on things of that sort, Gigi."

Georgette's shoulders drooped. "Perhaps it is not beneficial to dream, but at times dreams are my only escape. Reality is distressingly prosaic. Perhaps I should aspire to the stage."

Marianne glanced away. "I know you grow tired of hearing this, Gigi, but your burdens would seem much lighter if you would share them with God. He cares about your troubles and would help if you—"

"I know." Georgette crossed her arms over her chest in unladylike fashion. Her whalebone stays pinched. "I do think about what you tell me, Marianne. Truly I do. Sometimes I feel God's presence and I want to believe, but it is all so strange. . . ."

Marianne touched her arm. "Here comes your father."

Frederick Talbot strode toward them, appearing strangely pleased. "LaTournay, I have been looking everywhere for you." His eyes focused beyond the two startled girls. "Have you and Georgette already been introduced?"

"I have not yet had the pleasure." The calm reply came from directly behind Georgette. Her blood congealed. Uncrossing her arms, she hurriedly looked down to make sure nothing was showing that oughtn't, then met her father's hopeful gaze.

"In that case, Georgette, please allow me to introduce Mr. LaTournay," he said. "He and I have conducted business for several years, though only recently have we met in person. He and his grandfather before him have been our best suppliers of fine wool. Mr. LaTournay, my daughter Georgette."

Murmuring something polite and keeping her eyes lowered, Georgette turned and extended her hand. Long fingers squeezed hers. A kiss tickled her hand as the man bowed with continental elegance. Brown hair had been brushed back from his high forehead into a neat pigtail. He spoke quietly. "Miss Talbot, will you honor me with your next dance?"

Georgette glanced at her father, who nodded. "I. . .yes." Mr. LaTournay lifted his head and met her gaze. She jerked her hand from his grasp and placed it over her heart. To her horror, his dark eyes followed the motion before he quickly looked away. Even after her father introduced LaTournay to Marianne, Georgette trembled in reaction. Instead of lilting violins, she heard blood pounding in her ears.

The men moved away. Georgette dragged her gaze from the back of LaTournay's emerald velvet coat and stared at the floor, struggling to check her scrambled thoughts and emotions.

"We have actually been introduced to Mr. LaTournay—and he asked you to dance!" Marianne said. "My mother says he is one of the most eligible bachelors in the entire colony. He is acquainted with Governor Tryon and with, oh, everyone of importance."

Georgette recovered her voice. "I care nothing for his connections. When he looked into my eyes, I felt. . ." Her vocabulary failed. "He has a huge mole on his face, and he wears a *beard*. Why would Papa wish me to know such a person?"

Marianne waved her fan before Georgette's eyes. "Many pardons, but do we speak of the same man? Mr. LaTournay is far from ugly. It is true that he seldom smiles, and his manners are somewhat stiff, but you could make him smile if anyone could, Gigi. He is a man with a great future, my father says."

"And a wicked past." Georgette rubbed her arms. "As if

Apollyon himself took the form of a man. I do not wish to dance with him. I would rather stand here all evening than allow that fiend to touch my hand again." She backed up toward the wall.

Following, Marianne shook her head. "You are allowing imagination to nullify discretion. Just dance, Gigi. You will probably never see him again. Keep in mind that he has honored you with his request, and relax."

"I wonder how much of our conversation he overheard. He was standing behind us, Marianne, eavesdropping."

"Did we speak of anything shocking? Gigi—"

A British officer approached Marianne to request a dance. She accepted, fluttering her fan, leaving Georgette alone. With vague thoughts of escape, Georgette turned and bumped into LaTournay's brocaded waistcoat. Heat enflamed her body and face.

"Miss Talbot." He bowed and extended his arm.

Forcing herself to smile, she placed her hand on his velvet sleeve, and he led her to the dance floor. The musicians struck up a lively country-dance tune. Although her feet performed the dance steps, Georgette's mind went blank. Her careful training in the art of conversation was for naught.

Other couples chatted throughout the dance. Georgette and her partner remained silent. Crazed imaginings flitted through her mind. Sometimes women allowed men to escort them into the gardens. What would she do if Mr. LaTournay suggested such a move? Scream?

"How tragic that I have conducted business with your father these many years and never before met you."

His comment startled her into missing a step. He guided her back into place. Before she could reply, he continued. "Instead of bemoaning my loss, I should take pleasure in the moment. New York is privileged to have you, Miss Talbot, and I am delighted to make your acquaintance."

She avoided his eyes. "Although my father has traveled to these American colonies numerous times, my mother and I first arrived in this province with the trade ships last April. I know of you by repute."

"My usual practice is to summer in the country and return to town for trade with foreign merchants," he said. "Winter will soon be upon us, so I must return north before the river becomes impassable. Alas, I am expected home before November. In these remaining days before my departure, may I call upon you, Miss Talbot?"

Georgette welcomed winter's approach. "We are unlikely to meet again. My family will return to England as soon as my father has completed his business here. We long to see home. Are you native to New York, sir?" She bit her lip, but the question had already escaped. She hoped he would not misconstrue her curiosity as personal interest.

"My mother was born in the Hudson River Valley."

She smiled cautiously at the nonanswer and tried to imagine this virile Mephistopheles ever having a mother. "Your name is French. You must be descended from the Normans. My mother loves everything about France—except the government. I was tutored in Paris, but since I have the face of a pug dog, nothing succeeded in making me fashionable."

"Lapdogs are de rigueur in Paris, I hear." His voice quivered. Was he amused? She dared not meet his eyes to see.

"I once owned a spaniel, but my father refuses to buy me another."

"You prized this dog?"

"I adore animals," she said, eyes narrowing.

"I meant no offense, Miss Talbot. I, too, esteem dumb beasts."

The dance concluded, and he escorted her from the floor. "May I call upon you before I leave town, Miss Talbot?"

Georgette avoided his gaze. "Perhaps." She curtsied.

Someone bumped her from behind. Unbalanced, she pitched forward and bounced into Mr. LaTournay. The American's gloved hands gripped her bare shoulders and pulled her upright. Overpowering sensations whirled through her mind and body, and something pounded against her palms.

A man's embarrassed voice apologized. Georgette vaguely heard LaTournay give a sharp reply. Then his voice near her ear prompted another shiver. "Are you well, Miss Talbot?"

She felt his breath upon her face. Opening her eyes, she nodded. The hint of a smile curled his mustache. He released her shoulders to grip the hands pressed flat upon his chest—hands Georgette suddenly recognized as her own.

"Oh!" She snatched her hands from his grasp and pressed them to her cheeks. With a whirl of skirts, she hurried blindly away. At last, in the recesses of a drawing room, she paused to wipe tears from her cheeks. "What has come over me? Dear God, hide me from this evil!"

☙

"No sir, the master is out, and I am ordered to tell you that Miss Talbot is ill with the headache and cannot receive callers," the butler, Montrose, said in a monotone.

"Give these to Miss Talbot along with my best wishes for her return to health."

Georgette listened from just inside the parlor door, clenching her teeth in guilt. That somber voice held unmistakable disappointment. When would the man give up? For five days in a row, he had attempted to see her.

As soon as the front door closed and Georgette heard Montrose pass the parlor on his way to the kitchen, she peeked around the door. After a late night out, her parents had not yet risen for the day, although it was nearly noon. Padding toward the stairs in her bare feet, she stopped short.

A bouquet of asters lay upon the entry table beside a plain calling card. "'J. M. A. LaTournay,'" she read softly. Her fingers brushed the delicate blue petals. Such lovely flowers were difficult to abandon, but one of the maids would surely put them in water soon and carry them up to her "sickroom." For now, she had better return to bed before anyone suspected the truth.

☙

Late that night, Georgette snuggled into her featherbed, reading a novel by candlelight. Eyes wide, heart thumping, she sat up with a start when a knock came at her chamber door. "Who is there?" Then, recalling her role, she shoved the book under her blankets and lay back with one forearm across her eyes. "Enter."

The door opened and hesitant footsteps crossed the room to pause near her bed. "Miss?" It was Biddy, the elderly chambermaid.

"Yes?" She put a pathetic quaver in her voice.

Biddy whimpered like a puppy. How odd. Georgette lifted her arm slightly.

A puppy goggled down at her, kicked its dangling legs, and whined again.

Georgette's eyes opened wide, and she sat upright. Biddy held the fawn-colored pug pup at arm's length. "The man told me to give it to you, missy. I am sorry to disturb you, but your parents are out, and Agnes hates dogs."

"Oh, he is adorable!" Georgette reached for the pup and clutched him close. The puppy's pink tongue washed her cheek. Laughing, she held him away from her face. "Where did you say he came from?"

"A man, missy. Just now, at the front door. A cloak concealed his face, but he left this card."

The puppy tugged at Georgette's braid while she read the inscription. "To Miss Georgette Talbot from a devoted admirer."

She flung the braid back over her shoulder. "Is he still here?"

"I doubt it, miss."

But even as Biddy spoke, Georgette scrambled out of bed, rushed to the window, and opened it wide. The street lamps below revealed a mounted horse standing in the middle of Broad Street.

"Hello!" She waved. The cloaked rider lifted his head.

"Missy! You'll catch your death standing at the window in your chemise. Your mother will be angry."

Biddy's outrage discouraged her not a whit. "Thank you," Georgette called down, cupping her hand around her mouth.

The rider lifted his hand. The horse wheeled and broke into a canter. Hoofbeats echoed down the empty city streets.

Georgette turned to meet Biddy's irate gaze, her hands clasped at her breast. "This is the most thrilling day of my life. Are you certain the man was a stranger, Biddy?"

The maid propped both hands on her scrawny hips. "You get back into that bed, missy, or I shall tell your mother about your showing yourself at the window in your chemise!"

"Oh Biddy, do not be foolish. I am certain he saw only a billowing white object. What did his voice sound like? Did he seem young or old?" A dreadful suspicion struck. Might her admirer be Mr. LaTournay?

"He sounded foreignlike. Not English like you, but maybe French or Spanish."

An accent could be feigned. Georgette pulled on her bedgown, watching the pup waddle toward her across the tumbled counterpane, his curly tail wagging. No matter his origin, she loved her gift. When he reached her, she scooped him up and kissed his velvety head. "I must take my puppy to the garden, then find him something to eat. What is your name, pup? You are entirely sweet."

Chapter 2

For what fellowship hath righteousness with unrighteousness?
and what communion hath light with darkness?
2 CORINTHIANS 6:14

April 1775

For two hours Georgette sat and listened to a stand-in for the regular minister drone about the evils of disobedience to Mother England. Occasionally he referred to a Bible passage. Georgette tried to focus on the sermon, but her eyes kept straying toward a visitors' box across the church. The man seated there seemed familiar, though she could not see him clearly.

She was certain he had been watching the Talbot box. Perhaps he knew her father. She hoped he was not one of her father's gambling friends come to ask for payment. Papa never spoke of financial matters, but Georgette knew the situation at home was rapidly worsening. Montrose and two footmen had been let go over the winter, leaving only Biddy, Agnes, and Cook to keep the household running. For a family of high standing, two maids and one flighty Italian cook were insufficient household staff.

A disturbance outside sent a stir through the congregation. People glanced around, giving hushed exclamations of dismay. *Crack! Pop! Bang!* Cheering filled the streets, and the hoofbeats of running horses clattered along Broadway, yet the good reverend made no sign that he heard. Georgette decided the man must be deaf.

Several men slipped out of their boxes and headed for the door, among them the tall visitor. Georgette felt as though the minister would never stop, but eventually he wrapped up his oratory with a prolonged benediction.

Members of the congregation questioned each other in hushed

tones, hurrying for the exits. Georgette followed her father into the churchyard as her mother stopped to chat with a friend. Firecrackers popped in the middle of the street. Boys in ragged clothes shouted. Although she was curious about the cause of this clamor, Georgette knew she could not barge into her father's conversation with a group of men. She glanced about in search of Marianne.

"Good day, Miss Talbot."

Lifting one hand to shade her eyes from the spring sun's glare, she looked up. Her eyes widened, and heat rushed to her cheeks.

The visiting gentleman was Mr. LaTournay. "It is good to see you looking well," he said quietly. "I trust you passed a healthy and profitable winter?"

She avoided meeting his gaze. "I—I am well, Mr. LaTournay. You are back in town?" Too late she realized the absurdity of her question.

"For a time. Have you heard the news?"

"No. What has happened?" Eager for information, she looked into his eyes.

"Four days ago, American and British troops fought a battle at Concord and Lexington, two villages not far from Boston. A courier brought the news just minutes ago. It was a defeat for the British, by his account."

"Oh!" She covered her mouth with one hand and extended the other as if to ward off disaster. "How dreadful! What will become of us? Papa must agree to return to England now."

LaTournay grasped her outflung hand. "I hope not too quickly."

She yanked it away and glared at him. "It cannot be soon enough for me."

The flicker in his eyes told her that her shaft had struck home; still he persisted. "May I call upon you sometime this week?"

Her fingers seemed to burn where his had touched them. "I—I shall be busy."

"Mr. LaTournay! How delightful to see you!" Her mother arrived amid a rustle of petticoats and ribbons. Georgette wanted to groan.

"I hope you plan to call on us again soon," she said, dimpling and nodding. "As you can see, Georgette is now quite well and able to receive callers."

LaTournay's shrewd glance brushed Georgette. "Thank you for the invitation, Mrs. Talbot. Ladies." Touching his tricornered hat, he bowed and walked away.

Georgette exhaled slowly and closed her eyes. *Dear Lord, please let him never return!*

❧

"When next he calls, you will receive him." Her father's voice held the ring of steel. He paced the sitting room, hands clasped behind his back. "Biddy tells me LaTournay attempted to call upon you last fall and you turned him away." He jabbed a finger at Georgette. "Never again will you feign illness to avoid him. Attempt it, and I shall drag you downstairs in your shift to entertain the man!"

Georgette felt her facial muscles twitch as she fought back panic. "Papa, surely you would not force me to marry. I dislike Mr. LaTournay. He is evil."

Her father swore, grasped her arm, and jerked her forward. Eyes narrowing, he hissed through clenched teeth. "LaTournay is a leading citizen in this province. His past is none of your concern. You will encourage his suit in every way possible. Do you understand?"

Georgette tightened her lips. Her father tightened his grip.

"Oww! Yes. I shall receive him."

He let go. Georgette rubbed her arm as tears spilled down her cheeks. "But I shall never marry that man!"

Smack! The back of his hand against her cheek jerked her head to one side. He pointed a finger in her face. "Never speak so to me again! You will do as I say, and that is final."

Georgette fingered the welt left by his signet ring and felt her heart break.

❧

That evening several men arrived to visit with her father. Her mother retired to her chambers, leaving Georgette to her own devices. Shouts and occasional bursts of laughter from the parlor drifted up the staircase.

More gambling. Georgette flopped upon the bed. If her heart sank any lower, it would punch a hole through the bottom of Manhattan. With a wry smile, she visualized the entire island upending and sinking into the river.

Her little dog, Caramel, strolled across the bedclothes. "You sleep too much," she informed him, sliding his floppy ears between her finger and thumb. "But I adore you anyway. You mend my wounded spirits better than any physic." For weeks after Caramel's mysterious arrival, she had questioned her acquaintances about pug dogs. Did anyone have a dog with puppies? Had anyone recently sold a pup? Her investigation turned up no clues.

"I wish you could tell me about the man who brought you, Caramel. Did you like him? Is he kind to fat puppies? Or was the cloaked rider a courier for my real benefactor?"

Caramel snorted and leaped off the bed in search of a toy.

Hearing the crackle of fireworks, Georgette hurried to the window to watch them flame across the sky. A woman's hearty laugh rose from the street below, along with the clop of hooves on cobblestones. The tavern at the corner did brisk business. Lively band music drifted on the chill night air, and the glow of bonfires dotted the city. A sudden breeze held the promise of spring, the sting of sea salt, and a whiff of gunpowder and smoke.

Georgette inhaled deeply. Excitement flooded her veins. She craved adventure, thrills—and romance. Anything to escape the future her father planned for her.

"Lord Jesus? Are You listening to me?" Her recent decision to devote her life to God's service had provided little respite from boredom, and instead of miraculously disappearing, her problems had multiplied.

Caramel brought her a leather ball. Georgette tossed it. She heard his paws scrabble on the floor, and a thump indicated when the pug slid into the wall. Small wonder his face was flat.

"I do not understand Your refusal to answer my prayers, God.

Papa plans to marry me to a reprobate, and Mummy smiles and tells me not to worry."

She accepted the slimy ball and threw it again. "Why would You put this desire for romance into my heart, then threaten me with a husband like Mr. LaTournay? I know I am to love You first, and I do. But I also wish for a loving husband and children. If You care at all, please send the right man to me soon. If only the admirer who sent my dog would make himself known." A long sigh closed her petition.

Rising, she rang for a maid to help her prepare for bed.

No response came to her summons or her prayers. Annoyed, she shut Caramel into her bedchamber and padded down the back stairs to the kitchen. Biddy and Agnes bustled to prepare refreshments for her father's guests. "Where is Cook?" Georgette asked as Biddy passed her, carrying a loaded tray.

Agnes gave her a glance. "Gone to join the celebrations, miss. Biddy and me, we hold little store by such goings-on, and the missus promised us extra pay to stay the evening. Too bad you have no young man to show you a good time tonight. 'Twould be unsafe for a lady alone. Every man in town will be out and about." Her gap-toothed smile was meant to be kind.

Until that moment Georgette had not considered sneaking out, but Agnes's comment stirred her imagination. Who would know? She considered asking Agnes to sneak out with her but decided against it. The practical servant would go straight to Georgette's parents with her plans.

Other women managed to traverse the streets of New York unescorted. She was a strong, healthy girl. Why not? Surely the Lord would protect her from harm.

In her father's wardrobe, she found a woolen cloak. The guests' coachmen would see her if she used the front door, so she slipped into the garden and through the gate.

Eager and breathless, Georgette hurried her steps along Broad Street. Hearing footsteps behind, she turned but saw only a carriage passing on a crossroad. A shiver trickled down her spine, and she increased her pace.

There would be safety in numbers. Noise and glowing light from the direction of the common drew her on.

Sure enough, bonfires and fireworks illuminated a boisterous gathering on the green. A man stood on a podium delivering an address about the bright future of New York, frequently interrupted by cheers and whistles. The crowd surrounding Georgette consisted mainly of the lower classes, judging by attire and vocabulary. Yet she saw some well-dressed men and a few women in gowns finer than hers. Liquor flowed freely, and more than one interruption of the speech came from an overly enthusiastic drunk. The crowd laughed at such interludes and continued carousing. Some of the women exhibited themselves in ways no lady would approve, yet their gentlemen associates appeared to relish the display.

Are there no men left in the world who appreciate a woman of virtue? Or must a woman be vulgar to excite a man's genuine interest? Among the other young women, she had heard talk of men who lived double lives. Such men would wed none but ladies of quality, yet they took pleasure in the company of actresses and dancers, even fathering illegitimate children. Men like Mr. LaTournay, who preferred other men's wives.

If I marry, I want my husband to be satisfied with me alone. Most of these women are no more beautiful than I am. I could be as exciting to a man as they if I tried. She imagined embracing any of the rough men standing near the fire and grimaced. Many of them had not bathed in months, judging by the grime around their necks. Some appeared young and strong; a few wore fringed buckskin breeches and jackets; some were bearded and hulking. Perhaps she was too choosy.

One brawny fellow noticed Georgette. "What have we here? Are you alone, sugarcakes? This is my lucky day." He lurched forward and gripped her arm.

Georgette's yearning for romance took a plunge. She turned to escape, but the man twisted her arm and pulled her back. "Why so modest?" His filthy hand gripped her chin, and rancid breath filled her nostrils. "Give us a kiss."

Suddenly the fellow gave a yelp and fell away from her, his hands grasping at a black cord around his throat. As his back struck the ground, a hand gripped Georgette's shoulder, turned her about, and propelled her forward. "The lady, she is with me, monsieur," a heavily accented voice said in clear warning. Turning back, Georgette saw in profile a black-cloaked figure standing with feet braced, brandishing a driving whip.

The big man staggered to his feet, bellowed once, and charged like a bull. His challenger stepped aside and rapped him on the skull with the butt of the whip. He sprawled on the grass and lay there, moaning. His drunken companions laughed.

The victor replaced the whip in a waiting carriage. A voluminous hood concealed his entire head, giving him the appearance of the Grim Reaper.

Georgette turned to run, but the man's arm slipped around her waist. He pulled her away from the bonfire toward the dark streets. Squealing, she beat both fists against his forearm. "Let me go. You are no better than he to accost a lady so!"

"You need not fear; I intend you no harm," the Frenchman said, setting her on her feet in the shelter of a large tree. "Do you not know what manner of business is conducted on the 'holy grounds' just beyond the common? Crazed, I think the lady must be, to wander alone in the wicked city, and more so on this night when men's blood runs hot."

Georgette shook her head in confusion. "Business? Do you mean the church?"

His laugh lacked humor. *"Innocente."*

Understanding dawned. Georgette's entire body burned with shame. "Are you saying those women are...? That man thought I was...? That you—no, never!" Horrified, she struggled to escape.

Her captor restrained her. "No, never!" he mocked in falsetto. But then his voice deepened. "And yet perhaps mademoiselle craves romance."

Gooseflesh prickled Georgette's arms. She sought a glimpse of the man's face but caught only an occasional glitter in his eyes, the reflection of a street lamp. "If—if I yearned for romance, it would be with a gentleman, not a ruffian. You Frenchmen are infamous for perfidy and. . .and passion."

When he chuckled, she regretted her suggestive choice of words. His grip on her upper arms seemed effortless, yet she was powerless to escape it.

Lifting her chin, she tried to sound confident. "Do you know who I am? My father will have you flogged if harm comes to me."

"Should harm come to you tonight, I would deserve such penalty, *ma fille.*" With one fluid motion, he again wrapped his arm about her waist and hauled her close. Her hooped skirts ballooned behind her. Although she held herself rigid and put up both hands to prevent her body from contacting his, Georgette made no vocal protest beyond a gasp.

"Regardez-moi, s'il vous plaît, ma belle fille."

She recognized enough French to know he had called her beautiful. "Let me go." She pushed at his chest. Her elbow bumped what proved to be a large pistol shoved into his belt. Whip. Gun. What other weapons did he wield? Might he be a soldier? Not with that accent. A French-Canadian trapper perhaps, come to the city for excitement and liquor.

His waistcoat felt soft beneath her hands, pleasant to touch. Or was it a shirt? Puzzled, she slid her hands over the thin fabric. Fringe. He wore buckskin. She heard the man suck in a breath, and a flurry of French followed, none of which she understood. He trapped her hands in an iron grip.

"So free with the touching you are. And you would return the favor?" His thumb traced her jawline.

She flinched in pain as he touched her cheek. "What are you doing?"

With a soft exclamation, he turned her toward the streetlamp. Georgette blinked, cringing when he hovered too near.

"Eh, what has happened to your face?" His caress circled the welt on her cheek. "Did that dog strike you? I should have killed him."

"No—he did not do it." She recalled her father's cruel blow, and her breath caught, sounding much like a sob.

"Then who?"

Georgette felt her lips move, but no sound emerged. Feeling lost, she reached both hands to his chest as if to push him away. His thudding heart against her palms seemed familiar. His breath brushed her face—no hint of alcohol or tobacco there. What manner of man was this?

He released her and backed away. *"Mille pardons."* The hooded head bowed. "Such liberties are not mine to take."

Trembling, she searched for something intelligent to say. "Who are you?"

He caught her by the hand, turned, and began to walk along the street toward her parents' rented town house. "Promise you will never again venture into the city alone at night."

Regret pricked her conscience. "I was foolish to behave thus. I *am* a lady. You must believe me!"

Once more he exclaimed something indecipherable in French, and he slowed his pace. "I doubt not your purity of heart."

"What may I call you? I am Georgette Talbot."

"I know." His voice was quiet. "Did you like the dog?"

"The dog? Caramel! You gave him to me? But why? Who are you? Where have we met?" All too soon she recognized the brick town houses and storefronts of Broad Street. Had her parents noticed her absence?

"I first saw you dip your feet in the river and swing on a tree branch until I feared you would drop into the water."

"You saw me?" Georgette whispered. Like a child she had played that summer day, for once free of adult supervision. Or so she had thought. "The day my hat blew away."

"Your hair, it catches the sun and captures my heart. Your dog, he will remind, each time you look at him, that your devoted slave worships the earth beneath your feet. *Nuit et jour,* I dream of you."

"Oh–h–h–h!" Georgette's feet seemed to float well above the paving stones.

He stopped at the garden-gate and released her hand. "Carriages still wait out front. You might yet slip inside unnoted."

"You are leaving? Will you not come inside? I wish to see your face."

183

He backed away. She caught the edge of his cloak. "Will I meet you again?"

"Assuredly, yes."

"When?"

"Ma petite Georgette." His features remained shrouded in darkness. "So desperate you seem. *Pourquoi?*"

"My father gave me the welt on my cheek because I refuse to marry an evil man."

"Your father seeks an evil man to marry his daughter? Pray, tell why." Satire laced his voice.

"He has already chosen one, although I am uncertain the evil man is yet aware of my father's plan. Papa has extensive gaming debts, you see. He did not gamble when we lived in England; it is the influence of this wicked city. I suspect Papa might—" She fell silent rather than reveal suppositions that put her father in an even worse light.

"And who is this evil man?"

"You must know of him, a Mr. LaTournay."

"I know the name. In what way is this man evil?"

Angered by his mocking tone, she snapped, "He pursues the wives of other men."

"You know this as fact?" His tone was equally sharp.

"His reputation is foul. My mother advises me to overlook such behavior in a man, but I cannot."

"Nor should you," he said. "A philandering man makes a poor husband."

The adamant statement warmed her heart, obliterating his former irony from her memory. "Are you married?"

"Not as yet, but when I wed, my heart will belong to my wife alone for as long as I live."

Releasing her hold on his cloak, Georgette covered her mouth with one hand.

He stepped forward and gently pulled her concealing hand away. She felt his breath upon her face, then the quick pressure of his fingers upon hers. *"Bonsoir* and adieu, Georgette," he whispered and strode away into the night.

Chapter 3

But the LORD said unto Samuel, Look not on his countenance,
or on the height of his stature; because I have refused him:
for the LORD seeth not as man seeth;
for man looketh on the outward appearance,
but the LORD looketh on the heart.
1 SAMUEL 16:7

The hired carriage stopped before a mansion on the out-skirts of town. Lifting her skirts, Georgette followed her parents up the broad front steps. A fine mist fell, and the entire world seemed gray.

"Everyone of importance in the province will be here tonight," her mother predicted. "Remember to smile and be genteel, Georgette."

"Yes, Mum." Georgette's interest in social events had waned.

After handing their wraps to waiting servants, Georgette and her mother hurried to the ladies' chambers to repair damages to gown or coiffure. When they returned, they joined her father in the queue of guests and shook hands with their hosts, retired Colonel Weatherby and his wife.

"Is it true this Whig pretense of a congress threatens to outlaw dancing and parties?"

"How dare they attempt to force such bans upon the law-abiding public?"

Snatches of disturbing conversation reached Georgette's ears as she picked her way through the crowds and joined a fluttering bouquet of young ladies near the refreshment tables.

Marianne waved her fan. "Gigi! Over here."

"Marianne, how are you?" Georgette slid into an open place against the wall.

"Well enough. You look lovely!"

"This is a remake of one of my mother's old gowns, and it is too small for me. Mother had Agnes tighten my stays until I feel ill." Georgette covered her mouth with her fan. "Alas, I am complaining again. I shall never learn to be content, Marianne. How do you do it?"

Marianne smiled. "Give yourself time to grow in God's grace, Gigi. You are a newborn babe in Christ; you cannot expect perfection from yourself."

Georgette sighed and pursed her lips. "My parents wish to hear nothing about my faith in Jesus Christ. They tell me I have been a Christian since I was baptized as an infant."

"That is what they were raised to believe. Just keep speaking the truth in a loving, respectful way, Gigi. Your interest in the Bible might inspire them to search for answers, too."

"People must acknowledge questions before they see a need for answers," Georgette said. "And it is difficult to point out fallacies in my parents' beliefs without sounding disrespectful. Had I not always been such a difficult child, they might be more willing to listen to me now."

Marianne patted her friend's arm. "You cannot change the past, Gigi, but the changes God has made in you since Christmastide, no one can ignore."

Guilt swamped Georgette. "You would not think so if you knew what I did last Sunday night." The secret of her escapade seared her conscience. "I can scarcely believe it myself." She longed to tell Marianne, yet a crowded ballroom hardly seemed the proper setting for a confession.

"No matter what you do, I shall always love and admire you, Gigi."

Georgette gripped Marianne's small fingers. "You are my first real friend aside from my sister. Most women are spiteful and insincere, but you? Never."

"You are good for me as well," Marianne said.

A tall figure loomed over them. "Good evening, ladies."

"Mr. LaTournay, how nice to see you back in the city! A good evening to you." Marianne extended her hand in greeting. He bowed over it, then turned his gaze upon Georgette.

"I trust each of you ladies will honor me with a dance this evening."

Georgette couldn't force herself to smile, but she managed to acknowledge his greeting with a nod before realizing he would interpret the movement as an agreement to dance. While she struggled to think of an excuse, one of Mrs. Weatherby's daughters settled at the piano and played the introduction to a reel.

"I should be honored, Mr. LaTournay," Marianne answered after a brief silence. He took her hand and led her to line up with several other couples at one end of the crowded room.

LaTournay's claret-colored coat fit his shoulders perfectly. Georgette looked away, determined to find nothing admirable in the man. Dainty Marianne seemed a child beside that lanky scarecrow of a man, she decided.

Two figures blocked her view. "Georgette, this is Mr. Lester Pringle." Her father indicated a smiling young man. "I hear from reliable sources that he is a fair dancer."

Georgette stammered through a "Pleased to meet you." Her father moved on, leaving Georgette alone with the attractive young man.

"If we hurry, we may join this dance. Will you?"

She nodded. He led her to the dance floor and bowed as the music began.

"I understand you are come to New York from England a year ago. If that is so, you have already endured one summer's killing heat," he said as she rotated around him.

"And who spoke of me to you?"

Light sparkled in his eyes. "My friend LaTournay. It seems you have made a fair impression upon his sensibilities. He does not usually come to town early in the year, yet here we find him in April."

Georgette's smile faded. "I have no wish to impress Mr. LaTournay."

Mr. Pringle's brows lifted as he displayed healthy teeth in a grin. "Better and better."

"Do you like dogs?" She tried to imagine Pringle cloaked in the dark.

He laughed. "Once I was presented with a harrier pup, but I gave it away. Dogs are bothersome creatures—especially lap dogs. Utterly useless. Horses are my passion. LaTournay rides a brown mare I would give my eyeteeth to own. Have you seen her?"

"No."

He proceeded to wax eloquent on the finer points of this unknown horse. Georgette concentrated on her dance steps. The small floor seemed crowded with couples, and she noticed a stitch developing in her side. Mr. Pringle danced with more enthusiasm than grace.

"I see LaTournay observing us with something less than approbation," he confided against her ear, pulling her so close that their bodies nearly touched. "Shall we make him burn with jealousy? Do you long for my kiss as I long for yours?"

"No." Georgette jerked away in confusion. Again Mr. Pringle laughed aloud, causing stares of disapproval from nearby matrons. Georgette wished he had kept his mind on horses.

The ladies and men changed partners for a moment, and Georgette found herself curtsying to Mr. LaTournay. He took her hand. The room seemed uncomfortably warm. She was relieved to switch back to Pringle despite his impertinent behavior. For the duration of the dance, Georgette had trouble focusing on her partner due to her constant awareness of Marianne's partner.

When the dance ended, Pringle excused himself. Georgette caught the roguish twinkle in his eye as his hand brushed the length of her bare arm. Fanning her warm face, she settled upon a vacant chair. Another touch on her arm made her jump.

"Gigi, I saw you with Mr. Pringle. Does he dance like a dream?" Marianne's bright eyes begged for information.

"Mr. Pringle? He is pleasant enough, though forward. He laughs too loudly." Georgette flicked her fan. "Did you enjoy dancing with Mr. LaTournay?"

"He was polite, although I think he would prefer you as a partner, Gigi. He asked many questions. I told him about your puppy, Caramel, about how you like to read novels, and I even told him about your accepting Jesus as your Savior last Christmastide. I hope you do not mind."

Georgette sprang up. "My side aches. Would you care to stroll through the garden with me?"

Marianne laughed. "It is pouring rain out there, you goose! I may be warm, but I am not afire. I should think you would want to stay here where Mr. Pringle can ask you for another dance. At present, he is talking with Mr. LaTournay. I think his face expresses real depth of character." Marianne looked dreamy-eyed. Perhaps her personality held a touch of romance after all.

Pringle turned, caught them watching him, and approached, smiling. "LaTournay tells me you are to dance the next with him, Miss Talbot. Since this is the case, I would be delighted to meet your friend." He turned his gleaming smile upon Marianne.

Georgette made the proper introductions, and Mr. Pringle requested Marianne's next dance. "If you are available," he added.

Color flooded the girl's face. "Yes, Mr. Pringle," Marianne said. "I have no engagement."

He bowed, winked at Georgette, and walked away. Stunned, the two girls exchanged looks. "Gigi, this is my fondest dream come true! Does my hair look well?" Marianne fanned herself until her curls flew about her face.

So I am to dance the next with Mr. LaTournay, am I? Georgette brooded. *I shall show him.*

The pianist concluded a minuet. Dancers left the floor, and Mr. Pringle arrived to claim Marianne. Georgette saw him trail a finger down Marianne's arm, bring her gloved hand to his chest, and look deeply into her eyes. Georgette shook her head. The man was far too confident of his own allure. Nothing like her mysterious rescuer.

"Miss Talbot."

That stilted voice lifted the hair on the back of her neck. Mr. LaTournay offered his arm, and Georgette accepted it. In his presence, all thought of defying his wishes vanished. "Remarkable weather we are having," she blurted.

"So it must be, since you have remarked upon it."

She swallowed hard and tried again. "Do you always come to

town when the ships arrive from England?" She curtsied to begin the dance, thankful that her feet seemed to know the steps without her conscious direction.

"Usually. I also trade with the other colonies of course. But, as you know, many items can be obtained only from your homeland."

"I wonder if Boston and Philadelphia are cities of culture and refinement. New York is rustic, in my opinion. We were surprised by the pigs that scavenge in the streets. I was told the beasts keep the streets cleaner, but I suspect my source spoke in jest. Pigs?" She winced. "Oh dear, do you raise pigs on your estate? Or was it sheep? I should think sheep would be cleaner beasts to have roaming the streets."

Her nervous chatter held his attention, and she thought one side of his mustache twitched. She now realized that the raised mark just below his left cheekbone was a reddish birthmark, not a mole. "No doubt you are correct," he replied, "but sheep prefer clean grass and fresh air to rubbish. I share their distaste for city life."

"I should think a man of your refinement would find country life dull." Unless he kept a collection of female admirers in the country as well.

"I have always before found town life dull, yet this spring I could scarcely wait to return. You have brought life to this dreary city, Miss Talbot. Perhaps someday I shall be privileged to show you the delights of rural living."

She would prefer to have his penetrating eyes focused elsewhere. Was it fear that raised gooseflesh on her arms each time he touched her hand? It must be!

"You have traveled nowhere in America outside this city?" he inquired as they traversed a circle.

"Not as yet. My mother often speaks of seeing Boston, but Papa says this is not the time for travel. One cannot tell whom to trust these days; there are so many traitorous colonists terrorizing honest subjects of the king. I would like to travel more. I did attend school in France for a year." They separated to dance with different partners for a moment, and she recalled telling him about her Paris schooling once before. He might find her company tedious and lose interest. All the better.

When the dance brought them together again, he spoke softly. *"C'est fort intéressant."*

Without attempting to translate, she answered lightly, "I confess that I understand little French. Although I attended school in France, I never claim to have learned anything there. Have you traveled?"

"I have never been to Europe."

Did he think her frivolous? For the first time, Georgette regretted her squandered opportunities. "New York is a British province. I mean, since you live here, you have been to England. Is that not true?"

"I am certain King George would find such sentiments gratifying," he returned. When the dance ended, he bowed over her hand and kissed it, looking up at her with a quizzical challenge in his eyes. Georgette stared, openmouthed. Some extraordinary power emanated from the man. And those eyes. . .

"Miss Talbot," he purred, holding her gaze and squeezing her fingers. "You know, do you not?"

"I have no idea of what you are speaking!" Georgette snatched her hand away and unfurled her fan.

He straightened, eyes widening. Lifting his brows, he averted his gaze, and she saw his mustache twitch as if he fought a smile. "My mistake."

Georgette watched him walk across the room.

"Marianne, why is evil so alluring?" she demanded of her friend a few moments later.

The smaller girl allowed Georgette to maneuver her into an alcove. "Whatever prompts such a question, Gigi?"

Georgette's rapid fanning produced a gale. "That lord of the underworld. I want him to go away. I refuse to become one of his many conquests!"

"I thought you liked him. I tried to attract your attention while we danced just now, but you seemed absorbed in your partner."

"I hate him!" Georgette blotted out the memory of her fiery

response to his slightest advance. "He uses other men's wives for his own enjoyment. He probably considers matrimony now only to add respectability to his family line."

Her other possible explanation was too humiliating to mention. Was she so undesirable that her father resorted to extortion to provide her with a husband?

"My father is acquainted with Mr. LaTournay," Marianne said. "He came to dine at our house the other night, and I found him pleasant company. He associates with the leaders of our province and is respected by most if not all of them. Gigi, the man has no need to improve his status by marrying well."

Georgette stifled a wave of jealousy. Mr. LaTournay dined with the Grenvilles? Had he transferred his interest to Marianne?

"I mean no offense," Marianne continued, "but if the truth be known, I would not have thought he would consider you at all, Gigi. Yet even Mr. Pringle remarked while we danced tonight that you and Mr. LaTournay thought yourselves alone in the room."

Georgette covered her hot cheeks with both hands. "No! Oh Marianne, did you not tell me I should seek a godly man to marry? I am far too easily beguiled by worldly men." She attempted to draw a deep breath and nearly cried out at the sharp pain stabbing her side. Growing still, she waited for the discomfort to pass.

"You and I both know we may not be allowed to select our husbands. My parents will consider a man's religion before promising my hand, but I fear yours will not. You must be in prayer that God will guide their selection."

"I shall pray," Georgette agreed, nodding. "Have you seen my mother? I wish to go home. I can scarcely draw breath. Agnes laced me too tightly."

❧

Across the room, Pringle and LaTournay conferred. "You are correct: The blond in pink is a choice armful," Pringle observed. "Keep your eyes half-closed, and she is *très belle*. The little one also has appeal, though she is freckled. Her hair is like moonbeams."

"She is Howard Grenville's daughter."

Pringle brightened. "The Long Island merchant and land owner? Miss Grenville's appeal multiplies beyond the tally of her freckles. She is the more comely of the two, in truth. Miss Talbot's mouth makes me think of a frog wearing lip rouge."

"Her mouth is lovely," LaTournay snapped.

"Ah!" A slow smile curved Pringle's lips, and his blue eyes twinkled.

LaTournay folded his arms. "Leave Miss Talbot to me. She is not your type."

"She will soon bore you—she is no wit."

"She amuses me."

Pringle shrugged. "You have never before asked me to leave a woman alone. Will you dance with her again?"

"I hope to." LaTournay frowned. "Here comes Lady Forester."

"How can you sound morose? Delia Forester is a sensible recipient of your passions—safely married, husband away much of the time, and ever so willing!" Pringle elbowed LaTournay in the ribs. "Why the sudden loss of interest?"

"I would obtain a wife of my own." Leaving his friend to absorb this information, LaTournay stepped forward and bowed to Lady Forester.

"A wife!" Pringle's exclamation reached his ears.

☙

"Thank you for the dance, Miss Talbot." Mr. Pringle bowed. His blond hair gleamed in the candlelight, and mischief twinkled in his blue eyes. Georgette sat down as he turned to Marianne and asked, "Will you honor me once more?"

The girl fairly leaped to her feet. "Oh yes!" She took his extended hand and let him lead her to the floor.

Georgette was thankful to be rid of the arrogant fellow. The tales he told of Mr. LaTournay's exploits with married women verified her worst fears. To make things worse, she could not draw breath without feeling as if a knife pierced her side. She should never have accepted Pringle's invitation to dance a reel.

She searched the room for her mother only to observe Mr.

LaTournay talking with a dark-haired woman who laid a possessive hand upon his arm and gazed into his eyes with evident desire. How shameless! Jealousy scorched Georgette's heart. The one man who expressed interest in her just had to be the town lothario.

Turning her face away, she started around the perimeter of the crowded room. The pain increased with every step. To grip her rib cage and pant would be ill bred, but etiquette began to seem trivial compared to the agony in her torso. She was suffocating, possibly dying, and no one noticed. Finding a seat behind a potted tree, she toppled into it and wished for oblivion. She pressed one fist against her teeth and the other into her side. Tears burned her cheeks.

"Miss Talbot, allow me to help you."

"Please!" Her sanity reached out and clung to the quiet voice.

"Can you rise? Lean against my arm, and I shall take you to a drawing room where you can lie down."

The voice gave her courage. She nodded. The room swirled around her in waves of color, music, and conversation. Leaning heavily on her rescuer's arm, she concentrated on remaining conscious. They passed through a doorway, and the party's commotion receded. "We are nearly there," the man said just as Georgette's legs buckled. After a moment's scuffle with her recalcitrant hoops and yards of fabric, he lifted her in his arms. She peered up at a familiar bearded face.

Mr. LaTournay was as strong as he looked, and his musky cologne filled her senses. "My mother," she whimpered into his shoulder, feeling strangely secure.

"I shall bring her to you. Here we are." His shoulder shoved against a door. Carefully, he maneuvered Georgette's hoops through the doorway.

As awareness returned, panic rose. What did he intend to do with her? "It is dark in here!" She pushed weakly at his chest.

He stopped. "Can you stand while I light candles?"

Although she was not sure, she nodded. He lowered her feet to the floor, discreetly tugged the ruffles down to conceal her petticoats, then left her swaying in the doorway. Georgette closed her eyes and fought to remain upright. Soft light filled the room.

"Come, rest here, and I shall go in search of your mother."

Blindly, she reached for him and leaned into his strength, letting him guide her to a settee. Bending to lie down was agony. Once she lay flat, her grip on his coat lapel relaxed. He stepped back, and her hoop sprang up. Without looking, he dropped a large cushion atop the billowing fabric. It settled unsteadily on her legs.

Georgette wanted to die. He tucked a pillow behind her head. Feeling a soft handkerchief upon her tear-dampened cheek, she reached up to take it from him.

"Better?" He was a hovering shadow, composed and reassuring.

"Yes. I can breathe more easily now," she said. "Mum insists that my waist be as small as Juliette's, but I am fatter than my sister." As soon as the words escaped, she wished to take them back. Of all things, she did not wish to bring the man's attention to her figure.

"Perhaps it would be wise to loosen your stays."

Her eyes flew open and his face came into focus. No longer shadowy and comforting, he was again evil incarnate. She pressed both hands to her bosom. "My mother will help me!"

"Of course. I shall return directly." He backed away.

Had she misjudged him? No one could be entirely evil, after all. "Thank you, Mr. LaTournay," she said as he opened the door.

"It is my pleasure to serve you."

Her heart thudded against her concealing hands. When he was gone, the last of her composure disintegrated. It was too painful to sob, but more tears scalded her cheeks.

※

"Whatever do you see in the wench? Her nose looks like a little blob, and her mouth is immense like a—"

"—a frog wearing lip rouge," LaTournay said in unison with Pringle. "She says she has the face of a pug dog." He swirled the coffee in his cup.

Pringle guffawed. "She even has the mournful brown eyes!" His brows lifted. "Tell you what—give her a bauble or two, entice her into the garden during the next dance, and take your fill of those smooth white shoulders. Then you can forget her and return to normal. What do you say?"

LaTournay leaned both elbows on the coffeehouse's marred tabletop and fingered the corners of a newspaper. "Why did you dance with her again?"

"You mean after you warned me off? You needn't look murderous. 'Twas all for you, my friend."

LaTournay said nothing.

Pringle spouted profanities, half laughing. "'Tis the truth. Granted, I tried the garden tactic myself, but she complained of her side hurting. I left the field open for you to play the gallant rescuer—a part you bungled, if I read the ensuing scenes correctly. Whatever did you say to her?"

"Nothing untoward. I have only to approach, and she blanches as if I were a death's head."

"Hmm. No doubt your reputation precedes you. It is all over the city that you prefer to dally with married women. Everyone knows of your torrid affair with Delia Forester." His grin reached from ear to ear. "So I bent Miss Talbot's ear with a few embellished tales of your libidinous exploits. You should have seen her blush, you satyr!"

"Sincere appreciation for the character endorsement," LaTournay said. "No wonder she panicked when I attempted to help her."

"Women find rakish men exciting. Once she discovers your wealth, she will be eager clay in your hands."

"I find it difficult to believe that her father has failed to inform her of my financial standing."

Pringle flung his hands up in surrender. "Very well. I promise to keep my hands off until you have tired of her. Satisfied? My sights are set on richer game—Grenville's daughter. My government job is not paying as well as I expected, so I might have to sacrifice pleasure for the present and take the matrimonial plunge."

"Your government job?"

Pringle glanced up and down the long table to make sure no one was listening. "A colonel in Boston—old friend of the family—asked me to check out the situation here in New York and carry messages."

"I see."

"It is infuriating what these Whigs do while the governor is gone, and they think they can get away with it." His expression turned serious. "I need solid information about plans and munitions, about who can be trusted to support us."

"I just arrived in town."

"What use are you?" Only half joking, Pringle sat back on the bench and drained his cup. "Tell me if you hear anything. The occupation and embargo of Boston have nearly destroyed the Pringle shipping business, and Whig associates are making it impossible for my father to recoup his losses. I am in worse straits than Talbot, since I have no daughter to sell off to a susceptible dupe. He would have to pay me to take her off his hands."

"Miss Talbot probably does not know how to spin, weave, or cook," LaTournay mused, "but she could learn."

Pringle shook his head. "The maid is passing fair, but I have seen far better. And if you think Talbot will let you wed her without first defrauding you of a considerable sum, you are a greater fool than even I realized."

"She is far from plain," LaTournay's voice rasped.

Pringle cleared his throat. "Worst thing is to get attached to a woman. Forget about her. Think of her as an angler—her charms are the lure, and she fishes for any rich man who will take the bait. You must be like the wise old trout: Steal the bait and avoid the hook. Oldest game in the world."

"Far from attempting to lure me, Miss Talbot would banish me if she had the power. She has depth, Pringle, a sagacity and sincerity one rarely encounters in a woman."

Pringle snorted and thumped a fist on the tabletop. "Same old story. Desire overrides reason. The deceitful woman will demand all and give nothing, and when you have given all, she will take it and run, leaving you with that barbed hook in your heart forevermore."

"So you prefer to play hunter rather than hunted. Unlucky Miss Marianne Grenville," LaTournay said.

"She is just a woman with a rich father. I shall give her a few babies to occupy her mind, then start enjoying life again. Who are you to criticize? At least Miss Grenville does not belong to another man."

The dregs of LaTournay's cup were bitter.

Chapter 4

How long wilt thou forget me, O LORD? for ever?
how long wilt thou hide thy face from me?
PSALM 13:1

Hearing the bell ring, followed by voices in the front hall-way, Georgette rushed from her room to peer over the edge of the dark stair landing. Mr. LaTournay handed his hat and cane to Biddy. Morning sunlight poured through a leaded window above the entry door, bathing him in a pool of brilliance.

A few locks of loose hair dangled around his cheekbones, giving him an unkempt appearance. By contrast, his brown wool coat fitted his rangy build perfectly, its simple lines displaying quality.

Snorting and woofing, Caramel descended the stairs in a wild rush. LaTournay bent to greet him. "Ah, the diligent watchdog," he said, rubbing Caramel's sides while the dog fawned about his boots. LaTournay looked up—Georgette had no time to hide. The corners of his dark eyes crinkled, and he lifted a hand in silent salute. She tried to smile back.

"Mr. Talbot will see you. This way, sir." Biddy showed him into the study. He ducked his head to enter.

"Has insanity taken over this entire city?" Georgette heard her father ask after the usual greetings. "It is no longer safe to walk the streets."

"I am certain this unrest will soon pass and the streets will be safe once more," Mr. LaTournay said.

"I pray you have come to me with an offer, LaTournay—"

The door closed, ending Georgette's eavesdropping. Hope and dread warred within her pounding heart. "Help me, Lord." The feeble prayer was the best she could do.

Sometime later, while Georgette sat on her window seat, gazing blankly at a book, her mother's call rang down the hallway. "Georgette? Come here, child." Georgette rose, shifting Caramel from her lap to the cushions. He snored on.

As she entered her mother's chambers, Georgette crossed paths with her beaming father. He patted her cheek and winked. "Good girl." Grateful for his rare approval, she smiled.

Her mother sat up against a silk-padded headboard, her abundant hair cascading over plump shoulders. A wrap supporting her chin tied in a knot above her forehead. Ribbons on her cap rustled as she nodded and smiled. "You look well this morning."

Her mother's mornings began and ended late.

"Thank you," Georgette said.

"It appears that, despite your unfortunate illness, your appearance the other night was adequate to attract a serious offer for your hand. So you see, the stays served their purpose. Your father and I could not be more delighted." Her blue eyes glowed. "Think of it! Your sister's husband comes of good family and has excellent prospects, but he lacks the wealth of your Mr. LaTournay."

"I care nothing for wealth. I would marry for love, Mother." Her chest felt tight. *He asked! He truly asked for my hand in marriage!*

Her mother babbled on. "Juliette must economize, but you? Never! I shall plan your trousseau immediately, for there is no time to waste. As you know, our finances have been somewhat strained of late, but your betrothed promises to pay for anything you need. How thrilling to have my daughter snare such a catch! Although I had suspected an attachment earlier, I knew for certain Saturday night. I told Victoria Grenville that he was enthralled with you, and now I am proven correct. He could scarcely take his eyes off you even as you danced with other men, and I do not believe he asked more than one or two other ladies to dance all evening. Of course, he might have done so after we were obliged to leave, but it matters not, for you are the lucky maiden he chose as his bride!"

Georgette barely heard her mother's ravings while her thoughts and heart waged war. Her logical mind found voice. "I cannot believe that you and Papa would sacrifice your daughter to an immoral man."

"What nonsense!" she said, swinging her legs over the side of the bed and flinging on her bedgown. "You will marry him and do it with becoming modesty."

"I would rather die."

An outright lie, and her mother knew it, for her lips curved. "You should run away to the stage, my dear. Perhaps your father is right and I have spoiled you. A dutiful daughter will yield to the greater understanding of her elders and marry the suitor they select for her."

"Loving parents would not select a suitor whose behavior the daughter finds disgusting." Georgette did not have to fake the break in her voice.

"Child, you speak of things outside your understanding. Mr. LaTournay is no better and no worse a man than any other. You cannot be immune to his melancholy eyes? And such legs and shoulders! Were I but ten years younger, I should contend for the fellow myself! If you care anything for the honor of the Talbot name, and I believe you do, you will obey as a dutiful daughter should. The wedding will take place as soon as decently possible, and that is the end of the matter."

◈

Georgette looked up from the book she was reading. Her mother stood in the doorway. "Your father is away, and I am leaving for the church, dearest girl. Unforeseen difficulty has arisen regarding your wedding. Dr. Inglis is being unreasonable about the entire affair because of Mr. LaTournay's Catholic baptism, and I fear we shall have to convince another minister to perform the ceremony. One would think that in a progressive city like New York, a minister would not be so bound by tradition."

"He is Catholic?" Such a thing had never occurred to Georgette. Placing her book on the window seat, she rose, picked up Caramel, and strolled about the room. "If Dr. Inglis disapproves, should it not be taken as proof that this marriage is disapproved by God?"

Her mother shook her head. "Mr. LaTournay is a Christian, Georgette. I do not believe he is active in religion of any kind, so what should it matter to you? He has agreed that your children shall be baptized in the church of your choice."

Georgette decided she would prefer to know the worst. After placing Caramel on the floor, she confronted her mother directly. "Does Mr. LaTournay wish to marry me, or is Father forcing him into marriage using some threat?"

Her mother appeared insulted. "To say such a thing about your own father! Why must you disparage your charms, my child? Mr. LaTournay desires to marry you, and that is all you need to know."

Covering her mouth with one hand and holding her elbow with the other, Georgette shook her head. "The entire affair is distasteful, and I cannot comprehend why you and Papa seem pleased. Mr. LaTournay may plan to take over the Talbot estates or Papa's business."

"Stop hiding your mouth, speak clearly, and stand up straight. If you would cease questioning everyone's motives, life would be much happier for all of us." Without meeting her daughter's eye, she closed the door.

Biddy brought up a calling card moments later. "A lady to see you, missy."

Georgette read the name. "Lady Forester? Are you certain she wishes to see me?"

"She said your name clear enough, missy."

"I shall come down directly." Her thoughts spinning, Georgette checked her reflection in the mirror and hurried downstairs.

"She is in the parlor," Biddy whispered in passing. Squaring her shoulders, Georgette nodded at the wrinkled little woman.

Lady Forester turned as Georgette entered the room. Her bright green eyes blinked in evident surprise. "Miss Talbot?"

Georgette's heart gave a jolt of recognition. "Yes?"

At first glance, the woman was stunning—voluptuous figure,

raven hair, those amazing eyes, and a low voice. Yet as light from the parlor windows touched the lady's face, Georgette saw that her skin was rough.

The hint of a sneer curled Lady Forester's mouth. "I cannot believe it. There must be more to the tale than I am aware."

"Madam?" Georgette began to suspect the woman's purpose, and anger heated her face.

"LaTournay must have some ulterior motive for choosing you as his bride. Perhaps he wishes to allay my husband's suspicions." She perused Georgette's figure.

"If you intend only to insult me, I must request you to leave." Georgette spoke through clenched teeth.

"I came in kindness to warn you. LaTournay may avow fidelity, but he will not keep that promise. Such a man can never satisfy his needs with one ordinary woman." Her tone implied that she, Lady Forester, transcended the common female.

The parlor door opened and Biddy announced, "Miss Grenville to see you, miss."

Georgette had never been more pleased to see Marianne's angelic face. "Madam, have you met Miss Grenville? Marianne, Lady Forester. She is just leaving."

Lady Forester's lips disappeared into a tight line. Angry red blotches marred her complexion. Lifting her skirts, she brushed past Georgette.

As the front door closed with a thud, Marianne looked puzzled. "Did my arrival anger her, Gigi?"

"She was angry before she arrived," Georgette answered. "I am overjoyed to see you, dearest friend. You rescued me from a most unpleasant encounter. I thought the woman might rend me with her claws as well as her tongue."

Marianne's cheeks turned pink, and her eyes expressed sympathy. "She came concerning your betrothal to Mr. LaTournay. Word of the match has spread throughout town. I pray you are happy, Gigi."

"Come." Georgette linked her arm through Marianne's and led her into the garden. The girls strolled between beds of sprouting perennials. "What have you heard?" Georgette asked after a thoughtful silence.

"Only that the banns would soon be read for your engagement. Gigi, I have news of my own."

Grateful for the change of subject, Georgette brightened. "Tell all."

"Mr. Pringle has been calling upon me, and Papa has given permission for us to court. Yesterday Mr. Pringle took me riding into the country in his chaise. He tucked the lap robe around me and worried lest I take a chill. Imagine! The day was balmy." Marianne giggled. "His voice gives me the shivers, so sweet and mellow. Oh Gigi, I have admired him for years. Never dared I believe that he might notice me!"

"I am happy for you."

"And are you happy?" Marianne's gentle blue eyes held concern.

"I shall never know happiness again unless God provides a way to escape this nightmare."

"Gigi, you mustn't say such things. God cares for our needs, and He wants to fulfill our desires, but sometimes we desire wrong things. We need to have our hearts in tune with His perfect will."

Georgette gave a sharp laugh. "My parents pledge me to a soulless rake, and I am to see this as God's will?"

Marianne cringed yet refused to yield. "I think you should start asking God to give you love for Mr. LaTournay. God can use a wife's godly example to bring her husband to Himself. Mama says she did not love Papa when she married him, but she prayed to love him, and now she cannot imagine life without him. They adore each other."

"But your father is a good man. If your mother did not love him, at least she did not despise him when they married. Do you know why that Forester woman came to see me? She told me that Mr. LaTournay will still be hers even after I marry him."

Marianne looked wise. "That is what she wants to believe. I know better. Mr. LaTournay adores you, Gigi. You have the advantage over Lady Forester, no matter what hurtful things she says. Your love will make him forget her entirely."

Tears burned Georgette's eyes as longing burned her soul. Turning away, she covered her face with both hands. "I confess— I wish that were true. But never will I be able to trust him. He travels to the city often, Marianne, and she will be here waiting for him. I do not want to share my husband with anyone. I cannot marry him. I simply cannot!"

Marianne wrapped her in a tender hug. "If you refuse even to try to love him, all hope of happiness is gone. How my heart aches for you, Gigi!"

Arms about each other's waists, the two girls circled the garden at a slow pace, heads bowed.

Georgette sighed. "Very well. I shall attempt praying to love him."

☙

Mr. LaTournay joined the Talbots for dinner that evening. Georgette picked at her food and kept her gaze lowered while the men talked politics. More than once her parents tried to draw her into the strained conversation. When these efforts produced no response, she sensed their perplexity escalating into irritation.

Mr. LaTournay's presence was like an ache in her soul. Sorrow blocked her throat.

"Tell us about your home, Mr. LaTournay," her mother demanded. "Do you have servants?"

"There are many people living on the farm. Our servants work for hire; we keep no slaves. All speak at least some English, and several have children. We also have frequent guests drop in at Haven Farm. My wife will not lack for company when I am away on business."

Georgette winced inwardly.

"Haven Farm," her mother repeated. "How charming. Did you name it?"

"My grandfather, Piers Vanderhaven, settled the land and chose its name."

"Did you grow up there?" Georgette's father spoke around a mouthful of food.

"My mother was born on the farm," Mr. LaTournay said. "My

grandmother died when my mother was born, and Grandfather never remarried. He left Haven Farm to me and my sister, Francine."

"So your mother was Dutch?"

"My grandfather was Dutch, but my mother's mother was French, as was my father." He sounded uneasy.

Georgette sensed displeasure emanating from her parents.

"You seem so English," her mother said.

"Neither France nor Quebec claims my loyalty. New York is my home, and it receives my allegiance."

"As a colony of His Royal Majesty, George III," her father added.

Georgette sneaked a look at her fiancé across the table. He met her gaze as though he had been waiting for her notice. "I am deeply committed to country and family. My wife will have no cause for fear or complaint."

Despite a strong desire to roll her eyes, Georgette faked a smile and returned her attention to her filet of cod. Hearing a whimper, she noticed that Caramel was not in his usual begging spot beside her chair.

He sat beside Mr. LaTournay.

Mr. LaTournay stayed for only a short time after the meal ended. Her parents retired to the parlor; Georgette could hear them arguing as she climbed the stairs. In her room, she bathed and prepared for bed, then lavished extra attention on Caramel, throwing a ball until even he tired of the game. The little dog scrambled up on the bed and flopped to his side, panting with lolling tongue. "At least Mr. LaTournay likes you, my precious puppy. Some men do not care for lap dogs." Circling the pug with her arms, she rested her forehead on his heaving side. "Why must he be so attractive, Caramel? I despise him, yet I crave his attention."

Biddy rapped at the door for the second time that day and held out a folded paper. "Sorry to disturb you, missy, but a man asked me to give this to you."

"A man?" Georgette hopped to her feet and broke the seal. "Did you recognize him?"

"I should say 'twas the same man what brought that dog, miss. He wore a cloak and spoke quietlike, but I heard the foreign in his voice."

Georgette sucked in a deep breath as she read. "Biddy, do not tell a soul, but I am to meet him in the garden."

Biddy's watery eyes widened. "A rondyvoo, miss? I'll be quiet as the dead."

Not even the morbid simile could diminish Georgette's excitement. With Biddy's help, she dressed and hurried downstairs. Her father dozed over a book in his study. Georgette tiptoed past the door and rushed along the hallway.

Moonlight silvered the rose trellis and threw stark shadows on the stone walkway. Shivering, Georgette tightened her grip on her knitted shawl. Would he come? She peered through the wrought iron gate, but no cloaked figure waited outside.

"Georgette."

With a startled cry, she spun around. A shadow detached itself from the deeper shadows near the wall. "Hello." Her voice quavered. "You came."

"You thought I would not?"

"I know of your betrothal to Mr. LaTournay." He stepped closer, a looming specter. "You no longer believe him to be evil?"

She studied her own linked fingers. "I have no choice but to marry him."

"You have many choices, *petite grenouille*. Does he know of your father's coercion? What man would wish to marry a woman by force? Have you no affection in your heart for the poor wretch?" His voice held a caressing note.

"Lady Forester called upon me today." The words poured out before she thought them through.

A pause. "Indeed." Cracking ice sounded warm in comparison to his tone.

"She told me that Mr. LaTournay would not keep his marriage vows to me, that I could never satisfy him." Aghast, Georgette lifted her hand to her mouth. This was an unknown man, not a father confessor.

He turned with a swirl of his cloak and walked the length of the garden path, spun about, and returned. "Her words contain no truth. You heard the vengeance of a resentful woman, *bien-aimée*."

"And how would you know?"

"I know much about women and their devious ways. I also attest that any man of sense would be more than satisfied to have you as wife. LaTournay, for all his faults, is generally accepted as a sensible man."

"You are acquainted with him?"

"I am."

"You say 'any man of sense.' Does this mean that I appeal only to a man's brain?"

He murmured something in French. "You play with fire, *ma belle* Georgette."

"Yes, I feel that fire within each time you speak my name." She pressed her hands over her heart. "I do not understand myself! Why is it that my heart responds to a man even while my mind doubts him? My mind knows Mr. LaTournay to be an immoral and ungodly man, yet my heart yearns within me when he is near. And you—I know so little of you, not even your name, and yet. . ."

"Pray do not leave me suspended thus." His long arm reached out, and his warm hand clasped hers. She wrapped her other hand around his.

"And yet you. . ." She struggled for words. "You seem like one to whom I may safely bare my soul."

His grasp tightened, and she heard him sigh. "Georgette, this charade must—"

"Marianne, my friend, tells me that I must pray not only for Mr. LaTournay's salvation from sin, but also that God will teach me to love him. You and I must never again meet alone, kind benefactor, for I am pledged to another. From this time on, my loyalty and love must belong to Mr. LaTournay alone."

His hooded head bowed low, and silence stretched between

them. Rousing, he lifted her hand, turned it, and touched his forehead to her wrist. "I am your slave and your footstool. Be merciful, I adjure you, *belle grenouille.*"

Before she recovered her equilibrium, he disappeared into the shadows once more.

Chapter 5

If ye then, being evil, know how to give good gifts
unto your children, how much more shall your Father
which is in heaven give good things to them that ask him?
MATTHEW 7:11

Georgette dutifully prayed to love Mr. LaTournay. Although her fiancé's moral code still disturbed her, she began to appreciate the possible benefits of marriage to such an intelligent man. As spring passed into summer, listening in on LaTournay's conversations with her father stimulated Georgette's thoughts and broadened her understanding of the turbulent political conflicts engulfing the city of New York.

She depended upon her betrothed for protection from an uncertain future. Not only did he always possess the latest news about the fluctuation of power between Whigs and Loyalists, he also seemed undaunted by it. More than once, Georgette heard her father quote Mr. LaTournay's remarks or advice to associates, citing the younger man as a reliable authority.

One rainy afternoon, Georgette spread the Thursday edition of the *Gazetteer* on the library floor, scanning it for conversational material that might impress her fiancé. Most of the news centered on politics. Everything in life seemed to revolve around politics, since the Provincial Congress now prohibited most social activities. The possibility of war was no longer whispered behind hands in drawing rooms. Now it was shouted in the streets—insults to Mother England, threats to her loyal subjects.

Although the Talbots showed carefree faces to the world, Georgette observed her father's tension in his constant smoking and recognized her mother's fear in her strident tones. For the first time, Georgette saw her parents as frail beings seeking security in every possible place—except the one place they might find it. Her attempts to discuss God and the meaning of life with her mother met with sighs and rolling eyes of rejection. The one time Georgette spoke in her father's presence of seeing God's guiding hand in their present circumstances, she feared he might do her physical violence.

Would life be different with Mr. LaTournay? Despite Marianne's assurances that a godly wife might influence her husband to seek the Lord, Georgette knew such change was unlikely. Not that Mr. LaTournay was unkind—but then, he was not yet her husband. A man would reveal only his best side before the wedding. Georgette's probable fate would be a marriage of mutual toleration, as exemplified by her parents.

Mr. LaTournay spent much of his time away from the city, never offering explanation for his absence. Georgette had not seen him for more than a week. She feared he might be visiting Lady Forester, although the latest gossip, according to her mother, testified that the two had parted ways. Georgette did not have the nerve to ask if he had other female friends. If he did, she thought she would rather not know. But then again, she did want to know.

Of all things, she feared unrequited love. The torture of loving a man who cared for other women! Already Georgette suffered. If he never loved her in return, she would want to die.

Scowling, she attempted to concentrate on the news. Utterly ridiculous, how her thoughts could wander from war to love. As if the topics connected. No reasonable woman expected love in her marriage anyway. To become an interesting companion to Mr. LaTournay, able to support her end of a conversation—now that was a sensible goal. Hence the newspaper.

But Georgette's thoughts and gaze soon wandered off the page again. *"When I wed, my heart will belong to my wife alone for as long as I live."* The memory of that beautifully accented voice echoed in her dreams night and day.

Since the night she sent her mysterious visitor away, she had heard nothing from him. Although he spoke no overt words of love—at least, not in English—Georgette nevertheless knew that he cared for her. Would she ever see him again? Pressing her wrist to her lips, she recalled the warmth of his touch.

She flopped back on the rug, wrapped both arms over her head, propped her bare feet on the seat of a chair, and studied the ceiling's plaster moldings.

Her wedding day. One hand resting on Mr. LaTournay's arm, she emerged from a huge gothic cathedral. Her face like marble, cool and lovely, she bore her fate with dignified forbearance. Suddenly a giant black stallion pounded into the churchyard and reared. Its rider's cape flowed from magnificent shoulders as he leaped to the ground, drew a sword, and challenged Mr. LaTournay to a duel.

Mr. LaTournay, tall and deadly, posed with saber in hand, his shirtsleeves billowing. Swords clashed. Women screamed and fainted.

With blood staining his white shirtfront, Mr. LaTournay slowly fell to his knees, reaching one hand to her. There in the churchyard, for the first and last time, she held her husband in her arms and kissed him. After weeping for the love that could never be, she rode away with her romantic hero. . . .

But Mr. LaTournay could not die. Even in her imagination Georgette could not bear the thought of him suffering injury. Yet unless her husband died, it would be evil to leave him for another man.

She decided the cloaked hero should be wounded instead, and the confrontation must take place before, not after, the wedding ceremony.

Reeling from a gash in his side, her hero tossed her behind him on the saddle and galloped away. Clutching his broad shoulders, she begged him to stop and let her bind his wound. He slid to the ground, and she cradled him in her arms. Tenderly, eagerly, she reached for the concealing hood—

The library door creaked. "I am so pleased you came by. We were beginning to wonder what had become of you. I have many questions. Georgette, are you in here? She was here a moment ago. I cannot imagine where she has disap—Georgette?" Her mother gasped at the sight of Georgette scrambling to her feet.

Mr. LaTournay stood at her mother's side.

Georgette brushed her skirts, feeling guilty heat pour into her face. She had not bothered to don a hoop and stays that morning, and the pink-flowered gown was one of her oldest. Her hair must be a sight after her gyrations on the rug. "I was. . .I was reading this week's *Gazetteer.* Good day, sir."

He bowed. "Good day, Miss Talbot. Do not apologize, madam; your daughter had no warning of my arrival. It is not to be expected that she would sit in readiness at all hours. Today's news must make interesting reading. Did you learn of our governor's return?"

Although his manner remained stilted, his tone was kind. Georgette felt short of breath, knowing how ridiculous had been her imaginings. "I had not heard of it."

"I asked Biddy to bring us tea in the parlor," her mother said. "Please join us, Georgette." In a whispered aside, she added, "And fix your hair!"

When Georgette entered the parlor a few minutes later, the conversation broke off and Mr. LaTournay rose to seat her at the tiny table. Smoothing her skirts, she smiled in his direction as he settled into the chair across from her mother. Caramel plopped between Georgette's skirts and Mr. LaTournay's boots. Her father remained in his favorite chair across the room.

Georgette's mother lifted the teapot. "It is growing difficult to find tea. I fear our cook purchased this on the black market. Do you take cream and sugar, sir?"

"Both, thank you." Mr. LaTournay handled the fragile teacup with practiced ease. His tanned hands were clean, even to the fingernails. He seemed cool and neat, as always. Georgette never needed to pardon an unpleasant odor while in his presence. Even his teeth were nearly perfect. She studied his mouth as he conversed with her father.

Her parents faded away.

Mr. LaTournay and she, a married couple, drank tea together in a shadowy room. Noticing that her husband needed more cream, she rose to serve him and dropped a tender kiss upon his cheek before returning to her seat.

Or would she kiss the top of his head? Or his lips? Could any woman ever feel comfortable enough with this man to display affection freely? How would he react? Bearing in mind his reputation, she knew he could not be as cold and impervious as he seemed.

He dabbed his mustache with a napkin.

Georgette's mother cleared her throat.

Realizing she had been staring, Georgette took a sip of tea and burned her lip. Her mother glowered. Mr. LaTournay's expression remained neutral, although he appeared somewhat flushed.

Could he read her thoughts? Oh, the curse of an unbridled imagination!

"So Governor Tryon is returning? I have always wished to meet him," Georgette blurted. "I have seen the warship *Asia* lying at anchor off Governor's Island. Now I shall watch for the governor's ship."

"He is to return, and therein lies the city's dilemma," Mr. LaTournay said. "The new commander in chief of the American armies, George Washington, is scheduled to arrive in the city on the very day of Tryon's return. Both men will expect a parade and official welcome, yet it would be unfeasible to hold two parades at once. Only Broadway is large and straight enough to accommodate a parade."

"Hmph. Who cares about the illicit general of an illegal army?" her mother said.

"From all I hear, Washington is a man to command both respect and admiration," Mr. LaTournay said quietly. "I have a wish to see the most talked-of man in America."

"Yet he is not to stay in town more than a day," Georgette's father added from his armchair. "Governor Tryon, the king's official, is vastly more important. Surely the city will show him the welcome he deserves after more than a year's absence. Some thought he would never return at all."

"All will be well now that Governor Tryon is back," her mother said. "I hope he demands the return of the British soldiers to Fort George and disarms the dangerous rabble who have ruled the streets these many weeks."

"I should like to see a parade," Georgette said.

"Then I shall take you," Mr. LaTournay offered. "Both men are scheduled to arrive in midafternoon, but perhaps that will change. We shall walk, so wear sturdy shoes." He placed his empty teacup in its saucer and again blotted his mustache. "Thank you for the tea. Miss Talbot, I wish to speak with you of plans for the future. Will you walk with me in the garden?"

"I need to confer with you afterward, LaTournay," her father said in a languid yet pointed manner. "There are details yet to be settled."

Georgette's mother gave her a warning look. Nodding to assure her good behavior, Georgette rose, brushed crumbs from her skirts, and led the way outside into a gray and gloomy afternoon. The garden, dotted with rain puddles, seemed smaller than ever before. Caramel sniffed and snorted his way along the wall, pausing to dig beneath a flowering shrub.

Mr. LaTournay paced a short track between two planters. His stride reminded her of. . . She shook her head to dislodge the traitorous memory.

"The minister of the Methodist church has agreed to marry us," Georgette said quickly to conceal her overwrought nerves. "My mother prefers early September. I hope that will suit you. It must be a small ceremony, but we shall have a reception here afterwards."

He paused before speaking. "I am aware of your parents' plans, but I do not wish you to feel rushed into marriage. Take the time you need to fully prepare, both emotionally and physically. I must warn you that we live simply at Haven Farm. Your everyday attire will consist of woolens and strong boots. It would be best to travel north before winter sets in, but if you cannot prepare in time, I shall return for you at whatever date you choose."

"I am willing to comply with the current arrangements." She attained a tone of self-sacrificing humility. "The banns have been published, and the wedding date was announced in the *Gazetteer*. Besides, I already own a quantity of serviceable clothing."

Another pause. "If you are certain."

She turned away. "I would not wish to inconvenience you."

"You misunderstand my meaning." He grasped her shoulder. She shivered, barely restraining herself from ducking away. He turned her to him and lifted her chin, but she refused to look up. "Miss Talbot, you need never fear me. Your welfare is my foremost consideration."

Georgette nodded.

A long moment passed, and she heard him exhale. "If you please," he said in a whisper, "may I kiss you?"

Conflicting thoughts whirled in Georgette's head, disappearing into a void. Again she nodded, then closed her eyes. Warmth touched her lips, living, tender. Her lips parted, and he kissed her again. His strong arms slipped around her waist, pulling her close to his chest. She heard and felt his rapid breathing, tasted tea in his kiss. She craved more of these wondrous sensations, but the embrace ended abruptly. Georgette opened her eyes to meet his gaze. He removed her arms from around his neck and took a step back.

"Perhaps waiting would be foolish after all."

Georgette felt his thumbs stroke her wrists. "What?" Helpless to comprehend her own desires, she jerked her hands free and covered her burning lips, shaking her head.

Shame propelled her away and sent her stumbling into the house. She heard him call, but the numbness of her heart prevented any response.

⌘

Georgette scarcely noticed Caramel's snoring. Eyes wide, she lay upon her bed. Dried tears made her face itch. Evening sunlight painted golden windowpane reflections upon the slanted ceiling of her bedchamber. A rain-freshened breeze stirred the window curtains. She could hear gulls mewing as they wheeled over the rooftops, and light traffic rattled along Broad Street. The Bible lying open upon her chest rose and fell with her uneven breathing.

Someone rapped at her door. "Missy?"

"Come in, Biddy."

The wooden door creaked open. "I have a note for you, missy, from Mr. LaTournay."

"Is he still here?" Georgette closed her Bible and sat up. She reached for the folded pyramid of paper. Beside her, Caramel stretched and yawned with a squeaky sound.

"He's been talking with Mr. Talbot in the study. Mr. LaTournay looks sad, missy," the maid dared to comment.

Georgette unfolded the paper. Caramel shoved his nose in the way as if to read it first. She pushed him aside and studied the elegant script.

> *I humbly beg your pardon and await your convenience in the garden.*
>
> L

"Thank you, Biddy."

"You wish to send him a note?"

"No, I shall come down."

Georgette watched until the door closed behind Biddy. If she were to refuse Mr. LaTournay's summons, her father would demand an explanation.

Rising, she splashed her face with water from the basin on her dressing table. Her eyes felt gritty and probably looked swollen. She trembled at the thought of speaking to Mr. LaTournay, and the knot in her chest forced out yet another sob. Georgette cupped her mouth with one hand, then touched her lips, recalling his kisses.

Did Mr. LaTournay's kisses affect Mrs. Forester the way they affected her? The thought of that woman in his arms twisted like a knife into Georgette's heart. Once again, she prayed for release—either from her fears or from this betrothal.

She had recognized passion in his eyes—those unfathomable eyes that could scorch and chill in the same glance. Although being desired by a man thrilled her, Georgette knew it was not enough. Mr. LaTournay had desired many women, by all accounts, yet his passion never endured beyond a month or two.

"Dear God, spare me the pain of becoming the latest in his string of discarded lovers. Help me to love him no matter what." Her face crumpled, but she swallowed the sob. "Oh, how blessed I would feel if You were to cause him to love me as I love him!" Caramel led the way downstairs and waited for Georgette to open the garden door. He dashed over to greet Mr. LaTournay and grinned while having his sides thumped. Georgette heard Mr. LaTournay speak to the dog, though his voice was too low for her to discern his words.

He straightened to his full height as she stepped outside. His gaze seemed to pierce her.

She hoped her eyes were no longer red.

"Miss Talbot, can you find it in your heart to forgive my behavior?" Had his behavior been worse than hers?

She nodded shortly. "Even as God for Christ's sake has forgiven me."

"Ah." The response held elements of both admiration and amusement.

A wave of courage and resolve lifted Georgette. "Are you a Christian?"

"I was raised in the church."

"Do you believe that salvation comes through faith in Christ?" He blinked. "I do."

"Will you study the scriptures with me? I have a need to understand more about God, yet much that I read is beyond my comprehension. If we were to study together, perhaps I could profit through your superior understanding."

She read surprise and interest in his expression. "I am honored by your request," he said.

A certain hitch in his pronunciation caught her ear. Georgette found the apparent speech impediment endearing, though it seemed unfair that even the man's flaws attracted her.

" 'Twill seem strange to greet you on the morrow without revealing all that has passed between us," she said, taking a step closer to him.

Shadows darkened much of the garden, though the sky overhead still shone bright blue. Mr. LaTournay's bare head caught sunlight reflected from a window. His hair and beard reminded Georgette of a beaver pelt she saw once, thick and glossy brown.

He stepped forward. "I must be away but shall see you Sunday at church."

"And for the parade; do not forget your promise." She reached out one hand.

Georgette saw one of his brows twitch in response to her unskilled flirtation. Taking her hand, he bowed slightly. "I shall not forget."

His touch recalled vivid sensations. "Good evening, sir." Once again, Georgette pulled away and fled.

Chapter 6

A sound of battle is in the land,
and of great destruction.
JEREMIAH 50:22

LaTournay's gaze wandered across the sanctuary of Trinity Church until it rested upon Georgette in the Talbot family box. Although she appeared to listen to the sermon, he saw vacancy in her stare. Her mind must be far away. As if sensing his regard, she glanced his way. Her face grew rosy as her gaze fell from his. What did she read in his eyes to make her blush and look away? Blinking, he settled into his seat and pondered the matter.

Dr. Inglis read Psalm 147. LaTournay could not recall hearing this passage before, but then he was not as familiar with the Bible as he should be. Today the words caught at his heart. Opening the Bible he had purchased the day before for the purpose of serious study, he located the scripture and followed along.

"'He telleth the number of the stars; he calleth them all by their names. Great is our Lord, and of great power: his understanding is infinite. The Lord lifteth up the meek: he casteth the wicked down to the ground. . . . He delighteth not in the strength of the horse: he taketh not pleasure in the legs of a man. The Lord taketh pleasure in them that fear him, in those that hope in his mercy. . . .'"

LaTournay tried to picture God, infinite and almighty, caring for the needs of His creation. A being so powerful would remain unimpressed by the fastest of horses, the strongest of men, the greatest of battles. The one thing that brought Him pleasure, according to the psalm, was a man who feared Him and hoped in His mercy.

Although he acknowledged God's existence and supremacy, LaTournay had always assumed the Creator remained detached from His creation. Yet this psalm suggested that God desired a more personal relationship with people. With him.

Les Pringle, beside him in the visitors' box, snored. LaTournay elbowed him. Pringle turned another snort into a cough. "Thanks," he whispered from the side of his mouth.

When the service ended and the congregation filed outside, Pringle hurried to intercept Georgette and Miss Marianne Grenville. He slipped between the two young women, tucking an arm around each. "Lovely ladies, I am the luckiest man alive. To think that today I shall accompany the two of you to the welcoming parade for our governor!"

The spurt of anger caused by the sight of another man's hand on Georgette's trim waist startled LaTournay. He hesitated to approach the group, uncertain of his welcome.

"I believe Mr. LaTournay has other plans for today." Georgette stepped out of Pringle's reach. Her lips curled in annoyance. Sunlight filtered through her straw bonnet, dotting her face.

She glanced up, met LaTournay's gaze, and blushed. Her fair skin frequently betrayed the strength of her emotions, though he found it difficult to determine their course. Did this blush reveal pleasure or pain?

He watched as she stiffened her backbone and faced him. "I am pleased to see you here today, sir, although the sermon left much to be desired." She extended one gloved hand. He bowed over it.

"Gigi, you must not say such things!" Miss Grenville said. "People will hear."

Beside her, Pringle grinned and lifted a brow at LaTournay.

"Church is for sermons about God, not about politics," Georgette said, reclaiming her hand.

"I appreciated the scripture reading," LaTournay said.

Miss Grenville's frown vanished. "That is wonderful. A good day to you, Mr. LaTournay." She was a pretty woman, slender and blond. He understood Pringle's interest.

"Good day to you, Miss Grenville. What is this name by which you address Miss Talbot?"

"I call her Gigi, for the two letter *G*'s in her name," she answered, beaming at Georgette. She tucked one hand into the crook of Pringle's elbow. "I imagine we shall see you at the parade today."

After Pringle and Miss Grenville strolled away, Georgette made an obvious effort to be friendly and natural. "At what time shall we commence our walk?" She fingered her bonnet strings, pushed her gloves into place, and shifted her Bible from one arm to the other.

"I shall come for you at two o'clock. My landlady has promised to pack us a luncheon basket. If you prefer, I can hire a chaise, since it will be a long walk."

"The day is warm but not unpleasant. I shall enjoy walking with you." She lifted her sparkling brown eyes as high as his chin, then dropped her gaze to his boot toes. "My parents are pleased that we shall spend the day together."

"As am I, Miss Talbot."

She sucked in a quick breath and released it in a little burst. "Two o'clock then. I shall be ready." Giving a wave, she hurried to follow her parents from the churchyard.

Lucille and Frederick Talbot made a handsome couple— Frederick dark and dignified, Lucille blond and shapely. In LaTournay's estimation, Georgette exhibited the finest qualities of both parents. He had not realized the Talbots walked to church. Frederick probably could no longer afford to hire a coach.

He watched the family promenade along the street until Georgette's bobbing skirts disappeared around the corner. He headed for his boardinghouse.

"LaTournay, wait!" Running footsteps sounded from behind him.

Panting and grinning, Pringle caught him by the shoulder. "I have scarcely spoken to you these three weeks. What have you been doing? I seldom see you anymore."

"Business often takes me out of town. Politics are the ruination of profit."

Pringle gave a sharp laugh. "That I know. I assumed you were also wooing. I heard of your betrothal to the Talbot wench." He shook his head. "I still say you are crazy. The woman's head is a vacuum. Granted, she has the form of a goddess, but so does Lady—"

"Your pursuit of Miss Grenville's fortune prospers?"

Pringle winced. "It goes well enough, but I begin to have regrets. Though I am an unabashed scoundrel, I begin to think Miss Grenville is an earthly angel. She talks constantly about God. To appease her, I profess interest in such things, but my acting ability strains when it comes to praying and confessing sins and such."

"Because you have no sins to confess?"

Pringle chuckled at the jibe. "Sometimes I wonder if she loves me only because I present a challenge. I have an ambitious goal: Before this day ends, I shall coax a kiss from that saintly maid, and she will enjoy it. I hope the governor is late and doesn't come ashore until well after dark. He is scheduled to arrive at four o'clock, you know."

"Colonel Lasher has a militia company waiting at Coenties slip, where Governor Tryon is expected to land. Another company travels with four members of the Provincial Congress to Newark, where they hope to meet General Washington and detour him to the Hoboken Ferry," LaTournay said.

A burst of profanity indicated Pringle's loathing of the militia. "As far from Coenties slip as possible, eh? Trust New York to butter both sides of the bread. And where will the rest of Lasher's companies be?"

"At a halfway point, ready to greet whichever personage arrives first. Absurd, but necessary."

Pringle scowled. "Nonsense. No reason in the world to make a fuss over this Virginian upstart who dares take arms against England. I cannot help wondering what Parliament is thinking to let this rebellion linger on. Why do the *Asia* and the *Kingfisher* not send a few firebombs into the town and make them think twice about entertaining the enemy?"

"Either ship could burn New York to the ground, but what would such aggression accomplish? A ruined port is of no use to

England, and violence against these rebels seems to harden their resolve."

"Have you been asked to take an oath of loyalty to this provincial travesty they call a congress? I shall resist to my dying day. I may not be an upstanding subject, but my loyalty belongs to the king." Pringle's eyes flashed indignation.

"Beware how loudly you speak, my friend. I, too, have scant use for the Sons of Liberty, as they call themselves. Yet several members of the Provincial Congress are loyal British citizens who desire a peaceful resolution to this conflict. Their complaints against England are not without basis." LaTournay paused at the door of his boardinghouse and faced Pringle. "Enjoy your day with Miss Grenville. She seems a worthy young woman, and I would not like to see my fiancée's friend hurt."

"Point acknowledged. Perhaps we shall see you about town." With a roguish grin, Pringle sauntered on, swinging his walking stick.

At five minutes past two, Georgette sat waiting upon the front stairway, rolling her parasol between nervous fingers. The gauze tucked about her shoulders itched and tickled her neck. Sweat beaded on her forehead until she patted it away with a hankie.

Caramel brought his leather ball, dropped it at her feet, and backed off with a hopeful woof. Georgette obliged him by throwing it down the hall.

A knock came at the door. Caramel abandoned the ball chase and reversed course to thump his front paws on the front door and bark. When Georgette opened the door, the pug danced about Mr. LaTournay's feet and yammered. She raised her voice above the din. "Please come in. We no longer have a butler, and the maids are off this afternoon."

He obediently entered the hall and set down a laden basket. Caramel pushed his flat nose beneath the cloth, his curly tail wagging. Mr. LaTournay went down on one knee and pulled the dog away. "No, that isn't for you, unless you plan to come along on our walk. Then I might be convinced to share." Caramel rolled to his back and let his tongue loll from one side of his grinning mouth. After pulling off his gloves, Mr. LaTournay rubbed the dog's chest.

Georgette lifted Caramel's leash off its wall hook and paused to watch the man play with her dog. His gentleness surprised her.

What would he think of the way Georgette had acquired the pug? Would he be resentful of her secret beau? More important, would he have just cause for jealousy?

He glanced up. "Is anything amiss?"

"Why, no, not a thing." Except for her nerves. "Do you not think the day is too warm for him to join us? Caramel loves a walk, but his legs are short."

"I shall carry him if he grows tired." He took the braided cord from her and looped it through Caramel's collar.

"Very well. I am ready for our outing. Is this gown suitable?" The green-sprigged white linen was among her most becoming frocks. Georgette settled her straw bonnet over her curls and tied its ribbons beneath her chin.

"You are springtime itself," he said. "I shall be the proudest man in town." Lifting the basket with his left hand, he handed her the end of Caramel's leash and offered her his right arm. "Shall we?"

"Indeed, we shall," she said, slipping her hand into the crook of his elbow. She could hold both dog leash and parasol with her other hand. "My parents are entertaining guests for luncheon. They plan to attend the parade for Governor Tryon."

"I had thought we might join the crowd greeting Washington. I am acquainted with the governor, but this Virginian general will be a new face. Two other generals will arrive with him—Philip Schuyler and Charles Lee." He escorted her through the front door and closed it behind them. "Schuyler is an important man in the northern parts of this colony."

Georgette reclaimed Mr. LaTournay's arm and fell into step beside him as they headed north on Broad Street. When Caramel lunged toward a tree, her parasol whacked the top of her bonnet. Tugging the dog back to her side, she continued the discussion. "I cannot understand how these men who fought so bravely for our country during the war against the French and Indians could now turn traitor and fight against England."

"It is a different war and a different cause. Such men would not shift their loyalties lightly, you may be sure. Perhaps we should listen to speeches today and learn what we may about their reasoning."

"Would that not be treasonous?" She searched his stern profile for reassurance.

He pressed his lips together and gazed over her head across the rooftops. His eyes, she noticed, were a muddy brown in hue. Yet they were arresting eyes, with their thick dark brows and lashes.

"Do you wish to take a side in any controversy simply because of tradition and blind loyalty?" he asked. "Or would you prefer to understand the motives governing the actions taken by both factions, then choose the position most tenable in regard to your beliefs and convictions?"

Startled by the question, Georgette scrambled for an honest answer. "I would wish always to do what is right in the sight of God," she said.

"Exactly as I believed you would answer." He sounded pleased.

"But how could God be pleased by treachery? Is it not true that God puts kings in power? Our king is head of the Church of England. Dr. Inglis preaches that rebellion against the king is rebellion against God." Engrossed in the conversation, Georgette paid no attention to her surroundings. Her troubled gaze still searched LaTournay's face, and she clutched his arm like a lifeline.

"I understand the appeal of this argument to you." He patted her hand and slowed his pace. "Tyrants have used it throughout history to retain power. Although it is true that God raises and topples kings and kingdoms, it is also true that not all those He allows to rule are good and upright. If I understand correctly, Christ, not any human king, is head of the Church. When a king abuses power and oppresses his subjects, it behooves those subjects to protest such injustice."

Georgette considered his words. "What if the king will not listen?"

"There you have put into words the vital question that has been debated up and down the coast of this continent these many years past. A similar situation long ago brought about the Magna Carta and the beginnings of republican government."

"I have often heard you discuss politics with my father. Always you spoke of taxes and representation, but this is the first time I understand the reason why so many colonists have joined the rebellion. Not that it is important for me, a woman, to understand such things, but—"

"Au contraire! You must realize what is at stake." Right there in the street he stopped, looked down into her eyes, and spoke earnestly. "I want you to know, and I want you to think, pray, and consider. As my wife, you will be affected by every decision I make."

His defense of the Whigs sounded entirely too sympathetic to Georgette. Yet, transfixed by his stare, she could only nod, unable to voice her questions. Relaxing, Mr. LaTournay pulled her hand back into place upon his arm and continued their stroll. Caramel trotted beside Georgette's whisking skirts, his head and tail high.

"I do not intend to frighten you," Mr. LaTournay continued, "but you must be aware of the uncertain times in which we live. Look at the militia companies gathered here upon the common. Raw boys, most of them. Do they look ready to fight His Majesty's troops? And yet the Massachusetts militia, largely comprised of old men, farmers, and young boys, has fought admirably more than once these past months."

Georgette studied the uniformed troops drilling on the village green. Might her hero be among them? One of them, a handsome fellow, caught her eye and smiled, losing the beat of the march. The man behind him gave him a rough shove. Her heart thudding, Georgette turned away and attempted to portray scorn. "And these are the people this General Washington plans to lead against our British troops? How can he hope to win?"

Mr. LaTournay merely shook his head. Together they walked past the unsavory section of town, turned west on Read's Street to Greenwich Road, and headed north along the riverbank.

Carriages passed them on the road, and other couples and family groups meandered along the highway north. The crowds increased as they approached the ferry landing. Caramel no longer tugged at his leash, and his tail had lost its jaunty curl.

"Are you hungry yet?" Mr. LaTournay asked. "This might be our best opportunity to partake from this increasingly heavy basket."

Georgette laughed. "You ought to have spoken sooner."

"There are shady places here along the river. See? Others had the same idea." He indicated a family of five seated on a blanket near the shore.

"A lovely big tree stands at the top of that knoll, away from the road. May we dine there with a view of the river?" she suggested. At his nod, she hoisted her skirts and led the way.

Mr. LaTournay spread the blanket and waited while Georgette fluffed her skirts in a circle. "I shall set out the luncheon, if you like," she offered, reaching for the basket. Caramel flopped down on the grass to pant.

As soon as Mr. LaTournay was seated, she handed him a lamb pasty wrapped in cloth. "Will you ask a blessing on our food?"

He nodded and bowed his head. Belatedly, he removed his hat. Holding it to his chest, he spoke slowly. "Almighty God, You have provided this food for us. It amazes me that You would notice us humans, yet You say we are important to You. I ask that You will lead Georgette and me in Your ways. Teach us to fear You and to hope in Your mercy. Amen."

He slid his hat back upon his head and bit into the pasty. Georgette wondered at the contradictions of his character. How could a man of such ill repute pray so convincingly?

They ate in silence for several minutes, watching the pedestrians and carriages, squinting in the sparkle of sunlight off the Hudson River. Georgette wanted to learn more about Mr. LaTournay, yet she did not know how to begin questioning him. He seemed a private person, as if a high wall protected his inner emotions. The brief glimpses she'd had into his heart left her wary.

Why did she feel as if she knew her covert admirer more fully than she understood her overt fiancé? The question always remained: Why would such a man choose Georgette Talbot for a wife?

Caramel recovered when the aroma of lamb reached his twitching nose. Sitting up and pawing the air, he begged for pasty. Mr. LaTournay rewarded his antics with bits of meat, then took him down to the river for a drink.

When they returned, Georgette offered Mr. LaTournay the remaining strawberries. "I fear I have few skills that will be helpful on a farm. I cannot cook or milk a cow, and my sewing skills are merely adequate."

Settling back on the blanket, Mr. LaTournay lifted a brow, no doubt surprised by her abrupt comment. "My sister can teach you any household skills you wish to learn." He popped a berry into his mouth.

"Your sister lives on the farm?"

"Francine helps run the farm and estate." His long fingers fondled Caramel's ears.

"She is unmarried?"

"Francine recently married Jan Voorhees, our foreman; they live nearby on the property. She is my elder by two years. Before leaving home in the spring, I told her of my intent to marry. She will be pleased to have a sister. The main house will be ours alone, shared only with the servants. I hope to travel less often after we are married."

Georgette determined to make their home so pleasant he would never wish to leave.

⚘

When General Washington and his retinue arrived, an enthusiastic crowd greeted them. To Georgette's surprise, a member of the New York Provincial Congress introduced Mr. LaTournay to the officers. Mr. LaTournay was one of few men present tall enough to look General Washington in the eye while gripping his hand. The two men seemed to take each other's measure, and Georgette recognized reserved approval on both sides. Mr.

LaTournay was invited to join the group of dignitaries for a short reception at the nearby home of Lester Lispenard, a local brewer, but he graciously declined.

While the New York crowd waited for the parade to begin, Georgette and Mr. LaTournay wandered off a short distance and found a shady tree. Mr. LaTournay again shook out the picnic quilt and laid it upon the grass. Georgette flopped down too quickly to be graceful, dropped her parasol, and leaned her back against the tree trunk. Caramel watched the proceedings from his makeshift bed inside the empty picnic basket. He was a solid little dog, but Mr. LaTournay did not seem to mind carrying him.

"My father often speaks of your connections and influence, yet I remained ignorant of your true importance to this colony," Georgette said. Mr. LaTournay's apparent support for these traitors puzzled her.

"The importance of any farmer or merchant lies mainly in the commerce he undertakes. Do you mind if I remove my coat?"

Observing the sweat trickling down his face into his beard, she took pity. "No sir." She would have liked to remove her shoes. Mr. LaTournay laid his coat on the quilt and ran a finger beneath his cravat. "You may remove that also if you wish," Georgette said.

He whipped off the tie and opened his shirt at the neck. "Much better." He lay back on the quilt, folding his hands behind his head and crossing his ankles.

Georgette tried not to notice the wet patches on his waistcoat and shirt—or the flat expanse of his stomach. "I do not understand whether New York remains faithful to England or intends to join the rebellion."

He squinted at the sky through his lashes. "I wish I could tell you what New York will do, but I cannot read the future. God alone knows what will come."

More questions swirled through Georgette's mind, but she could not find words or courage to phrase them. Caramel snored in the basket. A louder snore informed her that Mr. LaTournay slept. Georgette leaned over to examine him. A pulse beat in his throat, revealed by his open collar. Her hands ached to touch him.

The flood of passion his proximity stirred had become familiar to Georgette, but this new camaraderie she felt for him took her by surprise. Could a husband be a friend? She enjoyed talking with him, being with him—and not always with romance in view.

Politics never concerned her in the past, yet recently she found the subject intriguing, no doubt due to Mr. LaTournay's influence. He seemed to hold himself aloof, as a dispassionate observer above the fray of political affairs.

Georgette felt confidence in his leadership. Although, now that she thought of it, she had no clear idea in which direction he intended to lead. Of course, Mr. LaTournay would never participate in treasonous acts. Of that much she felt certain. Perhaps his intent today was to become aware of the enemy's strengths and weaknesses through observation.

Noticing something, she peered closer. On the shaved skin at one side of his neck, what appeared to be a scar ran diagonally toward his chin, disappearing into the thick beard. The skin around it was slightly puckered. How had he acquired such a wound? Georgette would have liked to part his beard and see how far the scar extended. The thought of him sustaining painful injury caused her to frown.

Had they not been within easy sight of dozens of people, she might have been tempted to kiss him. How would he react? Her imaginings brought a wave of heat to her face.

Folding her arms over her middle, Georgette lay back against the tree and closed her eyes. The next thing she knew, a warm hand cupped her cheek. "Wake up, Georgette. The parade is about to begin."

She stirred and sat up abruptly. "What time is it?"

"An hour has passed while we dozed. Several additional militia companies have arrived." Mr. LaTournay was already wearing his coat and cravat, looking almost as neat and composed as ever. Caramel rambled about amid nearby shrubs, sniffing fascinating scents.

Georgette was still blinking sleepily when Mr. LaTournay took her hands and pulled her to her feet. She helped him fold the quilt and stash it into the basket. "Ready?" he asked as soon as she had settled her parasol over one shoulder. He plopped Caramel into the basket atop the quilt, and this time, instead of offering his arm, he reached out a hand. Despite her sweaty palms, Georgette clasped his hand and followed him back to the Lispenard mansion.

When they arrived, the parade was forming ranks. Mr. LaTournay gave Georgette a running commentary as it passed them. After the militia companies came the New York dignitaries, followed by the three Continental generals and their staffs. An honorary escort of Philadelphia's light horse came next, and the noisy crowd of New Yorkers fell in behind. Georgette found herself cheering for General Washington and the proud men in uniform, although she could not have told why. Perhaps the quiet dignity of Washington influenced her emotions—he was an awe-inspiring figure upon his prancing horse. And Mr. LaTournay seemed to respect him.

They followed the parade south along the riverbank into town, back to the common, and down Broadway. More people gathered to cheer as the parade passed. Georgette gripped Mr. LaTournay's hand, waving her folded parasol in the air. "I shall be quite hoarse and sunburned by the end of the day," she confessed laughingly. "The governor, whenever he arrives, will receive no cheering from me, I sadly fear."

The day was still warm, although evening approached. Long shadows of trees and buildings striped the road. Disheveled, sweaty, and happy, Georgette shouted to make herself heard. "This is like a holiday!"

Mr. LaTournay squeezed her hand and smiled. Pressed by people on all sides, Georgette nevertheless felt an emotional connection with him as though they were alone. The crowds provided opportunity to jostle against him without appearing obviously brazen.

"LaTournay!" A man elbowed his way through the throngs, waving and hollering. "What are you doing in this mélange?"

Chapter 7

The LORD lifteth up the meek:
he casteth the wicked down to the ground.
PSALM 147:6

Les Pringle gripped Mr. LaTournay and Georgette each by the shoulder and halted them in the middle of the boulevard. "Miss Grenville is waiting just over there. She spotted Miss Talbot's parasol, though I didn't believe her at first. Come out of this farcical parade and join us! The governor delayed his arrival out of pure politeness; he lands at eight o'clock. We've plenty of time to get over to the slip and greet him."

People bumped Georgette in passing, and one man shouted for them to stop blocking the way. Still, she was surprised when Mr. LaTournay followed Mr. Pringle's orders and shepherded her to the east side of the road.

Marianne greeted her with a hug. "Gigi! We looked for you two all over town and began to think you decided not to come. You're wearing your green sprig—I adore that gown!" She greeted Mr. LaTournay, saw the dog in his basket and wrinkled her nose in distaste, but made no comment. "What happened to you two? However did you get caught up in that pandemonium? We saw those uniformed men posing as officers. Is it not disgraceful? Mr. Pringle and I decided they are all decidedly gauche—especially the gaunt fellow with the pack of dogs following his horse."

"That would be General Charles Lee, late of His Majesty's army," Mr. LaTournay said.

Mr. Pringle spat on the ground. "His Majesty is well rid of the scoundrel."

"I think General Washington is a magnificent man," Georgette said. "I do not say that I think he is behaving wisely, but—"

"General? He is naught but Mr. Washington, and never forget

it," Mr. Pringle interrupted. "Come to Fraunces' Tavern with us for supper and a drink." He gripped each of the young women by the arm. "Miss Grenville's parents have given their permission. I cannot imagine Miss Talbot's parents objecting."

Although Mr. Pringle maintained eye contact with Marianne, Georgette felt his thumb caressing her wrist. She pulled out of his grasp and linked hands with Mr. LaTournay again, gripping his arm for extra protection. Had her fiancé noticed? His bland expression told her nothing.

Mr. LaTournay bent to speak into her ear. "Washington's parade is nearly over anyway. Are you hungry?"

"Not hungry, but very thirsty," she admitted. "We must take Caramel home." Georgette felt somewhat guilty about her disinterest in Marianne's company, but she would have preferred to spend the remainder of the day alone with Mr. LaTournay.

He turned to the others. "We shall join you. Thank you for the invitation. First, if you will pardon the delay, I need to leave this basket at my boardinghouse. We shall take the dog home after our meal."

Mr. LaTournay's boardinghouse was located on Broadway near Trinity Church. Georgette followed Mr. Pringle and Marianne into the parlor and seated herself on a worn chair. Caramel curled up on her lap. Georgette wondered why a man of LaTournay's wealth and reputation would choose this particular boardinghouse. It seemed clean and genteel but far from luxurious. The parlor rug showed evidence of wear.

Mr. Pringle and Marianne conversed in low tones across the room, ignoring her. Marianne seemed to lose her good sense and manners in that man's presence.

The landlady popped in and straightened a vase of flowers, all the while studying Mr. LaTournay's guests. "He's never brought people here before," she said to Georgette as if excusing her curiosity. "I always wondered if he had any friends besides his servant. He seems such a good man. 'Tis a pleasure to know he's found a fine lady to wife."

When Mr. LaTournay reappeared, Georgette felt certain he—

in record time—had washed up and changed clothing. He smelled fresh; she smelled like a dustrag.

He took Caramel from her and tucked the dog under one arm. She looked up at him. "You have carried him and that basket much of the day; your arms must ache."

A smile curled the corners of his mustache. "He weighs no more than fifteen pounds." He started to say more but appeared to reconsider. "Shall we go?"

During their light supper at the tavern, Georgette caught herself yawning. Her dog slept under the table, too tired even for begging. Feeling Mr. LaTournay's gaze, she looked up and smiled. "An excess of sun and exercise has fatigued both Caramel and me, I fear."

"You will have need of a wrap before the evening ends," he said. His warm regard gave her the desire to rest her head on his shoulder.

"Should have covered up better earlier today," Mr. Pringle remarked. He reached across the table and pressed three fingers into her skin. "Look at that—she is sunburned. What a pity."

Georgette jerked her arm away. Mr. Pringle's blue eyes mocked her.

"Georgette has flawless skin. A touch of pink won't hurt this once," Marianne said. "I hope it doesn't hurt, Gigi, but at least you don't freckle."

Georgette attempted to smile, inwardly seething. If that man touched her once more, she would kick him in the shin.

When they reached the Talbots' town house, Mr. Pringle joined Mr. LaTournay in the parlor while Marianne followed Georgette upstairs. Caramel hopped upon the bed and curled into a ball.

Georgette dropped her bonnet beside him. "Ugh, my gown is full of road dust." She gave her skirts a shake. "And neither Biddy nor Agnes is here today."

"I shall be pleased to brush it for you." Marianne unbuttoned Georgette's gown and helped her climb out of its folds. "You must have walked far today to get this dusty." She waved one hand before her face as if to dispel a cloud.

"We walked up the shore to meet the generals. You are a dear to do this for me. We shall probably meet my parents at the landing. They admire Governor Tryon." Georgette pulled out her hairpins and tried to brush dust from her hair.

"So do mine." Marianne paused with the clothes brush poised over Georgette's gown. "Gigi, are you certain Mr. LaTournay is a loyal subject of the king? At times he says things that make me uncomfortable."

Coming from Marianne, the implication annoyed Georgette. "Mr. LaTournay studies all sides of an issue before making a decision. He says we should listen and learn from men wiser than ourselves. He is admired throughout the province, Marianne." She almost told her friend that he had been introduced to General Washington but reconsidered. Marianne would not understand the tacit honor.

"I am pleased to see how fond you have become of Mr. LaTournay, dear Gigi, but I do wish you would be more discreet. You cannot know how it affects a man to have a woman touch him. Holding his hand may mean nothing to you, but that contact can mean unimaginable temptation to a gentleman, my mother says."

"If this is true, try keeping an eye on that man of yours," Georgette growled around the hairpin she held between her teeth.

A crease formed between Marianne's brows while she vigorously brushed at the gown. "Be patient with Mr. Pringle, and give the Lord time to work."

"You do not plan to marry him, I trust." Georgette stopped brushing her hair long enough to study her friend's face. "He is not good enough for you."

Marianne smiled. "You need not worry, Gigi, although you are sweet to care. I could never marry a man who did not love my Lord Jesus. Mr. Pringle knows this."

"He is insincere."

"He is a flirt," Marianne said. To Georgette's surprise, her friend's expression revealed indulgent amusement. "He tells me he originally sought me out because he heard that my father was wealthy. You see, his family business in Boston has come into hard times. But now Mr. Pringle has worked everything out with my father, who bought into the Pringle shipping business as a partner. Papa says he would rather be business partners with his future son-in-law than with anyone else."

Georgette felt stunned. "Your father has taken partnership in a failing business? Was that wise?"

"They have signed a contract with the army using Pringle ships and warehouses, you see. Papa knows a good business transaction when he sees one. Besides, he recognizes Mr. Pringle's skill with numbers and money. Mr. Pringle is smart and hardworking. He is dedicated to England and has nothing good to say about these traitors who are trying to destroy the empire. His current goal is to catch an informant they call the Frog, an infamous traitor they have reason to believe makes this city his center of operation."

"The Frog? What a ludicrous title!" Georgette's hair crackled with each stroke of the brush.

"Mr. Pringle says he is slippery and always one jump ahead," Marianne said with a smile. "I do not know who first thought up the epithet, but it seems to suit this slimy traitor. He wears a dark cloak and never shows his face. Some say he is an insane French soldier who believes he is still fighting the last war. Whatever and whoever he is, Mr. Pringle says he must be stopped."

Georgette's arm paused in midair. "Oh?"

"Mr. Pringle and two other men have set a trap to catch the Frog. Something to do with ammunition stores up in White Plains. For Mr. Pringle's sake, I pray they are successful. How he hates the rebels! Did you see his eyes flash at the mere mention of Washington? And, oh Gigi, the truth is I love him. He makes me feel special and beautiful. When I look into his wondrous blue eyes, nothing else in the world matters at all."

"I would not have thought he could appreciate you, dear Marianne." Georgette's arm felt limp. She let it drop to her side.

"It is amazing, the changes God can make in a man's heart—or a woman's," Marianne said. "I shall be happy with my reformed scoundrel, Gigi. I know his faults and love him dearly in spite of them."

Marianne chattered about Lester Pringle's virtues while Georgette gave herself a quick sponge bath behind a screen. Out of Marianne's sight, Georgette allowed her thoughts to wander. Surely this Frog could not be her mysterious admirer. Many men wore hooded cloaks; the coincidence was too unlikely.

Marianne helped her climb back into her gown, then fluffed its skirts. Georgette pinned up her own hair. "I hope you are right about Mr. Pringle, dear Marianne," she said softly. "I would hate to see you trapped in an unhappy marriage—you, the sweetest and most unselfish of all people!"

The men rose when their two young women entered the parlor. "Thank you for waiting." Georgette handed a silk shawl to Mr. LaTournay and turned for him to drape it over her shoulders. "I hope we are not too late for the governor's parade."

Mr. LaTournay glanced at the mantel clock. "We should arrive in time. It is just down the street."

◇

Governor Tryon, a fine-looking man of military bearing, climbed the slip's steps to the foot of Broad Street and glanced around at the respectable crowd waiting to greet him. With the rest of the Loyalist crowd, Marianne and Mr. Pringle put gusto into their hurrahs. Georgette cheered hoarsely once, then fell silent, studying the people around her. Catching sight of her parents, she waved. Her mother waved back, looking more like a young girl than a matron of forty-two. Her father, on the other hand, had aged during recent months.

A salty evening breeze tugged at Georgette's bonnet. She gripped her shawl at her throat and shivered. Recalling Marianne's observation about Mr. LaTournay, she studied his face while the governor briefly addressed the crowd. He had not cheered for Tryon, but she could not recall hearing him cheer for the generals either. Though he appeared to listen to the governor's speech, his gaze roved constantly. He seemed troubled.

Had Mr. Pringle told him about the Frog?

What would she do if Mr. Pringle captured her hero? Worse yet, what if Mr. LaTournay became involved in the pursuit? How unthinkable that her dashing admirer should be hanged or shot as a spy!

Governor Tryon and his party headed up Broad Street. Georgette turned to Mr. LaTournay. "The governor looks unhappy."

Before Mr. LaTournay could reply, Mr. Pringle rounded upon her. "And how would you feel, knowing that your city had just finished giving your opposition a welcoming parade? Did you expect him to look gratified that New York is under the control of a pack of scoundrels? He will soon set things right and punish that rabble the way he put down the Regulators when he was governor of North Carolina. You two took a risk, being seen with that mob today."

"I think not." Mr. LaTournay's voice sounded flat. "I saw Loyalist leaders in the throng."

Mr. Pringle's blue eyes glittered. "Did you hear the news about the battle in Boston? His Majesty's troops gave that rabble militia a good thrashing and chased them off Charlestown Neck. Boston is ours again. Now Pringle Shipping can resume business and life will return to normal."

"I hope your business improves," Mr. LaTournay said.

"I am certain Mr. Grenville will also be pleased to hear the news," Georgette remarked, "since he is now a partner in your family firm. Is it true that—?"

But Mr. Pringle had already turned aside to address Marianne. Embarrassed, Georgette fell silent.

"Is what true?" Mr. LaTournay asked quietly.

"Marianne said something about Pringle Shipping signing a contract with the army. If that is true, I imagine Mr. Pringle's financial worries must now be at an end."

Mr. LaTournay looked thoughtful.

"Has he told you about the Frog?" she asked.

He focused on her face, his brow furrowed. "I believe I misunderstood. Please repeat your question."

"Has Mr. Pringle told you about the spy he intends to catch? I thought you might know about this man they call the Frog. Marianne told me of plans to trap him."

Mr. Pringle and Marianne started to join the crowd trailing the governor's retinue, then stopped and looked back. "Are you two coming?" Marianne asked.

"To be honest, since we are so near my house, I thought perhaps I would forgo this parade," Georgette said. "Please enjoy it without me." Her feet ached now even when she stood still.

"But I told my mother you and Mr. LaTournay would be with us this evening," Marianne said. "It is unseemly for me to be out alone at night with a gentleman. Did any of you happen to see my parents pass us?"

Georgette thought she saw Mr. Pringle roll his eyes, but a moment later, he spoke reassuringly. "You will be safe with me, dearest. I am well able to protect you, if need be."

"Would you feel better, Miss Grenville, if I were to accompany you and Mr. Pringle until he leaves you at your parents' doorstep?" Mr. LaTournay offered. "I promise to be unobtrusive."

A fleeting smile touched Marianne's lips, and her lashes fluttered. Georgette could only imagine the exultation her friend must feel at the prospect of being escorted about the city by two prominent bachelors. At the moment, Georgette's feet hurt too much for her to begrudge Marianne the pleasure.

"I hardly think a chaperone will be necessary." Smiling, Mr. Pringle spoke between clenched teeth.

"I propose that you discuss the matter while we return to my house," Georgette suggested brightly. "This breeze is cool, and it begins to grow dark."

Mr. LaTournay offered her his arm. Behind them, Mr. Pringle and Marianne fell into step, arguing in muted tones. "Do you approve of my offer?" Mr. LaTournay asked quietly.

"With all my heart. I do not trust that man alone with Marianne at night."

He nodded. "I warned him away from you earlier. If he annoys you again, inform me immediately."

Georgette looked up at his shadowy face. "Thank you." Did

anything escape his notice? "I enjoyed this day."

"I am gratified to hear it. I hope our future together will hold many more such days." He placed his hand over hers as they climbed the steps of her town house.

Again Georgette wished they were alone. He might have kissed her in the garden once more had Mr. Pringle and Marianne not joined their party.

"Business will take me out of the city these coming weeks. Use your time to prepare for our new life together." He pressed a quick kiss onto Georgette's hand. "Miss Talbot, if ever it seems I neglect you, know that such is my duty, not my desire."

Emotion filled her throat and prevented any reply. If only his stilted words rang true!

He descended the steps and joined the others. Georgette watched as Marianne took the arms of both her escorts. Their voices and laughter floated on a summer breeze.

༄

Caramel's growls awakened Georgette. Lying on her back, half asleep, she wondered what had disturbed the pug. A rattling at her window brought Caramel to his feet with a *woof.* Was it raining?

Georgette climbed out of bed, pulling on her bedgown as she crossed to the window. The night was clear and bright. A cloaked figure stood in the pool of light beneath a streetlamp.

For an instant Georgette's blood ran cold. Her teeth began to chatter, and she clutched her gown at her throat. What to do?

Her feet took charge, carrying her swiftly downstairs and into the garden. Like a wraith, he emerged from the shadows. "I—I told you never to return," she gasped, still clasping both hands beneath her chin.

"I saw you at the parade today, petite grenouille, and my heart bade me try once more. Tell me you care naught for this LaTournay, this Loyalist fool."

Georgette's heartbeat thundered in her ears. That ardent voice aroused terrifying passions. "But I do care for him. I love him. Oh, how can you do this to me? It is true then—you are the

Frog? They say you are insane with hatred for the English, so how can you care for me?"

"If I am insane, it is for love of you, *charmeuse*. How can you love that—that stick, that empty shell whose tongue falters unless it speaks of government, profit, and taxation? Faugh!" Turning away, he strode to a raised flower bed, propped one booted foot on its edge, and leaned his forearm on his knee.

"You do not know him as I do," Georgette replied. His derogatory words about Mr. LaTournay cooled her ardor, arousing her protective instincts. "I want you to go. But first, because you have demonstrated kindness to me in the past, I must take this opportunity to return the favor."

The hooded head turned toward her. How tall he was, and such breadth of shoulder! She would have noticed so fine a man at the parade had she not been engrossed with Mr. LaTournay.

"Some Loyalists plan to set a trap for you. I know only that it concerns weapons or something stored in White Plains. Please, please, if you truly love me, forsake this conspiracy against the king and return to a quiet life at...wherever you come from."

When at last he spoke, his deep voice purred. "You do care, ma belle. Someday your *amoureux* shall be free to love you as you so richly deserve. Do not again risk your safety for my sake, bien-aimée."

He straightened, and she took a step closer, hands pressed to her cheeks as if to stifle improper behavior. "Will I see you again?"

"You have forbidden it."

"I am to marry Mr. LaTournay."

"If I am fated to worship from afar, then God's will be done. I shall never covet another man's wife. Adieu, Georgette."

A moment later she saw a dark shape atop the garden wall. Something landed at her feet. She bent to pick it up—a fragrant rose. When she looked up, he was gone.

Chapter 8

*It is good that a man should both hope
and quietly wait for the salvation of the Lord.*
LAMENTATIONS 3:26

After checking the identity of the visitor through a parlor window, Georgette hurried to answer a knock at the front door. "Marianne, dearest! It has been so long, nearly all summer since I saw you last." She pulled the smiling girl into the entryway and overwhelmed her with hugs. "I had feared never to see you again! I was told that your father returned to Long Island, to your family estate, while you and your mother took refuge upon a ship."

"We did, Gigi, but we plan to stay aboard only until this present crisis ends. Mama wanted to go with Papa, but he says it is not yet safe. Loyalists on Long Island are even more persecuted than we are here in the city. Today Mama and I came ashore to purchase fresh food. I begged leave to visit you, and here I am."

"Come sit down, and I shall ask Biddy to prepare coffee since we have no more tea. I baked cinnamon cakes this morning." Georgette led the way.

"You baked them? How charming!" Marianne seemed impressed.

"Biddy has been teaching me to cook and sew. I wish to be an excellent wife."

Caramel frisked about their skirts as they entered the drawing room. Georgette knew Marianne disliked animals, and it amused her to see the other girl attempt to ignore the pug's overtures of friendship.

"Caramel, come. Sit." The dog rolled to his back, but that was close enough.

"You have lost weight, Gigi. Are you well?"

"I am well enough. It is the strain. You know." Georgette gave her a significant look, and Marianne nodded. She did not need to know that Georgette's greatest strain was caused not by the threat of war but by Mr. LaTournay's extended absence. In the past month she had seen him only twice, and those visits were brief and prosaic. Her father frequently expressed the irate conviction that LaTournay's passion for Georgette had cooled, as if it were her fault.

"Tell me, how is your family? Do you see Mr. Pringle often?" In the drawing room, Georgette rang for Biddy.

"Mr. Pringle comes on a boat to visit me." Marianne's voice was too bright, and color filled her cheeks. "Papa has invited him to stay at our estate." She spread her yellow skirts on the settee. "Your wedding day rapidly approaches. Are you ready?"

"We are. It breaks my mother's heart to forgo the large reception she envisioned, but in these uncertain times, a quiet ceremony seems best."

"I am sorry for that, though I believe you are wise. May I see your gown?"

"You may. I would have liked to wear my mother's gown, but it is far away across the sea. We had this one made. It is simple brocade and satin with touches of Brussels lace at the. . .never mind. You will see it after we drink our coffee."

Biddy arrived, pushing a laden teacart. The aroma of coffee preceded her. "Why, thank you, Biddy. You anticipated our need. That will be all," Georgette said, and the elderly maid withdrew.

"Of our servants, only Biddy remains. My parents expect to sail back to England immediately after the wedding." Georgette poured the coffee and served her friend. "But I am content to travel north and leave all this talk of war behind. You will be pleased to hear that Mr. LaTournay is studying his Bible. Is that not marvelous?"

"Has he prayed to receive Christ's salvation?"

"He is a Christian. Although I do not know him well as yet, I am certain we are admirably suited. What about you, dearest? You do not seem happy."

Marianne twisted the folds of her skirt.

"What has happened? Is it Mr. Pringle? I heard unhappiness in your voice when you spoke of him earlier. Tell me," Georgette urged.

"I believe. . ." Marianne bit her lower lip and blinked hard. "I believe you were correct in your assessment of Mr. Pringle when you warned me of his insincerity. I blush to confess my wicked suspicions, but at the time I thought perhaps you were jealous that I had secured his affection. After all, he is most handsome, and at one time you thought Mr. LaTournay ugly."

The memory of her lies burned Georgette's cheeks. "What has Mr. Pringle done?"

"I sometimes hear him abuse the Lord's name, and his habit of flirting with every woman he meets has not abated with time. I tried to overlook these things, thinking the Lord would change him, but time has brought no alteration. He becomes irritable if I mention them to him, and he reminds me how faithfully he attends church. . .though he sleeps through every service. He also. . ." Her voice trailed away, and her eyes studied the floor.

Georgette patted her hand. "No need to tell me more, dear, if it makes you uncomfortable."

"But I must speak of it. I think my heart is breaking, Gigi. I did not realize how deeply I cared for him until I saw how little he truly cares for me. Mr. Pringle dotes upon me when we are together, yet I fear he forgets me as soon as we are apart. And. . . he prevailed upon me to. . . Oh Gigi, I am so ashamed! I must marry him now, for I allowed him to kiss my lips. There. I have told you. After all my lectures to you about propriety, I have given my first kiss to a man who cares nothing for me! You must think me a woeful hypocrite."

Georgette's heart melted. "I am sure God will forgive you a momentary lapse of restraint. You will find a man worthy of your love, and Mr. Pringle will then be but a sorry memory. He is worthy of neither your love nor your regret. And your humility only makes me love you more. I am not so spotless that I should look upon you with disdain!"

No one else would ever know how often Georgette lay awake

in bed at night remembering the heartbeat of her secret lover against her palms and his proclamations of undying devotion. Her pulse throbbed at any mention of revolutionary activities; always she wondered if the Frog might be involved, and she prayed daily for his safety.

Marianne shook her head. "No, I shall never find a man I could love more than Mr. Pringle. Plans are under way for our marriage, Gigi. I hope I shall have your blessing. You, of all people, know what it is to love a man despite his lack of moral principle."

"Dearest Marianne!" Wishing she had listened more and spoken less, Georgette embraced her friend.

⁂

Studying Pringle's face across from the coffeehouse table, LaTournay decided his companion had lost flesh. His cheekbones protruded, and a day's growth of beard shadowed his chin. His blue eyes still flashed when he spoke of recent atrocities committed against His Royal Majesty's sovereign property. "If the Provincial Congress truly intended to replace the *Asia*'s burned boat, it would have been done by now."

LaTournay sipped his coffee and swirled the dregs in his cup. "The carpenters building the second replacement boat say they were threatened."

"Precious little has been done to identify the culprits responsible for destroying both the boat and its first replacement." Pringle seemed to pulse with restrained energy. His leg jiggled beneath the table, vibrating the seat of every patron sharing his bench. "You cannot convince me that Sears and the other delegates do not know."

"If they do know, they are not telling."

Pringle's fingers drummed on the tabletop. "I want to know what they are thinking. What are they planning?"

"What makes you believe they are planning anything?"

"The very air holds tension. I have heard rumors—but then, it is not my place to speak. You will tell me if you hear anything suspicious? So far, every news item I have passed on to my superiors is old news by the time I give it."

"It cannot be profitable employment. Why have you not returned to Boston now that it is safely occupied?"

"Safely? I think not. Those raiders never sleep—burning warehouses, stealing weapons caches, taking shots at the army's guards. They must have ears everywhere."

"His Majesty's troops are invaders on foreign soil. Every tavern keeper, every serving maid, every errand boy is potentially their enemy."

Pringle sniffed. "This is civil war, not an invasion, but otherwise your observations are correct."

"You avoided my question. Why not return to Boston?"

"This life is more exciting." A hard light shone in his eyes. "We have information that may soon lead us to the Frog."

"I seem to recall hearing that exact claim more than once before."

Pringle swore. "He must have ears on every street corner."

"What has the amphibious fellow done to incite such antipathy?" LaTournay inquired. "Refuse to croak?"

Pringle apparently missed the jibe. "He cheats. Deceives. Pretends to be something he is not. I am determined to see that slippery wretch dangle from the end of a rope before I am through. I can think of no lower form of life than a spy."

"I understood you were doing investigative work for that colonel."

Pringle blinked. "Yes, but there is vast difference between a man working on behalf of the king and a traitor passing information that reveals His Majesty's army's plans to the enemy."

"I see."

After a short pause, Pringle added, "Besides, I cannot leave while Miss Grenville is aboard ship in the harbor. Her parents are planning our wedding."

"And you? Will you marry her?"

Pringle rubbed one hand down his face. "I cannot say. It should have been easy to discard the freckled creature as soon as Pringle Shipping rose from the ashes, and yet. . ." His sober expression darkened into a scowl. "There is the Grenville estate on Long Island to consider. Fine property. Slightly too rural for convenience, but its income is considerable. I am an unreformed character, mind you. No religion for me. If Miss Grenville loves me as she claims, she will take me as I am. I neither make nor demand assurances of undying fidelity."

"Marriage requires more than you are willing to give, Pringle. For Miss Grenville's sake, you should disappear and never look upon her again."

"Tell me not that you have confessed your entire past to Miss Frogface, for I shall believe none of it," Pringle mocked, visibly stung by the suggestion. "I am more honest than you, for I make no promises that I do not intend to keep." He grimaced. "Frogface. Frogs are my plague, it seems. First that slimy spy eludes my detection, and now this large-mouthed lady steals away my friend. Two of a kind they are, both destroying my happiness. I would introduce them if I could and thereby rescue you from a tragic fate. You still want me to stand up for you while you don your ball and chain next week?"

"I depend upon it. The Talbots will take ship the following day. My wife and I shall start north as soon as possible."

Pringle blurted an oath and slapped the table. "A shame it is to remove your strategic brain from the city at a time such as this. For a man with so many connections and so much influence to be wary of involvement in political affairs—it is beyond reason. The loyal citizens of New York need someone to follow, someone to help them resist and overthrow these Whig idiots. You could be that man, LaTournay. They trust you and would follow without question."

"If you believe that, Pringle, you have scant knowledge of human nature."

❧

The following day, LaTournay walked along the streets of New York, noting its atmosphere of suspense. Conditions had deteriorated during his absence. Furtive glances, hurried transactions, abandoned shops, light traffic for a fine Wednesday morning in August—the city seemed to hold its breath in fear. He had delayed too long, yet the prolonged assignation had been unavoidable.

His pace increased. Would Georgette be angry or pleased to see him? Ten days until their wedding. She undoubtedly suspected him of abandoning her. At times even he had wondered whether he would return. The wisest move would be to ship her back to England and sail after her once this conflict ended.

Mounting the front steps in two bounds, he pounded the knocker. Someone had scribbled a symbol over the door, and another ill-advised person had evidently tried to expunge it. Smeared charcoal looked even worse than the original artwork.

"Oh Mr. LaTournay, I cannot tell you how relieved we are to see you!" Lucille Talbot clutched his sleeve and towed him into the house. "Where have you been? Georgette could tell us only that you were away on business, but what sort of business would take you from town for so long? We are in an uproar. Mr. Talbot found a merchant ship that is due to sail to England before the scheduled wedding date, and he wants to board her now."

"Why is that?"

"It is no longer safe for us here, and Mr. Talbot swears he will not remain another week. Georgette kept telling us to wait for your advice, but you were not here to advise us, so we thought it best to pack."

Frederick Talbot joined them in the drawing room. Bags underlined his resentful eyes. "LaTournay. Hmph. We began to think you would leave our daughter at the altar." He managed to produce a fatherly tone of concern.

"And I wondered if you might be imprisoned. Have you been asked to be an officer in the traitorous army?" Lucille inquired. "I hear they have asked the sons of every important family in town. Winthrop Hardcastle, bless his heart, swore that if he were to take a commission in any army, it would be England's! My friend Myrtle Hardcastle is vastly proud of her son—yet now he has been thrown into prison, and the rest of the family has taken refuge on the *Kingfisher*."

Talbot jumped in. "Which again brings up the question of Georgette. Mrs. Talbot and I plan to board ship as soon as possible. The *Lily Fair* leaves for England August thirtieth."

"I told him already," Lucille inserted.

"It means a precipitate wedding, if you still plan to marry our daughter."

"Mr. Talbot!" Lucille gasped. "Of course he still wishes to—" Her husband cut her off with a sharp gesture.

LaTournay studied their apprehensive faces. Their inability to return to England on any ship unless he purchased their passage remained unspoken. He disliked rewarding Talbot's manipulations, and yet. . . "If Miss Talbot is receptive to the plan, I shall not refuse."

Talbot's brow smoothed, and he beamed. "Come, my boy. Sit down and take some coffee. Lucille, pour for him."

LaTournay took a seat opposite Talbot and sipped sweetened coffee. Talbot was a well-informed man, affable and clever. However, his selfish disregard for others, particularly his wife and daughter, precluded any attachment on LaTournay's part.

The man fidgeted in his chair. "I favor summoning the parson here and finalizing the issue today. The banks and shipping offices are open many hours yet."

"Why the haste? Has anyone threatened you?" LaTournay asked. Greatly though he desired to marry Georgette, the suggestion of coercion galled him.

"Nay, but a mob of seamen has thrown stones in the windows of several nearby houses. They attack only those people known to be loyal to the Crown, and nearly everyone knows us."

"Someone used charcoal to draw a strange black figure above our doorway. It looks like a frog to me, though Frederick claims it is an *X*," Lucille added.

"I saw it," LaTournay said. "Although these mobs intimidate good citizens, I have heard of them harming no one."

"But—but—the ships!" Lucille sputtered. "At any time the warships could fire upon the city and kill us all. There has been provocation for such an attack many times over. I cannot imagine why Governor Tryon waits!"

"The warships' captains are well aware that many loyal British subjects still reside in the city, and the New York citizenry still supplies water and food to their crews. Despite the tough talk and posturing, it is highly unlikely that shots will be fired in the foreseeable future, Mrs. Talbot. A burned and gutted New York would be of no use to the British. Anyone can see that Manhattan Island could be taken at any time by a sizable landing force, for how could it be defended? The rebels have no way to prevent such an invasion. England can afford to be patient and wait for events in Boston to run their course."

"I care not what you say; it is a matter of time." Talbot leaped to his feet. "I'm off to fetch that parson. Lucille, you prepare the girl, and LaTournay, you know your part of the bargain."

Lucille put voice to LaTournay's thoughts. "Mr. Talbot, you truly intend to marry off Georgette this very day?" The mother sounded bereft.

"I do. No sense in delay."

LaTournay rose to his feet. "I must first speak with Miss Talbot."

"Fetch the girl, Lucille. Let us aim for four o'clock. That gives us time to finish packing afterward." Talbot donned his coat as he spoke.

When the front door closed behind him, Lucille and LaTournay exchanged looks. The woman's cheeks and lips were colorless. "What shall we do?" she whispered.

"Georgette must be informed. Where is she?"

"In the garden, reading, I believe. I should have called her when you first arrived, but Mr. Talbot would not—"

"I shall go to her." He gave Lucille a pat on the shoulder. She burst into tears as he left the room.

He opened the garden door and stepped outside. The tableau he viewed brought a smile to his face and ease to his heart. Yes, without doubt, he wished to take Georgette Talbot as his wife.

She lay on her belly in the grass, engrossed in a book, her chin propped on one hand. A golden braid trailed along her shoulder and looped over a sleeping Caramel. Once again she had evidently dispensed with hoops, stays, bonnet, and shoes.

"Miss Talbot." He spoke softly, but she gave a little shriek and rolled to her back, staring up at him over the edge of the book clutched between her hands. Too late she tucked her feet beneath her skirts. Caramel sat up, blinking. The dog yawned, spotted LaTournay, and trotted over to greet him.

"Mr. LaTournay!" She closed the book, laid it on the grass, and sat up. "We—we were not expecting you today."

"Nevertheless, you have me today." He approached to offer assistance. She regarded his hands before placing hers within them. He hauled her up and gripped her elbows when she would have stepped away. "I must speak with you upon an urgent matter."

Her brown eyes studied his face, and she nodded.

"Your father wishes us to marry today instead of waiting until September second. I am willing, but I would not rush you. You do understand that your parents intend to return to England immediately?"

Her attempt to draw breath resulted in several quick sobbing gasps. "Marry to—today?" He watched her eyelids flicker as she stared at the wall behind him. Abruptly, she covered her mouth with one hand and turned away. Her braid hung down her back like a thick rope, its sway reminding him of a horse's tail.

"Miss Talbot, you doubtless know that your father's conditions for our marriage included the purchase of their passage home." He attempted to clear his throat, but the lump remained, splintering his voice. "I want you to know that, if you prefer not to marry me now or ever, I am willing to purchase passage for you as well as for your parents. I desire your safety and happiness above all else."

Her reply, spoken between her fingers, scarcely reached his ears. "I am ready to make my new life with you, Mr. LaTournay."

The volatile mixture of joy and guilt felt like an explosion in his heart. "You do not understand what this new life might entail."

She folded her arms tightly, and he saw the outline of her shoulder blades through the fabric of her gown. Her voice sounded almost sharp. "Yet I do know that I want to share your future, whatever trials it may hold. God will be with us, blessing our love and commitment."

His chest heaved like a bellows, and his knees turned to jelly. "Love. Do you love me, Miss Talbot? You cannot even call me by my given name."

She spun around, followed by her swinging braid. Her eyes sparked. "When I commit my love and life to you, it will be for always, Jean-Maurice LaTournay."

His voice rasped. "So be it. I shall marry you, Georgette, and leave God accountable for the outcome."

Chapter 9

For this cause shall a man leave his father and mother,
and shall be joined unto his wife, and they two shall be one flesh.
EPHESIANS 5:31

I do." Georgette spoke her vows and felt Mr. LaTournay's grip on her hand tighten. She cast a glance at his face. He swallowed hard, and his dark eyes glistened. Not once did his attention stray from the Reverend Mowbray's sermon. His tanned face made his beard and hair seem lighter—or perhaps they were sun-bleached. Whatever he had been doing these past many weeks, he had spent much time out-of-doors.

Georgette wanted to be angry with him for his secrecy. She wanted to be cold and unattainable and make him pay for his desertion. She wanted to dream of her mysterious lover and hope he would rescue her at the last moment. During the last days of Mr. LaTournay's absence, she had imagined spurning him upon his return. In her mind he groveled at her feet and begged her forgiveness, promising never to look upon another woman if Georgette would take him back.

How could a man be wicked yet appear honorable? Georgette had only to catch sight of him and her vengeful plans faded into oblivion.

At Georgette's left side, her mother sobbed into a handkerchief. Biddy stood nearby, gaunt and dignified in gray bombazine. Georgette could not see her father on the far side of Mr. LaTournay, though she heard him clear his throat. The Reverend Mowbray's gentle voice belied his long, wrinkled face.

Georgette's head ached. Sweat dampened her wedding gown. Did Mr. LaTournay even notice her gown? She had hoped his eyes would brighten when she entered the drawing room. To her profound disappointment, he hardly glanced her way.

If only Marianne stood by her side. Marianne understood the

heartbreak of loving an undeserving man.

At the minister's cue, Mr. LaTournay slipped a ruby ring upon her finger. His hands shook. The froth of neck cloth above his waistcoat also trembled. Georgette dared not look higher. He was shaking! The imperturbable Mr. LaTournay quaked like a nervous lapdog.

The minister pronounced them husband and wife. For better or for worse, Georgette was officially Mistress Jean-Maurice Antoine LaTournay. Her husband faced her while the Reverend Mowbray prayed. Mr. LaTournay's thumbs caressed the backs of her hands, and she heard him draw a shuddering breath.

Wishing to reassure him, she laid her cheek on his knuckles, then pressed their entwined hands to her heart. With all her being, she wanted to care for him and bring him happiness. As soon as the prayer ended, he would read her devotion in her eyes.

But when the minister closed his benediction, Georgette's father gripped Mr. LaTournay's arm and pulled him aside. Both men signed and sealed documents. Georgette watched as her new husband placed a wrapped parcel in her father's outstretched palm. Her father's eyes held an avaricious gleam.

Her mother tugged at her arm. "Do not embarrass your father, Georgette. His pride is injured enough without you watching this transaction. He would have preferred offering a dowry for you to accepting a bride price."

Although Georgette suspected the reverse, she obediently looked away. The warmth began to drain from her heart.

"Now that that is over, we'll have Georgette's trunk loaded into the carriage." Her father clapped his son-in-law on the shoulder and winked at Georgette. "Unless you plan to stay here tonight. You two might assist with our travel preparations since you'll have nothing better to do."

The more jocular her father became, the colder Mr. LaTournay's response. "We shall lodge at my boardinghouse."

The realization that she was leaving her parents' home, never to return, struck Georgette to the heart. She looked at her mother's tearstained face, studied her father's smug expression, and felt like choking. Was this their final parting? And Juliette—would she ever see her sister again? "What about Caramel?" Her question ended on a sob.

Her father stared as if she had lost her senses. "Her dog," Mr. LaTournay explained. He took Georgette's clammy hand and squeezed it gently. "You and I shall travel north in a few days by horseback and river. I plan to send my man Noel ahead with our baggage. It will be easier for Caramel to travel with him. Noel is kind; Caramel will like him."

Georgette felt her jaw quiver. "He will be afraid. He will think I have deserted him."

"Not for long. Think how pleased he will be when you join him at Haven Farm. It would be best to leave him here overnight. Noel will collect him along with your remaining trunks in the morning."

"Yes, dear," her mother added, taking Georgette's other hand. "Biddy will be packing up your remaining belongings tonight. She will pack everything your pet will need, I am certain. You go ahead and leave everything to me."

"All this bother about a dog. Dump the beast in the river and have done," her father huffed. "I must drive the parson home now. Oh." He paused and pulled a folded note from his waistcoat. "Nearly forgot to give you this. It arrived this morning. From the Grenville girl. Good night, daughter. Be a good wife if you know how and make your husband happy. We shall speak our farewells on the morrow, I've no doubt."

Watching him escort the minister outside, Georgette wondered if her father had ever loved her.

The carriage driver stood in the hall just outside the parlor. "You got a trunk I should carry out?" He ducked his head in a bow and twisted his hat between his hands. His widening eyes took in Georgette's gown.

"The one in the hallway at the head of the stairs," her mother said.

Mr. LaTournay headed upstairs, and the driver stumped after him. "God's blessings on you and your new missus," Georgette overheard the burly man say. " 'Pears to me like you done married an angel."

Her mother closed the parlor door and embraced her. "Darling, I shall miss you so! I never wanted it to be this way. Juliette had a lovely wedding with many guests, but this!" Fresh sobs wracked her frame.

"It was not your doing, Mummy. I know you wanted a fancy wedding for me, but the husband matters far more than the ceremony. I do love my husband, and I believe we shall be happy together."

She broke the seal, unfolded her note, and read quickly.

Dearest Gigi,

My conscience will give me no rest since I visited you the other day. You must be told. Both my mother and I have seen Mr. LaTournay aboard this ship in the company of Lady Forester, once late at night, and never when her husband was near. Please do not hate me. My heart breaks for you as yours does for me.

Marianne

Georgette folded the note.

"What is wrong, dearest? Is Marianne unwell?"

Georgette handed her the letter. She scanned the page and sighed. "Alas, I had hoped you would not hear of this so soon."

Georgette gaped. "You knew? You knew and did not tell me?"

Her mother would not meet her gaze. "I feared you would refuse to marry him. You know how essential it is for your father and me to return to England, Georgette. Any further delay would ruin us. You must learn to tolerate men and their weaknesses, my dear. Such things are part of life. But you will find compensation if you seek it." She dabbed her tears away with a soggy handkerchief. "I always have."

Regaining control, she wagged a finger in Georgette's face. "Marriage is for babies and security. Love is another thing altogether."

Georgette wandered to the front window and stared out at the street. Her chest heaved in the effort to maintain control. Waves of heat rose from the cobblestones. Muggy air blanketed the city—it seemed worlds away from a crisp spring night, sparkling stars, and romance. Right there, beneath that streetlamp, the Frog had waited, looking up at her window. His avowal of undying love rang in her memory. She had sent him away forever. Even if by chance her mysterious hero were now to appear, he would be too late to rescue her.

✍

LaTournay stared blankly at passing buildings and trees as the hired carriage rolled along the street. Not until he spoke them aloud had the full meaning of his wedding vows struck home. *Until death do us part.* Would he have the chance to grow old with Georgette? Would ever the day come when she knew him fully and loved him without measure? Or would his entire life be a lie, a charade, lived in craven fear of her ultimate rejection?

Georgette deserved better.

He turned to regard his wife's profile and noted her pallor. "Georgette, are you well?"

She gave him a weak smile, and regret twisted in his gut. Her wedding day, yet she looked frightened and ill. "My head aches, likely due to the heat," she said. "When did you say we shall travel north?"

"If you are well enough, I had thought to leave Saturday morning. My business in town is complete." He forced his voice to remain calm and sympathetic. "If you wish, you might rest your head upon my shoulder."

Eyes closed, she relaxed against his shoulder. Despite his concern for her health, LaTournay felt excitement stir within him. For weeks and months, he had denied himself the pleasure of her embrace—had denied even the thought of her kisses. Duties had kept his mind and body occupied, and determination kept his imagination from straying into forbidden grounds.

Would she welcome his attentions?

His valet, Noel Dimieux, greeted them at the door to LaTournay's apartments. A smile nearly split the man's wrinkled brown face. Georgette acknowledged the introduction and thanked Noel for his congratulations. LaTournay ushered his wife into the sweltering sitting room. The windows stood wide but caught no ocean breezes. Moisture beaded on Georgette's pallid face and dampened the ringlets at her temples. Her hands trembled as she attempted to untie her bonnet strings.

"If you want to remove that gown, the bedchamber is beyond that door," LaTournay said before realizing how she might misunderstand. He tugged at his tightening collar. "Your trunk is there. If you like, I shall request to have a bath brought up."

Georgette nodded. "A bath would be nice."

ℒ

While Georgette bathed, LaTournay paced the sitting room, flopped into a chair, and rose to pace again.

Noel laid a light supper, then prepared to withdraw. He spoke in French. "A message left for you not yet an hour past, monsieur." He handed over a twisted paper.

With muttered thanks in the same language, LaTournay frowned as he untwisted the note. Its contents darkened his frown. *"Folie."* Crushing it in one hand, he tossed it upon the hearth.

He sensed Noel's regard but refused to acknowledge the silent inquiry. "That will be all, Noel."

"Oui, monsieur. God bless you and Madame LaTournay."

"What do you think of my wife?"

"Who could not approve such a fine woman, monsieur? *Très belle.* I now understand your determination to wed the lady." Noel failed to conceal a fatherly smile. "Be patient with her, monsieur. I believe she suffers from emotional exhaustion—a common malady of new brides."

"Ah." The unsolicited advice startled him, coming from reticent Noel. *"Merci."*

"I shall prepare your people at home for madam's arrival," Noel promised with a toothy grin. "And you may assure madam that I will attend her dog as if it were my own. I shall enjoy meeting the animal again. God's richest blessings on your marriage, monsieur."

For nearly an hour after Noel's departure, LaTournay read the newspaper, stared out the window, or paced. More than once he started to knock upon Georgette's chamber door, then reconsidered. At last he could wait no longer. "Georgette?"

Silence.

He opened the door. Evening shadows dimmed the small chamber, but he could see her clothing heaped upon the floor. Soap filmed the water in the unoccupied tub. Georgette lay prone upon the bed, clad in something white. Her golden hair cloaked her shoulders and most of her face. LaTournay knelt and touched her forehead. Damp and warm, but not feverish. He let his hand slide the length of her hair, down her back to her waist.

She moaned and her eyelids fluttered. "Mr. LaTournay. . .so sorry. My head. . ."

"Hush." He dipped a handkerchief in the tepid water in his basin, wrung it out, and pressed it upon her forehead. Soon she slept again, her expression more relaxed.

LaTournay ate a lonely supper of cheese, bread, and sliced fruit. While prowling about his apartments, he cast occasional glances at the activity in the lamp-lit street below. Though the hour grew late, men headed toward the southern tip of the island, singly and in groups. LaTournay shook his head, refusing to believe, and turned away.

Shouts from below brought him to the window again. What he saw raised the hair at his nape. Making no effort at concealment, dozens of men hauled cannons up Broadway, grunting and groaning as they dragged at the heavy ropes. In defiance of reason, the rebels proceeded with their plot to purloin British cannons from the Grand Battery at Fort George.

LaTournay checked on Georgette. Candlelight revealed her peaceful face, turned her hair to a curtain of gold, and shimmered amid the silken folds of her garment. She would not notice his brief absence. Better to be occupied than to brood upon his wife's temporarily inaccessible charms.

While changing into dark woolen garments, he pondered the repercussions to this provocative move by the Provincial

Congress. The British must be aware of the rebels' movements. Until now, they had displayed remarkable forbearance with the Americans, but blatant thievery of sovereign property was another matter.

Leaving his candle behind, he slipped into the dark hallway and down the stairs.

⟡

Boom! The first earthshaking explosion pierced Georgette's fuzzy dreams. Several more salvos in rapid succession brought her eyes wide open. Darkness met her gaze. Shouts of panic reached her ears. "What was that? Where am I?" she asked aloud, struggling to sit upright. "What time is it?"

She sat upon a bed, clad in the scanty satin chemise her mother had insisted would be ideal for her wedding night. Wedding. She was a married woman. Memories of the ceremony flitted through her mind.

At least her head no longer ached.

"Mr. LaTournay?" She dimly recalled him bathing her forehead with cool rags, but that was all. She must have fallen asleep.

A thin line of light showed beneath the door. He must be in the other room. She groped around in the dark but could not find a bedgown. No matter. What had caused the noise outside? Was the city under attack? No further explosions had ensued, but now drums began to pound. Someone inside the boardinghouse screamed, and Georgette's heart thudded.

"Jean-Maurice?" Shoving open the door, she almost fell into the sitting room. A candle burned upon a table in the deserted chamber.

Georgette rubbed her bare arms. Perhaps her husband had stepped outside for a moment. Surely he would not desert her on their wedding night. Taking the candle back to the bedchamber, she located her lace bedgown. Mr. LaTournay must have removed the tub and straightened the room while she slept.

She dared to peer down into the street through an open window. A number of large wheeled objects—cannons?—lined Broadway. Men appeared to be towing them north toward the common, using ropes. The streetlamps revealed other people throwing their possessions into wagons, handcarts, and wheelbarrows. Many rushed along the street. Voices and traffic blended into a cacophony. Mounted horses pushed through the crowds, endangering pedestrians. Fear thickened the night air.

Feeling helpless, Georgette plopped upon the settee, nibbled at her stale supper, and watched the candle burn low. Should she dress herself and prepare for flight? If she were in any danger, Mr. LaTournay would return for her. He might be fighting even now to save New York from annihilation. Haven Farm suddenly sounded like heaven. "We must leave this dreadful place," she told the candle.

Her eyelids drifted shut despite the commotion outside. She awakened with a cry as flashes illuminated the room and explosions shook the night. *Boom, boom, boom*—one after another, in seemingly endless succession. An eerie whistle and a crash, sounding horribly close, followed each shot. Clapping both hands over her ears, Georgette slid to the floor and sobbed in panic. "Lord God, save us!" Could this be the end of the world?

Quick steps rang on the hardwood floor and strong hands pulled her into a secure embrace. "Georgette." Mr. LaTournay spoke between the blasts, making fervent entreaties to God. Scratchy wool rubbed her forehead and shoulders as she burrowed into her husband's chest. Lying beside her on the rag rug, he sheltered her with his body.

At last the barrage ceased. Outside, the city's stunned populace continued to wail and shout. "What was it?" Georgette whispered. Her candle must have expired, for the room was dark.

"The *Asia*, I would guess, expressing her captain's displeasure concerning the removal of His Majesty's cannons from the Battery. Stay down, my dear. I shall check for possible fires." He scrambled to his feet, and Georgette immediately wished him back. His silhouette appeared at the window.

"I see no flames, and no alarm has been sounded. I imagine the purloined cannons will remain where they are for the present. It was a foolish attempt, at any rate."

"The *Asia* fired upon us? Upon our city? But why? We might have been killed!" Georgette could not stop trembling.

"And yet the Lord has preserved us this night, my wife. You shiver. Come to bed; I believe it will be safest to remain here for the night. Chaos reigns in the streets below. I returned to you with difficulty." He pulled her to her feet.

"But where did you go? You left me here alone?"

"I intended to step outside for only a moment. The folly of that plan is now clear to me, but at the time it seemed wise. You slept, and I meant to return before you knew of my absence. I apologize, Georgette. I was wrong to leave you unprotected."

"Why did you wait so long to return?" Her teeth chattered.

"I attempted to come back after the first shots were fired, but a crowd of panicked humanity pushing me in the opposite direction delayed my return. The ferries must be inundated."

"My parents! Are they safe?"

"We cannot tell until morning. You must entrust them to God's care." He put his arm across her shoulders and guided her toward the bedchamber.

"What time is it?"

"Past three o'clock." He turned back the coverlet while Georgette slipped off her bedgown. Although the room was dark, she felt shy about climbing into bed in his presence. He tucked the coverlet around her. "Warm enough?"

"Mr. LaTournay, were you in this city last week?"

A pause. "I was sometimes in the vicinity. Why do you ask?"

"You were seen visiting Lady Forester on one of the merchant ships." The strength of her own voice amazed her. The truth could not be worse than her doubts.

"I did not board the ship intending to visit her."

"Then why were you there?"

"Conducting business. I am a merchant; it was a merchant ship. I spoke to Lady Forester only of business." His voice held the ring of truth.

"If you were in the vicinity, why did you not visit me?" She tried but failed to sound unconcerned.

"I have labored to complete my work in this area so that I may enjoy many uninterrupted months at home with my wife during the winter. My desire would be never to return here, though I fear this will prove impossible." His voice deepened. "I dreamed of you every night, Georgette."

Her eyes closed as passion flooded her veins. She longed to believe him. This was no time to reconsider the consequences of her decisions. A godly wife had but one choice.

"Now I am here," she said. "Are you not coming to bed? You must sleep, too."

"If you wish it."

She heard the rustle of fabric and a moment later felt him slide beneath the coverlet beside her. Fear vanished, leaving breathless excitement in its wake. "I am sorry for falling asleep earlier. My head ached so, I could not bear it."

"It no longer aches?"

"Due to your tender care, Jean-Maurice. Will you hold me again?" She scooted over, and his eager arms drew her close.

❧

The following afternoon, Georgette's parents hugged her good-bye and shook hands with their new son-in-law. "So the warships will not fire upon New York in the foreseeable future, eh?" her father said, savoring Mr. LaTournay's error one last time. Georgette had lost count hours ago of repetitions on the same theme.

"I thought I should die of fear," her mother said. "If only we had taken ship yesterday! Mr. LaTournay, I trust you will hurriedly remove our daughter to safety. I shudder to think of her in this treacherous city."

"I shall endeavor to protect my wife to the best of my ability, Mrs. Talbot. We covet your prayers on our behalf."

"And you shall have them." She hugged Georgette one last time, then allowed her husband to help her into the *Lily Fair*'s boat. Burly seamen applied the oars, and the boat slipped into the open harbor.

Georgette wiped away fresh tears and waved until the tiny figures disappeared from her sight. "Will they be safe, do you think?"

"Safer than we are here." Mr. LaTournay slipped an arm around her waist. She leaned into his chest and let a few tears dampen his waistcoat, grateful for his strong embrace.

"I wish we could leave today for Haven Farm." She wanted away from this horrible city surrounded by warships. Away from the drilling militia and ranting newspapers. Away from other women who might try to steal her husband.

"Saturday will be better. We shall soon be home, my wife."

Although they stood on the slip in public view, Georgette pressed closer to his side. "May we return home now?"

"Home?"

"To our boardinghouse. My home is wherever you are."

He wrapped her in a warm hug. Georgette could not bother to worry about her husband's past nor concern herself about the future. The present was enough.

Chapter 10

Every wise woman buildeth her house:
but the foolish plucketh it down with her hands.
PROVERBS 14:1

We are nearly home. Do you see the house?" Mr. LaTournay pointed ahead. "The large white building surrounded by elms."

"I see it." After days of travel by boat and horseback, Georgette was more than ready to settle in at Haven Farm. However, the thought of meeting her new family while in this bedraggled state held little appeal.

"The house on our left belongs to my sister, Francine, and her husband, Jan. There she is—Francine!" Mr. LaTournay waved an arm above his head and urged his tired horse into a canter. Georgette's gray gelding followed.

The woman in the doorway waved back and ran toward them down the sloping green lawn surrounding her house. Two dogs barked and leaped about her skirts. A flock of geese ran honking in the opposite direction.

"I thought you would never get here!" she shouted. "Welcome to Haven Farm, Georgette!" As the horses slowed, Francine fell into step between them and laid her hand on Georgette's knee, beaming an irresistible smile. "Did you have a bon voyage? You must be exhausted! Yvonne—she is Noel's wife—has prepared supper up at the big house. First you can have a hot bath, and—"

"Is a brother now beneath your notice? Or am I invisible?" Mr. LaTournay demanded.

Francine turned. "Hello to you, too, Jean-Maurice. I hope your wife keeps you from wasting another winter." She gave Georgette a grin. "Georgette, I cannot express my gratitude to you for marrying *mon frère*. Jan and I thought he might pine himself to death last year on account of you."

266

Georgette gave Mr. LaTournay a startled glance. He rose in his stirrups to study something across the fields, ignoring the remark. "Would you like a quick tour of the farm on horseback?" he asked.

"I would prefer to see the farm another time. I am tired." That promised hot bath beckoned.

"Of course you are. Jean-Maurice is not thinking clearly. He should know better." Francine patted Georgette's horse. "A fine animal this is."

"Royal was a gift to me from Mr. LaTournay," Georgette said. "I am pleased to meet you, Francine." Her return greeting felt awkward, coming so late in the conversation.

Francine smiled up at her again. "I am pleased to have a sister after all these years. May I call you Georgie?"

Georgette tried to conceal her horror. "My friend Marianne calls me Gigi."

"Gigi? *Eh, bien.* My husband, Jan, asked me to extend his apologies for not greeting you yet; he will join us this evening." Francine gave Royal's sweaty neck another pat and stopped, allowing the horses to pass as she called after them. "I shall give you time to settle in, Gigi, but later you will tire of my company. Yvonne and I have joyfully anticipated the arrival of another woman!" She waved and trotted back toward her house.

"Francine seems an exuberant woman," Georgette observed. "I think I shall enjoy her company." She read approval in her husband's smile.

A young black man emerged from the barn to take the horses, greeting Mr. LaTournay in rapid French. He extended a sealed note.

Mr. LaTournay thrust the letter inside his waistcoat without a glance. "Thank you. Georgette, this is Pierre Dimieux, son of Noel and Yvonne. Pierre, my wife."

Pierre smiled, bowed, and spoke in perfect English. "Welcome, Mrs. LaTournay. I pray you will be happy here at Haven Farm."

Georgette nodded. "Thank you, Pierre."

Mr. LaTournay hopped lightly to the ground. "Please give the horses both a good rubdown tonight. The new gelding belongs to Mrs. LaTournay."

"Oui, monsieur. He is handsome." Pierre held the horse while Georgette dismounted. She handed over the reins with relief, wondering if she would ever again be able to walk normally.

Pierre questioned Mr. LaTournay in rapid French. This time her husband replied sharply in French. Pierre's expression darkened. Not for the first time, Georgette wished she knew more of the language.

As her husband took her arm and escorted her from the barn, she asked, "Is anything wrong?"

"Nothing that need concern you." He looked up at the house, and his face brightened. "Your home, Madame LaTournay."

Georgette thought it looked like a barn with windows, but she dared not voice that opinion. "I have never before seen such a house."

"It is gambrel style. Dutch. My grandfather built it." He reached inside to unlatch the lower half of the door.

"Why are the doors split in half?"

"So we can let light and air into the house without also allowing hogs, dogs, and geese inside. All the outer doors are that way." Suddenly he scooped her into his arms and pushed the door with his foot. Gasping at the suddenness of his move, Georgette clutched at his neck.

"Now this I like to see," a rich female voice said from inside the house.

"*Bonjour*, Yvonne." Mr. LaTournay sounded at once embarrassed and exultant. Georgette looked up to see a woman with dark skin, gray-streaked hair, and white teeth.

"*Très bien* to have you home, and the new madam, too!" The woman wiped her hands on her apron.

Mr. LaTournay set Georgette down, keeping one arm wrapped around her waist. "Georgette, meet our housekeeper and friend, Yvonne Dimieux. Yvonne, this is Georgette, my wife."

Georgette nodded. "I am pleased to meet you, Yvonne."

Yvonne bobbed a curtsy.

"Yvonne grew up in Tobago; she dislikes our northern winters. She is an excellent cook and housekeeper, so every autumn I must convince her to stay."

Yvonne grinned. "Liar that you are, monsieur. The Lord Jesus keeps me and Noel here with you. We will never go where He does not lead." Without pausing for breath, she added, "Bath water heats in the kitchen, and the tub awaits madam in her chamber. You speak the word, and I'll send the boys up with the hot water. The beds are turned, the linens fresh. I shall unpack for madam while she rests. I have something of hers in the kitchen. I'll bring it with me when I come upstairs."

"Merci, Yvonne."

All this French talk startled Georgette. Of course she had known that Mr. LaTournay spoke French, but now it seemed to flow from his tongue and accent even his English.

The housekeeper's dark eyes twinkled. "If you do not realize it already, madam, this husband of yours speaks only half his thoughts and even fewer of his feelings. You must make the man talk." With a nod and a wink, she whirled about and left.

Bemused by the advice, Georgette stared up at her husband's face.

Stepping back, Mr. LaTournay smiled. "Yvonne has wisdom to equal her remarkable intellect and a loving heart like none other. Now, be at home and do whatever you wish. This house is yours, Georgette. You have first bath. I shall join you upstairs later."

"You will read your letter?"

He seemed startled by the question. "Oui. The letter. I shall read it, of a certain."

❧

Yvonne delivered Georgette's possession to her bedchamber. "For you, madam. He was asleep on the hearth when you arrived."

"Caramel!" Georgette held out her arms.

The pug's floppy ears lifted at the sound of her voice, and he struggled to get down. As soon as Yvonne placed him on the floor, he yipped and spun in circles near Georgette's feet. "I do believe he is crying," Georgette said, attempting to hold the frantic dog. Tears of relief burned her eyes. The pug looked hearty and plump; Noel had truly been good to him. Georgette had trained Caramel not to lick her face; but when she picked him up, his tongue darted in and out near her cheek as if to taste the air.

Yvonne watched the reunion with an enigmatic smile. "He will be a piece of your past to soothe your heart," she said.

Georgette's first impressions of her new home were of large, clean rooms with wooden beams and white walls, immense fireplaces, and handsome furnishings. She felt pampered by Yvonne, who bathed her, combed out her hair, and helped her dress for supper as if she were a princess. She found the woman's stream of accented conversation soothing, laced with tales of Jean-Maurice and Francine as children. She helped Georgette unpack and arrange her clothing and possessions.

"*Voyons,* but you have lovely things!" Yvonne stepped back to admire her handiwork. The room looked bright and homey with Georgette's possessions scattered about. Caramel had already claimed the rug on the hearth.

"I hope there is room for Mr. LaTournay's things," Georgette said. "My gowns take up so much space."

"Monsieur uses the adjoining bedchamber as his dressing room. Never you worry," Yvonne said. "This house has rooms and to spare for you and a brood of children."

Georgette tried to ignore that last comment. "Does Noel help him dress?"

"The master claims no need of a valet when he is home, so Noel helps me keep the household in order. Come to supper when you are ready."

Yvonne opened the door to reveal Mr. LaTournay in the hallway. He stepped back, allowing the housekeeper to pass, then entered Georgette's room. Caramel gave him a cheerful greeting, rolling on his polished shoes to beg a belly rub.

"You look fine," Georgette said. Her husband had changed into a blue coat, brocaded waistcoat, and buff breeches. His unpowdered hair was brushed into a neat queue.

He scanned the room. "Does this bedchamber meet with your approval? You may choose another if it does not suit."

"It is most satisfactory. Of a certain, I must adjust to sleeping in a cave."

He glanced at the alcove bed. "It is warm in winter. You will see."

"I am sure I shall. I also see that I needn't have packed my featherbed. You must own many, since my bed frame already holds two." She crossed to the window and gazed upon rolling, forested hills and green pastureland already wearing a tint of autumn color. Cattle and sheep dotted the fields. "The view is particularly fine."

His hands slipped around her waist from behind, and she melted against his chest. His breath and lips against her temple brought a relieved sigh. As long as Mr. LaTournay loved her, she could endure.

"You are wonderful, my Georgette. They all love you, as I knew they would. Come, we must go down for our wedding supper. Yvonne has prepared a feast in your honor."

"She is kind, Jean-Maurice, as are Noel and Francine."

"Are your fears relieved?"

"Most of them. You will not leave me alone tonight?"

"You need to ask?" He kissed her before escorting her downstairs.

✍

The outside world seldom touched Georgette's little paradise of Haven Farm that autumn of 1775. She diligently applied herself to ignoring the few concerns marring her happiness. True, the town church's minister was an unabashed proponent of the rebel cause, but he seldom allowed his political views to color his sermons. Talk of war filtered through town, and Georgette knew of several local families whose sons had joined the traitorous army, yet these things she could disregard.

One afternoon in November, Francine dropped by to give Georgette a weaving lesson. "Before we settle down to work, I would really like a refreshment," Francine said, linking arms with her new sister. "I hear via family gossip that Yvonne is teaching you to cook and clean house." She stepped back to allow Georgette to enter the hall first, since their two hoop skirts could not simultaneously fit through the doorway.

"I must have something to fill my days—"

Non, my dear sister, you misunderstand. I approve of your activity, as does mon frère." Her bright smile soothed Georgette's ruffled feelings. "Yvonne abandoned training me years ago, but enough of her skill soaked through my thick skull that Mr. Voorhees finds me a satisfactory cook."

A stack of letters on the hall table caught Georgette's eyes. She stopped to examine the addresses. "Mr. LaTournay writes and receives many letters."

Francine gave her a speculative look. "He is a busy man. Too busy, in the opinion of some. Not busy enough, in the opinion of others."

"So many letters addressed to my husband; none for me. Does mail no longer travel to England?" Georgette dropped the letters back on the table. "My parents must have received at least one of my letters by this time. Why do they not reply? And why does Marianne never write to me?"

Francine shook her head and looked sympathetic as she towed Georgette into the kitchen. At the worktable, Yvonne chopped vegetables with a huge cleaver. Bundles of onions, garlic, and herbs hung from the ceiling, and a great kettle steamed over a crackling fire.

"Would either of you like some cider?" Francine made herself at home in the great house.

Yvonne smiled and refused without breaking rhythm.

"Gigi?"

"Please." Georgette brooded over troubling thoughts. "Farming must be stressful work. Often Mr. LaTournay looks tired and troubled. Sometimes. . ."

"Sometimes?" Francine poured two pewter mugs full of cider.

"When we read the scriptures together, certain passages seem important to him, yet he cannot explain why. We read a story about a man named Gideon the other day, and Mr. LaTournay asked me to read it aloud twice. He has spoken of it several times since. Is your husband mysterious like that?"

"Jean-Maurice is more mysterious than most. Has he told you about his childhood?" Careful to keep out of Yvonne's way, the ladies sat upon a settle near the open hearth.

"Very little. He seldom speaks of the past. I know he was born in Canada and spoke French as his first language. I know that your father was French and your mother part Dutch. You both lived here for many years, so I assume your father died young."

"Papa was a French soldier—Claude-Albert François LaTournay, handsome, romantic, and silver-tongued. Grandfather disapproved of him, but Maman ran away to marry him and regretted it ever after. Papa took her to Canada with him until he tired of being husband and father. He brought Maman here when we were children and left us in Grandfather's care."

"How sad she must have been!" Georgette mourned the disillusioned young mother.

"Our mother tried to shield us from knowledge of our father's perfidy, but he made his own character known to us later. During the Indian wars, he returned to claim Jean-Maurice. Mercifully, he left me here with Grandfather."

"Your mother died?"

"The year before our father's return. Jean-Maurice was thirteen when she died, and he missed her terribly. He still mourns her loss, I believe. Before Maman's death, he was a mischievous boy, always in trouble yet smart enough to talk his way out of punishment. Her death took all the fun out of his life."

"He seldom smiles." Georgette sipped her cider, trying to imagine Mr. LaTournay as a lanky young boy.

"I have never seen him happier than he has been these last few months."

Georgette smiled. "That is good to hear. Sometimes I wonder how he can be pleased with me. You know how hopeless I am at any profitable chore. He might have married any one of a dozen other accomplished young ladies in Saratoga alone, not to mention the hordes of females yearning after him in New York."

"I shall let Jean-Maurice assure you of his undying love. Enough for me to say that he paid heed to no woman but his mother until you came along."

Georgette winced inwardly. Mr. LaTournay's dissolute reputation remained unknown at Haven Farm, and she had no wish to disillusion his family.

"His sun rises and sets on you, Gigi *fille*," Francine continued. "I would not wish to be wife to such a man, but you are the ideal woman for mon frére. You possess courage and tenacity. Loving Jean-Maurice for a lifetime will require both."

Confused, Georgette shook her head. Perhaps Francine knew of her brother's moral failings after all. "I am sure it must be as difficult for him to love me as it is for me to love him."

"J'en doute. Behind every great man stands an even greater woman, if you want my opinion," Francine said. "You be Deborah to his Barak, support him fully, and you will reap rich rewards. It is not my place to tell you things he chooses to keep secret, but I shall let you know that Jean-Maurice undergoes a struggle."

"Involving me?"

"Certainement. When principle strives against passion. . ." Francine paused and smiled. "It is time for me to hold my tongue. You cannot know how tempted I am to divulge certain facts. I say it is high time he told you many things about himself, but does he listen to me? Ha!"

❧

LaTournay stamped his boots on the stoop to remove muck and snow. Once inside the lean-to, he took off the filthy boots and hung up his overcoat. The stench of livestock clung to his clothing and skin. He could not greet Georgette while smelling like manure. Stocking-footed, he ran up the back stairs to his dressing room. A fire burned on the hearth in anticipation of his arrival.

The water in his basin was tepid, but it felt good on his chilled body. He toweled warmth into his skin and dressed quickly. Somewhere in this barn of a house, Georgette awaited his coming. Her eyes would brighten at sight of him, and she would greet him with a kiss.

"Jean-Maurice?"

"I am here." He ran a comb through his damp hair.

She opened the door between their rooms. "Francine was here today to teach me weaving." Georgette wore a gown he particularly admired, pink and white like her skin. Wisps escaped her upsweep of hair. Her welcoming smile was as warm and inviting as he had anticipated.

"I was dirty." He reached to tie off his pigtail with a string.

"You smell nice now." Just as he had hoped, her hands slid up his chest. "And you feel nice." Wonder of wonders, she returned his fascination and delight in equal measure. Would he ever tire of her soft form and loving embrace? A man would have to be dead.

The string fell to the floor, unnoticed.

⁂

That night after scripture reading, Georgette asked, "Jean-Maurice, why were you so sad when first we met?" She shifted the sock she was knitting and dropped the ball of yarn on the floor. Caramel picked it up and started to trot away. "No, Caramel, drop it!" she cried.

LaTournay caught the dog and retrieved the yarn. After a quick search, he located the dog's basket of playthings and selected a shredded leather ball. "Here, young fellow. Play with this."

"Thank you." Georgette tucked the yarn ball beneath her elbow. "Perhaps 'sad' is not the correct description. Your eyes held such emptiness, such unspeakable sorrow, as if. . ."

He tossed the ball for Caramel and watched the dog scrabble on the floorboards. "Speak on." The pit of his stomach felt hollow. He settled back in his chair and crossed one ankle over the other.

"As if you had looked upon hell itself."

He leaned down to tug the slimy ball from Caramel's mouth and threw it again. "You spoke of me with Francine today."

275

She tipped her head quizzically. Firelight danced in the hollows and curves of her face and throat. "I wish to know everything about you, Jean-Maurice. You are the favored subject of my conversation and my dreams. Does this annoy you?"

Her increasing perceptiveness with regard to his thoughts and emotions could become inconvenient. "Anything you wish to know, ask me, not Francine." He tried to keep his tone light.

"What happened when your father came back for you? Francine says he left her behind and took you with him. It must have been difficult for you to leave this place. Did you even remember your father, or was he a stranger to you?"

He focused on Caramel, letting the little dog wrestle him for the ball. Les Pringle's warnings about women flashed through his mind, followed by proverbs about bothersome wives. Why could she not be content in her ignorance?

"I think I did remember him vaguely. But now I am here, married to the loveliest woman in all America." He rose and moved behind her chair to rub her neck and shoulders.

She dropped her knitting to clasp his hands and look up with adoring eyes. "Are you content as a farmer, Jean-Maurice? Sometimes I cannot help wondering. You often seem troubled. I enjoy discussing the scriptures with you each night, but I cannot match your depth of understanding. You are so intelligent and gifted; it seems wicked to waste your talents upon dumb animals and a simple wife."

For a moment he wondered how it would feel to grant her admission to his deepest thoughts and feelings. But sharing his complete history was unthinkable. She must remain content with the portion of his life he was able to share.

Bending, he kissed her neck. "Have I complained about your conversation?" He parried question with question. "I enjoy discussing Samson, Gideon, Moses, and our other historical friends each night. I respect your knowledge of Jesus Christ."

"I know you read the scriptures on your own. You insist upon reading the Bible straight through when we read together, but you have been peeking ahead into New Testament books. I know because you have moved my markers. I wish you would discuss those passages with me as well as the Old Testament stories."

Taken by surprise, he muttered, "I am unprepared to discuss them."

When he tried to pull his hands away, she tightened her hold. "Jean-Maurice, if you are a Christian, God has forgiven whatever sins you committed in the past. And I could better demonstrate love to you if I knew more about you. Share with me these memories that haunt you, please? I believe it would help if you spoke of them."

He pulled his hands from her grasp as terror darkened his vision. Chest heaving, he swore in French. "You know not what you ask. Leave the past alone. Be content with the man I am; forget the man I used to be. We are happy here together, and I would keep it so. Do you understand?"

Turning away, he retreated to the adjoining room to prepare for bed. He almost decided to sleep in the smaller bed in the alcove of his chamber, but the memory of Georgette's bewildered expression brought him back to her. Shivering, he climbed beneath the covers and waited for her to join him. When she did climb into bed, he pulled her close with her back against his chest. Nuzzling into her neck, he tried to relax and absorb her sweetness. She did not resist him, but he sensed her sorrow like a barrier between them.

Chapter 11

A time to love, and a time to hate;
a time of war, and a time of peace.
ECCLESIASTES 3:8

Georgette awakened to darkness, her heart racing. Jean-Maurice thrashed and cried out. His fist struck her arm. Still disoriented from sleep, she struggled to sit up. "Jean-Maurice, you are dreaming. Wake up."

He emitted a snarl like an animal's. Georgette yelped in fright. Braving the cold, she climbed out of bed and held a taper to the banked coals of last night's fire. Wax dripped on the hearth before the wick caught. Her husband still moaned and gasped for breath. Cupping the flame, Georgette set the candle in a holder and placed it on the bedside table. "Jean-Maurice!" She threw off the coverlet to reveal her husband's quaking frame. His long arms spread wide, fingers grasping at the mattress, he lay on his back shaking his head back and forth, moaning. His hair straggled across his face. Sweat glistened on his brow; his damp nightshirt clung to his chest and gaped at the neck, revealing sinews knotted as if he strained against bindings. The scar on his jawline showed white beneath his beard.

The rush of cold air made his breath catch. His eyelids fluttered. Tears streaked his temples.

"You are suffering a night terror, Jean-Maurice. Relax. You are safe at home." She touched his clammy forearm, ready to evade another wild swing.

He blinked. "Georgette. You are safe?"

Her jaw quivered with cold. "I am safe, as are you. That was a dreadful dream. You yelled and thrashed and howled. Are you better now?"

"Oui." His voice was quiet.

"Come and change into a fresh nightshirt, dearest. You are drenched in sweat." Teeth chattering, she stepped into his dressing room to find a clean garment. When she returned, he sat beside the hearth, stirring up the fire. The slump of his angular shoulders touched her heart. "Jean-Maurice?"

He glanced toward her, running his fingers through his tangled hair. "Thank you, but I shall change in my room. Come and warm yourself beside the fire until I return." She picked up a woolen shawl, wrapped it around her shoulders, and obeyed. Caramel sat up in his basket, blinking and yawning. After a quick survey of his humans, he tramped circles into his blankets and curled up to sleep once more.

When her husband returned and took the chair opposite hers, Georgette noticed his neatly brushed hair. "Did you wash? The water must have been icy."

"It was, but I could not subject you to a malodorous husband." A wry smile touched his lips before his gaze returned to the fire. He wore a fine silk banyan robe over his nightshirt, but his legs and feet were bare like hers. After three months, Georgette still found the informality of marriage intriguing.

Rising, she approached and knelt before him, looking up into his face. "Is it well with you, Jean-Maurice?"

He tugged off her nightcap and rested his cheek atop her head, placing his hands upon her shoulders. "Georgette, I love you so. Forgive me!"

"For loving me?"

"For being unworthy. If anything ever happened to you. . ." His voice trembled into silence. The grip on her shoulders tightened.

She reached between the lapels of his robe and laid her hand over his pounding heart. "You must learn to trust our Lord with the future. He is the only one with power to save. Remember all we have read together about His redeeming love?"

He gripped her hand with his own and pressed it closer. His chilly skin warmed to her touch. After a long silence, he said quietly, *"Dieu ne peut pas m'aimer."*

Concentrating for a moment, Georgette interpreted "God cannot love me" and felt a shock. How could this be? From the depths of her spirit, she prayed for wisdom. "God loves everyone from the greatest saint to the lowest criminal. He loves you, Jean-Maurice. If I can love you, certainly God does."

He rose and stepped away to face a dark corner of the chamber, arms folded across his chest. "He knows all about me. You do not."

Fear of the anguish she had seen in his eyes haunted Georgette. Lady Forester's harsh warning rang in her ears. Had he been seeing other women even after vowing fidelity to her? She spoke calmly despite the pain in her chest. "God knows everyone's secret sins, and He promises to cleanse and forgive. In all our Bible reading, have we yet learned of a man whose sins were too great for God to forgive? Sometimes men refuse to repent; they scorn God's sovereignty and mock His gift of salvation. But that is their choice, not God's. Jesus came to die for all men. He associated with the worst sinners—murderers, thieves, and harlots."

"Why?"

"Because those people recognized their need of a Savior. They knew their unworthiness to approach God on their own."

He gave a grunt.

Was it a grunt of assent or of dissent?

Still kneeling before the empty chair, Georgette prayed. Had her words made any sense? She was groggy with sleep, and he was overwrought. She hoped God could use her feeble efforts.

He swung around and faced her. "Come to bed before you fall ill." She accepted his outstretched hand and let him pull her up. Together they turned the featherbed and climbed into its billowing folds.

Jean-Maurice wrapped his arms around Georgette and gradually relaxed. Soon his deep breathing told her that he slept. An ache deeper than tears settled around her heart.

⸎

"Miss Gigi." Yvonne laid a work-roughened hand on Georgette's shoulder. "You should get outside and take some fresh air. 'Twould do you good."

Georgette nodded, dragging her gaze from the coals on the kitchen hearth. "Perhaps I shall visit Francine." She closed the Bible in her lap and sighed.

Yvonne's skirts rustled against the wooden settle. "I should keep my place and mind my business, but I hate the sight of you and monsieur both moping about. Old Yvonne is good at listening to the woes of brides."

Georgette met Yvonne's sympathetic gaze and tried to smile. Tears sprang to her eyes; she dabbed at them with the corner of her apron. Yvonne sat down next to her. Georgette leaned on the older woman's sturdy shoulder, inhaling her scent of cinnamon and coffee. "Oh Yvonne, I am such a fool."

Yvonne pressed her wrinkled cheek against Georgette's forehead and rocked gently. "Ma fille, tell Yvonne your folly."

"Mr. LaTournay—" A sob choked her for a moment. "He claimed to be a Christian. Only now, after months of marital happiness, do I learn that he does not accept God's forgiveness and salvation." The last words came out as a wail.

Yvonne remained quiet.

"His past troubles him, Yvonne, but he will not speak of it to me. He believes God cannot forgive him. And I have disobeyed God's command by marrying an unbeliever."

Yvonne nodded. "Noel and I shall pray twice as hard for the boy. You must know, Miss Gigi, that not all past sin and pain should be spoken of between husband and wife. Let him choose what he will share. And yet I agree with you that he must face his past and release it into God's hands."

"I am dreadfully confused. I should not have married Mr. LaTournay, and yet I love him so dearly that I cannot regret my error. I realize now that we had different understandings of the term 'Christian.' After being christened, he naturally considered himself a Christian. He did not know that I spoke of salvation through faith in Christ. But, Yvonne, had I known he was not a believer, I might have married him anyway. Is it sinful that I do not regret pledging myself to him for life?"

Yvonne stared into her eyes and gave her a gentle shake. "For shame, to waste time and tears so! God does not condemn us for the sins we might have committed had the situation been otherwise. He has enough to do forgiving us for the sins we actually commit. You erred through ignorance, and the deed is done. Now you must live with what is and obey what you know to be God's will. Do you think God would have you stop loving your husband?"

"No," Georgette whispered.

"Until Jean-Maurice met you, he rejected God altogether and his life was an empty shell. You are exactly what the boy needed—you have adored him, played with him, prayed with him, studied scripture with him, and shared with him the depths of your heart. Your love is an essential piece to the puzzle of his questing soul. You have given him a taste of God's perfect love. Now we must trust that God will prevail in the end. Only He can complete your marriage. Only He can form Jean-Maurice into the godly man He intended him to be."

Georgette looked into Yvonne's eyes and felt hope for the first time in days. She hugged the elderly housekeeper and silently thanked God for providing her with wise counsel.

Three days later, Jean-Maurice looked up from his evening scripture reading to announce: "I am leaving for New York City tomorrow."

Georgette's mouth fell open. Unwelcome thoughts flashed through her mind—Lady Forester, the Whig rebellion and its accompanying dangers, the Frog. *Has my husband tired of me so quickly?*

He laid the Bible on a side table and took a deep breath. "Information of an urgent nature impels this sudden journey. I would not leave you for a lesser cause."

"I shall go with you." She scarcely recognized her own voice.

He shook his head, though she recognized a hint of indecision. "The journey downriver in summer is difficult; in winter it is more arduous still. And you know of the unrest in the city." His eyes and jaw hardened. "Atrocities have been committed in the name of patriotism, and the innocent suffer. I cannot subject you to such danger, Georgette."

"What are you keeping from me?"

The slightest dilation of his pupils verified her suspicion. A dreadful certainty struck her. "It is my parents."

His shoulders stiffened. "How do you know?"

"Jean-Maurice, you must tell me!" She flung herself at his feet and clutched his knees. "What has happened? Are they alive?"

"They are alive." He cupped her face between his hands. "Georgette, do you hear? They are alive. Calm yourself, *épouse chérie.*"

Looking into his solemn eyes, she attempted to control her panic. "Did they not sail for England? Did the ship sink?" Her mind began to spin wild schemes. She must go with him to New York, no matter what the cost.

"The *Lily Fair* never sailed." He lifted her to sit upon his lap. The skirts of her bedgown engulfed him.

"The ship never sailed? But why?" Georgette twined her arms around his neck.

He remained unyielding in her embrace, and his voice stayed formal in tone. "I do not know why. Their passage was never refunded. A radical element in the city seized your father, then tarred and feathered him."

Georgette gasped as though she had received a blow to the stomach. "But why? And Mummy? Where have they lived? How have they survived these months?"

"I know not how they survived at first, but they currently reside at the Grenville estate on Long Island."

"So Marianne helped them. Now, of course, I must come with you," Georgette said. "Caramel will remain here with Yvonne and Noel. What? Why do you gaze at me with such trepidation and censure?" She smoothed the lines on his forehead with one finger and gave him a lingering kiss. His lips clung to hers as if he were helpless to resist. "Do you not wish to have me along?"

He closed his eyes and buried his head against her shoulder. "Do not make sport of me, Georgette. Your safety is my concern.

If my desires alone were consulted, you and I would never part. This war escalates in scale and intensity. British troops are expected to invade New York soon, though no one knows when."

"I hope it is soon; then we shall all be safe." She felt tension in his neck muscles as her fingers stroked the smooth skin above his collar.

"Yet we cannot wait for that day, and should the invasion occur while we are there, our lives would certainly be endangered. Best to snatch your parents out of harm's way, a tactic easiest accomplished by one man alone. Before long the Hudson will close off with ice. If it happens too soon, we shall be obliged to travel overland."

She felt his hands roaming over her back, yet his mind seemed occupied with travel and tactics. Time to plant a suggestion. She spoke into his ear. "Jean-Maurice, you will make arrangements for our quick passage home while I care for my parents' immediate needs. Together we can accomplish more."

He kissed her neck. Maybe he was not completely preoccupied after all. Georgette lifted her chin and sighed her pleasure. "So I may come with you?"

His grasp tightened, and he kissed a trail up the side of her throat.

"Jean-Maurice?"

He lifted bemused eyes and a crooked smile. "I can deny you nothing, *ma petite.*"

If anything, Mr. LaTournay had understated the misery of winter travel. Great chunks of ice floated alongside the boats traversing the river, and a contrary breeze impeded progress while freezing the passengers' faces. Georgette huddled in the stern beneath layers of oilcloth, blankets, and cloaks. It must be late afternoon, but the sleety weather and gray gloom had changed little since early-morning hours.

A corner of her shelter lifted. Her husband squatted before her. "Georgette, we shall arrive on Manhattan Island in approximately two hours. There we must hire horses to carry us to the ferry landing. I know not what political climate we shall find in the city, but 'twould profit us to say nothing to anyone about our business."

She nodded. Though she would have liked to complain about her frozen extremities and the complete lack of privacy, coming along on this trip had, after all, been her idea. Mr. LaTournay seemed to read her mind. His eyes crinkled above the muffler wrapped over his mouth and nose. His cheeks were cherry red from the whipping wind and blowing snow. Dancing wisps of dark hair caught in his brows and draped over his nose. He lifted his three-cornered hat, brushed back his hair with one hand, and replaced the hat. "Solid ground will come as a treat, eh?"

Georgette nodded. "And a hotel." With a hot bath, if at all possible.

"I shall try to find us lodging at the boardinghouse."

She looked at his chapped hands clad in fingerless gloves. He must be as uncomfortable as she, yet he seemed accustomed to a harsh environment. Georgette felt weak and useless. No wonder he had not wished to bring her along. She was nothing but trouble for him.

"Might there be difficulty in renting a room for the night?"

He shifted position, setting one knee down. "The proprietor might have fled the city by now. Word is that many citizens have emigrated to other cities or colonies."

Georgette nodded mutely.

He reached beneath the oilcloth to touch her face with his icy fingers. "I shall find lodging for you, *ma belle épouse,* never fear. You have been most courageous." He winked one red-rimmed eye and dropped her cover back into place.

A moment later, she heard him speaking to one of the boatmen in rapid-fire French. These men seemed to know him well. Everyone seemed to know Mr. LaTournay, she realized with irritation. Often she sensed, with a surge of jealousy, that other people knew him better than she did. She had given herself to him completely; why must he be so tight-lipped and reserved? Even during their most private moments, she sensed times when he checked himself, as if he feared revealing too much of his soul.

Jean-Maurice desired her; Georgette held no doubts in that regard. He expressed sincere admiration and gratitude, and his eyes communicated ardor more eloquently than his tongue. She felt more beautiful than ever before in her life, and perhaps she should have been content. Yet she wanted more.

Whenever her husband spoke to her tenderly in French, her heart responded with an intensity that astonished her. Only one other man had ever affected her so—a man she endeavored to forget. It could not be the French accent alone, for none of the many Frenchmen she had met while living in Paris had caused such havoc to her emotions.

Occasionally she pondered the similarities between Jean-Maurice and her mysterious hero. Both men were French, both tall and vigorous, both kind and considerate. She knew the Frog to be a man of honor, despite his absurd appellation and traitorous activities. Notwithstanding his cynical, teasing behavior at their first meeting, he had treated her with respect. Even while declaring his devotion at their subsequent meetings, not once had he disgusted her with a suggestion of immorality.

Was the Frog still alive? Would he see her enter the city and find a way to contact her? Guilt swept over Georgette even as she allowed the treacherous thoughts.

⟋⟍

They took lodgings that night at Hull's Tavern. After making sure she would have the bath she craved, her husband donned his coat and cloak. "I must make arrangements for tomorrow and inquiries about your parents, Georgette. You will be safe here in the room. I shall return in time to bathe before supper."

"Take care," she warned.

His weather-burned face creased into a smile. "Always."

True to his word, he reappeared while Georgette combed out her hair beside the fire. "The water is tepid," she said. "We can request a kettle of hot water."

"I have already done so." He opened the door in response to a knock, and a boy carrying a steaming kettle entered. Without a word, the boy emptied the pot into the tub. Mr. LaTournay pressed a coin into his hand and closed the door behind him.

The room contained no privacy screen. Georgette watched her husband remove his cravat and waistcoat. Embarrassed, she averted her gaze until he submerged himself in the tub. Blowing and sputtering, he surfaced, hair and beard dripping. "Not quite hot enough but far warmer than the Hudson," he said. "Please hand me the scrub brush and soap."

Georgette obliged. Dark hair lay plastered on his exposed knees, forearms, and chest. His wet shoulders reflected the firelight as he applied the scrub brush to his sinewy back. He grinned up at her. "The last woman who watched me bathe was my mother."

Heat suffused her face. Turning to the mirror, she began to pin up her still-damp hair but could not avoid hearing his chuckle.

"I fear my gown is out of style."

"The trade ships from England did not arrive here in October, so everyone in the city is wearing last year's fashions." Splashes and thumps told her when he climbed out of the tub. She could not resist sneaking a peek in the mirror while he dressed. His twinkling dark eyes met her gaze as he tightened the drawstring of his drawers.

Although she wanted to be offended or shocked, Georgette found herself smiling. Judging by his reaction, it was not a bad thing that she found him good to look upon. "Woman, you are a distraction," he growled. Instead of pulling on his shirt, he approached her to claim a kiss.

Nestled in his arms, Georgette inhaled the fragrance of his clean skin. "I am glad I came with you."

"At the moment, I, too, am thankful. I hope I may remain so." He stepped back. "We must make haste if we are to dine tonight."

Georgette reluctantly let him finish dressing.

✑

Moonlight streamed through a window, unimpeded by the wisp of curtain. Although the bed was clean and vermin-free,

Georgette could not sleep. Voices from the taproom below were just loud enough to annoy without allowing her to distinguish one word from another. Her supper of fried ham and beans was not setting well.

Her husband's deep breathing told Georgette that he slept. Shivering despite layers of blankets, she snuggled up against his broad back and thought wistfully of the luxurious featherbeds back home. He rolled over to embrace her, encroaching on much of her bed space. The price of warmth. Georgette rested her cheek against his chest and let the strong beat of his heart soothe her.

Just as her mind drifted into sleep, a sharper beat awakened her. Mr. LaTournay sat up and placed a restraining hand on Georgette when she opened her mouth to inquire. The rapping sounded again.

With astonishing suddenness and silence, Mr. LaTournay positioned himself beside the chamber door. "Who is there?"

"Pringle. I need to talk to you."

"One moment." He hauled on his breeches as he spoke. His nightshirt gleamed white as it floated to the floor. Georgette lost sight of him in the shadows but heard evidence of his preparation. He suddenly loomed over her. "Never fear. I'll not be long."

She clung to him for an instant, returned his kiss, and released him. The door opened, admitting a louder volume of taproom clamor, then closed. Its latch clicked into place.

As soon as he was gone, Georgette thought of a dozen questions to ask.

Chapter 12

But if ye will not do so, behold, ye have sinned against the LORD:
and be sure your sin will find you out.
NUMBERS 32:23

"Y ou were in bed?" Pringle inquired as he led the way downstairs. "At this hour? My, how marriage has countrified
you, LaTournay."

LaTournay glanced into the small taproom in passing. "Does
not the Provincial Congress regulate the closing hour of taverns
as it polices everything else in town?"

Pringle gave an appreciative snort as he hauled on his overcoat.
"I imagine the taproom currently contains an associator or two.
Rules are made to be broken only by those who enforce them."

LaTournay observed while his friend hunched in the tavern
doorway and scanned the street. "Eyes are always watching,"
Pringle said. "You can have no idea what these past months have
been. Daily we hope and pray that Governor Tryon will succeed
in convincing General Howe to make New York his center of
operations."

Thinking of his warm bed, LaTournay reluctantly followed
Pringle. For all his efforts, Pringle moved with the finesse of a
rolling boulder. The heels of his shoes tapped on the cobblestones, and he could not seem to restrain a stream of conversation. "The associators have detained me more than once, insisting
that I take an oath of allegiance. I tell them I already signed and
swore it once and do not intend to do so again."

"It does seem an ineffective measure—coerced fealty. You say
you did swear it once?"

"Only to remove suspicion from myself. An informant is useless when he is suspected."

The men turned east on Crown Street. A blast of winter wind
struck, slicing through layers of clothing. LaTournay drew his

cloak together at the neck and hunched his shoulders. "So you still spy for the army?" he asked as they approached the docks.

"I work for Governor Tryon now. Since he moved his office aboard the *Duchess of Gordon*, he needs eyes and ears in town. I move with the stealth and quickness of a panther. That is my code name—the Panther."

"Selecting one's own alias offers distinct advantages." LaTournay dragged one hand down over his mouth and beard in an effort to keep a straight face.

Diverse structures lined the street, from rickety shops surrounded by heaps of refuse to brick town houses with manicured gardens. The scent of rotting fish blended with wood smoke and sea salt. Deep grunts and strident squeals divulged the presence of nocturnal garbage looters. LaTournay hoped the beasts were of a peaceable nature. Swine were his least favorite of God's creation.

"Why did Governor Tryon move to a ship?" he asked.

"He caught wind of a plot to kidnap him," Pringle replied. "Although the Provincial Congress swears it intended no such scheme, who can place credence in the assurances of traitors?"

"Who, indeed?"

Pringle stopped him suddenly. "We are followed. Come." He ducked behind the short hedge lining a town house's garden.

LaTournay crouched beside his friend. "Who could it be, do you think? An associator?" He and Pringle were being shadowed, LaTournay knew, but the real trackers would not so carelessly betray their presence.

Pringle made a hacking motion to halt the questions. Hooves clacked on the cobblestones, and two hogs trotted past, ears flopping.

Pringle let out his breath as the two men stood upright. "False alarm this time. LaTournay, you disappoint me. You must learn to practice caution if you're to survive in this city more than a day. I depend upon you to help organize our Tories into troops that should impress even Howe. You may know little about military matters, but your voice and demeanor will inspire confidence, which is a trait sadly lacking at present."

LaTournay followed Pringle back to the walkway. "I, organize troops? Pringle, you flatter me."

"I have something to show you. Come."

"I cannot become involved."

Pringle shook his head. "You think so now, but not when you have seen and heard all."

Gripping his friend's arm, LaTournay tugged him to a halt. "Listen. My wife awaits my return. I cannot stay out long. What is so urgent that you drag me from my bed into the frigid night?"

"Your sad fate motivates me. I have a long and tragic tale to relate. Will you not come with me to Queens? A boat awaits us at the landing."

LaTournay paused before answering. "Not tonight. My plans take me there tomorrow. To Grenville's estate in Queens County, where my wife's relations bide until our coming."

Pringle laughed aloud. "But of course! Better still to reveal all with the wench present. Your plan could scarcely be improved upon. Very well. I shall meet you there." Exuberant as ever, he prepared to bound away.

LaTournay caught his arm again. "Do not refer to my wife in disrespectful terms. Are you married?"

"Married?"

"To Miss Grenville. I had understood that nuptials were forthcoming."

Pringle laughed. "Never if I can help it."

"Have you yet apprehended the Toad?"

A pause. "I assume you speak of the spy I call the Frog."

"Frog, toad, it matters little." LaTournay waved it off.

"We have not apprehended him as yet, but I expect to shortly. We shall soon have the proper gig with which to snare frogs. I anticipate skewering this particular animal and frying its legs in butter."

"I pity the unwary creature you capture, Pringle. Are you not taking this matter too personally? With what 'gig' do you expect to entrap this frog?"

"That you shall discover on the morrow, my friend—to your

sorrow, I fear." Pringle's laugh held little mirth. "I am a poet, you see, as well as a prophet. We shall lure this cuckolding frog from out of his concealing fog."

✍

Georgette stiffened when the chamber door creaked open. She gripped her bedclothes beneath her chin.

"It is I; never fear."

At the sound of her husband's voice, she felt as limp as overcooked cabbage. "Where have you been?"

"Let me join you before I answer that question." Sounds of rustling fabric followed. His silhouette passed the window moments before he climbed into bed beside her.

"Ooh!" she gasped as his icy arms and legs pressed against hers. His entire body shivered. She let him pull her close and soak in her warmth. "Now tell me."

"Pringle wished to take me to Long Island."

"Tonight?"

"I explained our plan to travel there tomorrow."

"I assume he found that plan satisfactory." Georgette rubbed her husband's frozen forearms. "So he dragged you out into the cold night for no good reason. I do not comprehend your continuing friendship with that man, Jean-Maurice. He cannot be a good influence. Do you wish to return to your old lifestyle?" The question that had plagued her for days popped out, taking her by surprise.

"My old lifestyle?"

"The immoral lifestyle of an unmarried man. I am well aware of your reputation. My mother says a woman should never speak of such things or even acknowledge awareness of her husband's foibles, but I cannot imagine practicing deceit on that scale."

"On what scale can you imagine practicing deceit?"

"None whatever! A husband and wife should be honest with one another." She sat up and turned to confront him, although darkness negated the effect of her stare. "Do you wish to be unfaithful to me?"

He gave an incredulous huff. "You can even ask this?

Georgette, I desire no woman but you, ever." Anger tinged his voice.

She dared not yet relax in relief. "I find it necessary to ask for two reasons. One, because of your past indiscretions. Two, because I know that you hide much of your heart and mind from me."

"I hide none of my heart from you. I love you. I have never loved another woman. For reasons I cannot reveal, I allowed people to believe that Lady Forester and I were romantically linked. The fabrication was hers; I simply neglected to repudiate it, and people chose to believe the lie. Tales of my liaisons with additional women are entirely fictitious. Others of God's commandments I confess I have broken, but the seventh remains sacrosanct."

"Is this true?"

"Ask me again in daylight if you doubt. I can no longer maintain the charade before my wife, come what may."

He sounded defiant. Something about the confession seemed odd, but Georgette was too tired to ponder the matter. "I believe you. Oh Jean-Maurice, I love you so much! It hurt terribly to think that you would ever tire of me and seek another woman. My mother told me to expect it."

"Your mother does not know me." He tightened his grip around her waist, pulling her down. Georgette's tears dampened his nightshirt as she clung to him. "Are you crying?" he asked.

"Because I am happy," she confessed. He stroked her head, dislodging her nightcap. She felt a deep sigh expand his chest.

⟨⟩

Snow dusted the gloves holding the reins—Georgette could not think of those numb hands as hers. The roached mane of her roan horse held an extra frost, though the snow melted on contact with the beast's sweating shoulders. To her befuddled brain, the animal appeared to breathe like a dragon—twin jets of smoke emerged from its nostrils.

Georgette ached in every bone and muscle. A sleepless night followed by a day of riding, all coming at the end of a most uncomfortable journey—she could hardly remain upright in the sidesaddle.

"Not long now," Jean-Maurice encouraged her.

"How many times have you visited Grenville Grange?" she asked, nudging her horse alongside her husband's.

"Once or twice. Beautiful countryside here." He scanned the rolling farmland. "Pleasant villages, scenic vistas."

Georgette squinted at her surroundings. Even with its frosted, winter-bare trees and fields, the island held a lush beauty. "I like our home better. I hope my father is well enough to travel, for I wish to remain not a day longer than necessary. How I long for our cozy fireside and snug featherbeds!" The scarf she had wrapped around her nose and mouth felt stiff with the frozen condensation of her breath.

Jean-Maurice reached across to squeeze her hand. The pressure hurt, but at least she knew her extremities were still alive. "I, too." He winked at her, and his eyes crinkled above his knitted muffler.

Grenville Grange sat back from the main road, surrounded by a sweep of snowy turf. Towering trees framed its black, gabled roofline. Multiple outbuildings indicated Grenville's prosperity.

The powdery snow had not yet accumulated on the circular drive. Mr. LaTournay tied his horse to a ring before lifting Georgette from the sidesaddle. Her right leg gave way as soon as it touched the ground. "I cannot bear weight on it," she groaned, clutching her husband's forearm.

"The feeling will soon return." He walked her slowly in a circle. The skirts of her riding habit swept frost from the lawn.

Two young black men approached to take the horses. When Mr. LaTournay thanked them, they gave him wary looks of surprise and said nothing.

"Slaves," he said flatly. "And Grenville claims to be a Christian."

While Georgette's thoughts flurried, a door clicked open behind them. "Gigi! Is it really you?"

Turning, Georgette laughed. "I wish I could say yes, but at the moment I am uncertain even of my own identity."

"Mr. Pringle told us you were coming—he returned this

morning—but Papa thought this weather would delay your arrival. I imagine the ferry ride was miserable." Marianne picked up her skirts and stepped over muddy ruts to greet her friend. After bestowing a kiss upon Georgette's cheek, she stood back to look her up and down. "Come in and warm yourselves. It is also good to see you again, Mr. LaTournay."

"My pleasure, Miss Grenville." He bowed.

"Your parents will be delighted to see you, Gigi. Your father is still ailing, but his color is better and his hair begins to grow back." Marianne gripped Georgette's hand and led her inside. Mr. LaTournay followed.

"A servant is bringing our things, although we do not expect to remain long," Georgette said. "We must hurry home, for the Hudson will soon be impossible to navigate."

Marianne said nothing, but her expression gave Georgette an uneasy twinge. She escorted them into a large sitting room with a roaring fire upon the hearth. Three shawl-wrapped figures huddled in chairs around the hearth. "Mother? Mr. and Mrs. Talbot? Gigi and Mr. LaTournay are here."

Georgette's mother dropped her knitting and leaped up to greet her. Georgette clung to her, tears streaming down her cheeks. "Mummy, I thought never to see you again!"

"Darling girl, you look wonderful! So rosy and elegant. You are happy?"

"I could not be more so," Georgette said. "Mr. LaTournay is good to me, and our home is lovely. We plan to take you there. Papa should recover quickly in the fresh country air." She cast an apprehensive glance at her father, who had not yet lifted his gaze from the fire.

"And dear Mr. LaTournay." Her mother extended a hand to her son-in-law and accepted his dutiful kiss.

"Welcome to our home, Georgette." Marianne's mother spoke stiffly. "Welcome, Mr. LaTournay," she added with more warmth. "I shall retire at present to give you privacy, but we shall meet at dinner. Would you like chocolate brought to your chambers?"

"Yes, thank you, Mrs. Grenville. We are eternally indebted for your provision of a haven for my parents during their time of need." Georgette took the woman's offered hand and curtsied. Her legs cramped, but she managed to rise without grimacing. Mrs. Grenville swept from the room, chin held high.

"Let me show you to your chambers so you can freshen up." Marianne sounded too bright and cheery.

"Hello, Father," Georgette said. "I hope you are feeling better."

Her father gave her a cursory glance and focused on her husband. "You heard what they did to me?" He described his tormentors in profane terms. The three ladies exchanged uncomfortable glances.

"We were deeply disturbed to hear of it," Mr. LaTournay said. "Only the lowest individuals would perpetrate such abuse upon their fellow man. No excuse can be tendered for this dishonorable offense. If you please, I shall join you here by the fire so that you may relate details of the experience without further distressing the ladies."

"Come then." Her father indicated an empty chair.

Mr. LaTournay first took Georgette's elbow and bent to speak quietly. "Go ahead; enjoy your time with Marianne. Your father needs to vent his outrage to someone other than ladies."

Although her father's rebuff hurt, Georgette tried to feel sympathy. "He has endured great pain and indignity," she whispered. "Thank you."

A faint smile softened his expression, and he gave her arm a gentle squeeze.

Marianne chattered as she led the way up two flights of stairs. "I am sorry we have only third-floor chambers left for you and Mr. LaTournay, but your parents occupy our best guest rooms. You have windows overlooking our little valley, and the rooms should be warm, since I ordered Trixie to light fires in them this morning."

"I am certain we shall be comfortable. I cannot begin to express my gratitude to your family, Marianne. What would my parents have done without your care?" Georgette's legs wobbled as she neared the third-floor landing. "Exactly how long have they been here?"

"Papa found them in late October. Their ship put them off

and sailed to Jamaica."

"Without refunding their passage. Is that not criminal? Can we not report this to the shipping company and receive their refund?"

Marianne pushed open a door near the end of the upper hallway. "Here is your chamber. Mr. LaTournay's is adjoining." She stepped inside before responding to Georgette's question. "Gigi, your father says they did not refund the passage, but your mother says otherwise. They lived on the money until my father found them. They might have purchased passage on another ship. . . ."

"Except that my father gambled much of it away first, I imagine." Georgette completed the sentence with a sigh. "This is a fine room." She smoothed the counterpane on a large four-poster bed.

"Gigi, are you happily married? Please tell me the truth." Marianne looked grave. "Mr. Pringle has told me terrible things. . . ."

"I am content, Marianne. My husband is good to me, and we love each other. We have our disagreements, naturally, and there is much I still must learn about him, but on the whole I would say we are well matched. What can Mr. Pringle have said that is so terrible?" Georgette untied her bonnet and dropped it upon the bed. Until her trunk arrived, she would have to remain in her riding habit.

"I am thankful to hear of your contentment," Marianne said. She strolled about the small room, tugging at the curtain, poking the fire, straightening a candlestick. "Ah, here is Trixie with your chocolate." Marianne relieved the slave woman of the tray. "You may go."

Trixie bowed her turbaned head and slipped into the hall. Georgette could not help comparing her with effervescent Yvonne.

Marianne poured a cup of the steaming beverage. "Do you take sugar?"

"Two spoonfuls, please. When is your wedding date?" Georgette asked as she accepted the cup, cradling its warmth in her hands.

"We have set no date. I am uncertain the wedding will ever

take place, Gigi. Mr. Pringle is busy with prepar—" She broke off, gave Georgette a nervous glance, and continued. "He is so busy these days with business that we never speak of love." Her blue eyes held deep sadness.

"I am sorry." Georgette did not know what to say.

Marianne hurried to the door. "Dinner is served at six; we dine early in the country." She paused. "Oh Gigi, had I not promised secrecy, I would warn you of what is to come. Your father is so angry—yet I am certain it cannot be true. No, do not importune me to tell you, for I cannot. Pray for wisdom and courage, my dearest Gigi. I shall be praying for you."

She slipped into the hallway, leaving Georgette to wrack her brain for an explanation.

☙

Les Pringle bounded in during the meat course, apologizing profusely as he seated himself at the table. He had not even bothered to change out of his riding clothes. "An eventful, auspicious day. Good evening to you all. Ah, Mrs. LaTournay."

He rose from his seat again and approached Georgette to bow. "Welcome to Grenville Grange. As you see, we have given your worthy parents the best of care. I had not the pleasure of congratulating you upon your marriage before Mr. LaTournay swept you off north. Allow me now to express my sincere wish that your future brings the amount of happiness you deserve." He kissed her hand with moist lips. The look in his eyes and the tone of his voice disturbed Georgette.

When Pringle returned to his seat, Georgette glanced across the table at her husband. Mr. LaTournay looked as baffled as she felt. Forks and knives rattled against porcelain dishes. Mr. Grenville sent the veal back to the kitchen, complaining that it was overcooked. The pungent aromas of heavily spiced mutton and broiled oysters competed for precedence. Georgette picked at her vegetables, longing for the moment she and her husband could retire for the night. A wave of homesickness struck her.

Dinner conversation revolved around farming and the shipping business. Mr. Pringle spoke with brilliance and animation, drawing the ladies into the discussion whenever possible. Mr. and Mrs. Grenville seemed enamored of him, but Georgette noticed a decided coolness on Marianne's part. She could not help feeling relieved. Marianne must finally have seen through the man's handsome mask to the scoundrel he truly was.

During the sweetmeat and cheese course, Pringle raised a hand to draw attention to himself. "Before another moment passes, we must clear the air and place all our cards upon the table."

A hush followed the announcement. Pringle's face expressed unaccustomed dignity and remorse. "It grieves me to cause pain to anyone, let alone to a good friend, but it must be done for the good of all. Mr. LaTournay, I have the grim obligation of informing you that your wife is untrue. While pledged to you, she entertained and gave comfort to another man. She is traitor both to you and to England."

Georgette choked on a bite of almond tart, coughed into her napkin, and took a quick sip of perry. The sparkling pear juice burned in her stomach.

In the deathly silence following her coughing attack, Mr. LaTournay turned to Georgette. "Is this true?" His eyes held a watchful calm.

"I—I—yes, I did see another man, but only to tell him that I could no longer receive him." Her tired mind spun in circles of conjecture. "If I betrayed England in any way, it was unwittingly done."

Pringle tossed a few raisins into his mouth and emitted a sharp laugh, talking while he chewed. "The man must have been slow to understand, for you saw him several times last summer. Is it not true that your dog was a gift from this man and that you once entertained him while clad only in your nightclothes?"

Heat flooded Georgette's face. "No! I mean, well, yes, but not in the way you imply. He came into the garden one night, and I ran down to tell him he must leave."

"And did you or did you not warn this man, a spy and traitor known as the Frog, that we Loyalists had laid a trap for him?" Pringle's voice rang through the room. "Hardly an 'unwitting' treachery."

Georgette's gaze skittered across the other accusing faces to focus upon her husband's dark eyes. They seemed empty, devoid of expression, as if he were a stranger she had never met and would never know. "Jean-Maurice, you must believe that I have never been unfaithful to you! This man had been kind to me; I could not allow him to be captured without warning him of the plot."

Mr. LaTournay looked at Pringle. "How do you know these things?"

Pringle snapped his fingers at a footman. "Bring in the woman called Biddy."

"Biddy!" Georgette breathed the name aloud.

The tiny woman entered, wide-eyed and apologetic. "Missy Georgette, I never would have told if not for the way that Frog has hurt our soldiers. Please forgive me for spying on you, missy!"

"Tell these people what you told me, Biddy," Pringle demanded. "How did Mrs. LaTournay react when you brought her the notes from this Frog spy?"

"Forgive me, missy—but she smiled so bright it seemed like the stars lit in her eyes. I said to myself that the lady must be in love to react so. And the dog, he represented that lover to her, no doubt in my mind. When that Frog first brought the puppy, she showed herself at the window in her chemise. Shocked, I was, and thinking she must have known this cloaked man before."

"No! I never did." Georgette gasped for breath, feeling smothered.

Mr. LaTournay slid back his chair and rose. "You deliberately aided a Whig spy? You entertained another man at night? That dog you treasure was a gift from this Frog?" Never before had he addressed Georgette in such lifeless tones. "And you accuse me of keeping secrets."

Turning to his stunned host and hostess, he said, "Please excuse me. I must have time to think. I shall take a room in a nearby town." After a bow to the room in general, he made a quick exit.

Georgette felt her heart shatter into jagged shards.

Chapter 13

Then said Jesus unto the twelve, Will ye also go away?
JOHN 6:67

"How can I do this thing?" Georgette pleaded. "I am no siren to lure a man to his capture or death!" She pushed the paper aside and turned away from the writing desk. Scattered about the parlor, the Grenvilles and the Talbots watched the proceedings in condemning silence. Georgette felt new sympathy for martyrs of the Inquisition.

"You care more about this traitorous spy than about your husband," Pringle accused. "I warned LaTournay, but he refused to listen."

"Love for my husband does not mean I will sign the death warrant of another man. Do you think me a heartless monster?"

"Yes, in fact, I do." Pringle grinned. "Write the note, woman, before I find it expedient to take more forceful measures." He slapped his gloves against his thigh.

"Mr. Pringle, you would not strike Gigi," Marianne said, her voice shaking.

"I would strike a woman only if provoked. My patience wears thin." His smile did not reach his gleaming blue eyes. "This woman deserves only contempt and harsh treatment until she makes restitution for her breach of faith. I shall keep constant watch upon her while she remains in this house."

"Mr. LaTournay demands this of me?" Georgette picked up the quill and studied its point. "That I play false to a friend?"

"He expects this and much more before he will again welcome you into his home and affections. A man once betrayed will not easily be fooled again."

Thoughts rambled through Georgette's mind as she toyed with the goose quill. Recently Jean-Maurice had been pondering God's forgiveness; she knew because she had seen him deep in study of scripture when he believed himself observed by no one. Had her apparent perfidy soured his perception of Jesus Christ? Had her weakness for romance destroyed her husband's hope for salvation?

She did not want or need any lover besides Jean-Maurice. Even so, her heart quailed at the prospect of bringing harm to her secret friend. Would the Frog come to her if summoned? Perhaps he would be out of town. Perhaps he had found another love and would scorn an invitation from a married woman. He might have forgotten her by now. Georgette could only hope.

Dipping her quill into the ink, she penned a short plea for aid. "I do not know how it will be delivered," she remarked after sealing it with a few drops of bayberry candle wax. "One can hardly address a missive to a frog."

"Leave that to me." Pringle snatched the note from her hand. "You should not have sealed it until I read it." He broke the seal and scanned her note, nodding in approval. "The very thing. Seal it again. I shall send a courier to town this night. Within two days we shall have this Frog in hand, I swear it!"

Later, despite a fire on the hearth and Trixie's application of a warming pan between her sheets, Georgette felt chilled to the bone. She wept alone in the four-poster bed. Inarticulate prayers poured from her heart, a longing for forgiveness and a return to love. "I shall confess all, if he will but grant me opportunity. Dear Lord, only You can bring good out of this terrible evil. Please protect the Frog, and please bring my husband back to me."

An icy draft awakened her during the night. Blinking away sleep, she rolled over, pulled aside the bed curtains, and stared at the window, visible as a pale smudge in the darkness of her chamber. As coals flared weakly on the hearth, Georgette beheld white draperies sweeping into the room like grasping ghostly arms. Someone or something had opened the window.

She sat up. "Who is there?" The window clicked shut, and frigid silence returned.

Georgette thought her heart might batter its way through her ribs. Dread and cold brought on a wave of nausea. Her limbs trembled uncontrollably, and her teeth chattered.

A black shadow tossed a faggot into the coals. A flame burst forth to lick at the bundle of dry sticks. The sight of a swirling cloak and gleaming boots brought Georgette intense relief—her midnight visitor was human, not goblin. "Frog?" she whispered.

"Bon nuit, ma petite grenouille. Pleased am I that you do not scream at sight of me." He approached the bed as silently as he had entered the room, speaking just above a whisper.

Georgette clutched her coverlet beneath her chin. "How. . . ? Why are you here? You cannot already have received the note. If you are found in my chamber, your life will be forfeit and mine forever ruined."

He pushed the bed curtain fully open. "I come on an errand of mercy, ma belle." Backlit by the crackling fire, he made an impressive figure. "I cannot leave you in ignorance even one more hour, though it cost me everything. I come to confess." He knelt beside the bed and caught her hand. Rough leather gloves abraded her fingers as she twisted them in his grasp. His other hand reached to cup the back of her head.

"No!" She panicked. "You must leave! This is not right."

He shifted upward to sit on the edge of the bed frame. "Hush, ma épouse chérie, trust me. This is very right." He hauled her into his lap and cradled her close. A frosty beard brushed her cheek, and melting snow dampened her nightshift. He smelled of wet horse, fresh air, and coffee. His cool lips pressed against hers, warming rapidly at her response. Understanding broke over Georgette like an avalanche, and she clutched her husband's broad shoulders in a fever of excitement. He kissed her cheeks, her neck, murmuring endearments in French.

She touched his beloved features. "Jean-Maurice, you still love me? I do not understand—you—are you the Frog?"

"Always I shall love you, Georgette. This Frog and I are one and the same, although I did not choose the name." His cold nose pressed into her neck. "You betrayed me with myself, beguiling woman that you are."

She struggled in protest. "I never betrayed you! Recall how I sent you away." She paused, frowning. "Why did you deceive me so? Jean-Maurice, I have been in agony this day, thinking you no longer cared for me!"

He groaned softly. "That is why I have risked all to come this night. Tomorrow, if you love your husband, you must play the actress and feign a broken heart."

"But you are a traitor to England?" Georgette began to apprehend the implications of his deception.

A quiet knock at the chamber door stunned them both to silence. "Georgette?"

Georgette flung herself at the door and opened it a tiny crack, jamming her foot at its base to keep it from opening wider. "Yes, Mother?"

A candle's flame lighted her mother's features. She blinked in evident surprise at Georgette's vigorous response. "Are you well? I heard movement; our chamber is beneath yours. Would you like me to sit with you tonight?"

"I want to be left alone," Georgette answered in her best petulant tone. "My life is ruined, and I wish to see no one. Go away." She closed the door.

"Very well, dearest. Despite all you have done, I love you."

Georgette leaned her forehead against the door. "I love you, too, Mummy." She assuaged her guilt by determining to be extra kind to her mother in the morning.

Turning, she scanned the room. Had she dreamed Jean-Maurice's appearance? Shivering, she hurried to climb back into bed and nearly screamed when her hand touched flesh. "Surprise," a deep voice said.

"Your boots," she whispered, imagining spurs shredding the linen sheets.

"Maman taught me never to wear shoes in bed. Come join me." When he rolled to his back and reached for her, she realized that he lay crosswise on the bed with his feet hanging off the far side.

"Can you stay awhile?" She climbed in beside him, wrapped her arms around his body, and rested her head upon his buckskin-fringed shirtfront. He embraced her gently.

"*Quel dommage!* How I wish it could be so." His beard tickled her forehead as he spoke.

"Mr. Pringle said he would have me watched," Georgette whispered. "Are you certain no one saw you enter my window? How did you climb up here? The roof is steep and high!"

"The Frog is part squirrel, and the trees are close." He caressed her back. "Pringle is unaware that Grenville's slaves are friendly with my servant Pierre Dimieux. They watched me enter and they keep guard."

"Pierre—Yvonne's son." Georgette remembered the handsome young hostler.

"And Noel's son. My closest friend since childhood, my faithful bodyguard, and the finest woodsman I know. Georgette, I request you to play the brokenhearted woman tomorrow and display strong feeling for the Frog. My mission depends upon you. Do you trust me?" He caught her face between his hands.

Although doubts crowded into her thoughts, Georgette nodded. "I shall do whatever you say, Jean-Maurice. But I am no actress. How can I do this?"

"Imagine how you would behave if this Frog were your lover and you had betrayed him to his doom." Jean-Maurice sat up, cradled her in his arms, and kissed her. "Pray for guidance and pray for me, ma petite grenouille."

"Always. I love you." She reached to touch his back as he scooted off the far side of the bed. Despite the boots, his tread on the floorboards was nearly inaudible. He lifted the window sash and slipped outside with startling suddenness. Georgette rushed to the window and peered through the frosted glass, but he might have taken flight for all the evidence of him visible below.

The following day seemed an eternity. Georgette helped her mother untangle yarns and knitted part of a sock. Her mind kept wandering, and she unraveled at least three socks' worth of work before ending up with less than one finished product. Her father still had not addressed her, and she feared he never would. Her mother chatted nervously, avoiding the subject that weighed heaviest on all minds.

During the noon meal, her father leveled his leaden gaze and his fork at Georgette. "If not for your stupidity, LaTournay would have purchased passage to England for your mother and me by now. You had better make this right. Do not expect us to take you in if LaTournay throws you out."

Georgette stared in disbelief at this new evidence of her father's disregard for the feelings of others. The Grenvilles attempted to brush over the awkward moment, but Georgette saw her mother's hands shaking as she buttered her bread. Georgette wished she could offer her mother sanctuary at Haven Farm. Her appreciation for Mr. LaTournay's kindness increased with each passing day.

As Georgette entered the drawing room shortly before dinner, a maid brought her a note: *"Come to the apple orchard at midnight."* A drawing that must be intended as a frog served as signature.

A hand reached from behind Georgette and snatched the paper out of her fingers. Pringle scanned it. "Ah, he is drawn as a moth to the flame." He scrutinized Georgette. "I never understood why LaTournay fell for you, although you do have your. . . assets." He lifted a brow. "This Frog must share LaTournay's weakness."

She drew her shawl closer around her shoulders and turned away from his crude gaze.

Paper crackled. "The apple orchard at midnight." Mr. Pringle sounded displeased. "Difficult to conceal men there, but we shall have to contrive a way. If you give this spy so much as a hint of warning, I shall shoot you down like a. . .a frog. It is fitting that a frog should find you appealing. One large mouth must attract another."

"Mr. Pringle!" Marianne stepped into the room, her face crimson. "How cruel! You are no gentleman to speak so to a lady."

Chagrin flitted across his face. "This is no lady. She is a spy, Marianne—a spy who betrayed her husband and her country. Such a woman deserves no courtesy."

Georgette produced a sob and a few tears. Burying her face in her hands, she rushed out of the room and upstairs, pausing to catch her breath on the first landing. To her surprise, Marianne had followed her.

"Darling Gigi! How your heart must be breaking!" Marianne led the way into her own drawing room and closed the door.

Georgette sighed. "Marianne, why must life be so confusing? Why does God allow certain prayers to remain unanswered?"

"He answers every prayer, Gigi, but sometimes His answer is 'no' or 'wait.' From our limited perspective, these prayers appear unanswered. Do you love this Frog so much? I thought you loved Mr. LaTournay."

"But I do! Oh Marianne, I cannot explain."

Marianne sat on a settee and patted the seat. "Is the Frog handsome?" she asked as Georgette sat down.

A twinge of jealousy pinched Georgette. Then she nearly laughed aloud at her own folly. "His face is always concealed. He is a tall, active man with a beautiful voice. He speaks of love to me in French."

In French. How blind she was! Georgette decided that had she been married to Jean-Maurice when first she met the Frog, he would not have deceived her so easily. He would not have deceived her at all.

"I detect tenderness for him in your voice." Marianne sounded close to tears. "Do you wish me to warn him in some way? I could ride to meet him at the ferry and warn him away."

So Marianne wished to impress the dashing Frog, did she? Georgette savored the power of possession. "I cannot allow you to endanger yourself. Besides, how can I convince Mr. LaTournay of my faithfulness to him unless I betray the spy?"

"But, Gigi, Mr. Pringle has twenty-five men ready to seize the Frog tonight. They plan a public hanging."

Fear licked like flames at Georgette's confidence. What did Jean-Maurice plan to do? Only now did it occur to her to wonder why he planned to meet her in the orchard. Would he needlessly expose himself to danger? She shook her head. "He has always escaped their traps before. I pray he will find a way of escape tonight."

"I, too, will pray for his safety," Marianne whispered.

Before he left the house at eleven that night, Pringle gave Georgette explicit instructions about when, where, and how she should leave the house and make her way to the orchard. "We will be watching you, and any deviation from the plan will cost you dearly." He narrowed his eyes. "Any hint of warning, and that Frog of yours takes twenty-five musket balls in his gut. *My* shot just might miss its target and find you."

"I understand."

Marianne and Georgette held hands and prayed while they waited for time to pass. Georgette heard running horses outside. Would Jean-Maurice be prepared for this unfriendly welcome? Surely he did not depend solely on the Grenville servants to protect him. Why bother coming at all? What ulterior motive directed his movements?

Several shots rang out. Men shouted. Horses neighed.

The women exchanged startled stares. Running to an upstairs bedroom window, Marianne and Georgette looked toward the Jamaica road, seeing torches and milling figures. Georgette's mother and Mrs. Grenville joined them.

"What has happened?" Mr. Grenville spoke from the bedroom doorway. Receiving no answer, he pushed his way to the window. "Something has gone awry. This disturbance would alert the enemy."

Calling for a servant, he stormed from the room and thundered downstairs. Out in the road, the torches moved slowly into the distance and disappeared from sight.

The women followed him, conjecturing among themselves. Georgette checked the grandfather clock in the front hall. Soon it would be her appointed time to meet the Frog in the orchard. Would the meeting ever take place?

A liveried man rushed through the front door, bent to gasp for breath with his hands on his knees, then ran into the parlor. The women followed him, hoping to overhear his news.

"What is it, Toby? Stop puffing and tell me what you have

discovered," Mr. Grenville ordered.

The man struggled for breath. "I run clear from the crossroads, suh. Mr. Pringle's men, they was captured by a band of associators. They be taken back to New York City tonight. Mr. Pringle, he went crazy and shot the leader spy, the one he calls the Frog. Then somebody shot Mr. Pringle, but he ain't hurt bad. Somebody carried that Frogman off somewheres, but nobody knows what become of 'im or who he was."

Chapter 14

Neither is there salvation in any other:
for there is none other name under heaven
given among men,
whereby we must be saved.
ACTS 4:12

Georgette lowered herself into a chair and laid her head back.

Dear Lord God, I beseech You to protect my husband and bring him home to me. Jean-Maurice believes he is doing right in Your eyes, I am certain. Forgive his unbelief and make Yourself known to him in an unmistakable way. Please make me worthy.

The Grenvilles and Georgette's parents discussed the subverted plan in hushed tones. Marianne brought Georgette a cup of chocolate and knelt at her feet, looking up with worried eyes. Georgette held her cup with one hand and reached to squeeze Marianne's hand with the other. "I am certain Mr. Pringle will recover. Toby's report indicated that he was not seriously injured."

"Yes, but the Frog." Tears turned Marianne's eyes into sparkling blue pools. "He was so brave and daring. No wonder you loved him. I wish such a man would take interest in me."

"You speak as though he were dead." Georgette snatched her hand back and sipped at her chocolate. "I do not believe it." The enormous lump in her throat could not be swallowed or ignored.

"I pray you are right." Marianne inspected her fidgeting fingers. "You say you never saw his face, yet you loved him. Did he ever kiss you, Georgette?"

Georgette lifted a brow. "How romantic you have become, Marianne. At first he only touched my hands, but his voice held a passion that set my soul aflame. He called me 'ma belle grenooj' or something like that."

Marianne's forehead wrinkled. " 'My beautiful frog'? But he was the Frog, not you. Are you certain he said 'grenouille'?"

Georgette wanted to laugh and cry at once. The rogue! How dared he call her a frog! Setting down her chocolate, she rose with a rustle of petticoats to walk across the room. She covered her lips with one hand and propped her elbow with the other, her old habit. Did Jean-Maurice think her mouth too large? Or did he call her his frog because he had always intended her to be his mate—one frog admiring another?

Her thoughts flitted from one concern to another. Small wonder he had been secretive all these months of their marriage. Georgette recalled several instances when she had reviled Whig leaders and condemned the revolutionary forces. How could Jean-Maurice know that his wife loved him far more than she cared about politics? Whatever course he decided upon was the right choice as far as Georgette was concerned, knowing as she did that her husband would dedicate himself to no cause without careful deliberation.

In the wee hours of the morning, Georgette retired to her chamber and drew the curtains around the cold bed. Tonight she would receive no visit from an audacious frog. Still praying for her husband's safety and salvation, she drifted into sleep.

❧

Just past noon the following day, while Georgette sat knitting in the parlor in the company of her parents and the Grenvilles, the servant Toby burst into the room. "Mr. Grenville, suh!"

"What is it, Toby?" Mr. Grenville growled, looking up from his newspaper.

"Mr. LaTournay—he rides up the lane."

Georgette's father sat up, knocking his wig askew. "Ah! Hope returns with him." Casting a burning glare upon Georgette, he ordered, "You will do and say nothing to further alienate the man."

"Yes, Father." Georgette could scarcely conceal her elation. Her Frog was alive and well! Clasping her hands amid the folds of her gown, she strove to control her breathing. The lace ruffles upon her breast rose and fell much too violently. Staring at her lap, she reminded herself of the role she must play: the penitent wife.

The front door opened, voices sounded, and footsteps crossed the hall. Mr. LaTournay paused in the parlor doorway. Georgette took in a quick breath. Flawless attire and polished boots proclaimed him the fine gentleman, although a stray lock of hair dangled beside one of his high cheekbones. She resumed breathing with conscious effort.

"Welcome, LaTournay." Mr. Grenville bowed and offered a chair. "Your return signifies the return of hope to this household. You are no doubt aware of the attack upon our loyal citizens? Pringle has been taken captive. A dram of whiskey to dispel the chill?"

Mr. LaTournay bowed to the ladies, accepted the chair, and declined the drink. "Take heart. City leaders are already protesting the detainment of your townspeople. I doubt their incarceration will be of long duration. A more significant loss was the cache of gunpowder hidden in Mr. Johannes Smythe's barn. Had you heard of that calamity? The Whigs confiscated all."

"And Pringle's plot to capture that infamous Frog spy has been foiled," Mrs. Grenville added. "Do you think Mr. Pringle is badly injured?"

"I had not heard that his injury was severe. Some say he killed the Frog; others say the spy escaped unscathed." Mr. LaTournay held his hands to the fire, leaning his elbows upon his widespread knees. Georgette thought his face looked pale.

"A ship sails for England next week," her father said.

Mr. LaTournay studied his father-in-law dispassionately. "Whether or not you sail on that ship depends upon your daughter. I hear she took part in Pringle's plot to apprehend the spy. Was her participation voluntary? That is the pertinent question."

His enigmatic gaze turned upon Georgette. Despite her certainty, doubts assailed her. Jean-Maurice was the Frog. . .wasn't he? Could it be possible that he possessed a double, a twin? Who was this hostile stranger, after all?

"I—I wrote a note to bring the Frog here. It is not my fault that the plot failed."

His fixed stare brought heat to her face. "I shall never betray you, Mr. LaTournay," she added. Somewhere behind that forbidding mask must lurk her Jean-Maurice.

A sneer curled his lip. "Never—as long as I never turn my back upon you. We shall discuss this matter further in private." His voice held an ominous note. Georgette heard Marianne inhale sharply.

LaTournay rose. "Talbot, almost I am tempted to send your daughter back to England with you until this military conflict ends, but that would not serve my purposes. She will do penance at my pleasure. I shall purchase passage for you and Mrs. Talbot before my return north." He turned to Mrs. Grenville and Georgette's white-faced mother. "Pardon my blunt speech, ladies. Disillusionment brings out the worst in a man. I promise that my wife will suffer no physical harm, Mrs. Talbot; you need not fear."

Mrs. Grenville sputtered into speech. "You are always welcome to lodge here, Mr. LaTournay. The third-floor chamber still awaits your pleasure."

"I am grateful for your hospitality." His burning gaze once more focused upon Georgette. "Hence I shall retire until dinner. Mrs. LaTournay, you will accompany me."

Wilted beneath his stare, Georgette rose, excused herself, and led the way upstairs. As they passed into the front hall, her father's comment followed: "What that girl needs is a flogging. Her mother always pampered her. Deceitful, she is. No respect for authority."

Jean-Maurice said not a word as he followed Georgette up two flights and into her chamber. "Yours is the adjoining room," she said, but he closed her chamber door and leaned his back against it, eyes closed, chest heaving.

"Maybe tar and feathers were not too harsh after all," he mused aloud. "Almost I wish I had not already purchased his passage to England. Yet, for your mother's sake and to remove him from your vicinity, the fee was well spent."

Georgette regarded her husband from a distance, still uncertain. "You look pale, Jean-Maurice. Are you ill?"

"No, I am shot," he said softly.

"What? Where? Are you dying?" Georgette watched as he

313

staggered over to collapse upon her bed. "Has a doctor seen your wound?"

"Pull off my boots, woman, and cease that incessant weeping!"

Georgette leaped to obey, trembling in surprise and hurt. Footsteps sounded in the room below, and a door closed.

After his boots hit the floor, Jean-Maurice smiled up at her. "Hush, *ma chérie*—speak softly. My injury must not be known. Pierre bound it and applied a poultice. The damage is not serious, I think. The ball entered my shoulder from the side and exited through the back. Pierre thinks it bounced off my shoulder blade. I have suffered worse injury in the past." He closed his eyes and sighed. "Pierre shot Pringle through the arm."

"You should have stayed in bed instead of riding over here today to play the angry husband," Georgette scolded, wiping tears from her face with the backs of her hands. She dipped a handkerchief in her basin, wrung it out, and placed it upon his forehead. "Do you have a fever? Do you need your bandage changed?" She bent to lay her cheek against his.

"At present I need only rest and you." His eyes opened. "I could not leave you to wonder if I were dead or alive. Now we are together, all will be well." He lifted his right arm in invitation. "Come and 'do penance at my pleasure.' Rest with me. You look peaked."

"Where is Pierre?" Georgette covered him with a blanket and slid in beside him. Her hoop skirt rose behind her, admitting a draft. She tried to push it down, to no avail.

Jean-Maurice smiled. "You will seldom see Pierre, but he is near. Like a guardian angel."

The question must be asked. "Will you ever tell me how you received that scar on your throat and why you have nightmares?"

A pause. "Some tales are best left untold."

"When I heard that you had been shot, I prayed for your safety, but mainly I wondered. . . Please tell me, Jean-Maurice: Had you died last night, what would have become of your soul?"

He squeezed her gently. "The angels would have carried me to the Holy City. Never fear."

"So you know that God has forgiven you?" Georgette lifted her head to get a clear look at his face.

His dark eyes glimmered at her from beneath their thick lashes, and a double chin formed as he tipped his face down. "I am forgiven for Christ's sake, not for any worth in myself. Like the apostle Peter, I at last came to realize that, short of inventing my own god and religion, I had no choice but to abandon my pride and accept God's gift."

"When did this happen? Why did you not tell me?" She crossed her hands over the solid muscles of his chest and rested her chin upon her fingers, trying to pretend her voice did not wobble with emotion. "What do you mean about Peter?"

"I would have told you sometime." He looked uncomfortable. "It happened gradually since our talk that night. I refer to the Gospel of John, chapter six. 'Then Simon Peter answered him, Lord, to whom shall we go? thou hast the words of eternal life. And we believe and are sure that thou art that Christ, the Son of the living God.' And also in the book of Acts chapter four: 'There is none other name given among men, whereby we must be saved.' Jesus Christ is my Lord and my God, and I shall serve Him all my days. That is all."

Georgette hid her face against his broad chest and wept. "Oh, thank God, thank God! Jean-Maurice, I love you so."

⚜

If the Talbots and Grenvilles wondered about the amount of time Georgette and Jean-Maurice spent upstairs, they made no comment. Pierre's prompt attention to the injury and Jean-Maurice's iron constitution collaborated toward quick healing. Georgette winced at the holes and bruises marring her husband's skin, but she rejoiced at his uneventful recovery. She hid away the soiled bandages until Pierre could collect and wash them for her. Each night the nimble servant availed himself of Jean-Maurice's entry—the gable window.

Although her husband slept much of the time, he dressed carefully for meals. No one could possibly have guessed at his injury. He conversed with the men about current affairs, rejoiced at rumors of the captive farmers' imminent release, and chuckled at her father's jokes concerning the pitiful Continental Army. To Georgette, he maintained in public a polite, guarded behavior.

After four days of rest, Jean-Maurice decided he was strong enough to travel home, overruling Georgette's protests. "All reports indicate that the Hudson is still open. I am well enough to ride in a boat. I weary of this house and these people, and we should depart before Pringle's return."

The morning of their departure, Pierre loaded their trunks upon a cart and brought a new pair of hired horses. Georgette kept a worried eye on her husband during their travel preparations, but Jean-Maurice showed no sign of weakness.

Marianne drew her aside in the hallway. Georgette returned her friend's hug, feeling guilty for the lack of attention she had given her. Marianne's blue eyes brimmed. "I shall miss you, Gigi. I see the wary glances you give your husband, but truly I believe you need not fear. When he thinks no one is looking, Mr. LaTournay still gazes upon you with affection. Your marriage can be saved if you set your mind to forget about the Frog and strive to become a submissive wife. I shall pray for your complete reconciliation with Mr. LaTournay."

Humbled and slightly amused, Georgette bowed her head and squeezed Marianne's hands. "Thank you, my dear. I shall pray that God will bring a great love into your life—a man worthy of you." She kissed Marianne's soft cheek.

Her mother waylaid her next. "Dearest girl, I am so thankful your husband purchased our passage instead of simply giving Mr. Talbot the money. He is so generous and kind." She leaned close and lowered her voice. "He gave me extra money in case of another emergency; your father does not know. Do try to value Mr. LaTournay and forget that dreadful Frog. He is handsome from some angles, and I believe he cares for you. How distinguished he is! Do you not think his eyes are fine?"

Georgette restrained a smile. "Very fine, indeed. He has been kind and patient with me this week, Mummy, despite his harsh words. I believe I do care for him, after all. Our home in the north is lovely; I wish you could see it. I anticipate our home-coming with pleasure." She found it difficult to restrict her speech to such glaring understatements.

"I am gratified to hear it. Although your marriage was arranged, it does not necessarily follow that it cannot be felicitous."

They linked arms and entered the front hallway where the others waited. "This time I shall make certain they sail with the ship," Mr. Grenville was saying in a hearty tone. "You can count on me."

"I do, sir," Mr. LaTournay returned with a respectful bow. He shook her father's hand and accepted her mother's embrace. Georgette wondered if he was remembering the last "final" farewell. Despite her cynical thoughts, she wept once again while hugging her mother.

As they rode side by side along the ferry road, Jean-Maurice reached across the intervening space and grasped Georgette's hand. "Are you sorry to take leave of your parents?"

Georgette pondered the question and sighed. "Somewhat. I long to be home again with you. And Caramel."

"Ah, yes, that love offering from my rival, *le Grenouille*."

His harsh tone startled Georgette until she caught the twinkle in his eye. "A little uncertainty would do you good," she returned. "And I am reminded to inquire why you call me your frog. Marianne translated for me." Her irritation increased when he laughed aloud. "Do I resemble a frog? Does my large mouth amuse you?"

He caught her mount's reins and stopped both horses. "Ma épouse chérie, can you believe that I find anything about you objectionable? In my eyes, you are altogether lovely. I behold your lips to think of only one thing."

Putting his weight in his left stirrup, he leaned over to kiss her. Smiling, he returned to his seat and released her horse. "Now that we have scandalized the populace of Queens, shall we proceed?"

Swallowing hard, Georgette nodded. The joy in her heart must have glowed on her face, for every time Jean-Maurice looked her way that entire day, he smiled.

Chapter 15

And the angel of the LORD *appeared unto him, and said unto him,*
The LORD *is with thee, thou mighty man of valour.*
JUDGES 6:12

Firelight flickered on the oak beams and plaster walls of Georgette's bedchamber. A log fell in a shower of sparks. Jean-Maurice rose to brush the hot ashes away from Caramel's basket and rebuild the fire. Straightening, he flexed his shoulders and glanced up to meet Georgette's gaze.

"Does it ache?" she asked.

"Not too badly." He sat down across from her.

"What will you do after you are fully recovered, Jean-Maurice?" Georgette rose to stand behind his chair and rub his shoulders. Six weeks after the shooting, he had regained much of his former strength, though he had not yet regained full mobility in his left arm. He used it to toss a ball for Caramel. The little dog pounced on the toy and brought it back.

"I am uncertain." Jean-Maurice picked up the slimy ball and threw it again. "Because my identity yet remains unknown, my superiors wish me to organize further spy operations. British spies are everywhere. If we intend to win this war, we must fight fire with fire. I have also been requested to train regular troops in the art of bayonet warfare."

"You would fight in this war?" Georgette tried to sound brave.

"I had hoped never again to join in combat."

"Again? You have fought before?"

Silence. Caramel dropped the ball at Jean-Maurice's feet and woofed for attention. Jean-Maurice obliged by throwing the ball, but his thoughts were obviously elsewhere.

"Did you fight in the Indian wars? Is that what happened when your father returned for you? And you must have fought on the side of the French. But you were only a boy at the time!"

His shoulders tightened. Georgette watched him run one finger up the scar from his collar to his chin. "My childhood ended the day my father came to this house. In the name of war, I have committed atrocities of which I can never speak. As a spy, I was obliged to accept the reputation of a womanizer and pretend to woo another man's wife, a mistake that nearly cost me all I hold dear. Mere words cannot express the remorse I suffered when you scorned my suit."

"I recall the Frog defending your reputation to me," Georgette said in an attempt to lighten his mood.

He shook his head. "Yet you believed me an immoral man even after our marriage, being too innocent yourself to recognize my inexperience with women. I deserved your suspicion, for I had deceived you, lied to you. For all this evil, God has forgiven me, just as you said He would. But how can I fight another war or engage in further intelligence work, knowing I may be obliged to repeat sins of my past?"

Georgette kissed the top of his head. "You would not repeat the past, because now you belong to God. The torment that once burned in your eyes is gone; God's peace fills you."

He caught her hand and brought it to his cheek. "Georgette, you are God's wondrous gift to me. I do not deserve you." His broken whisper brought tears to her eyes.

"Neither do I deserve you. I know it is difficult for you to speak of your past, but it helps me to understand you better. Whatever comes in our future, Jean-Maurice, I want to enjoy each moment we spend together so that I shall have no regrets. We are one now, and I shall endeavor to assist in any task the Lord assigns you, whether it is to spy for the Whigs or to fight for their army."

He pulled her into his lap and buried his face in her loose hair. "Woman, if ever I conceal my activities from you again, rest assured that I think only of your safety. I trust you completely. In the past you have been my unwitting accomplice; now you are my mate in every sense."

Their future loomed cloudy and uncertain, yet Georgette's heart was at peace. "One *bonne grenouille* deserves another. Um, Jean-Maurice, how does one say 'tadpole' in French?"

"*Tetard.* Why?"

Georgette merely smiled.

Jill Stengl is the author of numerous romance novels including Inspirational Reader's Choice Award- and Carol Award-winning *Faithful Traitor*, and full length historical *Until That Distant Day*. She lives with her husband in the beautiful North Woods of Wisconsin, where she enjoys spoiling her three cats, teaching high school literature classes, playing keyboard for her church family, and sipping coffee on the deck as she brainstorms for her next novel.